P9-EAJ-857

THE BORZOI SERIES OF STORIES AND TALES

FRENCH STORIES AND TALES *edited by Stanley Geist*

GERMAN STORIES AND TALES *edited by Robert Pick*

SPANISH STORIES AND TALES *edited by Harriet de Onís*

These are Borzoi Books
published by Alfred A. Knopf in New York

GERMAN STORIES AND TALES

GERMAN STORIES AND TALES

Edited by Robert Pick

New York

Alfred A. Knopf

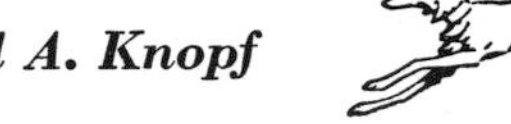

1954

Acknowledgment is hereby made for permission to reprint the following: *Youth, Beautiful Youth* by Hermann Hesse, from SCHÖN IST DIE JUGEND, S. Fischer Verlag, used by permission of the author. *An Episode in the Life of the Marshal de Bassompierre* by Hugo von Hofmannsthal, from SELECTED PROSE, Bollingen Series XXXIII, copyright 1952 by Bollingen Foundation, Inc., used by its permission. *Lukardis* by Jakob Wassermann, from WORLD'S END, copyright 1927 by Boni & Liveright, Inc., used by permission of Liveright Publishing Corporation and George Allen & Unwin Ltd. *Cardiac Suture* by Ernst Weiss, from HEART OF EUROPE, edited by Klaus Mann and Hermann Kesten, copyright 1943 by A. A. Wyn, Inc., used by permission of the publisher and the author's estate. *The Message that Failed* by Moritz Heimann, from WINTERGESPINST, S. Fischer Verlag, used by permission of the publisher; lines from Ruth and Thomas Martin's translation of THE MARRIAGE OF FIGARO included in this story, copyright 1947 by G. Schirmer, Inc., used by permission of the publisher. *Rock Crystal* by Adalbert Stifter, from ROCK CRYSTAL: A CHRISTMAS TALE, copyright 1945 by Pantheon Books, Inc., used by permission of the publisher. *The Bachelor's Death* by Arthur Schnitzler, from MASKEN UND WUNDER, S. Fischer Verlag, used by permission of Henry Schnitzler. *Mona Lisa* by Alexander Lernet-Holenia, from DREI GROSSE LIEBESGESCHICHTEN, copyright 1950 by Morgarten Verlag, Conzett & Huber, used by permission of the author and the publisher. *Zerline, the Old Servant Girl* by Hermann Broch, from DIE SCHULDLOSEN, copyright 1950 by Rhein Verlag, A. G., used by permission of the publisher and Ludwig Krafft-Kennedy, administrator of the Estate of Hermann Broch. *The Friend in the Closet* by Hermann Kesten, used by permission of the author. *The Metamorphosis* by Franz Kafka, from THE PENAL COLONY, copyright 1948 by Schocken Books, Inc., and also published as *The Transformation* in the volume, IN THE PENAL SETTLEMENT, by Martin Secker & Warburg Ltd., used by permission of both publishers. *A Little Legend of the Dance* by Gottfried Keller, from THE PEOPLE OF SELDWYLA AND SEVEN LEGENDS, E. P. Dutton & Co., Inc., and J. M. Dent and Sons Ltd., used by permission of both publishers. *Death in Venice* by Thomas Mann from STORIES OF THREE DECADES, copyright 1930, 1936 by Alfred A. Knopf, Inc., and also published by Martin Secker & Warburg Ltd., used by permission of both publishers.

L. C. catalog card number: 53-9481

THIS IS A BORZOI BOOK
PUBLISHED BY ALFRED·A·KNOPF, INC.

 Published simultaneously in Canada by McClelland & Stewart Limited. Manufactured in the United States of America.

FIRST EDITION

EDITOR'S NOTE

When the publisher asked me to edit this collection of German stories and tales, we agreed that its contents should be, above all, good reading. This volume was not intended to be—and is not—an anthology representative of the five or six generations of modern German storytelling.

In reading a great number of stories, I tried to put myself in the place of a person eager to listen to a teller of tales, but concerned little with the teller's renown, and even less with the historical or esthetic significance of his story. Subjectivity, of course, entered into my final selection—though no larger measure of it, I hope, than any editor makes himself guilty of when gauging the merits of new material.

Although some of the present stories are classics, I cannot claim to have assembled "the greatest stories" of German literature. But I am confident that the primary criterion of my choice did not diminish the literary quality of its result. Mediocre stories, no matter how successful on their first appearance, stop being good reading after a very short time.

•

The one genre that German fiction can boast as its very own is the *Bildungsroman,* the novel of the education, inner development, and maturing of a young man. Because of its very nature, this kind of novel had only a limited influence on the shorter forms of fiction. Still, there are stories, fairly long as a rule, which follow that tradition with the happiest results. Hermann Hesse's "Youth, Beautiful Youth" is one. When the story opens, the young man knows little about himself despite all the pictures of life he has gathered on travels and winnowed from books. When the beautiful summer days are over, experience has taught him the difference between pleasant self-deceit and genuine feeling; with as poignant a farewell to youth as you are likely to encounter, he sets out on his road to manhood.

"The Message that Failed," by Moritz Heimann, is another account of a young man's reaching self-knowledge through a single experience. That serious theme is coupled, in this story, with a motif whose comedy might have amused its "inner hero," Mozart himself. Its ultimate subject—the ironical precariousness of human communication—emerges from the intertwining of the two themes and raises the very special experience of this very special young man to the level of general importance.

Irony is one of the most felicitous strains in German storytelling. The reader will find it in various disguises in some of the most dissimilar tales in this book: in Clemens Brentano's puzzling "The Picnic of Mores the Cat"; in Gottfried Keller's irreverent "Little Legend of the Dance"; in "The Bachelor's Death," that worldly-wise, melancholy *novella* by Arthur Schnitzler; in Alexander Lernet-Holenia's deceptively cool "Mona Lisa"; in "Cardiac Suture," Ernst Weiss's stunning *tour de force;* and in Hermann Kesten's "The Friend in the Closet," a story about the contemporary impasse of moral judgment.

Irony at its subtlest is also present in Thomas Mann's celebrated "Death in Venice." It now and then tinges the stylistic classicism of this story, whose intricate and yet limpid texture has made it one of the enduringly great experiences in modern European fiction. "Death in Venice" is really a morality play, with death appearing quite bodily three times to a man who all his life has drawn on forces he has not been aware of. It is also the crowning achievement of the German fictionists' long pursuit of the problem of art and the creative artist.

None pursued these problems with greater passion than the romanticists. The extraordinary attracted them in every field, leading them to the lyrically fanciful, the bizarre, the "Gothic"—but also to an enlarged, indeed deepened, concept of reality. They acknowledged the complexity of the human mind and the ambiguity of human action and speech; they sensed that forces of which man is not conscious affect his thought and his behavior.

The impact of this heritage on the writers of later periods—its diffused effect—has produced an impressive body of stories certain to engross the mid-twentieth-century reader. The "romantic feeling of reality," Joseph Conrad said, may in itself "be a curse, but, when disciplined by a sense of personal responsibility and a recognition of the hard facts of existence shared with the rest of mankind, becomes a point of view from which very shadows of life appear endowed with an internal glow." he grasp of the extraordinary in ordinary human existence—of the element of adventure and of the unheard-of within the ordinary business of living—this is the essence of the "romanticism" in not a few of the stories assembled here.

Take the most modern of them, Hermann Broch's "Zerline, the Old Servant Girl," and consider the romantic forest-and-castle scenery that turns up in this severe account of the tortures and bliss of adult love; and consider, further, the challenging use of the Don Juan myth in this narrative and its elusive ending. From a thoroughly credible situation involving thoroughly convincing characters the author has extracted an awareness of the existence of powers beyond the ken of reasoning, a feeling that fits superbly the subject-matter of his daring story.

Or watch the miraculous enter as scrupulously realistic a piece of writing as Adalbert Stifter's famous "Rock Crystal," if only through the mind of a half-awake child. This great mid-nineteenth-century author might have told his story of suspense without that fairy-tale coda and still have conveyed its Christmas atmosphere to the reader. But it is that brief episode which literally endows the whole narrative, in retrospect, with an "internal glow."

The fairy-tale, that most ancient medium of storytelling, still holds sway over German fiction. What makes "Lukardis," Jakob Wassermann's account of an incident in the Russian revolution of 1905, a memorable narrative is its being, in reality, the tale of the "royal children" of old, the ancient story of the doomed love of two pure young people.

Technically speaking, Hugo von Hofmannsthal's beautiful "Bassompierre" story is the romanticized version of a factual seventeenth-century report. Yet the latter-day story is by far the more real of the two. It transforms an "episode" in the life of a boastful great nobleman into a drama of human significance. The woman's elemental love dwarfs the figure of her self-assured lover, and her tragic fate strips his triumph over common human afflictions of any trace of grandeur.

Franz Kafka's "The Metamorphosis" begins with lines that demand the complete suspension of our disbelief. But the utterly implausible thing that has happened to the story's hero dulls our sense of reality as little as his. In actual fact, our sense of reality becomes sharpened, and we gain a second vision of everyday human relationships and a feeling of truth that obliterates the manifest unreality of the tale's point of departure.

Recently a critic suggested that the unheard-of calamity that befalls the protagonist of "The Metamorphosis" occurs only in his imagination—an idea significantly reminiscent of the reaction of children eager to persuade themselves of the "unreality" of some gruesome Grimm tale that keeps haunting them. The chickens have come home to roost: in listening to a teller of tales who (to use Plato's definition of poetry) causes a thing to emerge from nonexistence into existence, the mid-twentieth-century reader, for all his sophistication, finds his emotion as deeply engaged as that of a child or of his own early ancestors.

•

No historical principle governed the arrangement of the stories in this volume. Nor does this Note, though it tries to point out certain traits common to many of them (as to many of all German stories), aim at a division according to type or group. I do not pretend to say that every story printed here is *sui generis*. But few of them are true to any one type; few follow strictly the technique of any one school of writing. German stories are, on the whole, highly individual. One reason for that individuality may be the failure of nineteenth-century realism to establish a firm, dominant tradition in German storytelling.

Marie von Ebner-Eschenbach's quietly humorous "Krambambuli" has its share of the shortcomings of what is often referred to, with one qualification or another, as late-nineteenth-century German realism. It is a parochial story, a slightly sentimental one. Yet it is still likely to move the reader. This tale of conflicting loyalties, which is also a parable of the call of the wild, has survived both the idealized social background and the author's determined politeness. When all is said and done, techniques and "schools" matter little—the story's the thing!

Like the traveling journeyman in Johann Peter Hebel's "Kannitverstan," the reader of fiction is left to draw his own conclusions from the images of reality shown him. Although he is far better off than that good fellow—grasping so much better what he is being told, and being told so much more—he still must arrive at truth in his own way. Stories that make good reading may smooth that road and spare the reader the journeyman's detour of error.

—Robert Pick

CONTENTS

GERMAN STORIES AND TALES

YOUTH, BEAUTIFUL YOUTH

by Hermann Hesse

Even my Uncle Matthäus was pleased, after his fashion, to see me again. When a young man who has been in foreign parts for several years comes back home one day and turns out to have done rather well for himself, even the coolest relations will smile and gladly shake his hand.

The small brown suitcase in which I was carrying my worldly goods was still brand-new, with a sound lock and gleaming straps. It contained two clean suits, plenty of underwear, a new pair of boots, a number of books and photographs, two handsome pipes, and a small pistol. In addition I had with me my violin case and a knapsack full of trifles, two hats, a cane and an umbrella, a light coat, and a pair of overshoes. All these things were stout and new, and moreover, sewed into my breast

---

Born in Swabia (1877), Hermann Hesse became famous through his novel Peter Camenzind, *the story of a youth who after many adventures discovers where he belongs.* Unterm Rad *and* Nachbarn *are two of the other novels of Hesse's earlier period, which was marked by loving descriptions of small-town life and nature. In 1911 he traveled to India, where both his father and his grandfather had worked as missionaries. The First World War threw him into a grave crisis, and he finally adopted Swiss citizenship. Indian philosophy and psychoanalysis had a decisive influence on his later production* (Siddharta, Demian, Steppenwolf). Narziss und Goldemund, *his most beautiful novel, deals with the old German theme of man's dual nature. The offerings of Hesse's old age, particularly the much-discussed* Glasperlenspiel (Magister Ludi), *combine independent thought with the imagery of German romanticism. Hesse's poetry and the small body of his literary criticism have won distinguished places. A Nobel Prize winner, he lives in Montagnola, in the Swiss canton of Ticino.*

pocket, I had more than two hundred marks in savings and a letter promising me a good position abroad for the coming autumn. It all made quite a respectable outfit. And now, with my journeyman's years behind me, I was returning with all this equipment. I came back a man of the world to my home town, which I had left as a diffident problem child.

With creeping caution the train descended the hill in great winding curves, and with each turn the houses, streets, river, and gardens of the town below came closer and grew more distinct. Soon I could distinguish the roofs and pick out the familiar ones; soon, too, I could count the windows and recognize the stork nests. And while childhood and boyhood and a thousand precious memories of home were wafted toward me out of the valley, my sense of arrogant triumph at the homecoming slowly melted away. My desire to make a big impression upon all those people down there yielded to a feeling of grateful astonishment. Homesickness, which in the course of the years had ceased to trouble me, assailed me powerfully in this last quarter-hour. Every clump of broom near the station platform and every familiar garden fence became strangely precious to me, and I asked each to forgive me for having been able to forget it and get along without it for so long.

When the train passed above our garden, I saw someone standing at the topmost window of the old house and waving a large towel. That must have been my father. And on the veranda my mother and the maid were standing, also waving, and from the top chimney faint blue smoke from the fire for the coffee flowed up into the warm air and out over the little town. All this now belonged to me again; it had all waited for me and was now welcoming me.

At the station the bearded old platform attendant ran about just as excited as he had always been, herding people away from the tracks, and among the people I saw my sister and my younger brother looking for me expectantly. For my baggage, my brother had brought along the little express wagon that had been our pride all through our boyhood. On it we placed my suitcase and knapsack. Fritz pulled and I followed along behind with my sister. She reproved me for wearing my hair so short now, but thought my mustache handsome and my new suitcase very elegant. We laughed and looked into each other's eyes, and from time to time clasped hands again and nodded to Fritz, who went on ahead with the little cart, but kept turning around to look at me. He was as tall as I and had filled out nicely. As he walked ahead of us, I suddenly remembered that when we had been boys I had sometimes hit him in the course of quarrels. I saw again his child's face and his offended or sorrowful eyes, and I felt something of the same painful penitence I had always felt in those days as soon as my anger had ebbed away. Now Fritz strode along, tall and grown up, and already with blond down around his chin.

We went down the avenue of cherry and rowan trees and passed the upper footbridge, a new store, and many old, unchanged houses. Then came the corner by the bridge, and there as always stood my father's house, with open windows, through which I could hear our parrot chortling, and my heart pounded for joy and for all the memories. I went through the cool, dark stone gateway and down the wide stone walk and hurried up the stairs. My father came down them to meet me. He kissed me, smiled, and patted me on the back. Then he led me silently by the hand to the upper door of the vestibule, where my mother was waiting and took me in her arms.

Then the maid, Christine, came running up and shook hands with me, and I went on into the living-room, where the coffee stood ready, and greeted Polly, the parrot. He recognized me at once, climbed from the edge of his cage roof onto my finger, and lowered his beautiful gray head for me to stroke. The room was freshly papered, but otherwise everything remained the same—from the portraits of grandparents and the china closet to the tall clock with its old-fashioned decorations of lilacs. The cups stood ready on the set table, and in my cup was a small bunch of mignonette, which I took out and stuck in my lapel.

Opposite me sat my mother, looking at me and putting soft rolls on my plate. She admonished me not to talk so much that I should forget to eat, and then she herself asked me one question after another that I had to answer. Father listened in silence, stroked his beard, which had turned gray, and looked at me through his glasses with an air of kind scrutiny. And as I reported my experiences, acts, and successes—without being excessively modest—I could not help feeling that I must thank these two for the best of all.

This first day I wanted to see nothing but my dear old home; there would be time enough tomorrow and later on for everything else. And so after the coffee we went through all the rooms, through kitchen, corridors, and bedchambers, and almost everything was just as it had been before. The few innovations I discovered already seemed old and obvious to the others, and they disputed over whether these changes had not already been made in my day.

In the small garden that lies on the slope of the hill between ivied walls, the afternoon sun fell upon neat paths and rough limestone edgings, upon the half-filled water barrel and the beautiful, vivid flower beds, so that everything seemed smiling. We sat down on the veranda in comfortable chairs. The sunlight flowed, muted, warm, and pale green, through the large transparent leaves of the syringa. A few bees that had lost their way buzzed about, heavy and intoxicated. In gratitude for my return Father bared his head and said the Lord's Prayer. We stood still with folded hands, and though the unusual solemnity dampened my spirits slightly, I nevertheless heard the old and sacred words with gladness, and I spoke the Amen gratefully.

Then Father went to his study, my brother and sister ran off, and the whole house became quiet. I sat alone at the table with my mother. This was the moment I had long been looking forward to, and also dreading. For though my homecoming was glad and welcome, my life in the past several years had not been entirely pure and innocent.

Now Mother looked at me with her beautiful warm eyes and read my face. Perhaps she was considering what to say and what to ask about. I sat in embarrassed silence, playing with my fingers. I was prepared for an examination that on the whole would not be altogether inglorious, but which in certain of its details was bound to make me feel abashed.

For a while she looked quietly into my eyes. Then she took my hand in her fine, small ones.

"Do you still pray a little sometimes?" she asked softly.

"Not any more of late," I had to say, and she gave me a slightly troubled look.

"You'll learn how again," she said then.

And I said: "Perhaps."

Then she was silent for a while, and at last asked: "But you do want to be an upright man, don't you?"

To that I could say yes. And now, instead of putting awkward questions to me, she stroked my hand and nodded to me in a manner that meant she trusted me, even though I made no confessional. And then she asked me about my clothes and laundry, for in the past two years I had taken care of myself and no longer sent things home to be laundered and repaired.

"Tomorrow we will look through everything together," she said after I made my report, and with that the interrogation was over.

Soon afterward my sister came out to the veranda and asked me to come into the house with her. In the parlor she sat down at the piano and took out the music we'd played long ago, which I had neither sung nor heard for so long, but had not forgotten. We sang songs of Schubert and Schumann, and then we set to singing German and foreign folksongs until it was time for supper. My sister set the table while I talked with the parrot, who was supposed to be a male in spite of his name, Polly. He could say a great many things; he mimicked our voices and our laughter and accorded each of us a special and precisely graduated degree of friendliness. He was most intimate with my father, who could do anything he wanted with him; then came my brother, then Mamma, then myself, and last of all my sister, of whom Polly was a little chary.

Polly was the only pet in our house, and was just like one of the children, having been with us for twenty years. He loved conversation, laughter, and music, but not in his immediate vicinity. When he was alone and heard people talking animatedly in the adjoining room, he listened sharply, joined in the conversation and laughed in his good-natured, ironic fashion. And sometimes when he sat alone and quite unobserved on his climbing bars, when everything was silent and the sun shone warmly into the room, he would begin in deep, contented tones to hail life and praise God. His song sounded like a flute; it was solemn, warm, and heartfelt, like the self-forgetful singing of a child at play.

After supper I spent half an hour watering the garden. When I came in again, wet and dirty, I heard from the walk a half-familiar girl's voice speaking inside the house. Quickly I wiped my hands on my handkerchief and entered. There, in a lavender dress and a big straw hat, sat a tall, beautiful girl. When she stood up, looked at me, and held out her hand, I recognized Helene Kurz, a friend of my sister's, with whom I had once upon a time been in love.

"So you still recognize me?" I said smugly.

"Lotte told me you'd come home," she said pleasantly. But I would have liked it better if she had simply said yes. She had grown tall and very pretty indeed. I could think of nothing else to say and went over to the flowers by the window, while she chatted with Mother and Lotte.

My eyes gazed out on the street and my fingers toyed with the geranium leaves, but my thoughts were elsewhere. I saw a slate-cold winter evening; I was ice-skating on the river between the high alder bushes, sweeping in timorous semicircles as I followed at a distance the figure of a girl who scarcely knew how to skate and was being guided by another girl.

Her voice, grown much fuller and deeper than it had been, now sounded familiar and yet almost unknown to me. She had become a young lady, and I felt not in the least her equal in age and station. Rather, it was as though I were still fifteen years old. When she left, I shook hands with her again, but made a needlessly low and ironic bow and said: "Good night, Miss Kurz."

"So she's back home again?" I asked afterward.

"Where else should she be?" Lotte wondered, and I preferred to drop the subject.

At ten o'clock sharp the house was locked up and my parents went to bed. As he kissed me good-night, my father laid his arm around my shoulders and said softly: "It's good to have you back home again. Are you glad, too?"

Everybody went to bed—the maid, too, had bid us good-night some time before—and after doors had opened and shut a few times, a profound nocturnal silence settled over the entire house.

Beforehand I had got myself a mug of beer and chilled it. I now set it on the table in my room, and as smoking was not permitted in the living-rooms of our house, I filled a pipe now and lit it. My two windows looked out over the dark, quiet courtyard, from which stone steps led uphill to the garden. Up above I saw the pines silhouetted black against the sky, and above them the stars twinkling.

I stayed up for more than an hour, watching the moths flitting around my lamp, and slowly blowing my clouds of smoke toward the open windows. Long, silent processions of images passed through my mind, countless memories of home and boyhood days—a vast, silent host rising and glimmering and vanishing again like waves on the surface of a lake.

Next morning I put on my best suit as a token of respect for my native town and my many old acquaintances, and to make it quite clear that I had done well and not come home a poor devil. Above our narrow valley the summer sky was radiantly blue. A haze of dust rose from the white avenues. In front of the near-by post office stood the mail carriages from the forest villages, and in the street small children played with marbles and soft balls.

My first stroll took me over the old stone bridge, the oldest structure in the town. I contemplated the small Gothic chapel on the bridge, which in former days I had raced past hundreds of times. Then I leaned on the parapet and looked up and down the swift green river. The cozy old mill with the white wheel painted on its gable end had vanished, and in its place stood a large new brick building. But otherwise nothing was changed, and, as of old, innumerable geese and ducks swam about on the water and waddled on the banks.

On the other side of the bridge I encountered my first acquaintance, a schoolmate who had gone into the tanning trade. He was wearing a shiny orange-yellow leather apron. He gave me a groping, uncertain look, but did not quite recognize me. Pleased, I nodded to him and strolled on, while he looked back after me and kept trying to recall.

At the window of his workshop I greeted the coppersmith with the marvelous white beard. Then I looked in on the turner, who let the belt of his lathe hum and offered me a pinch of snuff. Then came the market square with its big fountain and the quaint town-hall arcade. The bookseller's shop was there. And though the old fellow had long ago given me a bad character because of my ordering Heine's works, I dropped in and bought a pencil and a picture postcard. From here it had never been far to the school buildings, and so I took a look at the old barracks as I passed. At the gates I scented the familiar, nervous smell of schoolrooms, and scurried on with a sigh of relief to the church and the parsonage.

By the time I had drifted around a few more of the narrow streets and had been shaved at the barber's, it was ten o'clock, time to pay my visit to Uncle Matthäus. I went through the handsome courtyard into his fine house, dusted off my trousers in the cool passageway, and knocked on the door of the living-quarters. Inside I found my aunt and her two daughters sewing. Uncle was already at his office. Everything in this house breathed a spirit of pure, old-fashioned industry, a bit austere and emphatically utilitarian, but also serene and reliable. It was a house of eternal sweeping, dusting, washing, sewing, knitting, and spinning, and nevertheless the daughters found time to make music, and do it very well. Both played the piano and sang, and if they did not know the more modern composers, they were all the more familiar with Handel, Bach, Haydn, and Mozart.

Aunt jumped up to greet me. Her daughters finished their stitches first and then shook hands with me. To my amazement, I was treated quite like a guest of honor and taken into the visitors' room. Moreover, Aunt Berta could not be dissuaded from offering me a glass of wine and assorted pastries. Then she sat down opposite me in one of the company chairs. The daughters stayed at their work in the other room.

This time I was partly subjected to the examination that my kind mother had spared me yesterday. But here too I was not required to embellish an unsatisfactory state of affairs in the telling. My aunt was passionately interested in the personalities of certain well-known preachers, and she questioned me at length about the churches and ministers in all the towns I had lived in. A few small embarrassments cropped up, but with good will we glossed over these and joined in lamenting the death some ten years before of a famous prelate whose sermons I might have been able to hear in Stuttgart if he had lived.

Then the conversation turned to my fortunes, experiences, and prospects, and we decided that I had had good luck and was well started.

“Who would have thought it six years ago?” she remarked.

“Was I really so badly off then?” I could not help asking.

“No, I wouldn’t exactly say that. But still your parents were really worried then.”

“So was I,” I wanted to say, but on the whole she was right, and I did not want to revive the quarrels of the past.

“I guess that is true,” I therefore said, and nodded soberly.

“I gather you have tried quite a number of trades.”

“Yes, certainly, Aunt. And I regret none of them. For that matter, I don’t intend to keep my present one indefinitely.”

“You don’t say! Do you mean that? When you’ve just got yourself such a good position? Almost two hundred marks a month—why, that is splendid for a young man.”

“Who knows how long it will last, Aunt?”

“What a way to talk! It will last all right if you stick right to it.”

“Well, let us hope so. But now I must go upstairs to see Aunt Lydia, and then drop in on Uncle at the office. So good-by for now, Aunt Berta.”

“Yes, adieu. It has been a great pleasure to me. Be sure to come around again.”

“Of course.”

I bade good-by to the two girls in the living-room and from the doorway called another farewell to Aunt. Then I climbed the bright, wide staircase. And if before I had had the feeling that I was breathing an old-fashioned atmosphere, I now entered one positively antique.

In two tiny rooms upstairs lived an octogenarian great-aunt who received me with the delicacy and gallantry of bygone times. There were water-color portraits of great-great-uncles, antimacassars, purses with bouquets of flowers and landscapes embroidered on them in beads, oval picture frames, and a fragrance of sandalwood and delicate old perfume.

Aunt Lydia was wearing a purple dress cut very plain. Except for her nearsightedness and a faint shaking of her head, she was amazingly youthful and spry. She drew me down on a narrow settee, and instead of talking about the distant past asked me about my life and my ideas. She was interested in everything, attentive to everything I said. Old as she was, and remote and ancestral though her rooms smelled and looked, she had gone on frequent travels up to only two years before. Though she did not wholly approve of it, she had a clear and by no means entirely unfavorable conception of the contemporary world, and she liked to refresh and fill out her view of it. At the same time she possessed a charming and graceful adroitness in conversation. When you sat with her, the talk flowed on without pauses and was somehow always interesting and pleasant.

When I left, she kissed me and dismissed me with a gesture of blessing which I have never seen anyone else employ.

I looked up Uncle Matthäus in his office, where he sat bent over newspapers and catalogues. I had made up my mind not to sit down and to leave shortly, and Uncle made it easy for me.

"So you are back in the country again?" he said.

"Yes, back again. It's been a long time."

"And now you are doing well, so I hear?"

"Quite well, thank you."

"You will drop in and say hello to my wife, won't you?"

"I already have been to see her."

"Oh, you have. Good boy. Well then, that's fine."

Whereupon he lowered his gaze to his catalogue again and held out his hand toward me. As he had picked approximately the right direction, I shook his hand quickly and went out with a contented feeling.

Now the official visits were done with, and I went home to dine. In my honor there were rice and roast veal. After dinner my brother, Fritz, took me aside and led me up to his room, where my butterfly collection hung on the wall under glass. My sister wanted to chat with us and stuck her head in at the door, but Fritz importantly waved her away. "No, we have a secret," he said.

Then he scrutinized my face, and when he saw me looking sufficiently curious, he drew a box out from under the bed. The lid of the box was covered with a sheet of tin and weighed down by several good-sized stones.

"Guess what's inside," he said in a low, crafty voice.

I thought about our former hobbies and experiments and guessed: "Lizards?"

"No."

"Ring snakes?"

"Not a bit."

"Caterpillars?"

"No, nothing alive."

"No? Then why is the box shut so tight?"

"There are things more dangerous than caterpillars."

"Dangerous? Aha—powder?"

Instead of replying he removed the lid and I saw inside the box a good-sized arsenal: packages of powder of varying fineness, charcoal, tinder, fuses, lumps of sulphur, boxes of saltpeter, and iron filings.

"Well, what do you say?"

I knew that my father would have been unable to sleep a wink if he had known that a box of such materials was stored in the boys' room. But Fritz was glowing so with joy and the pleasure of having sprung his surprise that I expressed this thought only by a mild remark and instantly accepted his reassurances. For I myself had a certain responsibility for all this, and I was looking forward to a fireworks display as eagerly as an apprentice to quitting-time.

"Will you go in with me?" Fritz asked.

"Of course. We can set the stuff off at night, in gardens here and there, eh?"

"Sure we can. Recently I set off a grenade with half a pound of powder in it, out on the meadows outside of town. It boomed like an earthquake. But now I'm out of money, and we still need all sorts of stuff."

"I'll contribute three marks."

"That's the boy! Then we'll have rockets and giant crackers."

"But you'll be careful, eh?"

"Careful! Nothing's ever happened to *me!*"

This was a reference to a bad accident I had had with fireworks at the age of fourteen; it had missed by a hair costing me my eyesight and my life.

Now he showed me the supplies and the various pieces he had started, initiated me into the mysteries of some of his new experiments and inventions, and stirred up my curiosity about others that he intended to show me and was keeping a deep dark secret for the present. This took up the whole of his noon hour, and then he had to go back to work. After he left I had no sooner covered up the sinister box and stowed it away under the bed than Lotte came in and asked me to come for a walk with her and Papa.

"How does Fritz strike you?" Father said. "He's grown up, hasn't he?"

"Oh yes."

"And is a good deal more serious, don't you think? He's beginning to outgrow his childish pranks at last. Yes, now all my children are grown up."

Getting there anyway, I thought, and felt a bit ashamed. But it was a glorious afternoon; the poppies flamed in the grain-fields, the red corn cockles smiled. We walked along slowly, talking of nothing but enjoyable matters. Well-known paths and orchards, the familiar margins of woods, greeted me and beckoned to me; times past rose up once more, sweet and radiant, as though everything had been good and perfect in those days.

"Now I must ask you something," Lotte said. "I have been thinking of inviting a friend of mine here for a few weeks."

"Have you? Where from?"

"From Ulm. She's two years older than me. What do you think? Now that we have you here, that's the main thing, and you must tell me right out if her visit would bother you."

"What's she like?"

"She's taken the teacher's examination—"

"Oh Lord!"

"Not 'Oh Lord' at all. She's very nice and certainly no blue-stocking—not at all. In fact, she hasn't gone in for teaching."

"Why not?"

"You'll have to ask her that yourself."

"Then she is coming?"

"Stupid! It depends on you. If you think you'd rather have just the family all together, she can come some other time. That's why I'm asking you."

"I'll toss a coin."

"If you feel that way about it, say yes right off."

"All right, yes."

"Good. Then I'll write to her today."

"And send her my regards."

"That will hardly overwhelm her with pleasure."

"Incidentally, what is her name?"

"Anna Amberg."

"Amberg is nice. And Anna is a saint's name, but a dull one, if only because you can't make a nickname out of it."

"Would you like Anastasia better?"

"Yes—that could be shortened to Stasi or Stasel."

Meanwhile we had reached the top of the hill, which from one terrace to the next had seemed almost upon us, but had kept receding. Now from a rock we looked down across the queerly foreshortened, steeply sloping fields through which we had climbed, to the town, far below in the narrow valley. Behind us, on rolling land, the black pine forest ran for mile upon mile, broken here and there by narrow meadows or a strip of grainfield that gleamed in sharp contrast to the dark color of the woods.

"Really, no other place is so beautiful as this," I said pensively.

My father smiled and looked at me. "It is your homeland, son. And it is beautiful; that is true."

"Is your homeland more beautiful, Papa?"

"No, but wherever your childhood was, everything is beautiful and sacred. Haven't you ever been homesick, my boy?"

"Oh yes, now and then I have been."

Near by was a wooded spot where in my boyhood days I had often captured robin redbreasts. And a bit farther on there must be the remains of a stone fort that we children had once built. But Father was tired, and after a short rest we turned back and descended the hill by another road.

I wished I could find out a little more about Helene Kurz, but I dared not bring up her name for fear of exposing myself. In the peacefulness and idleness of being home, and with the happy prospect of several weeks of a lazy holiday before me, my youthful heart was beginning to be stirred by longings and plans for romance. All that was needed was a handy pretext. But that was just what I lacked, and the more I was haunted by the image of that beautiful young lady, the more difficult it became for me to ask without embarrassment about her and her circumstances.

As we walked slowly homeward, we gathered large bunches of flowers from the margins of the fields. This was an art I had not practiced for a long time. In our household Mother had established the custom of keeping not only potted plants, but also fresh flowers on all the tables and chests of drawers. In the course of years a great many simple vases, glasses, and jars had been assembled, and we children scarcely ever returned from a walk without bringing home flowers, ferns, or small branches of trees and shrubs.

It seemed to me that I had not even looked at wildflowers for years. For they look very different when you notice them in passing, with an artistic pleasure, as islands of color in a world of green, and when you kneel or stoop to examine them singly and choose the finest for picking. I discovered tiny hidden plants whose blossoms reminded me of outings in my schooldays, and others that my mother particularly liked or had given special private names. These same flowers were all still to be found, and each of them awakened a memory. Out of every blue or yellow calyx my joyous childhood looked up at me, looked with unwonted dearness and nearness into my eyes.

In what we called the salon of our house stood several tall cases of plain pine. Stuffed into these, standing or lying in confused heaps, was a hoard of books dating back several generations. They were not in any kind of order and were rather neglected. As a small boy I had found and read here *Robinson Crusoe* and *Gulliver's Travels*, in yellowed editions with gay woodcuts. Then I had turned to old stories of seafarers and explorers, and later to a good many more literary works such as *Siegwart, Story of a Monastery, The New Amadis, The Sorrows of Werther*, and Ossian. Later still, I took up the many books by Jean Paul, Stilling, Walter Scott, Platen, Balzac, and Victor Hugo, as well as the small edition of Lavater's *Physiognomy* and numerous sets of pretty little almanacs, pocket-sized booklets, and popular calendars, the older ones illustrated with copper engravings by Chodowiecki, the later ones by Ludwig Richter, and the Swiss ones with woodcuts by Disteli.

Now on evenings when there was no family music-making or when I was not manufacturing firecrackers with Fritz, I could take one or another volume from this treasure store into my room and blow the smoke of my pipe into the yellowed pages over which my grandparents had sighed, raved enthusiastically, and pondered. My brother had gutted and consumed for his fireworks one volume of Jean Paul's *Titan*. When I had read the first two volumes and was hunting for the third, he confessed his crime, but claimed that the volume had been in bad shape anyway.

These evenings were always pleasant and entertaining. We sang; Lotte played the piano and Fritz the fiddle; Mamma told stories of our childhood; Polly fluted away in his cage and refused to go to bed. Father rested at the window or pasted away at a scrapbook for his small nephews.

But I did not at all feel it as a disturbing note when one evening Helene Kurz dropped in again to chat for half an hour. Again and again I looked at her with a sense of amazement at how beautiful and perfect she had become. When she arrived, the candles on the piano were almost burned down, and she joined in the singing of a two-voiced song. But I sang very low, so that I could hear every note of her rich voice. I stood behind her and looked through her brown hair at the candlelight gleaming golden, saw how her shoulders moved slightly as she sang, and thought how delicious it would be to run my hand just a little over her hair.

Without much logic, I had the feeling that we were linked by certain memories of former days because I had been in love with her around the time of my confirmation. Now her casual friendliness was a mild disappointment to me. For it did not occur to me that the relationship had existed only on my side, and that she had known nothing about it.

Afterward, when she took her leave, I picked up my hat and walked to the glass door with her.

"Good night," she said. But instead of taking her hand, I said: "I'll walk you home."

She laughed.

"Oh, no need of that, thank you. You know it isn't customary here."

"Isn't it?" I said, and let her pass. But then my sister took her blue-ribboned straw hat and called out: "I'll go along too."

And the three of us descended the stairs. I eagerly opened the heavy front gate and we stepped out into the warm dusk and walked slowly through the town, across the bridge and the market square, and up to the steep outlying hill where Helene's parents lived. The two girls chattered away like starlings, and I listened and was glad to be with them and one member of a trio. Sometimes I walked more slowly, pretending I was looking up at the sky for weather signs, and lagged a step behind so that I could see how straight and freely she carried her dark head and how firmly and evenly her slender body stepped forward.

At her house Helene shook hands with us and went in. I saw her hat gleaming for a moment in the dark vestibule before the door clapped shut.

"Yes," Lotte said, "she really is a fine girl, isn't she? And there's something so sweet about her."

"There certainly is. How do things stand with your girlfriend? Is she coming soon?"

"I wrote to her yesterday."

"Hm, I see. Well, shall we go home the same way?"

"Oh, we might go by the way of the gardens, at that."

We walked down the narrow lane between the garden fences. It was already dark, and we had to watch where we were going, for there were many sagging plank steps on the path and loose pickets leaning out from the fences.

We had almost reached our garden and could see the living-room lamp burning inside the house. Suddenly a low voice said: "Pst! Pst!" and my sister was frightened. But it was our brother, Fritz, who had hidden in the garden to meet us.

"Stand still and watch!" he called to us. Then he lit a fuse with a sulphur match and came over to us.

"Fireworks again?" Lotte scolded him.

"There won't be much of a bang," Fritz assured her. "Just watch, it's my own invention."

We waited until the fuse had burned down. Then it began to crackle and shoot out small reluctant sparks, like wet gunpowder. Fritz was glowing with pleasure.

"Now it will come, in a second, first white fire, then a small bang and a red flame, then a pretty blue one!"

It did not turn out as he expected. Instead, after some jerking and shooting of sparks the precious invention went up all at once, with a loud boom and blast pressure and a white cloud of smoke.

Lotte laughed, and Fritz was unhappy. As I tried to console him, the dense smoke drifted away with solemn deliberation over the dark gardens.

"We did get just a glimpse of the blue," Fritz began, and I admitted that. Then, almost tearfully, he described in detail the making of his pyrotechnical triumph and how it should have gone off.

"We'll try it again," I said.

"Tomorrow?"

"No, Fritz. Let's make it next week."

I might just as well have said tomorrow. But my mind was full of thoughts of Helene Kurz and was lost in the dream of some wonderful happiness that might dawn for me tomorrow—perhaps that she would visit again in the evening or that she might suddenly take a liking to me. In short, I was now engrossed in things that seemed to me more important and more exciting than all the fireworks in the world.

We crossed the garden to the house and found our parents at the backgammon board in the living-room. It was all so simple and natural and could not be any different. And yet everything has turned out so differently that today it all seems infinitely remote to me. For today my old home no longer exists for me. The old house, the garden, and the veranda, the familiar rooms, furniture and pictures, the parrot in his big cage, the dear old town, and the whole valley have become strange to me and no longer belong to me. Mother and Father are dead, and my childhood home is nothing but memories and homesickness. No road leads me back there any longer.

Around eleven o'clock at night, when I was sitting over a fat volume of Jean Paul, my small oil lamp began to grow dim. It sputtered and made tiny, anxious noises; the flame became red and sooty, and when I examined it and turned the wick up and down, I saw that it was out of oil. I felt sorry about the fine novel I was reading, but it would not do to go groping around in the dark house now, looking for oil.

And so I blew out the smoking lamp and went to bed in a bad temper. Outside, a warm wind had sprung up and was blowing gently through the pines and the lilac bushes. In the grassy yard down below, a cricket was chirping. I could not fall asleep and again began thinking of Helene. I could hope for no more from this well-bred, beautiful girl than to go on looking at her with vain longing, and that was as painful as it was pleasurable. I felt hot and wretched when I imagined her face, the sound of her rich voice, and her walk, the firm and energetic rhythm of her footsteps as she had walked down the street and across the market square this evening.

Finally I jumped up out of bed. I was much too warm and restive to sleep. I went to the window and looked out. Among wispy strips of cloud the waning moon floated pallidly. The cricket was still singing in the yard. What I would have liked best was to go out walking for an hour or so. But our front door was always locked at ten o'clock, and if it ever had to be opened and used after that hour, this always signified an event, something unusual, disturbing, and adventurous. I did not even know where the door-key hung.

I remembered again bygone years when as an adolescent I had sometimes thought our home life was virtual slavery. And at night, with a guilty conscience and adventurous defiance, I had slipped out of the house to have a mug of beer at a tavern that stayed open late. To get out I had used the back door to the garden, which was fastened only by bolts; then I would clamber over the fence and reach the street by way of the narrow lane between the adjoining gardens.

I put on my trousers—the air was so warm that no more clothing was necessary—took my shoes in my hand, and stole out of the house barefoot. Clambering over the garden fence, I set out on a slow stroll through the sleeping town, walking upstream along the river, which flowed along with muted whispers and played with small quivering reflections of the moonlight.

To be up and about outdoors at night, beneath the silent sky and beside quietly flowing water, is always mysterious and stirs the soul to its very depths. At such times we are closer to our origins; we feel a kinship with animals and plants, feel dim memories of a primeval life before houses and towns were built, when man, the homeless wanderer, could regard the woods, streams, mountains, wolves, and hawks as his equals and could love them as friends or hate them as deadly foes. Night also removes our customary sense of community life; when lights are no longer burning and human voices can no longer be heard, one who is still awake feels solitary and sees himself parted from others and thrown upon his own resources. Then that most terrible of all human feelings, that of being inescapably alone, of having to live alone and to taste and endure alone sorrow, fear, and death, underlies our every thought—to the young and healthy only an intimation and a warning, to the feeble a real dread.

I too felt something of this. At least my ill humor faded and gave way to quiet contemplation. It pained me to think that beautiful, desirable Helene would probably never think of me with emotions like those I felt toward her; but I also knew that the grief of an unrequited love was not going to kill me, and I had a vague premonition that life, mysterious life, held darker abysses and worse vicissitudes than a young man's vacation sorrows.

Nevertheless, my stirred-up blood remained warm and, independently of my will, created out of the sluggish breeze caressing hands and a girl's brown hair, so that this walk late at night made me neither tired nor sleepy. So I walked over the rowen grass of the pale fields on the banks of the river, removed my light clothing, and plunged into the cool water. The swift current instantly forced me to put up a stiff resistance. I swam upstream for a quarter of an hour. Depression and melancholy streamed off me with the refreshing river water. Cooled and somewhat tired, I found my clothes again, slipped into them still wet, and returned home and to bed in a light, tranquil frame of mind.

After the excitement of the first few days I gradually fell in with the quiet normality of life at home. How I had roamed around in the outside world, drifting from city to city, knowing many different sorts of people, sometimes working, sometimes dreaming, sometimes studying, and sometimes spending nights carousing, living for a while on bread and milk and then for a while on books and cigars, a different person every month. And here everything was the same as it had been ten and twenty years before. Here the days and weeks ran on in a serene, even tempo. And I, who had become estranged from all this and accustomed to an unstable life of variegated experiences, fitted into this again as if I had never been away. I took an interest in people and things that I had completely forgotten for years, and missed nothing of all that the outside world had meant to me.

The hours and days ran along for me as easily as summer clouds, without leaving a trace behind; each was a colorful picture and each a floating emotion, rising in a rush of music, sounding forth, and soon fading dreamily away. I watered the garden, sang with Lotte, firecrackered with Fritz, chatted with Mother about foreign places and with Father about the latest events in the world; I read Goethe and Jens Peter Jacobsen, and one thing passed into another and went well with the other, and nothing seriously mattered either way.

At the time what seriously mattered to me was Helene Kurz and my feeling for her. But that too existed like everything else; it moved me for hours at a time, then was submerged again for hours. Constant alone was my pulsating, joyous feeling of being alive, the feeling of a swimmer who moves along in smooth water, unhurried and aimless, without effort and without a care. In the woods the jay shrieked and the bilberries ripened; in the garden, roses bloomed and fiery nasturtiums. I took part in it all, thought the world glorious, and wondered what life would be like when eventually I too would become a real man, old and sensible.

One afternoon a large raft came floating through the town. I jumped aboard it, lay down on a pile of boards, and floated downriver for a few hours, past farms and villages and under bridges, while above me the air quivered and sultry clouds seethed with faint thunder, and under me the cool water of the river slapped and laughed fresh and foamy. I imagined that Helene was along; I had abducted her, and we were sitting hand in hand and showing each other the splendors of the world from here all the way downstream to Holland.

When I left the raft far down in the valley, I jumped short and landed in the water up to my chest. But on the warm walk home my steaming clothes dried on my body. And when I reached the first houses of the town again, dusty and weary after my long tramp, I met Helene Kurz wearing a red blouse. I lifted my hat and she nodded, and I thought again of my daydream, of her traveling down the river with me hand in hand and speaking to me as an intimate, and then for the rest of that evening it all seemed hopeless to me and I thought myself a silly dreamer and stargazer. Nevertheless, before going to sleep I smoked my handsome pipe, with two grazing deer painted on its porcelain bowl, and read *Wilhelm Meister* until after eleven o'clock.

The following evening at about half past eight I went up to the Pinnacle with my brother, Fritz. We had a heavy package with us, which we took turns carrying. It contained a dozen giant crackers, six skyrockets, three large grenades, and a variety of small things.

The air was tepid, blue-tinted, and filled with shreds of cloud in motion, which drifted gently away over the church tower and the peaks of the hills, frequently covering the pallid first stars of evening. At the Pinnacle we first rested for a short while after our climb, and I looked down on our narrow river valley lying below in its pale twilight colors. As I looked at the town and the next village, at the bridges and mill-dam and the narrow, shrub-lined river, the twilight mood and the thought of that beautiful girl stole upon me together. I would have preferred to be dreaming there alone and waiting for the moon. But that could not be, for my brother had already unpacked and startled me by exploding two crackers from behind my back; he had linked them with a string, tied them to a pole, and held them out close to my ears.

I was a little annoyed. But Fritz laughed so uproariously and was so pleased with himself that I was quickly infected and joined in. In quick succession we set off three extra-powerful grenades and listened to the tremendous reports booming up and down the valley and dying away in long, rolling echoes. Then came more firecrackers, squibs, and a large catherine-wheel, and to finish it off we slowly sent one after another of our fine skyrockets mounting into the now black night sky.

"You know, a real good rocket like that is almost like worshipping God," said my brother, who sometimes liked to use figures of speech. "Or like singing a beautiful song, don't you think? It's so solemn."

On the way home we tossed our last firecracker into the shingler's yard, at the nasty yard dog, who howled in terror and went on barking ferociously after us for a quarter of an hour. We came home high-spirited and black-fingered, like two young rascals who have been up to all sorts of tricks. And to our parents we sang the praises of our lovely evening walk, the view of the valley and the star-strewn sky.

One morning while I was at the window cleaning out my pipe, Lotte came running up and called: "Well, my girl-friend is arriving today, at eleven."

"Anna Amberg?"

"Yes. You'll come with me to meet her, won't you?"

"All right."

I was not particularly pleased at the prospect of this guest, to whom I had not given a thought. But there was nothing to do about it, and so toward eleven o'clock I went to the railroad station with my sister. We arrived too early and walked up and down in front of the station.

"Perhaps she will be riding second-class," Lotte said.

I stared incredulously at her.

"She might be. Her family are well to do, and though she hasn't any airs . . ."

I shuddered. I imagined a fashionable lady with mincing manners and a pile of baggage stepping out of the second-class car and finding my father's comfortable home pitiful and myself not at all good enough for her.

"If she's traveling second-class, she may just as well travel right past here, for all I care."

Lotte was annoyed and was going to answer me sharply, but then the train pulled in and stopped, and Lotte ran quickly toward it. I followed her at a leisurely pace and saw her girl-friend getting out of a third-class car, armed with a gray silk umbrella, a traveling-rug, and a modest suitcase.

"Anna, this is my brother."

I said hello, and because in spite of the third class I didn't know what she would think of my taking her suitcase myself, light as it was, I beckoned the porter and handed it to him. Then I walked along into the city beside the two girls, wondering at how much they had to tell each other. But I took a liking to Miss Amberg. Of course, I was a bit disappointed that she was not especially pretty, but to make up for that there was something pleasant about her face and voice that was soothing and awakened confidence.

I can still see the way my mother received the two of them at the glass door. Mother had a knack for reading people's faces, and anyone whom she welcomed with her smile, after a first searching look, could be prepared for a good time in her home. I can still see how she looked into Anna Amberg's eyes and then nodded to her and gave her both hands, taking her into her heart and making her at home without saying a word. My suspicion that the stranger would be an intruder promptly vanished, for she took the proffered hands and friendliness with quiet cordiality, and from the very first hour became part of our household.

With all the acumen of my young years, I decided that first day that this pleasant girl had an innocent, natural serenity. She might not know too much about life, but she was a worthwhile chum. I had a dim suspicion of the existence of a higher and worthier serenity that some can acquire out of trouble and suffering, and some never acquire at all; but this I did not really know from experience. For the time being, I remained unaware that our guest possessed this rare kind of tranquil cheerfulness.

Girls with whom one could chum around and talk about life and literature were not often met with in my sphere of life in those days. Up to now I had regarded my sister's girl-friends either as objects to fall in love with or as creatures of no importance at all. To associate with a young lady without constraint, and to be able to chat with her about all sorts of things as if she were one of my own friends, was something new and delightful to me. In spite of being on equal terms with her, I sensed in her voice, language, and way of thinking the feminine tone, and I found this warm and sweet.

Quite incidentally I was rather abashed to notice how quietly and skillfully and with what absence of fuss Anna fitted herself into our life and accustomed herself to our ways. For all of the friends I had ever brought home as vacation guests had always made a bit of a to-do and brought with them an alien atmosphere. Even I myself had been louder and more self-important than was needful in the first days after my homecoming.

At times I was amazed at how little special consideration Anna seemed to require. In conversation I could even be almost rude without seeing any sign that she was offended. How different it was with Helene Kurz, by contrast! Toward her, even in the most animated talk, I would not have dared to use anything but the most careful and respectful phrases.

As it happened, Helene Kurz came to see us quite often during this time, and seemed to be fond of my sister's friend. One day we were all invited to a gathering in the garden at Uncle Matthäus's. Coffee and cake were served, and afterward gooseberry wine; in the intervals we played harmless children's games or strolled decorously along the garden paths, whose neatness and precision of themselves imposed dignified behavior.

It was strange to me to see Helene and Anna together and to talk with both at once. With Helene Kurz, who as always looked wonderful, I could talk only about superficial matters, but I did so in the prissiest tone, while with Anna I could chat about even the most interesting subjects without any agitation or sense of strain. And while I was grateful to her, finding conversation with her relaxing and reassuring, I kept glancing away from her to the other, the far prettier girl whose looks ravished me and yet always left me unsatisfied.

My brother, Fritz, was wretchedly bored. After he had eaten as much cake as he could hold, he suggested several rougher games; some we would not enter into, and others we quickly abandoned. In between he drew me aside and complained that the afternoon was terribly insipid. When I shrugged, he alarmed me by confessing that he had a firecracker in his pocket which he intended to set off later on when the girls would, as usual, take their time about bidding each other good-by. I had to argue hard to dissuade him. He then took himself off to the remotest corner of the big garden and lay down under the gooseberry bushes. But I betrayed him by laughing with the others over his childish bad temper, though I was sorry for him and understood his feelings very well.

My two cousins, Aunt Berta's daughters, were quite easy to handle. They were altogether unspoiled and drank in with grateful eagerness jokes that had long since lost all sheen of newness. Uncle had withdrawn immediately after the coffee. Aunt Berta stayed with Lotte most of the time; she was quite willing to dismiss me after I had a few words with her on the art of putting up berries, which made her very pleased with me. And so I hung around the two girls and in pauses of the conversation wondered why it is so much more difficult to talk with a girl you are in love with. I should have liked very much to pay some kind of homage to Helene, but I could think of nothing. Finally I cut two of the many roses in the garden and gave one to Helene, the other to Anna Amberg.

That was the last entirely unclouded day of my holiday. The following day I heard from a casual acquaintance that Helene Kurz had recently been a frequent visitor to such and such a family, and that an engagement would soon be announced. He mentioned this incidentally, among many other items of news, and I was careful not to let on that it meant anything to me. But even though it was only a rumor, I had in any case scarcely dared to hope for much from Helene, and was now convinced that she was out of reach entirely. I returned home utterly unhinged and fled to my room.

Under the circumstances and with my youthful resiliency, I could not go on sorrowing for very long. But for several days I refused all amusement. I took long, lonely walks in the woods, hung around the house feeling sad and vacant, and spent evenings behind closed windows improvising on the violin.

"Is something the matter, my boy?" Papa said to me, laying his hand on my shoulder.

"I didn't sleep well," I replied quite truthfully. I could not manage to tell him any more. But he said something then that I have often recalled since.

"A sleepless night," he said, "is always a bad business. But it is endurable if we have good thoughts. When we lie still and do not sleep, we easily become vexed and turn our mind to vexatious things. But we can also use our will and think good thoughts."

"Can we?" I wondered. For in recent years I had begun to doubt the existence of free will.

"Yes, we can!" Father said emphatically.

I can still remember distinctly the very hour when, after several days of being bitter and gloomy, I came to myself again, forgot my unhappiness, and began living with others and being gay again. We were all sitting in the living-room over afternoon coffee; only Fritz was not there. The others were merry and talkative, but I kept quiet and did not participate, though secretly I was already feeling once more a need to chat and be lively. As young people will, I had surrounded my sorrow with a wall of silence and defiant obstinacy. After the considerate custom of our household, the others had let me alone and respected my obvious low spirits, and now I could not get up the courage to tear down my wall. A short while before, my feeling had been genuine and necessary to me; now I was pretending it, boring myself with it. Moreover, I was ashamed because my period of penance had lasted so short a time.

Suddenly the tranquillity of our afternoon coffee was shattered by a jaunty flourish of trumpets, a bold and challenging run of rapid tones that made us all leap to our feet.

"There's a fire!" my sister cried out in alarm.

"That would be a funny fire alarm."

"Then soldiers are going to be quartered on us."

Meanwhile we had all rushed headlong to the windows. On the street, right in front of our house, we saw a swarm of children, and in the midst of them, seated on a huge white horse, was a trumpeter clad in scarlet, his horn and habit resplendent in the sunlight. This remarkable person looked up at all the windows as he trumpeted; he had a tanned face, with a tremendous Hungarian mustachio. He went on frenziedly blowing his horn, mixing his themes with all sorts of random improvisations, until all the windows in the vicinity were crowded with onlookers. Then he put down his instrument, stroked his mustache, placed his left hand on his hip while with his right hand he reined in the restive horse, and delivered a speech. He was passing through, he said, and only for this one single day would his world-famous troupe be stopping in the town. On the earnest pleas of the citizens he would give a "gala performance" that very evening on the meadow near the marsh. There would be "trained horses, elegant balancing acts and a grand pantomine as well." Admission for adults was twenty pfennigs, children ten. Having given his announcement and made sure that all understood, the rider blew one more blast of his shining horn and rode off, followed by the flock of children and a dense white cloud of dust.

The laughter and the joyous anticipation that the circus

rider's appearance had stirred up among us was a great help to me. I took advantage of the opportunity to drop my gloomy airs and join in the excitement of the others. Promptly I invited the two girls to the evening performance. After some demurring Papa gave us his permission, and the three of us at once sauntered down to the meadow to take a look at the show. We found two men busy marking off a round arena and fencing it in with rope. Then they began putting up a high scaffolding. Near by, on the steps of a green van, a frightfully fat old woman sat knitting. A pretty white poodle lay at her feet. While we were looking on, the rider returned from town, tied the white horse behind the van, removed his flashy red garments, and in shirtsleeves helped the others set up the scaffolding.

"Poor fellows!" Anna Amberg said. But I said I couldn't see what there was to pity about them. I took up the defense of the circus performers and praised their free, merry gypsy life to the skies. There was nothing I would like better than to go with them, I said; to walk the tightrope and after the performance take the plate around.

"I'd love to see that," Anna laughed merrily.

Whereupon I took my hat instead of a plate, made the gestures of a man taking up a collection, and humbly asked for a small contribution for the clown. Anna put her hand in her pocket, fumbled for a moment, and then threw a pfennig into my hat. I thanked her and dropped it into my vest pocket.

The gaiety I had been repressing burst out of me with stunning force. I was high-spirited as a child all that day. Perhaps being aware of my own fickleness had something to do with this.

In the evening we took Fritz along and went to the performance. Even before we got there we were akindle with excitement and anticipatory pleasure. At the meadow a crowd was surging aimlessly hither and thither. Children stood about, silent and blissful, their eyes wide with expectancy; young rapscallions teased everybody and knocked one another over in front of people's feet; onlookers settled down in the chestnut trees, and the constable strode around with his helmet on. Around the arena a row of seats had been set up; in the center of the arena stood a four-armed scaffold with cans of oil depending from its arms. These were now lit; the crowd pressed closer; the row of seats slowly filled; and above the arena and the many heads swayed the sooty red flame of the kerosene torches.

We had found places on one of the plank seats. A hand-organ sounded out, and the ringmaster appeared in the arena with a small black pony. The clown came in with him and began a conversation, punctuated by many slaps in the face, which evoked loud applause. It began with the clown's asking some insolent question. Answering with a slap in the face, the ringmaster said: "Do you think I'm a camel?"

To which the clown replied: "Now, sir, I know quite well what the difference is between you and a camel."

"Oh, you do, clown? What is the difference?"

"Why, ringmaster, a camel can work for a week without drinking. But you can drink for a week without working."

Another slap, more applause. And so it went on, and even as I marveled at the crudeness of the jokes and the simplicity of the grateful audience, I myself laughed along with everybody else.

The pony made leaps, jumped over a bench, counted to twelve, and played dead. Then came a poodle that jumped through hoops, danced on two legs, and did military drill. In between, the clown constantly reappeared. Then came a goat, a very pretty little animal that balanced itself on a chair.

Finally the clown was asked whether all he could do was stand around and crack jokes. Whereupon he quickly threw off his bulky clown's costume, appeared in red tights, and climbed up the high rope. He was a handsome fellow and did his act well. But even if he had not, it was a fine sight to see the red figure illuminated by the flames of the torches suspended far up under the dark-blue night sky.

Since the performance had taken longer than planned, the pantomime had to be cut out. We too had stayed out beyond our usual hour, and we set off for home at once.

All during the performance we had kept up a lively chatter. I had been sitting next to Anna Amberg, and though we had made nothing but casual remarks to each other, I had been aware all the time of her warm closeness, and now on the way home I missed it a little.

Because I lay in my bed for a long time without falling

asleep, I had time to think about that. And as I did so, I became uncomfortably and shamefully conscious of my faithlessness. How had I been able to give up beautiful Helene Kurz so quickly? But with the help of some sophistical reasoning that night and during the next few days, I settled the matter quite neatly and solved all the apparent contradictions to my own satisfaction.

That night, before finally going to sleep, I lit the lamp again, found in my vest pocket the pfennig coin that Anna had given me in jest, and studied it tenderly. It bore the date 1877—in other words, it was just as old as myself. I wrapped it in white paper, labeled it with the initials A. A. and the day's date, and placed it in the innermost slot of my wallet, as a lucky penny.

Half of my holiday—and the first half of a holiday is always longer than the second—had long since passed, and after a week of violent thunderstorms the summer began to grow gradually older and wiser. But I, as though nothing else in the world was of any importance, steered lovelorn, with fluttering pennons, through the almost imperceptibly shortening days; I charged each day with a golden hope and in gay bravado watched each one coming, shining, and going without wishing to stop it and without regretting its passing.

Certainly this bravado sprang from the amazing insouciance of youth, but my mother was also partly to blame for it. For without saying a word about the matter, she let me see that she was well disposed toward my friendship with Anna. Associating with this intelligent and well-mannered girl had certainly done me good; there was no denying that. And it seemed to me that Mamma would also approve a deeper and closer relationship with Anna. So there was no need for worry and concealment, and I behaved toward Anna as I would have toward a dear sister.

Such a situation, however, was far from what I wanted, and after a while this static chumminess between us at times became almost painful to me. For I wished to emerge from the well-fenced garden of friendship into the broad, unbounded fields of love, and had no idea how I could imperceptibly lure my unsuspecting friend out on the open roads. But out of this very conflict there arose, during the last part of my vacation, a deliciously free state of suspension between contentment and desiring more which remains in my memory as a state of great happiness.

So we passed pleasant summer days in our fortunate household. With Mother I had meanwhile returned to the old relationship of a child, so that I could talk to her about my life without constraint, could confess past faults and discuss plans for the future. I still remember one morning how we sat in the arbor winding yarn. I had told Mother what had happened to my belief in God and had finished by asserting that if I were ever to become a believer again, someone would have to come along and convert me.

At this my mother smiled and looked at me. After meditating for a while she said: "Probably no one will ever come along and convert you. But gradually you yourself will learn that it isn't possible to go on through life without faith. For knowledge is good for nothing, you know. Every day you are apt to see someone whom you thought you knew through and through do something that proves how little you really know people or can be certain about anything. And yet people need something they can rely upon; people need certainty. And then it is always better to turn to the Saviour rather than to some professor or Bismarck or anyone else."

"Why?" I asked. "After all, there isn't so much that we know for certain about the Saviour."

"Oh, we know enough. And then too—in the course of ages there have been individuals here and there who were able to die with self-confidence and without fear. It is said that Socrates was one, and there were some others—but not many. In fact, they were very few, and if they were able to die calmly and composedly, it was not because of their wisdom, but because their hearts and consciences were pure. Very well, let us say that these few people were right—each one right for himself. But how many of us are like them? As against these few, you see on the other side thousands upon thousands of poor, ordinary people who have nevertheless been able to die willingly and with composure because they believed in the Saviour. Your grandfather lay suffering terribly for fourteen months before he was granted relief; yet he did not complain and suffered all that pain and death almost cheerfully because the Saviour was his consolation."

And finally Mother said: "I know quite well that I cannot convince you. Faith does not come through reason, any more than love. But you will some day learn that reason does not cover everything, and when you have come to that point, then in your extremity you will snatch at anything that seems to offer support. Perhaps then you will remember some of the things we have said today."

I helped Father in the garden, and often when I went for walks I would bring back for him a sackful of forest soil for him to use on his potted plants. With Fritz I invented new fireworks and burned my fingers setting them off. With Lotte and Anna Amberg I spent whole mornings or afternoons in the woods, helping to pick berries and look for flowers. I read aloud to them from my favorite books and discovered new places for strolls.

The fine summer days ran into one another. I had become accustomed to being about Anna all the time, and when I thought that this would soon come to an end, dark clouds blackened the bright blue of my vacation sky.

And as all loveliness and sweetness is mortal and has its destined end, day after day of this summer, too, slipped through my fingers—this summer which in memory seems to have brought my youth to a close. The family began to talk of my impending departure. Mother once more went carefully through my stock of clothing, mending a few things, and on the day I packed she presented me with two pairs of substantial gray woolen socks that she had knitted herself; neither of us knew that it was to be her last gift to me.

Long dreaded and yet surprising when it came, the last day finally arrived. It was a fair, blue late summer day, with lacy clouds and a soft southeast breeze that played in the garden among the roses, still blooming in great numbers—a breeze that gathered all the fragrance of the summer until, toward noon, it grew tired and went to sleep. Because I had decided to make the most of the day and not to leave until late evening, we young people decided to spend the afternoon on an outing. That left the morning hours for my parents, and I sat between the two of them on the sofa in Father's study. Father had saved a few farewell presents for me. Now, with a kind of joking tone that concealed his emotion, he gave them to me. There was a small old-fashioned purse with a sum of money in it; a pen to carry in the pocket; and a neatly bound notebook that he had made himself and in which he had written in his austere hand a dozen good maxims. He advised me to be sparing but not stingy with the money; to use the pen to write home frequently; and if I found any more good maxims that my experience had tested, to set them down in the notebook beside those others which in his own life he had found useful and true.

We sat together more than two hours, and my parents told me a good many stories of the past, of our own childhood, of theirs, and of the lives of their parents; stories that were new to me and struck me as important. I have forgotten much of what they said, and as at intervals my thoughts kept wandering away to Anna, I may well have not listened to all of the earnest and weighty things they said. But what has remained with me is a vivid memory of that morning in the study and a feeling of deep gratitude and reverence for both my parents, whom today I see in an aura of purity and holiness which no other human beings have for me.

But at the time the farewell I had to take in the afternoon touched me far more deeply. Soon after lunch I set out with the two girls along the road over the mountain. Our destination was a lovely forest gorge, a steep-walled tributary valley of our river.

At first my solemn mood made the other two silent and thoughtful. But when we reached the peak of the mountain, from where the winding valley and forested hills could be seen through the tall red trunks of the firs, I wrenched myself out of my depression with a loud whoop. The girls laughed and instantly started to sing a hiking song. It was *"O Täler weit, o Höhen,"* an old favorite of Mother's, and as I sang along I recalled many joyous outings in the woods in my childhood and on past vacations. Just as soon as the last notes of the song died away, we began, as though by agreement, to talk about those times and about Mother. We spoke of those times with gratitude and pride, for we had had a glorious youth, and I walked hand in hand with Lotte until Anna, laughing, took my other hand. Then we strode along the whole length of the road that ran on the ridge, the three of us swinging our hands in a kind of dance, and it was a joy to be alive.

Then we climbed down a steep, slanting footpath that led to a brook at the bottom of the deep gorge. From a distance we could hear the brook leaping over stones and ledges. Farther upstream along the brook was a favorite inn of ours, where I had invited the two girls to have coffee, cake, and ice cream with me. Descending the hill and along the brook we had to walk in single file, and I remained behind Anna, looking at her and trying to think of some way to speak alone with her before the day ended.

Finally a pretext occurred to me. We were close to our destination and had arrived at a grassy spot covered with wild pinks. I suggested to Lotte that she go on ahead to order the coffee and have a nice garden table set for us, while Anna and I gathered a big bouquet of ferns and flowers, this being such a fine spot to pick them. Lotte thought this a good idea and went ahead. Anna sat down on a moss-covered rock and began plucking fronds of fern.

"So this is my last day," I began.

"Yes, it's too bad. But you will surely be coming home again soon, won't you?"

"Who knows? Not next year, at any rate, and even if I do come again, it won't be the same."

"Why not?"

"Well, it would be if you should happen to be here again!"

"You know that's not altogether out of the question. But, after all, your coming home this time had nothing to do with me."

"Because I didn't know you then."

"Yes, of course. But you aren't even helping me. You might hand me a few of those pinks over there."

I pulled myself together.

"I'll pick them by and by. But at the moment something else is more important to me. You see, now I have a few minutes alone with you, and that is what I have been waiting for all day. Because—since I must leave today, you know—well, I wanted to ask you, Anna—"

She looked at me, her intelligent face grave and somewhat troubled.

"Wait!" she interrupted my stumbling speech. "I think I know what you want to say to me. And now I must ask you sincerely not to say it!"

"Not say it?"

"No, Hermann. I cannot tell you now why that cannot be, but I don't mind your knowing. Ask your sister some other time, later on. She knows all about it. We have so little time now, and it's a sad story; let's not be sad today. Let us make our bouquet now, until Lotte comes back. And for the rest, let us stay good friends and be jolly together for the rest of this day. Will you?"

"I would if I could."

"All right, then listen. My case is the same as yours: there's someone I care for and cannot have. But when that's how it is, there's all the more reason to cling to the friendship, kindness, and fun that come your way from other quarters, don't you think? That is why I say let us stay good friends and for this last day at least have fun together. Shan't we?"

I murmured yes, and we shook hands on it. The brook sported in its bed and sprayed drops of water up at us; our bouquet grew huge and vivid; and before long we heard my sister's voice approaching us, singing and calling out. When she reached us, I pretended I wanted to drink. I knelt by the brook's edge and dipped my forehead and eyes into the cold, flowing water for a short while. Then I took up the bouquet and we walked together the short distance to the inn.

There under a maple tree a table was set for us, with ice cream, coffee, and cookies. The innkeeper's wife welcomed us, and to my own surprise I found I could talk and answer people and eat as though all were well. I became almost gay; I made a little after-dinner speech and laughed unforcedly when the others laughed.

I will never forget with what simplicity and kindness and amiability Anna helped me to get over my humiliation and sadness that afternoon. Without betraying the fact that something had occurred between us, she treated me with a wonderful friendliness that helped me to act normal. I was filled with the greatest respect for her older and deeper sorrow and for the serene manner in which she bore it.

The narrow forest gorge was filling with early evening shadows when we started out again. But on the ridge, which we reached after a quick climb, we caught up with the sinking sun and walked for another hour in its warm light before we lost sight of it again as we descended to the town. I looked back at the sun one last time as it hovered, large and pink among the tops of the black pines, and I thought that tomorrow, far from here, I would see it again in foreign places.

In the evening, after I had taken my leave of all in the household, Lotte and Anna walked with me to the station and waved after me as the train slid away into the darkness.

I stood at the window of the car and looked out on the town, where street lamps were already lit and windows glowed brightly. As the train approached our garden, I caught sight of a powerful blood-red flare. There stood my brother, Fritz, holding a Bengal light in each hand. At the very moment that I waved to him and rode by, he sent a skyrocket shooting straight up into the air. Leaning out, I saw it mount and pause, describe a gentle arc, and vanish in a rain of red sparks.

Translated by Richard and Clara Winston

KANNITVERSTAN

by Johann Peter Hebel

In Emmendingen and Gundelfingen, as well as in Amsterdam, a man has the opportunity every day, I dare say, to reflect on the inconstancy of all earthly things—if he wants to—and to learn how to be satisfied with his lot even though life is no bed of roses. But it was by the oddest roundabout route that a German journeyman in Amsterdam came, through error, to the perception of this truth.

After he had come to that great and prosperous city of commerce, full of splendid houses, heaving ships, and busy people, his eye fell upon a house larger and more beautiful than any he had ever seen on all his travels from Tuttlingen to Amsterdam. For a long time he gazed in wonder at this costly building, at the six chimneys on its roof, at its beautiful cornices, and at the high windows, each larger than the front door to his father's house.

Finally, yielding to an impulse, he addressed a passer-by. "My good friend," he asked, "can you tell me the name of the gentleman who owns this marvelous house with the windows full of tulips, asters, and gilliflowers?" But the man, who probably had something more important to attend to and, unfortunately, understood just as much German as his questioner did Dutch—to wit, nothing—growled: "*Kannitverstan,*" and whisked by. This is a Dutch word—or three of them, if one

---

Born in 1760 in the duchy of Baden, the son of a manservant, Johann Peter Hebel studied theology and became a teacher and school principal. From 1807 to 1814 he annually published an almanac, Der rheinische Hausfreund*—short stories and anecdotes from which, collected in a volume,* Schatzkästlein des rheinischen Hausfreundes, *established his fame. He also wrote poems in the Alamannic dialect. Elevated to the prelacy, he lived in Karlsruhe until his death in 1826.*

looks at it properly—and means no more than "I cannot understand you."

But the good stranger thought it to be the name of the gentleman he'd asked about. "That must be a mighty rich man, that Mr. Kannitverstan," he said to himself, and walked on.

Making his way through the narrow streets, he came at length to the estuary that is called Het Ey, meaning "the Y." There stood ship after ship and mast after mast, and he was beginning to wonder how he could ever manage to take in all of these marvels with his own two eyes, when his glance fell upon a large merchantman that recently had put in from the East Indies and was being unloaded. Whole rows of piled crates and bales stood side by side on the wharf, and more were being rolled out: casks full of sugar and coffee, full of rice and pepper, and with them—pardon—mouse droppings too.

After he had watched for a long time, he asked a fellow who was carrying a crate on his shoulders the name of the fortunate man to whom the sea had brought all these wares. "*Kannitverstan*," was the answer.

Then he thought: "Aha, so that's how it is! If the sea floats him such riches, no wonder he can put up houses with gilt-potted tulips in the windows." So he went away, sorrowfully reflecting how poor a man he was among so many rich people in this world. But just as he was thinking: "I wish I, too, would be as well off some day as this Mr. Kannitverstan," he turned a corner and saw a great funeral procession. Four black-draped horses were pulling a black-covered hearse slowly and lugubriously, as though they were aware they were carrying a dead man to his peace. A long cortege of friends and acquaintances of the departed followed behind, pair after pair, muffled in black cloaks, and mute. A solitary bell sounded in the distance. Our stranger was seized by the melancholy feeling that no good man can suppress at the sight of a funeral, and he remained standing reverently, with his hat in his hands, until all was over. Then he attached himself to the last mourner (who was just figuring how much he would make on his cotton if the bale price should rise ten florins), tugged at his coat, guilelessly begged his pardon, and said: "He must indeed have been a good friend of yours, the gentleman for whom the bell is tolling, that you follow his coffin so grieved and pensive."

"*Kannitverstan,*" was the answer.

A few large tears descended from the eyes of our good journeyman from Tuttlingen, and he felt sad and relieved at once. "Poor Kannitverstan," he exclaimed, "what have you now of all your riches? Exactly what I shall get one day from my poverty: a linen shroud! And of all your beautiful flowers, you have, perhaps, a rosemary on your cold breast, or some rue." With these thoughts he accompanied the funeral procession to the grave as though he belonged with it, and saw the supposed Mr. Kannitverstan sink down to his final resting-place, and was more moved by the Dutch funeral oration, of which he understood not a word, than by many a German one to which he had paid no attention.

He left with the others and went away with a light heart, and at an inn where German was understood, he ate, with relish, a piece of Limburg cheese. And whenever afterward his heart became heavy because so many people in this world were so rich and he was so poor, he only thought of Mr. Kannitverstan of Amsterdam—of his big house, his opulent ship, and his narrow grave.

Translated by Paul Pratt

AN EPISODE IN THE LIFE OF THE MARSHAL DE BASSOMPIERRE

by Hugo von Hofmannsthal

At one time in my life I had, in the course of my service, to cross the little bridge (the Pont Neuf not yet being built) fairly regularly several times a week at the same hour, and as I did so, some laborers and others of the common people came to recognize and salute me. But the most insistent and regular greeting came from the very pretty shopkeeper whose shop bore the sign of the Two Angels. Every time I passed during those five or six months, she dropped me a low curtsy and watched me out of sight. Attracted by her behavior, I returned her look and acknowledged her salutation with care. Once, toward the end of winter, I was riding from Fontainebleau to Paris, and as I mounted the little bridge, she came to the door of her shop and said, as I rode by: "Your servant, sir." I returned her greeting and, looking back from time to time, saw that she had leaned yet farther out to keep me in sight as long as she possibly could.

Among English-speaking people Hugo von Hofmannsthal (1874–1929) is known chiefly as the author of the librettos for many of Richard Strauss's operas and as the man who adapted Everyman (Jedermann) *for the Salzburg festivals. On the Continent his fame as a poet, dramatist, writer of fiction, and man of letters far transcends that renown. He was born, the descendant of Jewish merchants, Austrian peasants, and Italian patricians, in Vienna, where he was to live until his death. He published his first verse drama, a masterpiece, at the age of seventeen. Probably his two most accomplished works are* Andreas, *the fragment of a novel, and the drama* Der Turm. *The story reprinted here was first told by Bassompierre himself (1665); in 1795 it was retold by Goethe in his* Conversations of German Émigrés.

Behind me I had my man and a postilion, whom I had meant to send back to Fontainebleau that evening with letters for certain ladies. On my order, my man now dismounted and approached the young woman, telling her in my name that I had remarked her eagerness to see and greet me, and that if she desired to make my closer acquaintance, I would wait upon her at any place she appointed.

She replied to my man that he could have brought her no more welcome message; she would herself come to any place I would name.

As we rode on, I asked my man if he knew where I could meet the woman. He replied that he could take her to a certain procuress's, but this man of mine, William of Courtrai, being a most careful and conscientious creature, at once added that there was plague here and there in the city, and as it had already carried off not only men and women of the mean and dirty sort, but a doctor and a canon too, he would advise me to have my own mattresses and bedclothes with me. I fell in with his proposal, and he promised to prepare me a good bed. Before we dismounted, I added that he should take to the place a proper washbasin, a small bottle of sweet-smelling essence, and some cakes and apples; he should also see that the room was thoroughly warmed, for it was so cold that my feet were frozen stiff in the stirrups, and the sky was heavy with snow-clouds.

That evening, going to the appointed place, I found a very beautiful young woman, some twenty years of age, sitting on the bed, while the procuress, her head and bent old back muffled up in a black shawl, seemed to be urging something upon her. The door stood ajar; in the fireplace big fresh logs were blazing noisily. The women did not hear my approach, and I remained standing a moment in the doorway. The young woman was gazing steadily into the fire with wide-open eyes. A single movement of her head seemed to have put miles between her and the old crone; in the movement a few locks of her heavy dark hair had burst out from under the little nightcap she wore, and, twining in natural ringlets, had fallen over her shift between her shoulder and bosom. She also wore a short petticoat of green woolen stuff and slippers on her feet.

At that moment I must have betrayed my presence by some noise; with a sudden movement of her head she turned toward me a face so haggard with expectation that it would have looked fierce but for the radiance of devotion which streamed from her wide-open eyes and burst like an invisible flame from her speechless mouth. She was inexpressibly beautiful. In a trice the old crone was banished from the room and I was with my mistress. When, in the first rapture of this unexpected possession, I ventured a few liberties, she shrank from me with unspeakably anxious pleading both in her look and in her rich, low voice. But in a moment her arms were about me again, and the upturned gaze of her fathomless eyes, straining upon me, clasped me more close than her lips and arms. Then again she seemed to be struggling to speak, but her lips, quivering with kisses, formed no words, and from her pulsing throat there came no sound more distinct than a broken sob.

Now, I had spent most of that day on horseback on freezing highroads; later I had been party to a very annoying and violent scene in the King's antechamber, and then, to overcome my ill humor, I had both drunk wine and fenced vigorously with a two-handed sword, and so, in the midst of this lovely and mysterious adventure, as I lay with soft arms round my neck and perfumed hair pouring over me, I was overcome by a fatigue that was almost a swoon, so sudden and irresistible that I could no longer remember how I had come into that room. For a moment I even imagined the woman whose heart beat so close to mine to be a totally different one I had known earlier in life, and at once fell into a deep sleep.

When I awoke, the night was still dark, but I at once felt that my mistress was no longer by my side. I raised my head and in a faint glow of the dying embers saw her standing by the window. She had pushed open one of the shutters and was looking out through the crack. Then she turned round, saw that I was awake, and called (I can still see her raising the palm of her left hand to her cheek to toss back her fallen hair): "It is not day yet—not for a long time." Only then did I really see how tall and beautiful she was. I could hardly wait until one or two steady, long steps of her beautiful, glow-reddened feet had brought her to my side again. On her way she moved to the fireplace, bent down, took the last heavy log lying in front of it in her shining bare arms, and flung it into the embers. And then she turned, her face sparkling with flames and joy; in passing, she snatched up an apple from the table, and was again in my arms, her limbs still bathed in the fresh heat of the fire, then dissolving, as it were, in the yet fierier flames that pulsed through them from within. Clasping me with her right hand, she bit into the cool fruit in her left, then held it to my mouth, offering the fruit, offering her face. The last log in the fireplace flamed higher than all the rest. With a shower of sparks it sucked in the flames, then hurled them up again in a furious blaze, and the firelight broke over us like a wave dashing against the wall, flinging our shadowed embrace up and down upon it. The great log crackled, feeding from its heart fresh flames that danced upward, dispelling the darkness with sheaves and fountains of glowing red. Then, all of a sudden, the flame sank; a breath of cold air pushed open the shutter like a hand and revealed the livid, hideous gray of dawn.

We sat up, knowing that day had come. But the light outside was like no day. This was no awakening of a world, and what lay outside was like no street. Things had no outlines. It was a world without form and void, where only shapeless, timeless things could move. From somewhere distant as a memory came the chime of a church clock, and a raw wind, which had no home in day or night, poured into the room until we clung together, shuddering. She leaned back, her eyes fastened on my face; her throat quivered, something rose in her and surged to her lips, but no word came, no sigh and no kiss, but something which, unborn, was like all three. In the growing light the changing expressions flitting across her face grew yet more speaking. Suddenly, in the street outside, shuffling footsteps and voices approached the window so close that she bent and turned her face to the wall. Two men passed; for a moment the light of a little lantern carried by one of them brightened the room; the other man was pushing a barrow, whose wheel creaked and groaned. When the men had passed, I stood up, closed the shutters, and lit a candle. Half an apple was still lying there; we ate it together, and then I asked whether I could see her once more, as I was not to leave till Sunday, while this night had been the night from Thursday to Friday.

She replied that she certainly desired it more ardently than I, but that unless I could stay over Sunday, she could not see me again, for she could only meet me in the night from Sunday to Monday.

A number of hindrances flashed through my mind, and I raised some objections, to which she listened without a word, but with a most painful questioning in her eyes, while her face grew almost ghastly in its somber hardness. Then, of course, I promised to stay over Sunday, and added that I should come to the same place again on Sunday evening. She looked at me steadily and said, her voice quite harsh and broken: "I know very well that I have entered a house of shame for your sake, but I did it of my own free will because I meant to be with you, because I would have done anything and gone anywhere. But now I should feel like the last and lowest woman of the town if I brought myself to come here again. I did it for your sake, because for me you are what you are, because you are Bassompierre, because you are the one human being in the world whose presence could make this house my house of honor."

She said "house"; for a moment it seemed as if a more contemptuous word were on her lips; as she said it, she cast upon the walls, our bed, and the bedclothes, which had slipped off onto the floor, such a look that, in the sheaf of light that flashed from her eyes, all these mean and ugly things seemed to start and cringe away from her, as if the wretched room had really grown bigger for a moment.

Then, in an inexpressibly gentle and solemn voice, she added: "May I die a wretched death if I have ever known any man but my husband and you, or desire any other in the world," and bending forward a little, her whole life in the breath of her parted lips, she seemed to be waiting for some answer, some assurance of my faith. But because she did not find in my face what she sought there, her eager, searching look clouded, her lashes opened and closed, and in a moment she was at the window, her back turned to me, her forehead pressed against the shutter with all her might, her whole body so shaken with noiseless but horribly violent weeping that speech died in my mouth and I did not dare to touch her. In the end I took one of her hands, which were hanging nerveless at her sides, and with the most endearing words I could command succeeded, after long effort, in soothing her until she turned her tear-stained face to me again and a smile broke out like a light from her eyes and around her lips, instantly drying up her tears and bathing her whole face in brightness.

And then it was the most delicious game to watch her begin to speak to me again, with endless variations on the one theme: "You will see me again! Then I will let you into my aunt's house," speaking the first part in a dozen different ways, now with sweet insistence, then with a pretense of childish suspicion, then whispered in my ear as if it were the greatest secret in the world, then again thrown over her shoulder with a shrug and a pout as if she was making the most commonplace appointment in the world, and in the end caressingly reiterated as she clung to me, laughing up into my face. She described the house to me in long detail, like a mother telling her child the way when it must cross the road to the baker's alone for the first time. Then she drew herself up, turned serious, and bent her radiant eyes on me with such force that they could have raised the dead to life, and went on: "I shall be waiting for you from ten o'clock till midnight and even later, and yet later still, and the downstairs door will be open. First you walk along a little passage, but you must not stop there, for my aunt's door opens on it. Then you come to a staircase leading to the upper story, and there I shall be." And, closing her eyes as if dazed, she threw back her head, spread out her arms, and embraced me—and a moment later was out of my arms, fully dressed, strange and grave, and out of the room, for now day had come.

I made my arrangements, sent some of my men ahead with my baggage, and by evening of the next day was a prey to such vehement restlessness that, soon after vespers had rung, I crossed the little bridge with my man William, whom I forbade to take a lantern, so that I might see my mistress in her shop or in the adjoining lodging and give her, at any rate, some sign of my presence, though I hoped for nothing more than perhaps to exchange a few words with her.

To avoid attracting attention, I stopped at the bridge, sending my man ahead to reconnoiter. He was away for some time, and on his return wore the moody and despondent look that always meant that he had failed to carry out one of my orders. "The shop is shut up," he said, "and there seems to be nobody in it. Indeed, there is nobody to be seen or heard in any of the rooms looking on the street. You can only get into the courtyard over a high wall, and there is a big dog growling in it. But there is a light in one of the front rooms, and you can see into the shop through a chink, though I fear it is empty."

I was put out by this and made up my mind to go home at once, but all the same crept slowly past the house again, while my man, in his eagerness, applied his eye to the chink, which let out a thin ray of light, and whispered to me that the woman was not in the shop, but that her husband was. I was anxious to get sight of this shopkeeper, whom I could not remember ever having seen in his shop, and whom I imagined by turns as fat and shapeless or withered and decrepit. I approached the window and, to my extreme surprise, saw walking about in the well-furnished, paneled room an uncommonly tall and well-built man, who was certainly a head taller than I, and who, when he turned round, showed a very handsome, very grave face with a brown beard, silvered here and there, and a forehead of almost rare sublimity, with temples more spacious than I had ever seen before in a human face. Though he was quite alone in the room, his eyes wandered, his lips moved, and as he paused from time to time in his pacing up and down, he seemed to be carrying on an imaginary conversation with some other person; once he made a gesture with his arm as if brushing aside some objection with half-indulgent authority. There were ease and an almost contemptuous pride in his every movement, and as he turned in his solitary pacing up and down the room, I could not but call vividly to mind a very illustrious prisoner whom I had had under guard in the King's service when he was held in an apartment in the tower of Blois Castle. The resemblance became still more noticeable when the man raised his right hand and looked down on his upturned fingers with a searching, even grim look.

For it was almost the same gesture that I had often observed my august prisoner make when gazing at a ring that he wore on the first finger of his right hand and never removed. The man in the room then approached the table, pushed the water-globe in front of the candle, and placed both his hands, with outstretched fingers, in the circle of light; he seemed to be examining his fingernails. Then he blew out the candle and went out of the room, leaving me with a dull feeling of sullen, angry jealousy, for my desire for his wife was rising steadily within me, feeding like a spreading fire on all it encountered, and fanned, in some bewildering fashion, by this unexpected vision as it was by every snowflake that was blown by the raw wind to hang and melt, single, on my eyebrows and cheeks.

I idled away the next day, unable to bring my mind to bear on anything, bought a horse I really did not care for, waited after dinner on the Duc de Nemours, and spent some time there at cards and in the silliest and most disagreeable conversation imaginable. For it all turned on the plague, which was spreading rapidly in the city, and there was not a word to be got out of any of these gentlemen but of the hasty burial of the bodies, the straw fire that must be lit in the room where anyone had died, to consume the pestilent vapors, and so on. But the silliest of all, in my opinion, was the Canon de Chandieu. Fat and hearty as ever, he could not refrain from keeping one eye fixed on his fingernails to see if there were to be seen there any trace of the suspicious blueness that was generally the first sign of the plague.

Disgusted with it all, I went home early and retired to bed, but could not sleep. In my impatience, I dressed again and resolved at all costs to go and see my mistress, even if I and my men had to force our way in. I went to the window to call them; the icy night air brought me to my senses and I realized that my plan would mean certain ruin to the whole affair. I threw myself fully dressed as I was on my bed and at last fell asleep.

I spent Sunday in similar fashion till evening came, and arrived long before the time in the street named, but forced myself to walk up and down a near-by alley till ten struck. Then I soon found the house and the door she had described. The door was open, as she had said, and the corridor and staircase were behind it. But upstairs the second door at the head of the staircase was shut, though a thin streak of light shone from beneath it. So she was inside, waiting, standing perhaps with her ear to the inside of the door as I with mine to the outside. I scratched on the door with my fingernail; then I heard a noise within which sounded like the shuffling, unsteady steps of bare feet. For a time I stood breathless and then began to knock, but a man's voice replied, asking who was there. I pressed back into the shadow of the doorway without uttering a sound. The door remained shut, and I crept downstairs on silent feet, step by step, then along the passage out into the open air, and with beating temples and clenched teeth, afire with impatience, walked up and down a street or two. In the end I could not resist returning to the house. I did not mean to go in yet. I felt, I knew, that she would get her husband away. She would, she must, succeed, and I should be able to go to her at once. The street was narrow. On the other side there were no houses, but only the wall of a convent garden; I stood flattened against it, trying to guess which was her window from the other side of the street. Suddenly, in one that stood open in the upper story, a light flamed up and died down. I seemed to see it all before my eyes; she had thrown a big log on the fire, as on that other night. As on that other night, she was standing in the middle of the room, her limbs bathed in the firelight, or sitting on the bed, listening and waiting. I would see her from the doorway, with the shadow of her neck and shoulders rising and falling on that invisible wave on the wall. I was already in the corridor, on the stairs. The door had been opened. Standing ajar, it allowed the flickering light to come out. I had stretched out my hands toward the door-handle, when I seemed to hear the steps and voices of several persons inside. But I would not believe it and took it for the pulsing of my blood in my temples and in my neck, and for the blazing of the fire within. That other night, too, it had blazed noisily. My hand was on the door-handle when it really came home to me that there were people in the room—several people. But now I no longer cared, for I felt, I knew, that she was there too, and that as soon as I had opened the door, I should see her, take her in my arms, and, though I should have to wrench her out of the hands of others, hold her to me with one arm, cutting a way for her with my sword, with my dagger, through a melee of shouting men and women. The one thing that seemed quite intolerable was to wait longer.

I pushed the door open. This is what I saw:

In the middle of the empty room I saw a few people burning bed-straw, and in the flames, whose light flooded the room, I saw scaling walls whose plaster lay on the floor, while against one wall there was a table on which two naked bodies lay stretched, one very big, with covered head, the other smaller, lying against the wall, with the black shadow of its outline rising and falling beside it.

I reeled down the stairs, and in front of the house encountered two gravediggers. One held his little lantern up to my face, asking me what I wanted; the other pushed his creaking, groaning barrow against the door. I drew my dagger to fend them off, and went home. There I at once drank three or four glasses of heavy wine and, having slept, set out on my journey to Lorraine.

All my efforts to discover something about the woman after my return were vain. I even went to the shop with the sign of the Two Angels, but the people who kept it did not know who had kept it before them.

Translated by Mary Hottinger

LUKARDIS

by Jakob Wassermann

In the course of the long-drawn-out revolution that afflicted the Russian Empire in the last decade but one, a brawl took place in the streets of Moscow. The immediate cause of this brawl was the exile to Siberia of thirty-five students of both sexes who had been celebrating with excessive exuberance the jubilee of a professor whom they revered and who was the object of police suspicion. A contributing cause was the fact that the preparation for this celebration had been made in a series of secret meetings. Certain of the most highly respected families of Moscow were affected by this harsh measure, and the sorrow and indignation of so many previously peaceful citizens created an atmosphere more fraught with danger than if it had resulted merely from the instigation of political agitators.

Among the students deported with such cruel haste was a girl named Anna Pavlovna Nadinsky. She had a brother living in Moscow, Eugene—or, as the Russians say, Evgen Pavlovich—who was an officer in a regiment of dragoons. Eugene was a proud, handsome young man, twenty-three years old, and apparently assured of a brilliant future. He was exceedingly fond of his sister, who had been his close friend and confidante throughout his life. When he saw her now lost to herself and to the world, a prey to the want and humiliation that the years

---

Jakob Wassermann (1873–1934) was born in Fürth, Bavaria. After an unhappy childhood and youth, he moved, still very poor, to Vienna, where he was to live until retiring to the Styrian countryside. His numerous books—historical novels (The Dark Pilgrimage, Alexander in Babylon, Caspar Hauser), *works of psychological fiction* (The Goose Man, Gold), *and long novels about basic social problems* (The World's Illusion, The Maurizius Case)*—made him in the 1920's and 1930's one of the most widely read European authors.*

in Siberia would bring, his sorrow was so great, his sense of justice so deeply outraged, that the very foundation of his existence crumbled, and he determined to protest against the institution in whose services he had, until now, been so eager.

What followed seemed to happen of its own accord, and astonished him as much as anybody else. A few days after the arbitrary action of the police, his regiment was ordered out to quell a revolt in the streets. Of a sudden he left the column at the head of which he was riding, jumped down from his horse, and ran toward a barricade that had been hastily erected out of paving-blocks, wheelbarrows, baskets, and articles of furniture. As he ran, he gestured frantically to its defenders in a way they could not misunderstand, particularly as desertions from the army to their ranks, even in the midst of battle, were not uncommon. But scarcely had Nadinsky reached the top of the barricade from whose shelter he hoped to fight against the real enemies of his country, when he was struck by two bullets from the guns trained on him by his dragoons. Hands stretched toward him, eyes filled with enthusiasm welcomed him; he seemed to hear a chant of thanksgiving which stilled his last doubts. Even his name was called aloud, as if some of these revolutionists knew him. Despite his weakness, the joy in their voices seemed to him sufficient reward. He turned, drew his revolver, fired upon the assailants, his former comrades, then plunged forward on his face, the fingers of one hand caught in a cane chair wedged into the barricade.

He was seized immediately by two young men who bore his unconscious form away and laid him on the stone stoop of a house near by. Hastily they ripped open his coat and shirt, bound up his wound, which was bleeding freely, and looked about in search of help. A peddler's cart stood at the curb. Its owner had vanished, and its lean little horse seemed frozen in the shafts. Quickly they laid the officer on a bed of vegetables and greens and covered him with leaves. One of them returned to the barricade, while the other led the cart down the street, through numerous alleys, and finally into the open square where stood the University Hospital. He went on into the courtyard and called an intern, who gave orders at once to place Nadinsky in one of the wards.

His wound was severe. One of the bullets had merely grazed

his throat, but the other was lodged in his lung and had to be removed by an operation. On the third day Nadinsky awoke out of a feverish unconsciousness. It was some time before he knew where he was and what had befallen him.

Meanwhile, all Moscow had been talking of the young officer's desertion, and the police, through one of their numerous spies, had discovered his hiding-place. An *ispravnik* turned up at the hospital to arrest the fatally wounded man. Although the critical condition of the patient was clear even to the policeman's eye, he flourished his written order and insisted upon taking Nadinsky away. An intern was still arguing with him when the surgeon stepped forward, glanced at Nadinsky's apathetic countenance, was touched by his youth, and said: "If he is removed now, he will die within fifteen minutes. The police will do better to wait." The *ispravnik* stood irresolute. He was still a novice and not yet hardened. Moreover, in the maze of his multiple orders and commissions, he had lost his head. He thought awhile and then declared himself willing to leave the officer in the hospital until his strength had returned in sufficient measure to permit of removal.

Thus a few days were gained by Nadinsky. During these days the surgeon's sympathy for him grew greater, and he made efforts to interest others in the fate of his patient. Friends appeared who were willing to help him escape. One morning he was taken into a private room. In the evening a young man arrived with an orderly's uniform in which Nadinsky was to be conveyed to Sokolnikin, a park in the environs of Moscow. In his weakened condition, there was still a life-and-death chance of saving him. Nadinsky agreed to accompany the young man, for to remain meant the certainty either of death or of life imprisonment in remotest Siberia.

In the dead of night, amid snow and ice (for it was the middle of March), he was taken to Sokolnikin, where he lived in the villa of a scientist who was presumed to be above suspicion by the police. But twenty-four hours had scarcely passed when messengers appeared from the city who, after strolling casually and unconcernedly about, entered the villa and announced that the police were again on Nadinsky's track and were planning to swoop down and arrest him the following night. No choice remained, therefore, but to seek another refuge.

This scientist, who was of German birth, had living with him his sister, Anastasia Karlovna, a woman whose courage was as great as her kindly spirit. She had been living in Moscow for more than forty years, enjoyed a great many influential and benevolent friends in high positions, and was, besides, greatly loved by many of the common folk. It was she who kept house for her brother, nursed the young officer, tended him, and arranged cleverly to conceal his presence in the villa. Her first concern now was to procure for Nadinsky a new disguise. Having attired him as a laborer, she conveyed him, with the aid of a total stranger who had offered his services, to the house of a wood-turner in the suburbs. He was able to remain there only the night, for by morning the wood-turner had become fearful for himself and his family and refused to harbor the fugitive any longer. Nadinsky was dragged in this way for five days from one house to another, to a coachman's, a widow's, a gardener's, and finally to a laboratory worker's. Each time, at the end of a few hours these people realized to whom they were giving asylum. Fear of the police outweighed considerations of pity and hardened them against the eloquence of Anastasia, whose zeal never flagged. She spent her nights with Nadinsky, for he was not in a condition to be left by himself. He had to be washed and dressed, and have his bandages changed twice a day; the irregularity and excitement of his mode of living prevented his wound from healing rapidly. And now that the laboratory worker, who had been plied with gold and eloquence, refused any longer to shelter Nadinsky, Anastasia Karlovna feared that there was nothing more to be done. Those friends who had stood by her until now could do no more; the police were on their track, and every fresh step led in the direction of their ruin. Anastasia felt she was being spied upon herself. She tried for the last time, by prayer and entreaty, to soften the laboratory worker: would he not practice Christian indulgence for only one night more? The life of her brother—for so she represented Nadinsky—was at stake. But her words served only to increase the man's distrust, and she secured merely a respite of three hours. If, at the end of that period, Nadinsky had not been removed from the house, the man would go to the police.

It was now three o'clock in the afternoon. By six, therefore,

Anastasia would have to find another hiding-place for her ward. She drifted for a time through the streets, stopping first before one house and then another, but turning back each time at the door in fear of an unfavorable response, or even of betrayal. At last, in her distress, she fell back upon the idea of taking Nadinsky to one of those assignation houses in which rooms are let out to lovers. Only in such a place could she introduce a man who carried no papers. Given two days of rest and care, he would pull through, the doctor had told her that morning. Thereafter, he could get to the frontier by himself.

But to carry out this plan she would need an accomplice, a creature who could make the love-affair seem plausible, who was strong, discreet, and intelligent. She thought of all the young women she knew, but none of them seemed suited to such an undertaking. Anastasia had no friends among the revolutionists; moreover, it would be folly to confide in a person who might be under police surveillance. Nor was it possible to consider a woman of the lower class, or any woman to whom one might offer money; it had to be a lady or a girl of good family.

The exertion of the past few days had wearied her. Rather more to be seated somewhere than for refreshment, she went into a little pastry-shop and stepped into a twilit back room. Two women sat at a small table, drinking hot chocolate. Anastasia took a seat absent-mindedly, but she saw presently that the elder of the two women was looking in her direction and greeting her with a friendly nod. She recognized the woman as Anna Ivanovna Schmoll, the deaf-mute wife of a retired general. With her was her daughter Lukardis, a nineteen-year-old girl of unusual beauty. Scarcely had Anastasia glanced at Lukardis when she said to herself: "There is the only girl who can do it." Years before, she had been a frequent guest at the Schmolls', when Lukardis Nikolaievna had been a little girl. She had often played and chatted with the child, and remembered her well. She remembered that, already at the age of thirteen, this child had impressed her as do only those people who possess a peculiar quality, a peculiar strength. What sort of quality or strength it was, she never had been able to fathom, much as she had reflected upon it. The mother, Anna Ivanovna, was a rather simple-minded person, pious, apathetic, harmless, conscious in a vague way of her infirmity.

Anastasia took a seat at their table and, having inquired by look and gesture about the health of the general's wife, began to speak to Lukardis Nikolaievna in a low tone. The general's wife looked inquiringly at Anastasia's lips, but, unable to follow the conversation, she lowered her eyes modestly and refrained from interrupting their speech by any sign of curiosity.

Anastasia was conscious of the boldness of her design. She had no time to lose. It was essential that she speak briefly. In a few sentences she had to tell her story, make an extraordinary demand, arouse Lukardis's innermost sympathies, and at the same time move with care and cunning, for one word, one awkward gesture, could frustrate the whole plan. Lukardis knew nothing of revolutionary intrigues. She suspected much, but she had no information about these matters. She lived in a sphere of gentle dreaming, with the dolls of her past and the jewel-cases of her present, with echoes of the comical gallantries of married men and the careful protestations of scented unmarried men. Yet there was something in her of the young animal in the forest which listens to the sounds of the distant hunt, the tremendous commotion of pain and blood and death. She was ready for action, but unaware of her expectancy. There were moments when she was seized by a vehement unrest, an unreasoning desire, an impulse to escape from the realm of hypocritical calm in which her life was taking shape. But she was afraid of the world, of people; she trembled at each strange hand that was stretched forth to her. It seemed to her that everything that lay outside her home, even outside her room, was troubled, soiled. She never overheard people in conversation in the street without a shudder; never opened a newspaper without the sense that, side by side with all that was savage and mysterious to her in the outer world, there was something unclean, something that would soil her. Even the books she read, or a snatch of verse, a street song, a jest, awakened in her this terrible, unconquerable impression.

Motionless, she listened while Anastasia spoke. There was no lure for her in the story; she felt no girlish impurity or lust for excitement. All that she could read in the stern features of Anastasia Karlovna was a call to duty. She had no decision to make. What there was for her to do was immediately and unalterably clear to Lukardis.

Lukardis had been engaged these six weeks past to a Petersburg nobleman, a privy councilor named Alexander Mikhailovich Kussin. Her parents and their friends felt that an enviable future lay before her as the wife of this rich nobleman; and indeed she herself was happy about it.

If anything could make her hesitate now, it was the thought of him to whom she felt herself bound by a sisterly affection. But when Anastasia, who divined her preoccupation, suggested that she might be tranquil on this point, Lukardis wrinkled her forehead and replied that she did not need this assurance. Her fiancé, she said, would never dream for a moment that she might do anything evil or ugly.

"I take it, then, you have made up your mind to do it," said Anastasia in a low voice, her gray eyes fixed on the girl.

"I have made up my mind to do it," Lukardis answered in an equally low tone without raising her eyes. "But there is one difficulty— How am I to explain my remaining away from home for two days and nights?" she asked, crossing the fingers of her white hands.

Anastasia stared, gloomily pondering, at a plate of cakes.

Lukardis went on in a whisper: "The only thing possible is to disappear quietly, to leave a letter for Mother—"

"Yes, yes. A few lines. Anything. And beg them to keep it secret. Say you will explain everything on your return. But you too must be silent, Lukardis Nikolaievna," she added almost menacingly. "You must be as silent as though it had never happened."

Lukardis merely nodded. Her eyes were now wide open and gazing straight in front of her. Anastasia explained down to the last detail how she was to dress and act. After telling her where to come and at what time, she added to their serious conversation—which despite its gravity had lasted but a quarter of an hour—a few jesting remarks, in order that Lukardis might smile and divert any suspicion that might have arisen in the mind of her mother. Then she rose with a lighter heart and went her way.

She returned to Nadinsky and told him what she had planned.

He lay on a sofa in the wretched room of the laboratory worker and pressed her hand. "My life," he said, "is no longer worth such great effort, Anastasia Karlovna. It is a lost life."

She retorted that she had hoped for livelier thanks than were contained in these spiritless phrases, and set about changing his dressing.

Nadinsky sighed. "What is the use?" he said in a tired voice. "Everything about me is changed, eye, hand, and emotions. I seem to be surrounded by ghosts. I do not seem to mind being cut off from the world. I can see my mother on our estate. As yet, she suspects nothing. I see her opening a locket and looking at a picture in it. It is a picture of me. She does not know that she will never see me again, she has no idea of that, and yet she sheds tears on the locket. But I have no feelings whatever. The world is to me unreal, because I can no longer love anything."

To Anastasia these words were the ravings of a feverish mind. She shook her head indignantly.

After a while, when it had grown dark, a carriage drove up before the door. Anastasia had bought some handsome clothes for Nadinsky and had helped him with his toilette, and now she looked at him critically before, once more, escorting him downstairs. In the carriage sat Lukardis Nikolaievna Schmoll, heavily veiled. Anastasia handed her a package of gauze bandages, and said to Nadinsky that she would be waiting for him on the second morning thereafter at a certain hour and at a particular place in the railway station. Meanwhile, she added, she would set about procuring him a passport. She gave an address to the coachman, waved her hand in farewell, and the carriage drove off.

Lukardis and Nadinsky sat in silence. Their situation was too unreal, too threatening, too fateful for embarrassment.

When the occasional street lamps lit up the interior of the carriage, Lukardis saw that Nadinsky's eyes were closed, his face was pallid. He had given her his hand on first sitting down beside her; that was all. She discovered that his proximity was not frightening her and that silence was easy.

The house to which they drove stood in a remote street. Nadinsky had to summon all his strength to get out of the carriage. He offered Lukardis his arm, but it was rather she who supported him than he her. He asked for two rooms, and was received with great assiduity. Dragging himself with an effort up the stairs, he strove to preserve the air of a man of the world engaged in a passing adventure.

In accordance with the custom of the house, a servant was placed at their special disposal. This person, suffocating in silver-embroidered livery, had malicious popeyes, wore an unvaryingly insipid smile on his thick lips, and was obsequious in his humility. Lukardis felt her heart contract at his glance. He set the table and stood listening in a doglike manner while Nadinsky, exhausted and indifferent, ordered the dinner, the wines, the champagne. His appraising glance seemed to insist that they be really what they pretended to be.

Lukardis was rouged and wore a low-cut gown. It was difficult for her to be anything else than herself. She was forced to put off the childlike innocence that shone ordinarily in her face, and put on an air of frivolity. She had to chatter, coquette, laugh, throw her arms about Nadinsky, and sit from time to time on his knees. She had to sketch passionate, wanton, seductive gestures. All those things which she had never noticed, never wished to see, never thought about save with horror, known only through careless words and pictures, the things from which she had hitherto averted her mind and her eye, she had now to do in order to deceive this man who came in with plates, bowls, glasses, and bottles, who chilled the champagne, served the food, and then, silently, smilingly, spying from under lowered eyelids, awaited further orders. She had to fit herself into the voluptuous lights, the multicolored cushions, the mirrored walls, for this house with its sham and glitter put her mind in a tumult. Nor was that all. She had to act so as to arouse no doubt about the reality and naturalness of her behavior. Everything had to be done casually, cunningly, and transparently, with no overt shudder or haste. She had to eat what was set before her, to drink the wines placed before her, and not only the wine in her glass but, when the waiter was out, that in Nadinsky's, too, for he might neither drink nor leave his glass filled. She was entirely unaccustomed to drinking, and it filled her with fright and depression to have to continue in this role, which she played instinctively and out of a spirit of self-sacrifice.

Whenever the waiter left the room, she got up. The terrific

tension that strained the muscles of her face gave way to an expression of bewilderment and even of frightened recollection, for it seemed to her that many years had elapsed since she had driven away from the home of her parents.

Nadinsky gazed at her in pain and astonishment, sought her as behind a mask, pitied her dumbly, accused himself in a gesture—and then, with an effort, brought back the studied smile to his lips and continued his acting when the fellow returned.

After the table had been cleared away, a maid came in, wearing a little white cap. She was young, but she appeared old. Her face had grown gray from this life in lamplight and in badly aired rooms. She brought water, tended the fire, asked if there was anything else she could do. Her voice was sweet, but her features were stony with hatred of the upper world, hatred of those who came to this house to indulge themselves in contemptible, quickly snatched pleasures. Lukardis's knees trembled whenever her glance fell on the maid. She was ashamed of her feet, her hands, her neck, and her shoulders. At last this trial too ended, and she was able to lock the door.

They were alone. A clock in a tower somewhere struck ten, its tones vibrating through the apartment. Nadinsky went into the adjoining room, where stood a double bed with a blue satin counterpane stretched over it. Bereft of strength, he fell upon the bed, and it was only after he had rested a quarter of an hour that Lukardis could help him undress. The cover drawn halfway up, he lay there with his chest bare.

"This is a human thing," said Lukardis to herself. Suddenly the tears started in her eyes and she thought with a kind of fright of the red-cheeked face of Alexander Mikhailovich, her fiancé. She bathed Nadinsky's wound and bound it.

As in a dream one sees perfumes, so Nadinsky saw her delicate hand. He was incapable of thanking her. He was afraid to catch her eye, afraid that a glance of gratitude might offend her. He wished she might be able to look upon him as nothing but a body, a thing devoid of feature and of feeling. And while Lukardis, half shocked and half in pity, was thinking: "A human being!" he, half blissful and half in fear for her, thought: "An unearthly being!"

He fell asleep. Lukardis sat motionless in an armchair. She

had brought a book in her little bag, but she knew she would be unable to read. She tried to think of her mother, her father, her friends, the last ball, of the opera she had last heard, but she could think of nothing. Everything faded out, everything eluded her. She heard Nadinsky's deep breathing, saw his pale, fine face, wearied by pain—but he too, he whom she was to tend and guard, seemed out of reach of her thoughts. It was as if miles separated her chair from his bed. She heard tittering on the stairs and shuffling steps in the hall. Voices, women's voices and men's voices, pierced in muffled tones through the walls, from above and from below. Glasses clinked. Then came the sound of a waltz played on a piano with, doubtless, one string missing, for at a certain point there was a hole in the melody, like a gap between two teeth in a smiling mouth. Shrieks arose. The piano was silent. Beyond the wall to the left arose a creaking, and then a sighing note at the sound of which Lukardis's blood curdled in her veins. The smell of perfumes came in from the locked rooms; garments rustled; doors banged open and shut. Every sound called up a picture from which she could not turn away. She trembled, yet, trembling, she had to look. She had never imagined that the world was like this, that this was life. Encounters in the darkness, strange hands clasping one another, forms reeling against suddenly illuminated mirrors, consent given in shameless words, the unknown unveiled, the crypt of mystery emptied, the consecrated soiled, the secret treasures of the imagination cheapened. She covered her face with her hands; the blood rushed to her rouged cheeks and her heart filled with horror.

Nadinsky opened his eyes and moaned. She walked the many miles to his bedside and held forth a glass of water. His forehead was hot. She put a damp cloth over it. At that moment he awoke and began to speak. He spoke in broken sentences of the hospital, of the surgeon, of Anastasia Karlovna. Whenever he paused, Lukardis interjected a timid word. He said: "Tomorrow I shall be strong enough to leave here!" to which she replied:

"That is impossible. You are still feverish. Besides, Anastasia Karlovna is not expecting you until the morning after, early, at seven o'clock."

These softly spoken words seemed suddenly to show him her

soul, her hitherto unclouded youth, her strong clean instincts; but he could not see that she had not stopped trembling.

Once more the piano was being played, but this time by a different hand, a rough, riotous, drunken hand. Throughout the performance Nadinsky and Lukardis gazed in torment into each other's eyes. It was past midnight. Out of the silence that fell came a hollow knocking at the street door. Nadinsky half raised himself. His fingers stiffened and his face was full of dark expectancy. Lukardis stood up and listened breathlessly. It was long before the door was opened. Steps sounded on the stair. They gazed in fear at the latched door, waited for the knock that was to decide their terrible fate. Voices reached them from the hall in a hurried exchange of words. Then all grew calm again, and their pulses commenced once more to beat regularly. In these three or four minutes they felt themselves strangely united; their strength and their fear were directed against a common enemy. It was as if they had been lifted into the air by a hurricane, propelled against one another breast to breast, and had thrown their arms about each other in order to help avert the crash that threatened. Lukardis forgot herself; Nadinsky forgot himself. He felt only the intensity of her fear, the forfeiture of her happiness, the shame and the misery of her. She, for her part, was thinking courageously of his fate, realizing now for the first time why his life hung in the balance.

Meanwhile sleep had once more overcome the feverish man. But he could not sleep soundly while the glaring electric light shone upon him. He said nothing about his desire for darkness, out of consideration for Lukardis, but she saw the nervous flicker of his eyelids and guessed what the matter was.

She lighted a candle in the adjoining room and switched off the lights. She too was weary. The late hour was like a paralyzing poison, and she sought a place to lie down. There was no bed in this room, merely a sofa, whose plush covering filled her with repugnance. She was repelled also by the chairs and the carpet. She rolled back the carpet from the threshold of Nadinsky's room, spread her fur coat on the floor, and lay down. The candle still glowed, but it seemed to bring nearer to her each sound in the house that had until now been vague—a call, a laugh, a single word. And she heard also the beating of the snow on the windowpane; its mildly crackling noise quieted her. She heard the breathing of Nadinsky, and was reminded of her responsibility. Each breath chained her more closely to his destiny. The things that had once been significant became meaningless to her; what she had done, wanted, and been in the course of her life now seemed childish and frivolous. She gazed back longingly, as from the deck of a ship, to the home that faded into the distance. She was asleep, and yet not asleep. Nadinsky had spoken words of comfort and encouragement to her—that was a dream; his throat had rattled feverishly—that was a fact. In dream she bent over him, nursed him; in fact she was chained to the floor, listening to the Bacchic cry of a woman. In the gray light of dawn she saw a rat running across the carpet. It seemed to her fantastically large, and it moved, she thought, like a ghost. She rose to her knees and sought the sky in the parting of the curtains, but all that she could see was a vague blot of gray and below it a window out of which peered an angular face. There was a second of crushing helplessness, and then she crept, nay fled, to Nadinsky's bed. His right arm was hanging limp. Beads of perspiration stood on his forehead. He looked frighteningly strange. A painful sense of hatred flared up in her. Yet there was no longer anybody in the world at whom she could look in this fashion. She had much to demand of him, everything, in fact; except for him, her world was but this house.

They had said nothing on their arrival about how long they wished to remain in these rooms. It was customary to let them only for the night. Anastasia's plan had been that they should lock themselves in until noon, and then declare their wish to spend a second night in the house. A gold-piece to the waiter and another to the chambermaid would suffice for this. But fresh water was needed for Nadinsky's wound; his condition demanded nourishment. If they rose early, how were they to justify staying all day? Nadinsky, who had been lying open-eyed and silent, was the first to broach this subject. He asked her to hand him his coat, drew out his wallet, and gave it to her. Two gold-pieces, he thought, would not be enough; fifty rubles would be better. Lukardis remarked that such extravagance would create suspicion and induce the proprietor to spy upon them. She held the note between trembling fingers. Never had money seemed to her at once so real and so incomprehensible. They were behaving with outward coolness, but their voices seemed smothered. Lukardis said something about the nastiness in the waiter's face, which induced Nadinsky to retort, more spitefully than he intended, that she had certainly led a life sheltered in cotton-wool, seeing that none of these people who lived in dirt and squalor could please her. He was revolting against the yoke of gratitude which she had laid upon him, and at the same time trying to draw her out of herself and let light and darkness play about her features. But she gazed sadly at the floor. She granted his point, and thus disarmed him. Her gentleness touched him, but also it goaded him into further cruelty. He protested against the idea that chance alone was responsible for making her his companion during these twenty-eight hours; she seemed to him guilty herself of the humiliation she was suffering, and he was angry with her because of that. He thought of her as having worn, before she met him, only robes of purest white, as having spoken, with those beautiful lips, only meaningless words, the dregs of her pampered class. It was only now, beside her, that he became a true revolutionist. His flight and concealment seemed to him now ignominious, and he imagined that very likely they lowered him in Lukardis's eyes. And therefore he declared suddenly his determination to get up and leave the house. He was trying to show her that it meant nothing to him—indeed, it was his duty—to share the lot of so many of the condemned, who had accomplished more and dared more than he. Once across the frontier, to whom could he be of use? Not to the Russian people, not to his friends, not to his unfortunate sister!

Lukardis begged him to control himself and tried vainly to reason with him, though she had only a child's reasons to present. Then, seeing that he remained obdurate, she assumed a tone of command. Of a sudden she was silent. She had heard steps. She raised her finger and pressed it to her lips. Someone stood listening at the door. Her proud glance became a plea for protection, and Nadinsky hung his head. Then Lukardis accepted the inevitable. She tiptoed to the door, unbolted it, hurried back to the bed, and slipped quickly in beside Nadinsky. Pulling the covers up under her chin, she reached for the electric bell-cord and rang. They lay breathless until a knock came. It was the maid. She stood in the doorway with an air of Nornlike gloom and took Nadinsky's order to bring fresh water and call the waiter so that breakfast might be ordered. Back she came with two jugs of water, followed by the waiter. His watchful eye took in the first room and as much of the next as it could see, and to Lukardis it appeared as if he were seeking the clothes she wore as she lay in bed, a circumstance she thought apt to arouse his suspicion. She shut her eyes, for the sight of this man was horrible to her.

Nadinsky held out the fifty-ruble note. "Twenty for the maid and thirty for you," he said in a tone of studied indifference. "We shall stay until tomorrow morning, if it can be arranged." The waiter bowed nearly to the ground. He had not looked for so generous a tip. The maid, who was feeding the fire, came over and tried to kiss his hand, but Nadinsky warded her off. "If it please the lady and gentleman, and there is nothing against it," said the waiter with a catlike gesture and a wink. Nadinsky ordered breakfast, and at the end of a quarter of an hour the tea and things were brought in.

Meanwhile, Lukardis lay on coals of fire. Her whole body was penetrated with something for which she found no name, a feeling composed of grief and fear which clouded her face with a deathly pallor. Nadinsky lay motionless, sharing her sensation. He understood her agony and averted his eyes from her. The waiter had set the table, bowed again to the ground, and left. When the maid had gone, Lukardis threw back the cover and rose as if fleeing from flames. She bolted the door and opened a window. Her hair had come unbound, and she let it hang freely, for it covered her bare shoulders. An hour earlier she would have resented appearing thus before Nadinsky, but since she had lain beside him, uncovered despite all covering, immeasurably his, her blood now revolted at the notion of his mercy. It was no longer improper for her hair to hang loose about her shoulders.

When the room was filled with fresh air, she shut the window and said to Nadinsky that it was time to change the dressing. Silently, he drew down the sheet. Even to Lukardis's untrained eyes it was clear that the wound was healing rapidly and that Nadinsky's fever had passed. She was already more adroit than the day before in the dressing and the binding of the wound.

When she had finished she offered him bread and milk. He asked to have a little tea in his milk, and she gave it to him. She herself swallowed something in great haste, as if she begrudged her body its hunger. The house was strangely silent. In the street, wagons rolled and children shouted. Nadinsky fell asleep, and Lukardis went into the other room. She pulled off her slippers in order to make no noise, and walked back and forth for hours, holding the strands of her hair in both hands. From time to time she would stand still and muse. Then she would stare at the pictures on the wall without really seeing them. One represented a Leda, holding the swan between her knees. By the door hung another: a German student with a rucksack on his back, flourishing his cap in the direction of a girl with two long braids, looking out of a window. The two rooms were reflected on both sides in the mirrors with the effect of an endless succession of rooms, all of them peopled by the fat, ugly nakedness of Leda, the sentimental student, the bed in which Nadinsky lay asleep, and the portrait of Czar Nicholas that hung above it—endless, multiple reflections, far into the dim, dim distance. Often, too, she would stand at the window and look at the vehicles and the children, at the snow on the ledges and the faces seen faintly behind windowpanes, and it would seem to her that all this, too, was endlessly repeated in the faint distance. Where had the world vanished to? Where was everything she had loved, embraced with harmless affection? Where was she herself, Lukardis, who had spent her life in the elegant boudoir of a general's daughter? Where was Alexander Mikhailovich, ever ruddy and ever smiling? And where was brilliant Moscow, with the tempting displays of its shops, the friendly acquaintances who turned up on every hand, the distinguished young officers, and the gay women? Where had the world vanished to? She could see only the man who lay before her in the many mirrors of the many rooms; she could see only his wound on his white skin, his wound which was like a flitting flame that she, with an enchantment put upon her, was forced to follow.

The chimes struck twelve, and it was a long time thereafter—how long she could not judge—before Nadinsky awoke. He sat up, and she came forward with some hesitation. More determinedly than she had expected, he said that she must leave this same evening. He felt strong enough now to stay alone and would intimate to the waiter that she would be back later in the night. And in the night nobody would bother to think about it again. Lukardis shook her head and said that it was as much for her own sake as for his that she preferred to stay. The scar had only just begun to form, and the wound would need to be dressed at least twice again before he could stir. If she left and he met with an accident, she would never forgive herself.

Nadinsky gazed searchingly into her face; then he stretched forth his arm in such fashion that she held out her hand to him. At that moment they both grew frightened. It was like some blissful but disastrous transformation that each underwent in the eyes of the other. Then Lukardis stepped with beating heart before one of the mirrors and pinned up her hair. Her fingers shook. If at this moment he had ordered her to leave, she would probably have gone without protest. But instead he began to lament that he had not died an honorable death in battle; what was he to do in foreign lands, eternally wandering, gnawed by grief and by the ever present thought of his tortured comrades, worried by the business of earning a bare living? For he was not rich. He had many debts. His mother's estate belonged to his creditors, really. Discouraged by so much discouragement, Lukardis stood still before the mirror and examined her tired face. He went on. He reviled his deed: he had not known what he was taking upon himself; it had been the result of impulse, not of decision; heroes did not act this way, did not deliver themselves up to chance, in order to be crushed. And here was she who had fled with him to this sewer: had she acted with a clear sense of what she was doing, or had she not, in reality, allowed herself to be swept away by sentiment, by pity, by the temptation of the unusual, the seduction of an enthusiastic friend? Had she not been uprooted and shaken, robbed of all her strength by Medusa-like visions? "So are we all," he cried, throwing himself back upon his pillows; "all of us, delivered up, cast down, beggars of fantasy, sacrifices to the moment, deceived by our actions!"

Lukardis moved over and sat on the edge of his bed. Quietly and firmly she looked into his face. Her eyes gave the lie to his words: there was a soulful harmony in the expression of her features.

It was as though, in the simple silence of bewilderment, a godlike nature had come to the aid of his heart. A beam of happiness sped across Nadinsky's brow. His skeptical spirit bowed in shame before the confidence and serenity of this girl, who was able to take him out of himself, out of this house.

Night fell. They sat in silence amid the darkness. When it came time to continue the comedy demanded by their situation, Lukardis switched on the light, drew the curtains together, and went out of the room in order that Nadinsky might dress. He called to her after a moment to help him on with his coat. Dinner was served as on the previous evening by the liveried waiter, with even more humility, with a smile even more insipid, and an eye even more alert behind his evil grimaces than before. They sat at table mirthlessly and avoided each other's glance. Only their hands moved—mute obedient spirits, passing to and fro, pretending a casual innocuousness under the eyes of the spy. This evening Lukardis was playing her part badly. Her laughter was artificial, her frivolity was even less convincing. Nadinsky came to her rescue by whispering, when they were alone, that they should pretend to quarrel. He invented the name of a Countess Shuilov and insisted that the collar of pearls she had worn at Princess Karamsin's last reception was false. Lukardis contradicted him. He persisted peevishly in his opinion, and with such success that a crimson glow overspread Lukardis's cheeks. She was astounded at this hypocrisy within hypocrisy, and suddenly was afraid of Nadinsky. The waiter came and went, poured champagne, with a look in his face that seemed to implore them to be friends, as if he were afraid of anything else than dovelike cooing. Finally Nadinsky got up ill-humoredly and ordered the waiter to clear out. He was amazed by Lukardis's pleading glance. Acting as though he regretted his impetuosity, he stepped toward her with outstretched hands. The waiter grinned with joy. Lukardis too stood up. She let her head fall on his shoulder, but only in order to whisper to him not to forget that the carriage must be ordered for the next morning.

All at once a piercing shriek resounded through the house, followed by a second and then a third cry. Lukardis clasped her hands in fright, while Nadinsky looked uneasily in the direction of the door. The waiter stood with a metal tray in the open doorway. A half-naked woman ran by. "Shut the door," breathed Lukardis faintly. A shot sounded and the ghostly howl of a man filled the air. Nadinsky pushed the servant out and slammed the door. In a few minutes all was quiet; then steps ran to and fro, voices murmured, a tone of command arose from below and was answered by a wail of lament from above. This was followed by sobs so heart-rending that Lukardis ran, wringing her hands, to the sofa, and flung herself face downward upon it. A lively tumult arose in the street, in the midst of which the voice of a policeman was clearly audible. Heavy feet through the hall indicated that someone was being carried out. The waiter came in with a look of contrition in his face and said: "I beg Your Excellency to be without anxiety. I beg the lady to calm herself. It is nothing. An insignificant accident has occurred. Your Excellency will not be disturbed again." With this he vanished.

Nadinsky went over to Lukardis and sat down beside her, stroking her hair with a trembling hand. She shrank from his touch and moved her head away. He withdrew his hand.

A storm rattled at the windows. As if in defiance, the piano sounded again; someone was playing the same waltz, the same gap-toothed melody. Was it only one day, one day and one night, since they had last heard that air? Had not years elapsed?—years filled with images and moods, joy and pain, splendor and wretchedness, expectancy and disappointment, greed and deprivation, dream and death? And was this already the end? Was not another night imminent? An endless, mysterious night? To Nadinsky it seemed that in the moment when he had climbed the barricade and been shot, he had stepped into another existence, conditioned by previously unknown laws and demands; and that his earlier existence with all that it comported had been shed like a cloak; that on coming into this house he had taken upon himself his destined life, divorced from past and future, devoid of bridges leading either backward or forward.

Oppressed and nerve-racked, he fell upon his bed. Lukardis came in. A lamp burned in the sitting-room, but in this room there was no light. The rooms repeated themselves in the mirrors, gray and vague. Lukardis found that one jug of water was still full, and again she dressed Nadinsky's wound. In drawing the fresh bandage from her bag, she pulled out a book, and when Nadinsky had been bandaged he asked if she would read to him. The book was a volume of Lermontov's poems. Lukardis, in her chair, had read only for a few minutes when her arms fell to her sides, her head sank, and sleep overcame her. Thus without resistance or transition do children fall asleep.

Nadinsky was careful not to stir. His eyes clung to her face, and it seemed to him that his own face must follow the change of expression to which her features were being subjected. A sense of ineffable peace entered his soul. He stretched his legs and breathed deeply. Her lips were moving. She was whispering, smiling gently. Her hands opened and the book fell from her lap. She started, opened her eyes, glanced in horror at the dim room, and slept on. Sleep mastered her completely, and her body lost its equilibrium so that she would have fallen to the floor had not Nadinsky caught her in his arms. He laid her across his bed, her feet on the chair. Her head rested on his knees, her arms were crossed above it, and her breast rose and fell in a powerful rhythm. Gradually Nadinsky commenced to feel her weight; the blood ceased to circulate in his thighs, and it was hard for him to remain motionless. He let himself fall back on his pillows, slipped his hands under the covers and under the girl's back, and tried thus to hold up her unconscious body. In this way the burden fell in rotation on his arms, his thighs, and his knees. A glow of happiness went through him. He felt that he was repaying her care and trouble, and also he was happy because she was so close to him, so utterly under his protection. His eyes dwelt long on the sleeping girl, while his mind was filled with a rapturous gratitude. Her life, her slumber, the lines of her relaxed form, each of which seemed a sort of spiritual barrier against the chaos of the world, filled him with a sense of limitless bliss and poured new strength into his heart.

She had been asleep for hours when she was awakened by the drums of a military patrol marching through the street. Nadinsky was pulling himself up to a sitting posture when he saw that her eyes were full of dull astonishment. They seemed to be trying to glow serenely, and then to be covered by a veil of shame. Lukardis uttered a little cry and sprang up. Her face was suffused with blood. She pressed her hands to her breast and looked mutely ahead; and though Nadinsky spoke to her, she continued to appear embarrassed. He made an effort to speak casually, inquiring about the weather and the hour. She answered absent-mindedly, her face revealing alternately shyness and fright, and gratitude and secret questioning.

For the last time she washed and bound Nadinsky's wound, maintaining, meanwhile, her composure with difficulty. The world outside seemed to her like the open jaws of a savage beast. It was a quarter to six. They had to make themselves ready. Nadinsky was growing more and more calm; he was very pale when, having dressed, he went into the other room, where Lukardis stood. They sat opposite each other at the table. Lukardis was wearing her hat and fur coat; her handbag lay at her feet. Thus they waited in silence and with averted eyes for the time of their deliverance.

The clatter of wheels sounded finally in the street, and in a moment there was a knock on their door. The waiter came in, wearing not his livery, but a greasy bathrobe. His hair hung in oily strands over his forehead, and his face was sullen and evil. He presented the bill, which Nadinsky paid, including at the same time the coachman's fee. They went downstairs. Two pails filled with sweepings stood at the foot of the stairs, and in the entrance lay a black dog. The dog followed them, sniffing, to the carriage. Not a soul was to be seen in the streets as they drove the long way to the station.

In one of the waiting-rooms stood Anastasia Karlovna, beside a pillar. She greeted them and asked about Nadinsky's condition. Then she handed him a passport and a filled traveling-bag, they hurried out to the platform, and Nadinsky took his place in the train. After a moment he came back, walked over to Lukardis, and stretched forth his hand. An unaccountable lack of muscular response prevented Lukardis's lifting her head and turning her face toward him. He took both her hands in his, and the four hands lay together like the links of a chain. So they remained for a moment and seemed to themselves figures in a dream. Anastasia Karlovna gestured warningly. With a dragging step, Nadinsky turned back to the car and climbed in, placing himself at the window, where, in the black frame and the gray of the fog, his face was a chalk-white blot.

The whistle blew, and the train rolled slowly out of the station.

When Lukardis reached home, she found her mother dissolved in tears. The poor woman had not dared tell her husband of Lukardis's letter and had been at great pains to keep her disappearance from his knowledge. A strange argument ensued between daughter and mother, a scene in which the deaf-and-dumb mother gesticulated in her most excited and imploring manner while the girl merely shook her head and told nothing. Bit by bit the general's wife grew uneasy about Lukardis, and this uneasiness grew into dismay when the girl refused to see her fiancé, who had turned up for a few days in Moscow. Even her father's anger could not move her. She spoke no word, but looked calmly at the ground.

The engagement was broken; and even more deliberately than before, Lukardis persisted in avoiding other people—friends, strangers, parents, sisters. She retired deep within herself, became a different person. The doctors having counseled travel, her mother took her first to Paris and then to the sea in Brittany. One night the general's wife came upon her daughter unexpectedly as she lay out on the flagstone terrace of her room. Hands folded behind her head, the girl was gazing with wide-open indescribably brilliant eyes, upward at the starry heavens. In her face was an expression of infinite loneliness.

Nadinsky had vanished. Several people insisted that he was living on a farm in western Canada. But Lukardis never heard his name spoken, nor he hers.

Translated by Lewis Galantière

KRAMBAMBULI

by Marie von Ebner-Eschenbach

One takes a fancy to all sorts of things; but genuine, imperishable love comes to a person, if at all, only once in a lifetime. So, at least, thought Gamekeeper Hopp. How many dogs had he had and been fond of! But only one of them had been really dear to his heart, unforgettably dear—Krambambuli.

Hopp had bought him at the Lion's Inn in Wischau from an unemployed deputy forester—or rather he had bartered for him. At the first sight of the dog he had been seized with the affection that was to endure to his last breath. The eyes of the beautiful animal's owner bespoke the rascal. He sat at a table in front of an empty brandy glass and railed at the innkeeper for not giving him a second drink for nothing. A small fellow, still young, though frayed as a dead tree, with auburn hair and a sparse beard. His hunting jacket, probably left him when he quit his last position—the remains of past glory—bore traces of a night passed in a wet ditch.

Although Hopp was not eager to mix with such doubtful company, he took a seat beside the fellow and started a conversation with him. He soon found out that the good-for-nothing had already delivered his rifle and gamebag to the innkeeper as pledges, and that he now wanted to pawn the dog; the innkeeper, however, the dirty usurer, wouldn't hear of a pledge that had to be fed. At first Mr. Hopp made no mention of his interest in the dog. He ordered a bottle of Danzig cherry brandy and began to pour drinks.

Marie von Ebner-Eschenbach (1830–1916) was an Austrian poet, novelist, and playwright. Her stories deal either with the landed gentry, into which she was born, or with the peasantry of Moravia, then part of Austria-Hungary. A staunch Catholic, she was a conservative, yet critical of her class. In the 1880's she was considered one of the masters of novella-*writing.*

Well, in an hour's time it was settled. The gamekeeper bought twelve bottles of the brandy and turned them over to the fellow; and the vagabond handed over his dog—not easily, it must be said to his honor. When he fastened the leash around the animal's neck, his hands trembled, and it seemed as if he'd never finish.

Hopp waited patiently, and quietly admired the wonderful dog. At most he was two years old. In color of hair, he was only a few shades darker than the scoundrel who was giving him away. On his forehead he had a mark, a white stripe that ran right and left in small lines like needles on a fir twig. His eyes were great, black, and gleaming, bordered with small light-yellow streaks, clear as dew; his ears were long and faultless. And faultless, in fact, was everything about the dog, from the claws to the fine sensitive nose, the powerful, supple figure, and the stance, which indeed was beyond praise: four living pillars that might have borne the weight of a stag, yet weren't much thicker than the legs of a hare! By Saint Hubert, this creature must have had a pedigree as old and pure as the family tree of a knight of the Teutonic Order! The gamekeeper's heart leaped with joy over the bargain he'd got. He rose, took the leash, and asked: "And what's his name?"

"The same as the brandy for which you got him—Krambambuli," came the reply.

"Fine, fine, Krambambuli! Let's go! Come on, come on! Forward!"

Yes, long might he call, whistle, tug at the leash—Krambambuli didn't seem to hear him. The dog turned his head toward the man he still considered his master, sidled up to him, and only howled when the latter shouted at him: "Beat it!" and gave him a kick. Only after a fierce struggle did Mr. Hopp succeed in getting possession of the dog—who, bound and gagged, finally had to be stowed into a sack. For the several hours it took Hopp to hike to his home, he had to carry the sack with Krambambuli over his shoulder.

It was two full months before Krambambuli, beaten half to death—and chained to a sharp spiked collar every time he tried to run away—finally realized to whom he belonged. But when his subjugation had been completed, what a dog he was then! No tongue could describe, nor word measure, the height of perfection that he achieved—not only in the practice of his calling, but also in daily life as a zealous servant, a good comrade, and a true guardian and friend. "He lacks only speech," it is said about other intelligent dogs, but Krambambuli didn't lack it: his master, at any rate, carried on long conversations with him.

The wife of the gamekeeper became downright jealous of "Buli," as she disdainfully called him. "Have you nothing to say to me, only to Buli?" she said one night. "For all your talk with that animal, you are forgetting how to talk to humans."

The gamekeeper admitted to himself that there was some truth in what his wife said, but he didn't know how to help matters. What should he talk about with his wife? They'd never had children, they were not allowed to keep a cow, and domestic fowl do not interest a huntsman at all in a living state, and not very much when roasted. And in tree-farming and hunting stories, again, his wife took no interest. Hopp finally found a way out of his dilemma: instead of talking to Krambambuli, he would talk about him, about his triumphs everywhere and the general envy his possession excited, about the "ridiculous sums" offered him for the dog, which he of course had refused.

Two years had thus gone by when one day the Countess, the wife of Hopp's employer, appeared at the gamekeeper's home. He knew at once what the visit meant, and when the good and beautiful lady began: "Tomorrow, Hopp, is the Count's birthday—" he softly broke in with a little grin:

"And Your Grace would like to make a gift to his lordship and are convinced that Krambambuli would be appreciated more than any other present."

"Yes, yes, dear Hopp." The Countess blushed with pleasure at this obliging attitude, and said how grateful she felt, and asked him just to name the price to be paid for the dog.

The old fox of a gamekeeper chuckled, looked very humble, and then came out with his proposition: "Your Grace, if the dog remains in the castle, does not bite through his every leash or break his every chain, or, if he can't, does not strangle himself in the attempt, then Your Grace may have him gratis, for then he'd no longer be of value to me."

The experiment was made, but it didn't come to anything like a strangulation. The Count had lost his joy in the obstinate animal before things came to this pass. In vain had they tried first to win him by love, and then to tame him through coercion. He bit everyone who came near him, more often than not left his food untouched, and—though a hunting dog doesn't have much weight to lose—wasted away. After a few weeks Hopp received the message that he should come and fetch his hound. He didn't hesitate; and when he went to the kennel to get the dog, there was a reunion of boundless rejoicing. Krambambuli let out a wild howl, sprang up on his master, propped his forepaws on the gamekeeper's chest, and licked away the tears running down the old man's cheeks.

In the evening of this happy day, they walked together to the inn. There Hopp played cards with the doctor and the Count's overseer, and Krambambuli lay in the corner behind his master. From time to time Hopp looked around at him, and then the dog, though apparently deeply asleep, would immediately beat the floor with his tail, as if he wanted to announce: "Present!" And when Hopp, forgetting himself, would triumphantly hum the little tune "How goes my Krambambuli?" the dog would sit up in dignified respect, and answer with his light eyes: "All goes well with him."

In those weeks a band of poachers were carrying on their activities, in a really reckless and brazen fashion, not only in the Count's forest, but in the whole district as well. Their leader was supposed to be a dissolute fellow. He was called "Red" by the woodsmen who'd seen him in saloons of evil repute, by the foresters' helpers, who, though already on his track here and there, had never succeeded in catching him red-handed, and finally by his own informers, of whom he had several among the riffraff in every village.

Damage to the game and woods reached a record high, and the aroused forest employees grew increasingly irritable. Thus it occurred only too often that little people, caught at some insignificant woodland offense, suffered harsher treatment than they would have at other times, and harsher than was properly justified. This caused great bitterness in all the villages. The hatred first turned against the head forester. He received many warnings: the outlaw gunman, it was said, had sworn he'd take vengeance on him.

The head forester, an audacious man and also a rash one, brushed aside the talk. Undaunted, he let it be known far and wide that he had asked for the most uncompromising ruthlessness from his subordinates, and that, in the case of dire consequences, he himself would assume the responsibility. He repeatedly exhorted Hopp to the strict performance of his duties, and sometimes reproached him with lack of "pluck"—at which, of course, the old man only smiled. He would wink down at Krambambuli on such occasions, and the dog then would yawn loudly and with obvious disdain. Neither he nor his master took offense at the head forester.

The head forester was the son of the unforgettable man who had taught Hopp the noble art of hunting, and whose own son as a small boy had, in turn, been initiated by Hopp into the rudiments of the profession. The vexations the boy had caused him, Hopp considered, even to this day, a joy. He was proud of his former pupil and loved the head forester despite the rough treatment that he, like anybody else, experienced from him.

One June morning Hopp was with him once again, this time at one of his police actions. It occurred in a stand of linden trees at the edge of the manorial park that bordered the Count's forest, and in the neighborhood of the tree farm—which the head forester, had it been up to him, would have surrounded with land mines! The lindens stood in their most beautiful bloom, and a dozen small boys were crawling around on the branches of the magnificent trees like squirrels, breaking all the twigs they could reach and throwing them down. Two women were promptly picking up the twigs and stuffing them into baskets already more than half filled with the fragrant loot. The head forester fell into an immense fury. He had his assistants shake the boys from the trees, unconcerned about the height they fell from; and while they crawled around his feet, whimpering and crying, one with a battered face, another with a dislocated arm, a third with a broken leg, he soundly beat the two women with his own hands. In one of them Hopp recognized, with an eerie feeling, the wench rumor had marked as the sweetheart of Red. And when the baskets and kerchiefs of the women and the hats of the boys had been confiscated, and Hopp had been ordered to take the stuff to the courthouse, he couldn't ward off a sinister premonition.

The order that the head forester shouted at him, wild as a

devil in hell—and, very much like the Devil himself, surrounded by tormented, lamenting sinners—that command was to be the last he ever gave to Gamekeeper Hopp.

A week later Hopp met his superior again in the linden forest—dead. From the condition of the body, it could be seen that it had been dragged through marsh and scree in order to lie in state at this place. The head forester lay on cut boughs, his forehead adorned with a large wreath of linden blossoms, and a linden-blossom garland was wound around his breast as a bandoleer. His hat lay near him, upside down, filled with wildflowers. His gamebag had been left him by the murderer, only the cartridges had been taken out and linden blooms stuffed into the bag instead. The beautiful breech-loader of the head forester was missing and had been replaced by a miserable shooting iron, whose strap had been slung, in mockery, across his shoulder. (Later the bullet taken from the chest of the murdered man proved to fit exactly the barrel of this shooting iron.)

At the sight of the disfigured body, Hopp had grown stony with horror. He could not have moved a finger, and his brain was as if numbed. He stared and stared, and at first thought nothing. Only after a while did he manage to look beyond the corpse and at once asked himself: "What is the matter with the dog?"

Krambambuli was sniffing the dead man, running around him with his nose to the ground as though he'd gone crazy. He'd whimper, and then again let out a shrill yelp of joy, or make a few leaps, or yowl—and it was as though a memory, long dormant, had been awakened in him.

"Here!" called Hopp. "Come here!"

And Krambambuli obeyed, but looked at his master in the greatest excitement and, to put it in the gamekeeper's parlance, "said" to him: "I entreat you, above everything in the world, don't you see it? Don't you smell it? Oh, dear master, look! Use your nose! Oh, master, come! Come over here!" And with his nose he nudged the gamekeeper's knee, and then slunk back to the body, looking over his shoulder repeatedly as if to ask: "Are you following me?" Then he'd begin to lift the heavy gun and push it, and finally tried to seize it in his teeth.

A shudder ran down the gamekeeper's spine, and all kinds

of suppositions began to dawn upon him. But speculations were not his business, and, too, it was not up to him to enlighten the authorities with guesses; rather, it was his duty to leave things as he had discovered them and go straightway to the courthouse. So he did simply what was his duty.

Before all the forms prescribed by the law in the case of such catastrophes were complied with, the whole day and also a part of the night had elapsed; and only then did Hopp, before he went to sleep, turn to his dog.

"My dog," he said, "now the police are on the move and now there will be raids without end. Shall we leave it to others to cleanse the world of the renegade who shot to death our head forester? My dog knows the dirty tramp, knows him, yes indeed. But nobody needs to know that, and I've told no one about it. I, haha!—I would bring my dog into this affair! No, sir—not me!" He bent over Krambambuli, who sat between his knees, and pressed his cheek to the animal's head and accepted the dog's grateful nuzzling in return. And he was just beginning to hum: "How goes my Krambambuli?" when sleep overtook him.

Psychologists have tried to explain the mysterious urge that frequently draws a criminal back to the scene of his crime. Hopp knew nothing about these learned theories, but nevertheless he kept wandering with his dog, without peace or respite, through the linden forest. On the tenth day after the head forester's death he thought for the first time of something else besides revenge, and occupied himself for a few hours in the Count's forest marking trees to be taken out in the next cutting.

His work finished, he hung his gun over his shoulder and took the shortcut through the woods toward the tree farm near the linden forest. When he turned into the path that ran along the beech-tree fence, he seemed to hear something rustle in the leaves. But deep silence reigned again in the following moment—deep, prolonged silence.

He might have thought it had been nothing out of the ordinary if it had not been for the dog, who stood with bristled hair, his neck stretched forward, his tail straight out, and stared transfixed at a place in the fence. "Oho!" thought Hopp. "Just wait, you killer, if it's you!" He stepped behind a tree and cocked his gun. His heart beat frantically—and his already short breath almost failed him completely when all of a sudden Red stepped onto the footpath. Two young hares hung from his gamebag, and over his shoulder he carried the breech-loader of the head forester. What a temptation to fell the ruffian from the safe ambush!

But never would Gamekeeper Hopp have shot at even the most vicious enemy without warning him first. With a leap he sprang from behind the tree, out on the path, and shouted: "Surrender, curse you!" And when the poacher ripped the breech-loader from his shoulder, the gamekeeper fired, the gun gave a click, but—oh, all of you saints!—no report. It had leaned too long against a tree in the damp forest with its bullet inside—it refused!

"Good night, so this is what death looks like!" it ran in the old man's head—and at the same time his hat flew into the grass. The outlaw had had no luck, either! Moreover, he'd wasted the one shot that he'd had in his gun. And no sooner had he pulled another cartridge out of his gamebag than Hopp shouted:

"Sick him, Krambambuli, sick him!"

"Here, to me! Come here, Krambambuli!" beguiled a tender, loving, and, alas, so familiar voice from the other side. "Come here. . . ."

But the dog—

What now occurred happened much faster than can be told.

Krambambuli had recognized his first master and ran toward him—halfway. Then Hopp whistled and the dog turned; Red whistled, and the dog turned again; and then, stunned and overpowered, he writhed in desperation on a spot midway between the gamekeeper and the poacher.

Finally the poor animal gave up the struggle and made an end of his doubt, though not of his agony. Barking, howling, belly to the ground, body taut as a tendon, head raised as though he were calling heaven to witness his anguish, he crawled to his first master.

Seized with a thirst for blood, Hopp took out a new cartridge with trembling fingers; but he inserted it in his gun with quiet assurance. Red again had his barrel aimed at him. This was it! And both men knew it as they looked at each other through their sights. But whatever their thoughts, they pulled the triggers as calmly as a couple of marksmen in a painting.

Two bullets flew: that of the gamekeeper to its mark, that of the outlaw into the air. For the latter had lurched: in the very split second he pulled the trigger, the dog had jumped up at him in a tempestuous greeting. "Beast!" the outlaw managed to hiss. Then he fell, backwards, and never moved again.

Hopp walked slowly up to him. "You have had enough," he thought; "it would be a shame to waste another shot on you." Yet he put his gun on the ground and inserted a bullet. The dog sat erect before him, his tongue hanging out, panting in short, loud gasps, and looked at him. And when the gamekeeper had loaded his gun and took it in hand again, they held a conversation, of which a living witness could have heard just as little as the dead Red.

"Do you know for whom this piece of lead is meant?"

"I can imagine."

"Deserter! Traitor! Perfidious, wayward cur!"

"Yes, master, yes."

"You were my joy. Now that's over. I can take no more joy in you."

"Understandable, master"—and Krambambuli lay down, put his head on his outstretched forepaws, and looked at the gamekeeper.

Yes, if only the accursed brute had not looked at him that way! Then he would have brought matters to a quick conclusion—and would have spared himself and the dog, too, a great deal of pain. . . . But you don't shoot a creature that looks at you that way! Hopp murmured half a dozen oaths between his teeth, each more blasphemous than the preceding, shouldered his gun, took the young hares from the outlaw, and went away.

The dog followed Hopp with his eyes until he disappeared between the trees. Then he stood up, and his spine-chilling howl of woe rang through the forest. He turned around in a circle a few times and then once again seated himself bolt upright near the dead man.

And thus he was found by the investigating officers who, guided by Hopp, appeared at nightfall to inspect the body of the outlaw and to have it removed. Krambambuli yielded a few feet when the gentlemen appeared.

One of them said to the gamekeeper: "Why, that's your dog."

"I left him here as a guard," answered Hopp, ashamed to confess the truth.

What was the use? It came out anyway, for when the body was loaded on the wagon and moved away, Krambambuli trotted behind with his head lowered and his tail between his legs.

The next day the bailiff saw him roaming around not far from the room where Red lay. He gave him a kick and called to him: "Go home!" Krambambuli flashed his teeth at him and ran away—according to the man, in the direction of the gamekeeper's home.

Yet he never arrived there, but instead took up the miserable life of a vagabond.

One day Krambambuli, gone wild and lean as a skeleton, came skulking about the shacks of the cottagers at the end of the village. All at once he fell upon a child who stood in front of the last hut, and greedily tore from him the piece of bread he was eating. The child stood rigid with terror, but a small spitz came running out of the hut and barked at the thief, who then let go of his loot and fled.

The same evening, before going to sleep, Hopp stood at his window and looked out at the gleaming summer night. It seemed to him as if he saw the dog sitting on the far side of the meadow at the edge of the forest, steadfastly and longingly looking toward the abode of his former happiness—the truest of the true without a master!

The gamekeeper closed the shutter and went to bed. But after a while he got up and walked again to the window. The dog was no longer there. And again he tried to sleep. And again he could not.

He could stand it no longer. He could stand it no longer without the dog. So be it. "I'll bring him home," he decided, and upon this resolve he felt as if reborn.

He was dressed by the first gray of dawn. He asked his wife not to wait for him with the midday meal, and hurried off.

As he opened the door of the house, he found Krambambuli. The dog lay dead before him, his head pressed against the sill that he had never more dared to cross.

The gamekeeper never got over his loss. Sometimes he forgot

that he'd lost the dog, and at such happy moments, engrossed in thoughts, he would intone his familiar "How goes my Krambam—" But in the middle of the word he'd stop, shake his head, and utter, with a deep sigh: "A pity about the dog!"

Translated by Paul Pratt

CARDIAC SUTURE

by Ernst Weiss

The medical student Friedrich von B. was a tall, blond young man passionately in love with Major Surgery—but not at all loath to love others too, among whom a certain Hildegard Anneliese had played a large, if recently not always pleasant, part. Early in December he became an unpaid assistant in the surgical department of Geheimrat O., whom the students, because of his military bearing and imposing presence, called "the General"—an appointment aided by the fact that the professor and the student's father were fraternity brothers.

In the university clinic, without getting much attention from his father's friend at first, Friedrich von B. performed many small but indispensable and responsible services, such as general anesthesia, dressings, minor operations. Often, of course, he just stood idly about awaiting orders, or he presented patients at the lectures that took place between nine fifteen and eleven a.m., weekdays.

On one such occasion, on January 17, the professor lectured on malignant tumors. He proudly pointed out his permanent successes: cases on which he had operated three and five years earlier; even that of a patient from the start of his teaching and operating career in town, not less than seven and a half years before, who like the rest had remained in good health, without

---

Ernst Weiss was born, in 1896, in Moravia, then one of the provinces of Austria-Hungary. He became a physician and ship's doctor. Returning to shore, he lived first in Berlin, then (after 1933) in Prague, and finally fled to Paris. He was Jewish; and on the day the German army marched into Paris in May 1940, he drowned himself in his bathtub. Among his novels are Die Galeere, Tiere in Ketten, *and* Georg Letham, Arzt und Mörder. *He himself considered his unpublished diaries his most important work; the Nazis destroyed them.*

recurrence of symptoms. The operations had been serious ones, and it was a surgical triumph that the cures had lasted so long —the blessing of quick, radical measures.

The old patients had been recalled to the clinic by mail, and those who lived out of town received a mileage fee for travel expenses.

Now they were perched on a bench in the broad corridor leading from the wards to the auditorium. Five were men, three were women; four came from the city and as many from the countryside. Although the first associate had forbidden them to talk of their diseases, they had now talked of nothing else for an hour. Some had pulled their shirts up to show their scars, while others merely indicated the place and length of the incisions from outside, exaggerating the length. Then, smoothing their clothes, they proudly followed the student into the auditorium, and one of the women broke out in a sweat because in the hurry she could not get her gloves on fast enough.

The General reveled in surgical optimism. He compared the recovered patients' fate with that of others stricken with the same disease and now long resting in the cool earth. He held the shoulders of a frail, elderly woman between his huge arms and moved her about, right and left, like a little doll. Then he quickly turned away from the woman and with simple lines drew the diagram of the operation on a blackboard for the students, holding the piece of chalk in his right hand, and the chart, on which all required data were listed and which the associate had handed him, in his left. Then, with impeccable delivery, he described the advances in operational technique, critically illuminated the good and bad sides of each method, calculated the prognosis with the aid of careful statistics, and forgot entirely that the eight people concerned were standing in the auditorium—which also served as operating-room, by the way.

He was still deeply absorbed by his surgical observations when suddenly the old Associate Professor E. rushed in and whispered something in his ear. The excitement spread at once to the surgeon and appeared in his face, which looked as if bathed in vermilion, with only the old dueling scars of his youth standing out more brightly, cherry-red. A steep crease formed on the General's forehead, a sign of acute reflection, while the associate herded the eight healed ones out of the hall like a small flock of poultry.

The professor immediately turned on the water at a basin reserved for his use; he turned upside down the hourglass that stood on a glass shelf. The brown sands started trickling, to indicate ten minutes—the prescribed duration of hand-washing and personal asepsis.

The student helped to dress the General for the operation. The General was talking and washing by turns, while a big yellow waterproof apron was tied with a brass chain round the bull-neck that was as vermilion as his face; without looking, he stepped into black galoshes that came up above his ankles.

Instantly the academic teacher had become a different person. His voice, his bearing, his very glance were different. With the hard brush he scrubbed his fingers, palms, and the backs of his hands, and his forearms up to the elbow. By foot pressure he took soap from an automatic container, and soon the arms were covered with white lather. Then everything was rinsed off; the skin, of an increasingly vivid red, reappeared, only to vanish again in the froth.

By his side, the assistants did exactly likewise.

Now the General turned to the audience:

"Lucky, unfortunately rare coincidence. Suicide attempt near the hospital. A young woman, a young girl. Stab into the heart. A cardiac suture, I expect. Modern operation. Antiquated suicide instrument: an old-fashioned penholder with a common steel pen. Office girl. One relatively favorable circumstance, gentlemen—the ominous object has remained in the wound and so kept her from bleeding to death.

"Quite an achievement, by the way, to hit the heart with such a primitive weapon. The method I now hope that all of you, and that includes the gentlemen in the top rows (I urgently request everyone to remain seated, the dust is terrible and highly dangerous)—anyway, the method I now hope to demonstrate is new, and remains one of the many extraordinarily great merits of the late Professor Rehn in Frankfurt. First assistantship to you, Dr. E., as usual; second, Dr. Glicker, with the third going to Dr. Schillerling; anesthesia might be given by the young man here—one of your colleagues, gentlemen, who already anesthetizes quite nicely. In cases like this we need a very good anesthesia—*nota bene:* hyperpressure anesthesia, because, after all, the thing happens within the chest cavity.

"As I said, for some years now we have been no longer helpless against heart injuries. Since Rehn, we can attack punctured —in fact, though of course only in the rarest cases, even shot wounds of the heart. We can attack anything of the kind, provided, gentlemen, that the patient gets onto our table here alive. Out of five cases operated on in time, no less than three will recover. No doubt but that the Archduke, the Austrian heir presumptive, if his heart injury in Sarajevo at the time—well, let's drop this painful chapter; Head Nurse, have sodium-chloride solution heated, prepare adrenalin, solution 1:1000—yes, I just wanted to say we have methods against any kind of injury, but we have no method yet against the murderers. We stitch up the wound, but we don't heal the heart. Pulse to be checked by the anesthetist. Don't forget to bring the rib-dilator; in fact, all bone instruments.

"The indication is simple in such cases: you start operating as soon as you've got the patient. Prompt aid is decisive. Although there isn't a second to be lost, where have you got our patient? Bring her right in to us; formalities and red tape are unnecessary; I operate even without the consent of the patients —often dazed in such cases—or relatives, who haven't the faintest notion. All that doesn't matter here. Up and at 'em—but not without strictest observance of the rules of asepsis. We ask no quarter; we must and we shall stick exactly to the rules of asepsis, for we are about to open one of the most sensitive parts of the body, always prone to suppuration: the thorax and the pericardium. Well, here she is. Come on! Careful! Gently!"

The tall, light-blond, somewhat light-minded student of medicine Friedrich von B. saw again Hildegard Anneliese, who had played a large, if not always pleasant part in his most recent past.

Instruments were being sterilized on several electrically heated little stoves. Thick steam rose from the small kettles and evaporated in the amphitheater. Though it was close to noon, the auditorium was gloomy.

"Light," said the General.

Lamps, set in rows beneath the ceiling, hissed up, and a shadowless, almost pure white light fell on the operating-table, the professor and his aides, and the bottom rows of seats in the audience. A clock, the dial of which had been only indistinctly visible, now showed not quite two minutes after eleven. The General was silent. No sound was heard except the bubble of the seething water, the silvery tinkle of the instruments moving about in it, and the murmuring breath of the listeners.

The would-be suicide moaned dully. She did not scream; she seemed to hold her breath back, as every movement of her chest was painful. In the depths before them, brightly illuminated by the lamps on the ceiling, the students saw her face—framed in tumbled, moist, dark-blond hair, the upper lip drawn far over the lower, moist too. The light-gray eyes were shut tightly, then torn open again; the lids trembled, the irises shifted restlessly from one corner of the eyes to the other. Scissors had already cut the clothes from the upper part of the body, and a light gauze veil was spread over it; in one place the veil rose to a sharp point, and this place moved rhythmically.

Silence reigned. The General and the assistants had ceased scrubbing arms and hands with their brushes and were looking at the patient.

It seemed as though it were midnight. Stillness. Nothing but the hiss of the water, the gurgling of the sterilizers, the hiss of the lamps, and the muffled moans recurring with each exhalation.

The General had signaled to the head nurse. Gently, as if afraid to hurt the other woman, she removed the gauze veil with a sterile forceps. One saw the penholder under the patient's left breast; it bobbed with every heartbeat, as if depressed to a downstroke by an invisible force and rising again so as to trace a hairstroke.

"Above all," said the General, resuming the brush treatment of his already lobster-red arms with particular intensity, "above all, you see that consciousness remains quite unaffected. Aside from shock—only too natural in such cases. And: no hemorrhage. External bleeding has ceased. Ought to have been inappreciable, anyway."

His muscular male arm, gleaming like polished metal in the glare, waved the student Friedrich von B. closer to the sufferer.

"All right. Go ahead. Anesthesia."

The student shrugged his shoulders. He was trembling all

over with horror and had to strain every nerve to control himself. For hyperpressure anesthesia he needed a special apparatus, which should have been there long ago. It had been moved to another room, however, for a small adjustment, and now that every second counted, it was missing, and nobody dared tell the chief.

Large nickel-plated drums with coats, caps, towels, rubber gloves, and dressings were swiftly opened by nurses. Working in pairs, they took out white, square sheets, opened them and spread them under the patient, whom the head nurse lifted up with infinite tenderness. Below the waist the body was covered with sheets; only the upper part of the torso remained free, and the face, growing paler by the second. The hands were strapped down. A broad belt was drawn over the thighs.

Nine minutes had run off in the hourglass. The rustling big sieves with the instruments were taken from the seething water. Vapor steamed up in huge clouds. On small wheel-tables the head nurse deftly sorted the metal gear in systematic, orderly rows: similar instruments next to each other, larger ones to the right, smaller ones to the left. Scissors, straight and curved, four-fingered hooks, bone forceps, clamps, small pincers, needle-holders, boxes with sickle-shaped needles and others with straight needles, silk and catgut thread rolled on glass spools and arranged according to thickness.

The sands had all but run out of the upper glass; Friedrich von B. gazed about the room, but as yet the anesthesia apparatus hadn't arrived. The gurgle of the water ceased abruptly.

"Iodine," said the surgeon.

Now, in the last second, the contrivance rolled in—a complicated contrivance. The rust-colored tank with the rust-colored faucet was the oxygen tank; the blue one with the blue faucet held carbon dioxide, and the green faucet adduced the narcotic. Gleaming pressure-gauges and clear glass cylinders filled with liquids served to check every breath.

While the professor was helped into his surgical whites—white coat, white cap, white mask—the student held the reddish, closely adhering rubber mask over the young girl's nose and mouth. Great pearls of the narcotic, mixed with air, trickled through a transparent glass vessel. "Breathe deeply. Breathe deeply," the student told the girl in a toneless voice.

The girl shook her head silently, stubbornly. With feeble motions she pushed the mask away from her as well as she could. The mask followed her, but the pale face squirmed and sought to get away from it. She opened her mouth, she wanted to scream, she wanted to fight. But not a word, never anything but the same long-drawn-out dull moan came from the bloodless, skin-colored lips.

"Iodine," the General repeated, donning rubber gloves. A metallic purplish brown, daubed on the operating field with a broad piece of gauze, now covered the two breasts, the entire skin as high as the region of the throat and down to the navel.

In the center of the brown field bobbed the penholder—wearier now, faster and weaker, as if scribbling—driven by the helplessly trembling heart. The breath, distinct until now, became shallower. The eyes were wide open, despairingly but clearly roving through space.

Incredible that a human being so badly hurt was still clear in her mind, that she knew what she was doing, what she was suffering.

Already the General's face showed the peculiar, almost gay, virtually relaxed expression indicating that he had thought the course of the operation through to the last detail, taking into consideration all possible complications, so that nothing remained but the technical execution—but why was the patient still awake?

She was really almost livelier now than before, with her eyes seeking and at last finding those of her former lover.

Not a second to be lost, the student thought; it must be. But what should he tell her; how was he to make her understand, how to make her see reason, what could he remind her of? Whose fault was it? Who can make up for it—two minutes before death? Eleven o'clock and twelve minutes.

"And the pulse?" the General asked.

Friedrich von B. groped at the girl's soft, beautiful throat, the lines of which were familiar to him from times long past. Gently, with the tips of his index and second fingers, he touched the moist, soft, lukewarm skin. "Nothing at the carotid. I can feel nothing at the carotid." But the girl had felt his hand. Did she love him still? Did she want to live again? Did she repent? Was she still the one she had been a few minutes ago?

Her eyelids suddenly closed; the long lashes came close together and formed a dense, dark-blond line all but brass-colored in the glaring light. The lips opened softly; milk-white teeth, set in gums of a pale coral red, appeared as the student lifted the mask an instant. She was breathing toward him, drawing in the ether air in hurried, shallow breaths. Thirteen minutes past eleven.

"All right, we'll start anyway. Is she asleep? Not yet? Doesn't matter. Life is primary, anesthesia secondary. War is war. Up and at 'em. Keep the head quite low—avoid cerebral anemia; above all, supply the respiration center, medulla oblongata. The blood issuing from the wound presses on the heart from outside and congests in the pericardium. Heart tamponade, this was called by our genius Ernst Bergmann. Still a little lower—good, enough."

The table had been lowered soundlessly by a hydraulic mechanism. The student felt the girl's head, covered with moist, silken hair, descend on his knees. Was she alive? Did she suffer? She was no longer moaning. Was she asleep? Was she awake? Was she dead?

"All right now, please."

From a gleaming, alcohol-filled crystal bowl the first associate took a thin nickel scalpel bent like the fin of a fish, with a blue-glistening steel blade. The General seized the upper end almost as a painter grips his brush, and with the blade, as though merely experimenting with the design of an arabesque, he drew a curved line starting between the two breasts and circling the left one at its lower rim. The line was drawn in a pale red, as if breathed onto the skin. No real drop of blood. The assistants gripped the wound edges with their hooks from above and below and pulled them far apart. The patient moaned, then fell silent. The student gave ether. The knife disappeared from the surgeon's hand—you did not see how—and now the instruments in his right alternated between large and small, sharp and blunt, cutting and solving, grasping and releasing ones.

The hands of the surgeon and his aides were stuck into tight, reddish gloves of thinnest rubber, so tightly clinging to the fingers that the nail contours were visible through them. In the operating field nothing was seen but the one big, long-fingered hand of the General, whose every move seemed lax and casual but was in fact made with exact, methodical precision. The other hands were busy holding the wound edges, passing instruments or sponges, and carrying out all sorts of supporting measures, which the General directed mostly with his eyes, using his voice only for the most important commands. What he was saying was rather addressed to the listeners and intended to make them understand the course of his operation.

"You notice that there is virtually no hemorrhage. Unfortunately. Blood pressure is infinitesimal. Careful with the anesthesia. Better let her moan—just as much as is absolutely necessary, so she won't wake up. She's still under the influence of shock, will hardly feel pain. We hear a rustle in the subcutaneous tissue: air emanates, squeezed out of the injured thorax. What to do? We shall remove a piece of the breastbone here; here we'll fold up the ribs. We make a gateway to the heart, a sort of door. That means we must sever two, three, in fact a good four ribs—handling the periosteum with care, because later all this must grow together again. It does that quite easily. Keep your heads away—no germ must get in! Now more pressure for the anesthesia, please. Just a trace of ether and plenty of oxygen. Now we're engaging the enemy. Grip the suicide instrument from outside, with a forceps—just hold it like that. And here we go after it—this is the way the pen went, you can still see the ink marks. Now we mobilize it—twist a little from outside, good! Now pull—gently, stronger, more energetically—good! It's out. Good, take it away to the collection. There's idiocy for you; a desperate person takes anything that happens to be handy. Now for the ribs; look out now; rib scissors—yes, put it there, cautiously—first a finger underneath, now I press through, and now we pass on to the next. Finger underneath, and hold the whole skin-and-bone flap upward, cautiously, without force. One, two, and another one—one, two, ruck-ruck, keep going but don't slip—hold the flap quite still, damn it, take it easy, so, easy, ea-sy—good!"

The student von B. held his hand over the girl's mouth; he could scarcely feel her breath.

"Don't lift the mask! Hyperpressure must stay. She's breathing all right, don't worry; we know better up here, we can see the lungs expand. Just check the anesthesia; we have to take it as it comes. Watch it! Here's the pericardium. All right, forward! Sharp clamp. Clamp. Larger one. Smaller one! Medium size, damn it—pay attention and twist the thing outward a little! Another, and another, and so forth without a lot of talk! Here is the wound in the pericardium, serrated, zigzag—that's the way it must have gone through; not a simple cut, of course, because at the moment of the injury the pericardium tightened and turned, as at every heartbeat. Hollow probe—we want to get inside, we want to get deeper and deeper!"

The probe, a fingerlike instrument of nickeled steel, ribbed length-wise, slipped smoothly through the wound into the dark, bloody depths.

"All right. Hold the probe down, please. Now the scissors on top of it, please—straight ones are best—yes, and support it below; hold the probe exactly below the scissors. One cut! That's good. And now first of all a clear view! All full of blood clots. That must be removed. We'll clean it out. Wipe off, lightly—don't rub on the pericardium, it doesn't like that. Now we have a clear view, but it won't last long; we must see the wound without delay. It may be right before our eyes, but it doesn't have to be there, either. Where does it bleed? Where does it bleed from? Pretty gory, that. Sponge, please. Head up—only I must see; get out of my way! Sponge, don't touch it with your hand, just sponge with the forceps—gently—more energetically—gently, I said; gently and energetically at the same time, and don't rub, don't scrub! Watch it! Go on! Soon we'll see daylight. How's the pulse? Anything there? Nothing? Well, give her sodium-chloride solution, as much as possible—blood would be better, a blood transfusion; would take too long, though; we'd have to have the blood group first, takes too long—inject physiological sodium-chloride solution into the cubital vein at the elbow, as much as will go in! Life substitute, blood illusion! And one of the gentlemen determines the blood group in the laboratory—have we got a donor, then? You gave us blood once, Dr. B., what's your blood group? Watch it—just for another hundred seconds. Quiet! Forward, fixation of the heart. With the heart leaping around like that we can't do anything. It has to be kept still. It must come out of its lair. Out, I say, you coward! We have to hold it quite still, and we must have it accessible if we want to stitch it up. So; sutures up for fixation. Yes, a thread like that will do—thin silk, curved needle, this size will do. Give it to me, why the fooling around? Don't thread it too short after the eye and give me the needle-holder right away and you hold the pericardium clear and you take up the end of the thread, so it doesn't drag. Here, you see, I puncture the serous peri- and epi-cardium—left ventricle, apex—going in, and here I come right out again; now we have a loop, the brother here will hold it for us; and the same again a little higher up and a bit to the right, and one more loop over to the side—like this, you see, I catch the cardiac muscle with the needle, in, through, out, needle away, ends together, and it's all done. Pick the thread up—and now out with the heart, cautiously, from its cave. It bleeds? Let it bleed. Of course it bleeds. Lift it up. Faster, higher—more gently! Still a little more, perhaps. Don't be scared—over to the side, like this. On this heart wall: nothing. Nothing here, either. All right, now the other side. Lift it up a little, please, and over to the right. Hold it—and sponge again, very lightly, without pressure. Stop! Stop!

"Here we are. Here's the wound. Finger in the wound, you —finger *at* the wound, I mean. Hold the wound edges together, very gently, yield with your hand as the heart beats! Like this; good. But we want to see something, too! Don't press. Enough. It's good, it's all right. Well, and now on to the heart suture. Same silk as before. First suture crosswise. Left wound edge, right wound edge, out with the thread, make a knot, hang the thread on a clamp to be held off, like that. In order. Caught the top layers. Doctor, you take over the suture and hold the heart wall a bit toward me—no, a bit over to the right, and always yield to the heart movements. Good. Second suture. A little deeper, to be on the safe side. In, out, make a knot, pull it tight slowly, equally from both sides, and hang the thread up again. Hemorrhage is fading, but that isn't enough. Anything stir at the pulse? Not yet? How's the breath? Wretched? Just keep calm. Keep your hand away. Third suture. Got it. Hemorrhage has stopped. The heart wound is closed. Scissors—cut the threads of the three sutures. Not too short. But no tail, either! No. Good.

A fourth? No, that will do. Leave it alone. The suture is solid enough; it will hold even when the blood pressure rises and the vessels fill up normally. Pulse? No? It'll come. It'll come all right. Man lives if the heart lives. You can see how the heart muscle recovers evidently, beats get more marked, it contracts and dilates properly—not like the hysterical trembling and fluttering of a while ago. That was *in extremis,* you might well say. Good—just keep giving sodium chloride into the arm vein, but don't disturb us up here and don't come too close to us with the filthy stuff. Relax the heart rein, pull the threads out, everything in its proper order. You see how the heart muscle tears at the three reins, like a fresh colt; it is gaining strength before our eyes. Good, and the pulse? Hardly tangible. We'll fix that all right! Hand us the adrenalin now, we'll shoot her the injection right into the heart. Good. Got it. Well?"

"The pulse is back. I think."

"We think so too. Respiration?"

In a glass tube of the anesthesia apparatus the student saw pearls of exhaled air rising in a silvery, increasingly vivid stream. "Going all right," he said.

"Now to close the pericardium. We'll take catgut for that. For the heart we didn't dare; silk is safer. But the pericardium doesn't have to stand that enormous pressure. It'll work, it'll be all right. Now we put the ribs back into their old position; the periosteum we sew up quickly with a few stitches. Glass tube under the skin; here, down at the bottom. Muscle—fascial closure of the wound, that is to say: skin suture, fine silk, just a few stitches. Anesthesia?"

"Off for some time."

"Good. From now on, pure oxygen, three and a half, four liters—by and by. And camphor for safety's sake. Keep her head low, up in the ward too. Blood transfusion only if required. Rather yes than no. Which blood group? A? And you, Mr. von B.?"

"Also A, sir."

"Couldn't be better. Stay both with her. When did we start?"

"Eleven twelve."

"Operating time: seven minutes and a half. A hundred years ago Napoleon's personal physician could amputate a leg in that time, including everything, blood-stilling, et cetera. But those were other masters than we are. Well, pick the patient up carefully and lift her into the bed—or rather, let me do it. That's it—that's the way. Hot-water bottles ready? Cover her. Cover her! Everything all right. Everything else we'll leave to luck. Good morning, gentlemen, good morning."

Translated by E. B. Ashton

THE MESSAGE THAT FAILED

by Moritz Heimann

A young revenue clerk by name of Vincentius Hüttenvogel came home from the opera later than usual, and unusually excited.

He lived in a suburb blending into the countryside, in a cozily furnished room with alcove attached, which he rented from a slightly odd woman not much over forty. His circumstances were orderly but not lavish, and had trained him to a greater austerity than fitted his age. Though of good family, he managed without a valet and had the landlady attend to his domestic needs. He often visited the theaters, yielding passionately to all impressions and yet restrained from the unselective enthusiasm of youth by his own talent—a talent long self-evident to him, but also noticeable to other people of discernment.

On this particular evening he was far from the inspired and reflective mood in which he generally walked home from a performance. Always striving to consider a work of art in the entirety of its perceptible form, he could not help it that a single tune lodged in his ear like a ditty in the vulgarian's—Cherubino's aria: "You know the answer, you hold the key. . . ."

He carefully hung up his greatcoat, lighted the oil lamp, and half-abstractedly attended to some other chores. But now and then he interrupted himself to harken, somewhere, for the

---

Moritz Heimann (1868–1925) was born in the province of Brandenburg. Man of letters, playwright, and essayist, he left only one novelette *and a handful of short stories. For many years, and until his death, he was the editor-in-chief of a distinguished Berlin publishing firm. Devoting more and more of his time to the advice he gave its authors, he neglected his own work.*

The Vincentius Hüttenvogel of this story is Franz Grillparzer, the great Austrian dramatist (1791–1872). The poem is his.

quite personally provoking, mocking, importunate proposition: "Love's tender secret, share it with me. . . ."

When he sat down, his arms before him on the table, he noticed on the sleeve of his light-blue tailcoat a woman's hair, golden red in the mild glow of the lamp. He was astounded and, all at once, felt an outburst of the intoxicating confusion that had been stirring his blood for hours. True, this delicately coiled golden hair could have landed on his sleeve only by accident, probably in the crowded opera lobby; but it was strange how completely, in color and length, it resembled the hair that had gleamed in unveiled feminine abundance on the head of Cherubino, the page, in tonight's performance of *The Marriage of Figaro.*

Vincentius closed his eyes to review the evening once more. His neighbors, to the left and to the right, had been young men; a gray-haired old lady had occupied the seat in front of him; and in the lobby he distinctly remembered seeing in his vicinity only some strikingly light blondes and a brunette of Italian appearance. He had exchanged personal greetings only with his friend Altmüller—casual, perfunctory greetings appropriate to his relation with this luxury-loving young man about town.

Again Vincentius regarded the golden thread. With his fingertips he picked it off the sleeve, certain that he would have kissed it if it had indeed come from Cherubino's head. But then he felt suddenly revolted by the lone, dead, fallen hair; he rose and went to the half-opened window to let it fly out. Yet the stiff breeze instantly drove it back from his outstretched hand against the windowpane, and Hüttenvogel saw it gleam again in the brightness of the full moon, paler than previously. The sight seemed to cheer him; he closed the window, lowered the curtain, and, slowly pacing the room, felt the confusion of his blood resolve.

Nanette Luegg, who sang the part of Cherubino—a striking beauty whose looks rather than her talent made her a favorite with the public—had for the first time risen above Hüttenvogel's criticism. This night she had triumphed by the very qualities he used to censure. She had not even tried to impersonate a boy except in her costume, and even that had been so chosen as not to interfere with her feminine bearing and charms. She played the part exactly as though she were gratifying her own or a lover's whim, as gossip had it she was on occasions, by masquerading at home. Unconcernedly she trod the boards as a page, not in an attempt to seem like one, but solely in the service of the music in her charge and of her own beauty. While blithely singing out a boy's tender, passionate fancies, she tantalized with a bare throat, with a bosom heaving under the brocade jacket, and with her luxuriant woman's hair. Quite naïvely, she was boy and woman at once.

Vincentius, who had often seen and heard her, but had formerly resented her crude, naturalistic vocal style, was at first vexed and then enkindled by her Cherubino's ambiguity. Artlessness this time impressed him as superior art; no love song had ever had the elemental quality of this gay, careless outpouring from a creature who did not lure a woman with male wiles or try as a woman to seduce a man. This was no longer yearning or mere concupiscence. This was rapture itself in all of its sweetness!

On his way home Vincentius had sensed that this rapture was something less corporeal, and therefore more spiritual, than his experiences—even his experiences as a poet—had thus far showed him. He numbly surrendered to an emotion capable of doing away with the last vestige of his finical gentility. At times the boy-woman's figure stood all but bodily before his senses, and the page's aria rang unalterably in his ears, as boldly seductive as if, at the opera, it had been meant for him alone out of the thousands in the audience.

In that state of mind he had come home and found the hair on his sleeve. Now, though not fully sobered by the wind's refusal to abduct it, he regained sufficient control of himself to put a sheet of paper on his desk, grasp his quill firmly, and set down the title of a poem: *Cherubino.*

In a light, well-rounded handwriting marked by some old-fashioned letters, he wrote the first stanza almost without changing a word. (It did not venture far beyond a general lyrical address.) But then the peculiar situation took hold in his mind: the boy—the woman; and the ever changing Proteus became harder to grasp. Impatient to capture meter and rhyme both faster and more precisely than they would come to him, Vincentius relapsed into a mood of a quite personal impassioned feeling.

When there was a knock on the door, he mechanically called: "Come in," and did not even look up as his landlady set a tray with buttered bread and fruit on the small sidetable.

She tiptoed out, but in the doorway she cast another glance at her young gentleman, her countenance transfigured by veneration.

When Vincentius had finished the four stanzas of his poem, he read it aloud to himself, with resounding precision. It so convinced him of the potency of his sentiment that it seemed impossible to him to go to sleep. He dressed again, carefully, in view of the inclement weather, and set out to carry his burning head through the streets under the wintry stars—but not before he had conscientiously filed the poem with the rest of his manuscripts.

In the morning he took the sheet out again, and now the poem struck him with a new, unexpected, and, to his sense of delicacy, all but indecent impact. In bright daylight he felt as far from his poetic ecstasy after the opera as from the blissful ardor of writing the verses. What beset him now was a grimly serious reflection. In the past, his carping hesitancy had disparaged and spoiled his every chance of an amatory tie; whenever a woman's kindly face or sparkling eye or—this he liked best—free, regal bearing appealed to him, he had been quick to find this fault with one, and that fault with the other. Disdaining to ask, he had received no answers either, and had learned nothing about surrender. He had grown steeped in an arrogance that deprived him of the very first requirement of love: to be ready and willing.

Now he was ready and willing. The declaration of his willingness was in his hand, irrefutably recorded in verse. Yes, he had to admit it to himself: he desired the lovely singer who gave him nothing to censure because she left nothing to doubt. She was so clearly unvirtuous and so definitely insignificant that his ideal had to abdicate for lack of a field of endeavor. She was nothing but young, lovely, and ripe—and deep down within himself, beside the kings and heroes of his sketched dramas, Vincentius felt the stirring of a rake at this moment.

This was what made the situation serious, and this was what made an end of it. Vincentius knew that Mlle Luegg had wealthy lovers. And he, in wearisome circumstances made more oppressive by the reproachful bend of his pride, at present not even well equipped with clothing, and quite incapable of having his routine upset—he angrily dismissed the very idea of humbling himself. "That's out," he said to himself. For a moment he thought of sending her the poem anonymously, like an infatuated high-school boy. But he promptly realized that he was too much in earnest about the whole matter. So he put the manuscript back in its place and went to his office.

Somewhat later the landlady came in to do the room. Wrapped in a long gray apron, with her hair tightly secured under a kerchief, the good woman moved about the room as cautiously as if her revered young gentleman had been sitting at his desk. She hurried through the rough work, but dusted tables and closets tenderly and at length. Now and then she glanced at the desk, with longing. Finally, on the point of withdrawing to her kitchen, she could no longer resist the urge to find out whether the bottom drawer—the one with the manuscripts—might have been left unlocked. It had not been. She put the dustpan on the floor and knelt down, the broom under her left arm. With sighs of compunction she unhooked the key-ring from her apron-belt. She knew the right key, and with more sighs she unlocked the drawer, reached in cautiously, and brought out a sheaf of papers.

The one on top was the poem to Cherubino. "A new one," she muttered blissfully, and read the verses on her knees, while her face turned crimson.

Oh, she knew La Luegg. Working nights as a cloakroom attendant at the opera, she was familiar with all the theater gossip, and always listened eagerly to the torn, disembodied melodies floating through the closed doors. Last night she had thus heard *The Marriage of Figaro;* she knew what was meant by the words:

> The tender fullness of these members, marred
> By boyish garb, however richly gilt . . .

"That I must have," she said, and replaced the other manuscripts. Then, still clutching the broom and with the poem in her hand, she set out for her room and there took an album bound in embroidered satin out of her hope chest.

She carried this album back to Hüttenvogel's room, went to Hüttenvogel's desk, sat down on Hüttenvogel's chair—or on the edge of it, rather—and prepared for further action.

In the album she kept a strand of Hüttenvogel's hair, tied with a blue silk ribbon and recently obtained from his barber by a likely pretext. The volume also contained a libretto of *The Magic Flute*—and thereby hung a tale. At the first performance of that opera by the Hon. Concert Master and Royal and Imperial Chamber Composer, Wolfgang Amadé Mozart, at the Theater auf der Wieden, on September the 30th, 1791, a Friday of unforgettable memory, she had played one of the animals that frighten Prince Tamino—a monkey, to be exact—though she had been thirteen years old by then and owed the part only to her undeveloped figure. (She had not begun to fill out a little till she was seventeen or eighteen.) This libretto had accompanied her through all the vicissitudes of her life, as a sacred memento of her stage career. When the first page was slightly burned one day, through carelessness, she had cut it out, painstakingly transcribed it, and put the copy in its place. Having thus acquired a taste for the occupation with poetry, she had bought the voluminous album, bound it in satin, and used it henceforth to copy quotations and entire poems from newspapers and almanacs. Once she recognized Vincentius Hüttenvogel's worth, however, the album came to mean more to her than even the *Magic Flute* libretto. She soon had to add blank pages, to make room for all of the loot she obtained; at first—infrequently—from sheets her young gentleman left lying about, later—with scant success—from the wastebasket, until at last she did not shrink from outright burglary.

Now, at Hüttenvogel's own desk, she entered the "Cherubino" poem in her gilt-edge volume. Then she took pains to remove every trace of her crime and contentedly went back to her room.

It was there, rereading what she had written, that she came to appreciate the meaning of lines like these:

Allay this clash of feelings, these alarms,
This violently seething ichor purge;
Allow my gaze to wallow in these charms,
My lips to cool their fever and submerge
In coupled waves astir between these arms. . . .

She felt ashamed and at the same time very happy. She felt that words so fiery could not but be heeded. She really loathed Mlle Luegg, the brazen hussy. But it seemed to her as though the recipient of such verses could no longer be the woman whose lovers, tiffs, and luxuries were on everyone's lips, as though the verses were bound to transform this woman—into every woman. A confused notion made her copy the poem once more, on the cleanest sheet of note-paper in her possession.

Thus it came about that Nanette Luegg, awaking at noon, received, among other tokens of anonymous homage, a poem to Cherubino. In bed, drinking hot chocolate, she read the billets-doux that her maid had untied from gorgeous flower arrangements and the lengthier effusions bold enough to speak for themselves; she read a gay and forward epistle accompanying something precious that was to be worn around the neck and was presently locked away, and more billets and billets-doux. She read them all without excitement, with a kind of satiated, habitual, animal pleasure, as if receiving her due. Done with this business, she dressed—in a short time, for one so beautiful—and set herself for a tedious rehearsal-less day.

Her lover, a rich young man named Altmüller, turned up earlier than expected. He brought her flowers—which she laid with the rest—and complimented her on her beauty, her freshness, her hair, in words she felt she had been reading herself less than an hour before. He praised her performance of last night as so successful she might ask for a raise in salary before renewing her contract. All that he said with a cordiality not altogether free from the conceit of possession; and as he sat there in his Grecian chair, looking stocky and a little common, she watched him sideways, and suddenly raised hand and forefinger to interrupt him.

"Excuse me a moment, Xavier," she said, and went to her secretary, where the missives of this morning lay in a small pile. She thumbed through it, without knowing what exactly she was looking for, until she came upon the poem to Cherubino, read it, tucked it into her gown, and rejoined Altmüller.

"We got some snow overnight," he began again. "Shall we take a sleigh and go for a ride?"

"Was I really good last night as Cherubino?" she asked.

"Good? You were unusually good," he assured her. "You were in splendid voice, your costume looked charming, and in regard to certain other things I overheard some comments in the lobby that I found most flattering, Nanette. And coming straight from your dressing-room, I had to admit to myself they were well-founded."

The singer became suddenly glum and ill-tempered. "What you find flattering!" she remarked with disdain. He smiled, as was his habit when faced with one of her startling and not always sparkling moods, but this time his smile only added fuel to the fire. She felt he was far beneath her. "By the way," she said bitterly, "I am not interested in your own flattery, either. You have known me for four months, you go regularly to the opera, but I don't think you have an idea of what matters in art—what mattered to me in my part last night, for instance."

"Haven't I?" he merrily inquired, went to the piano, and began to play the tune of "You know the answer" with round fingers and harmoniously enough for dancing. Before repeating the refrain he turned around: "And then a doublet and trousers and a cocked hat. Oh, Nanette, it's you who have no idea! You've no idea how charming you are as the page—because no one believes you are he."

With these words he attempted an amorous approach. But she rebuffed him, and his refusal to take her struggling seriously made her only more frigid. At last she told him right out: "I'm in no mood for your jokes. I'm tired. I have to study. Please go."

"You mean it, Nanette?" he asked.

"I mean it," she replied.

"Good-by—and nothing more?"

"Good-by, and come back tomorrow."

"Well, that's some comfort," he said without resentment, amiably kissed her hand and lips, and left.

• • •

Coming back on the following day, he found the mood of his inamorata changed indeed, but not in his favor. A jesting reminder of her cruelty of yesterday was quickly interrupted:

"Listen to me, Xavier. I know you think I'm stupid. Don't deny it—you think I am at least as stupid as you are."

"Oh, now, Nanette!"

"And you may be right," she eagerly continued. "If a woman is healthy and lucky, I really don't see how she can help being stupid. There has never been anything wrong with me. I got over certain critical years easily and well. I have my voice and I've always enjoyed the good things in life—"

Altmüller could not hold back a meaningful glance and a grimace that made her smile for an instant. Then she went right on:

"But just what pleasure I get out of singing, for instance, *that* you don't know, my dear Xavier. And if I told you, you would think I'm crazy or at least, shall we say, indecent. Don't worry—I'm just suggesting to you that every woman knows a few things she only needs to remember to make you arrogant men look like little boys. We may be fools, but we can pull up our foolishness for moments, like a curtain, and what happens then to you and your kind is this!" And she briskly swept one flat palm across the other.

"Nanette, please leave the curtain down," he begged with comic exaggeration.

"Yes," she said, rising abruptly, and started to pace the room, "when I imagine myself in men's clothes again, I think —" She searched in vain for words to express an idea that she seemed to feel clearly enough. "If I were a man and got to see no other side of men than the one you show me as a woman, nothing in this world could bore me more than the lot of you." This was not exactly what she meant to convey, but it sufficed to baffle Altmüller.

"But you are not a man," he said.

"I'm nothing worse, I hope? Nothing inferior?"

"But, Nanette dear, do you have to ask me that? I, who know no other happiness than to read your every wish in your eyes? Who thinks of you as Fate's most precious gift to him?"

"And yet I'm to be satisfied with what would bore me if I were a man?"

"Such is love."

"That we show our silly sides to each other?"

"In heaven's name, what do you want? Seriously now, Nanette, do you want to join the bluestockings and swear off love?"

"I've been told," she answered with a touch of cynicism, "that the bluestockings know a good deal about love."

"Blowing hot and cold would not be your way," he rebuked her, sincerely chagrined. "Your way is strong and simple, like Nature's own."

"As if these were the only two ways," she proudly countered. "Here, read this!" She drew the poem from her bosom and handed it to him. He had the presence of mind to kiss the paper before weighing it in his hand, but she remained unmoved and urged him to read.

He read, looked at her, and shrugged. "Very pretty. Talented, it seems to me"

"Very pretty. Talented," she repeated, nodding after each word. "I might have known." She moved away from him, and he awkwardly dropped the sheet on the table.

But when he wanted to take his leave—unasked, this time—she grasped his lapel. "When you use a word like *talent,* it sounds as if nothing could be more ordinary. My chef has talent: he can cook. And my hairdresser has talent: he puts my hair up without hurting me. I am sure that's how you think the man who wrote this has talent—because it rhymes. But here" —she gestured vehemently at the paper—"here is a flame that makes me feel ashamed of having listened to the same compliments every day for four months. This here is love, this is feeling. This doesn't make me out a fool. Somebody I don't know knows more and better things about me than you do—more than till yesterday I knew myself."

"Nanette," said Altmüller, suddenly suspicious, "you know that our relationship, even if you don't call it love any more, was built on honesty. Be honest now. You know who sent you that poem!"

"Is that all you'll ever understand?" she triumphed. "I do not know who sent me the poem. I haven't a single clue as to who it might be. The handwriting looks almost like that of a schoolboy. . . ." Relieved and happy, Altmüller sought to take hold of her, but she withdrew her hand and threw back her head: "But I'll find him, this unknown poet!"

"How?" asked Altmüller. "In this case I'm afraid you could not count on my assistance."

She smiled at him. "You forget that tonight I'll sing Cherubino again."

He did not understand.

"My *song* will bring him to me," she explained. "You just come to the opera. And don't be surprised if I have at least another word from him tomorrow."

This stratagem worried Altmüller less than she thought, however, and he took his leave feeling reasonably safe.

As for the singer, their talk had further entangled her in the unusual romance. She was full of joy and definite expectations, as if everything else must happen according to plan. When she read the poem now, as she did several times during the afternoon, she could almost hear a real, familiar voice in it—and she was as good as ready with her answers.

That night she sang with a more sweeping success than she had ever scored. There was hardly a change in her acting. What confusion of sex the poem had left in her had given way to stage routine as soon as she put on make-up and costume. But her voice had never been so light, like a bird between heaven and earth, gladdening her and others. The ride home found her more fatigued than usual, more elated, but also warier of drafts and cold, and full of confidence in the development of her adventure.

Her confidence was dashed in the morning. Again she received letters and flowers, but nothing came from the unknown—not a verse, not a line. She had been so sure in her hope that its frustration completely upset her good spirits. She refused to see Altmüller and spent the day in a state of frenzy alternating with depression. Like a spoiled child who cannot accept the denial of any wish, she finally found comfort in persuading herself that, had the unknown appeared bodily in her room, he would not have differed much from other men. His very failure to appear lent him a thrilling new reality. It made her imagined colloquy with him more ardent, and her expectation more tempestuous and agonizing.

And when Altmüller, who was informed of everything that went on in his mistress's house, showed up the next day, hardly able to conceal his satisfaction, he had to discover that the spook was anything but gone.

Nanette was paler, paid less attention to him, and changed the subject when he cautiously began to praise her latest performance. "You've got to help me, Altmüller. Either it's all over between us, or you've got to help me. I've made up my mind. I've got to meet the unknown poet."

"What do you want of him?"

"That depends on what he wants of me."

"Well," he said, "the poem doesn't seem to leave any doubt, does it? If you mean to give him that—?"

"That—that and everything," she cried, and burst into tears.

It was the first time Altmüller had seen her cry, but he remained stubborn. "You wouldn't ask me, of all men, to console you in this grief, would you?"

"Then you can go at once," she blazed, "and if you don't change your mind, your time here is up. I've never asked you for anything. This is my first request, and you refuse it."

"But it's quite a request, Nanette." He tried to placate her.

She measured him with an ambiguous glance. "Figure out what I'm worth to you, Altmüller. It's the most you'll lose to anyone."

Altmüller could not get the words out of his mind. He was at home before he could think up a good reply, and he had to admit to himself that arguing with Nanette required more of an effort than he had been called upon to make in his past dealings with her and other women.

He called on her, without being admitted; he wrote to her, without receiving replies. He heard that Nanette shunned all company, and while the news relieved his most immediate anxiety, it proved that the fever kept consuming the beloved. His sudden exile from her surroundings, without actual deposition, made his thought grow all the fonder. He missed her in a way quite unlike the passing separation of, say, a journey. Eventually he could no longer chide her sentiment for a mere whim, and one night, at a weekly gathering of young men of divers occupations, he caught himself listening attentively to talk about theatrical and poetic subjects—talk that might shed some light on Nanette's mystery.

Among those present at this party was Vincentius Hüttenvogel, and Altmüller was tempted to confide in him. Like some of their friends, however, he found Hüttenvogel's thin, grave, suspicious face even more reserved and aloof than in the past; and with his own secret impressing him now as too frivolous, now as too complex for communication, Altmüller kept silent. Vincentius dominated the conversation and raised it to such lofty heights that everyone listened admiringly; only Altmüller was and remained distrait.

He felt lonely, like one who is homesick. However brilliant the lecture that rang past his ear, to him it seemed pompous and feeble—and he thought of Nanette, exactly as if she were his, and were thus giving more, in her freshness and warmth, than all original and counterfeit philosophers were capable of giving. His imagination grew livelier, his need of her increased, and he would not have been surprised to come home and find her there, awaiting him and ready to delight him.

"Nanette" (he wrote her that very night), "I will help you on one condition: if we do not find him within a month, you will marry me."

He sent her the letter in the morning, and before she had time to reply, he presented himself at their usual hour and was admitted.

Whether it was prudence or his zeal to serve her, he said not a word about the proviso in his letter. From the first uncertain greeting he proceeded directly to advice and suggestions: "We mustn't trust to chance. I haven't been idle all this time, you know. I kept my ears open as far as I discreetly could, but without success. After all, I number most of the young literary world among my acquaintances, and at our parties I couldn't possibly miss the most cryptic allusion—which had to come if our man should be known to anyone, for poets don't hide their light under a bushel, and virtually all of them know how I feel about you. So we'll just have to read the journals until we find a verse or a line that seems worthy of your poet."

It escaped Nanette that this tale signified nothing, and that the venture for which Altmüller so gladly volunteered was headed for futility. She was impressed by his seeming unselfishness, and for days and weeks the two of them bought all the newspapers, almanacs, and reviews they could lay hands on. For the first time in her life Nanette was not content to examine the fashion plates, the sketches of laces and bonnets, and to skim the society page. Instead, she eagerly tackled the rhymed stuff, looking for—she soon ceased to know for what.

Poetry was fatiguing, you could not deny it. The verses raised dust and made otherwise fresh views look gray. In the long run it was evident that one verse resembled another, and at close range you hardly saw the difference between good and bad.

Altmüller was shrewd enough to carry on more faithfully than Nanette—who might well have insisted some day on pursuing her unknown by other methods.

Just as she was about to voice this idea, however, it struck her that the waiting period would profit her in any event. Although as yet it had not been discussed between them, Altmüller's alternative was beginning to appeal to her. She felt like a child enamored of its instructor and uncertain whether or not he will come the next day—"I'll have a lesson tomorrow, or I won't; either way will be fun."

And then the month was over, and the poet had not been discovered. The lovers had to grant each other that they had tried honestly, to no avail. They looked at each other with feeling and sank one into the other's arms.

Thus the very sweetheart Altmüller had taken right off a predecessor's hand was now received by him almost as though from her parents' home.

Happier than ever, and more affably disposed by his manner of happiness, Altmüller, at a chance meeting with Hüttenvogel, could not resist the temptation to open his heart. He hardly bothered to ascribe a literary motive to his confidences, expatiating a little on the odd way in which the gift of poesy might flare at times, suddenly kindled, and then be extinguished forever. When the other looked doubtful, he immediately cited the example of Nanette's experience, and in the satisfaction of victory he bluntly stated that the unknown poet had missed the prize by a hair—for the opera singer had been on fire and unlikely to restrain her generous nature.

Hüttenvogel, with more than an inkling of the truth, inquired whether he might some time see the poem.

"You can imagine," said Altmüller, "that as a man of discretion I did not leave the powder next to the coals. But pouring it down the drain seemed too much of a pity." With these words he took the poem out of his wallet, and Hüttenvogel, as he had surmised, read his own verses.

His first reaction was one of overpowering irony. He could all but see the stream of life flow past his ungrasping hands, and in this lucid moment he foresaw the full measure of his lonely discontent. And yet: no mere disgruntled, disillusioned, lightless solitude. While his friend talked on and on, past—and yet not quite past—his ears and heart, the poet once more seemed to hear the song of Cherubino, and his raptured eyes saw the never tiring Eros in flight between heaven and earth.

Translated by E. B. Ashton

ROCK CRYSTAL

by Adalbert Stifter

Among the high mountains of our country there is a little village with a small but needle-fine church spire. Conspicuous above the green of abundant fruit trees, this spire—because the slates are painted vermilion—can be seen far and wide against the faint blue of the mountains. The hamlet nestles in the very center of a fairly wide valley, an almost perfect ellipse. Besides the church, a schoolhouse, and a parish-house, there are a few stately homes around a square with four linden trees and a stone cross in the center. These are not simple farmhouses, but a haven of handicrafts, providing the mountain people with essential commodities. In the valley and scattered along the mountainsides are many little huts of a sort common to such regions—whose inhabitants belong to the village, use its church and school, and support its craftsmen by buying their wares. Even more distant huts are also part of the village, but, hidden away in the mountains, cannot be seen from the valley; the people rarely come down among their fellow parishioners; often, indeed, they must keep their dead with them over the

---

"Here is still a world of beauty," Nietzsche said about the work of Adalbert Stifter. Born in 1805, the son of a linen weaver in Oberplan, in southern Bohemia, Stifter studied natural sciences, mathematics, and art, and then for many years supported himself by living as a private tutor in aristocratic households. At last he was appointed Supervisor of Primary Schools for Upper Austria. Tormented by an incurable disease, he committed suicide (1868). Besides his great novels, Der Nachsommer *and* Witiko, *Stifter published several collections of long short stories, of which the tale reprinted here is the most famous. He was also a landscape painter of distinction, and as such, significantly, a precursor of the German impressionists.*

winter till they can bring them to the valley for burial after the snow has melted. The great man of the village is the priest. The villagers regard him with veneration, and he, after a protracted stay in the valley, usually becomes used to isolation, stays on not unwillingly, and then just goes on living there. Since time immemorial no priest in the village has ever craved a change, none has been unworthy of his calling.

There are no highways in the valley, merely cart-roads with double wheel-tracks, along which the crops are brought home on one-horse carts. Accordingly, few strangers come to the valley; among these an occasional wanderer, a nature-lover who lives for a time in the prettily painted upper room of the inn, enjoying the mountain view; or possibly an artist who sketches in his portfolio the delicate church spire and beautiful rocky peaks.

The village people thus constitute a separate world; they know one another by name and are familiar with all the grandfathers' and great-grandfathers' tales. All mourn when anyone dies; all know the name of the newborn; they speak a language which is different from that used in the plain; they have their quarrels and settle them; they help one another, and if anything unusual happens, come flocking together.

South of the village you see a snowy mountain with dazzling horn-shaped peaks, rising, as it seems, from the housetops themselves, but actually quite far away. All year round, summer and winter, there it is with its jutting crags and white expanses, looking down upon the valley. As the most prominent feature of the landscape and ever before the eyes of the villagers, the mountain has been the inspiration of many a tale. There is not a man, young or old, in the village who has not something to tell about its peaks and crags, its caves and crevasses, its streams and torrents—something that either has happened to him or that he has heard about from others. This mountain is the pride of the village, as though the people had made it themselves, and, with due respect to their honesty, we can't swear to it that once in a while they would not fib for the honor and glory of their mountain. Besides being notable in itself, the mountain is actually profitable, for on the arrival of a party of mountain-climbers to make the ascent from the valley, the villagers serve as guides; and to have been a guide—had this or that experience, known this or that spot—is a distinction that affords anyone great satisfaction. When they sit together in the common room at the inn, they are always talking about their feats and strange adventures, never failing to mention what this or that traveler said and how much he gave them for their labors. The mountain also sends down from its snowy flanks streams that feed a lake in the forest, from which a brook emerges and flows merrily through the valley, driving the sawmill, the gristmill, and small machinery of various kinds, providing cleanliness for the village, and watering the cattle. The forest tracts afford timber and also break the force of the avalanches. Through subterranean channels and loose soil at these altitudes water filters and, coursing veinlike through the valley, comes to the surface in little fountains and springs, from which the people drink. And as time and again they offer strangers this unrivaled, much-extolled water, they never stop to think how useful it is, accepting it simply as something that has always been there.

With regard to the change of seasons on the mountain, in winter the two pinnacles called "horns" are snow-white and on clear days stand out in the dusky atmosphere with blinding brilliance; all the upland meadows at the base of the summits are white then, as well as their sloping shoulders; even the precipitous rock faces, or walls as the people call them, are coated with a white velvet nap of hoarfrost and glazed with ice-tissue, so the entire mass towers like an enchanted castle above the darkish weight of gray forest mantling the base. In summer as the sun and temperate winds melt the snow on the gradients, the horns soar up, as the mountain people say, black into the sky, their surface marked only by exquisite little flecks and snow veins. These veins, however, are not really white, but the delicate milky blue of the distant snow on the darker blue rocks. At higher levels in hot weather, the meadows about the horns never lose their blanket of eternal snow, and it shines down on the verdure in the valley; but on the lower levels the recent winter snowfall—a mere down—melts away, and iridescent blue-green tints appear in the glacier that, now bared, greets the people in the valley.

Ascent of the mountain is made from the valley. One follows in the southerly direction a smooth, well-made road that leads by a neck or "col" into another valley. A col is a mountain range of moderate height, connecting two larger, more considerable, ranges; and following it, one passes between the ranges from one valley into another. The col that links the snow-mountain with the corresponding range opposite is thickly studded with pines. At about the highest point of the road that descends into the farther valley stands a little rustic memorial. One time a baker, carrying his basket over the col, was found dead at this spot. A picture of him and his basket, with the pines about him, was painted on a tablet, fastened to a scarlet post, and erected to mark the scene of the tragedy. At this marker one turns off the road and follows along the col instead of making one's way straight down into the valley beyond. There is here an opening in the pines as if a road led into them, and indeed during part of the year there is a path leading to the rustic memorial by which timber is brought down and which afterward disappears, overgrown by grass. Proceeding along this path, which climbs gently, one comes at length to a clearing quite bare of trees, a barren heath with not so much as a bush, only scant heather, drought-inured mosses, and small, hardy plant-life. The ground then rises sharply and the ascent is long; one climbs in a worn groove or trench, which at least has the advantage of keeping one from losing the way over the vast sameness of heath. After a time, rocky towers as of a church rise from the grassy floor, and between these walls one keeps on climbing. Then more bare ridges appear, with scant vegetation, and one is breathing the air of the higher altitudes that lead direct to the icecap. At either side of the path is a steep wall, and it is this defile that joins the snow-mountain with the col. To scale the ice, one skirts the margin for some time above the rocks that surround it, until one comes to the packed snow bridging the crevasses, snow hard enough at most seasons to bear the traveler's weight.

At the highest point of the icefield the two horns rise from the snow. These peaks are difficult to ascend, moated as they are by snow, now wide, now narrow, and the *Bergschrund* or rim must be compassed by a leap. Since the sheer verticals offer only scant ledges for foothold, most climbers are satisfied with reaching the *Bergschrund,* and from there enjoy as much of the panorama as is not cut off by the horn. Those wishing to reach the summit can do so only with the aid of spiked shoes, ropes, and cleats.

There are other mountains besides this one on the southern horizon, but none so high. They too are covered with snow in the early autumn and on into late spring. Summer, however, eats the snow away, and the rocks gleam in the sun with a gentle allure, and the rich green of the lower forest is intersected by broad-lying violet shadows—a scene so lovely that one could look at it all one's life and never tire of it.

Along the valley in other directions—to the north, the east, and the west—the mountains stretch away into the distance, on and on, but lower, with occasional pastures and patches of tilled ground on the slopes and higher up forest clearings and alpine huts, the skyline marked by a delicate sawtooth edge that is an indication of the moderate height of the range; whereas on the southern horizon the mountains, though clothed with magnificent forest, sweep along with smooth outline against the luminous sky.

Standing in about the middle of the valley, one has the impression that not a single road leads either into or out of the basin—an illusion familiar to anyone who has spent much time in the mountains—while in reality not only are there several roads leading into the northern plains, but there is also the col path toward the south, where the valley is closed in by walls of perpendicular rock.

The little village is called Gschaid, and the snow-mountain that looks down upon its houses is called Gars.

On the other side of the col, with the beaten path from the wayside shrine leading down to it, there is a much more beautiful and fertile valley than that of Gschaid. As one comes into it, one encounters the stately market town of Millsdorf. It is a sizable town with several kinds of mills and a number of buildings in which trades and crafts are housed. The inhabitants are more prosperous than those of Gschaid, and though the valleys are only three hours' distance apart—a trifling matter to mountain people, used as they are to great distances and inured to hardship—manners and customs in the two valleys are so different and they are so unlike in appearance that one would think that untold miles separated them. This is often the case in mountainous regions, not only because of their varying positions—more or less propitious—with relation to the sun, but also as a result of character, which has led the inhabitants to choose differing occupations. But in one respect they are all alike: they cling to what is traditional and to the ancient ways of their forefathers, and never seem to miss the bustle of traffic; each loves his valley ardently, and could scarcely exist away from it.

Months, sometimes a year, may pass before anyone from Gschaid crosses into the valley beyond to visit the great market town, Millsdorf. And though the same is true of the people of Millsdorf, yet being in communication with other parts of the country around them, they are not so sequestered as the people of Gschaid. There is even a road that might be called a highway the length of their valley, and many a traveler, many a wanderer, goes on his way without a suspicion that north of him on the farther side of the lordly snow-mountain, lies a valley with a goodly scattering of houses, and a hamlet with tapering church spire.

One of the trades supplying this valley with needful commodities is the shoemaker's—indispensable the world over wherever human beings are no longer in the primitive stage. These valley people of Gschaid, be it said, are so far beyond it that they need the very stoutest and most durable highland footwear. The shoemaker is the only one in the valley. His house in Gschaid fronts on the square—among the better houses—and with its gray walls, white window-sills, and green shutters, looks out on the four linden trees. It has, on the ground-floor, the workroom, the journeymen's room, a large and a small living-room, the little shop, together with kitchen, larder, and such cupboards as pertain to them. On the second floor—that is, in the gable end—is an upper chamber, a formal best room, in which stand two imposing beds, well-polished and well-stocked wardrobes, also a china closet with dishes, an inlaid table, upholstered chairs, a little recessed wall safe or cupboard for savings, pictures of saints, two exquisite timepieces, and shooting-match prizes. Lastly, in a special cabinet of their own, with glass front, hang rifles for target practice and for hunting, with everything pertaining to them.

Adjoining the shoemaker's house is a much smaller one, separated only by an arched passage, built in the same style, and really a part of the other—a detail of the whole. It consists of one room with the usual adjuncts. It is for the use of the owner when he has transferred the property to his son or successor—a retirement-annex as it is called—in which he and his wife may spend their last years. Then again the small house will be vacant, awaiting a new occupant.

The shoemaker's house has a stable and barn at the rear, for everyone who lives in the valley—tradesman or not—tills the ground, thus obtaining subsistence. Behind the buildings, as with any of the better houses in Gschaid, is a garden that furnishes vegetables, fruit, and, for festive occasions, flowers. As in most mountain regions, beekeeping is customary, with straw hives in the garden.

Before he inherited his house, the shoemaker had been a chamois-poacher and in general, so people said, a not too model youth. In school he had always been one of the best pupils. Later he had learned his father's trade, then been a wandering journeyman, and had finally come back to the village. But instead of wearing a black hat as becomes a tradesman—such as his father had worn all his life—he perched a green one on his head, stuck every available feather in it, and strutted about wearing the shortest frieze coat in the valley, whereas his father had always worn a dark coat, preferably black—since he was a man of trade—and invariably cut long. The young shoemaker was to be seen on every dance floor and at every bowling alley. If anyone tried to reason with him, he just whistled a tune. He and his marksman's rifle were at every shooting match in the neighborhood, and sometimes he carried home a prize—treasured by him as a great trophy. The prize was usually a set of coins artistically arranged. But the shoemaker, in order to win it, had to disburse many more similar coins in his usual spendthrift fashion. He went to all the hunts in the neighborhood, and had quite a reputation for being a good marksman. Sometimes, however, he fared forth alone with his blunderbuss and spiked shoes, and it was rumored that he had once received a serious wound on his head.

In Millsdorf just where the town begins, as you come in by the road from Gschaid, there lived a dyer with a thriving business in which he employed many workmen; and—something unheard of in the valley—he even made use of machinery.

He was the possessor, moreover, of extensive farmlands. To woo the daughter of this prosperous dyer, the shoemaker of Gschaid would trudge all the way over the mountains. Noted far and wide for her beauty, she was also admired for her virtue, decorum, and housewifely accomplishments. Nevertheless, it would seem, the shoemaker attracted her attention. The dyer would not allow him to enter the house; and whereas the beautiful daughter had not previously gone to public places or taken part in festivities, and had rarely been seen away from home, now she went nowhere but to church or into the garden or from one room to another in the house.

Some time after the death of his parents, when he had become the proprietor of the house where he now lived all alone, the shoemaker changed into a wholly different person. Whereas till then he was always rollicking about, he now sat in his shop, hammering away day and night. He boasted that no one could make better shoes, and engaged only the best workmen, whom he nagged and pestered a good deal as they sat at their work, making them follow his instructions and do exactly as he told them. The result was that not only did everyone in Gschaid who had always before got footwear from neighboring valleys now come to him, but the entire valley did so as well. And as time went on, even people from Millsdorf and other valleys came to have their footwear made by the shoemaker of Gschaid. His fame traveled even into the plain, so that many people who intended to climb the mountains had their special shoes made by him.

He kept his house spick and span, and shoes, mountain shoes, and high boots gleamed on the shelves of the storeroom; and on Sundays, when folk from all over the valley flocked to the village and stood around on the square with its four linden trees, they liked to go over to the shoemaker's and peep through the windows at the people buying and ordering shoes.

In keeping with his love for the mountains, mountain shoes were his best work, and he used to say in the common room at the inn that no one could show him a mountain shoe made by anyone else that could compare with one of his. "They haven't the knack," he would add.

Now, though the dyer's beautiful daughter stayed at home most of the time and visited neither relatives nor friends, the shoemaker from Gschaid managed it so that she should catch a glimpse of him when she went to church, walked about the garden, or looked from the windows of her room. Because of this constant gazing, the dyer's wife by long, insistent, unremitting supplications induced her stiff-necked husband to give in, and the shoemaker (who had, after all, mended his ways) carried off the beautiful and wealthy maiden of Millsdorf as his bride.

The dyer, however, was a headstrong person. The right sort of man, he said, has an occupation, makes it thrive and grow, and thereby supports his wife, his children, himself, and servants; he keeps his house in order and lays by a goodly nest-egg, the only thing that gives a man dignity and standing in the world. Thus it was that the only dowry his daughter received was a well-filled hope chest; the rest was the husband's concern —for the present and in future. The dyeworks in Millsdorf with its farmland was a business worth while in itself, besides reflecting credit on its owner; and because all of it was, in a sense, capital, the dyer would give none of it away. But once he and his wife had died, the dyeworks and farmland would fall to their only daughter—namely, the shoemaker's wife in Gschaid—and the shoemaker and his wife might then do with them as they pleased; provided, that is, that the heirs were worthy. Should they be unworthy, they would get but the legal share, the inheritance going to their children, and if there were none, to other relatives.

Nor did the shoemaker make any demands, showing proudly that all he had wanted was to win the dyer's beautiful daughter, and that he was well able to keep her and care for her as she had been kept and cared for at home. And he dressed her, as his wife, not only better than any of the women of Gschaid and of the valley were dressed, but better even than she had been at home, and meat and drink and everything about the house had to be better and choicer than anything she had enjoyed in her father's house. And to spite his father-in-law, he bought more and more land, so that he came finally to possess a considerable property.

As the people of Gschaid seldom leave their valley and almost never go to Millsdorf, and as, furthermore, no one ever leaves his valley to settle in a neighboring one—though removals to great distances occur—and lastly as no girl ever leaves her valley except on the rare occasion when, as a bride, she follows her husband into another valley—so it came about that after the beautiful daughter of the dyer of Millsdorf married the shoemaker of Gschaid, she was still regarded by the people of Gschaid as a stranger; and though they were not unkind to her, and even loved her for her charm and virtue, there was always something, reserve or a sort of shy respect, that kept her from enjoying the same familiarity and warm intimacy that existed among the people who belonged to the valley. That's the way it was, and no use talking about it. And the finer clothes and easier domestic life of the shoemaker's wife only made it worse.

After having been married a year, she bore her husband a son, and several years later a daughter. She felt, however, that he did not love the children as much as she thought he ought to, and as she herself loved them; for he looked so serious most of the time and was always preoccupied with his work. He rarely petted or played with them, and always addressed them quietly as one speaks to grown persons. In the matter of food, clothes, and all material things, however, his care for them was above reproach.

At first the dyer's wife often came to Gschaid, and the young couple also at times went over to Millsdorf to attend church fairs and on other festive occasions. But after the children were born, things were different. Mothers may love their children and tenderly long for them when they are absent, but a grandmother's longing for her grandchildren amounts almost to a morbid craving. The dyer's wife would often come over to Gschaid to see the children, bring them presents, stay awhile, and then, after giving them some good advice, depart. But when age and health made these frequent journeys inadvisable and the dyer for that reason objected to them, a different plan was devised, everything was reversed, and the children visited their grandmother instead. Their mother herself would often take them in the carriage, or they would be entrusted to a maid-servant and driven in a buggy over the col, well bundled up because they were still of tender years. But when older, they would go on foot, accompanied by their mother or a maid; and when the lad had grown strong, knowing, and self-reliant, they let him take the familiar road over the col by himself, and even, when he begged to take his little sister along, if the weather was good would allow her to go with him. There was nothing unusual about this in Gschaid, for the people were hardy walkers, and parents, especially a man like the shoemaker, admired physical strength and were glad to see it in their children.

So it came about that the two children went over the col oftener than any of the other villagers, and in this way, like their mother, who had always been treated as a stranger in Gschaid, the children became strangers too, and were hardly Gschaid children, but belonged half to Millsdorf.

Conrad, the boy, already gave evidence of his father's serious disposition, and Susanna, the little girl, named for her mother and called Sanna for short, had unbounded faith in his knowledge, judgment, and strength and followed unquestioningly wherever he led, just as their mother accepted their father's guidance and never questioned his superior judgment.

On clear days the children could be seen early in the morning, making their way down the valley, crossing the meadow, and coming to the place where the col forest looks down upon it. Going up toward the forest they would keep to the path, finally reaching the highest point, and before noon be descending the open meadows on the other side, toward Millsdorf. Conrad then showed Sanna the ones belonging to their grandfather; as they walked across the fields, he told her about the various kinds of grain; they would look at the lengths of cloth hanging from poles under the rafters to dry, and swinging in the wind or blown into antic postures; then they would hear the fulling-mill and the pounding in the tannery built by their grandfather beside the brook; and now, turning a corner of the field, they were soon entering the garden through the back gate, where they were welcomed by their grandmother. She always seemed to know when they were coming, would watch from the window, and, seeing Sanna's bright red kerchief in the sun, would recognize them from far away.

She then led them through washhouse and press into the living-room, made them sit down, and would not let them open their neckerchiefs or spencers lest they catch cold. After the midday meal they were allowed to go out and play, run about the house, or do anything they liked, provided it was not indecorous or forbidden. The dyer, always at table with them, asked them about their school work, dwelling particularly on the subjects they should study. In the afternoon, even before it was time, their grandmother would begin urging them to start back, so that they would not be late reaching home. Although the dyer had given his daughter no dowry and vowed that until his death none of his fortune should be given away, his wife had no such scruples, and not only gave the children all kinds of things when they visited her, frequently even pieces of money of considerable value, but also and invariably made up two little bundles in which she put such things as she thought they might need or that would give them pleasure. And even if they had the same things in the shoemaker's house in Gschaid—as good as one could desire—their grandmother would give for the sheer pleasure of giving, and they would carry her gifts home with them as something very precious. So it always happened that the day before Christmas they would take home carefully wrapped, well-sealed packages, unaware that these were presents they would be receiving that evening.

Their grandmother's bundling them off always long before it was time merely resulted in the children's loitering at this spot or that along the way. They liked to sit by the hazel trees on the col and crack nuts with stones; or if there were no nuts, play with leaves or little sticks or with the pine-cones that drop from the branches in early spring. Sometimes Conrad would tell little stories to his sister or, coming to the wayside shrine, would take her a little way up the side road at the left toward the heights, saying that that was the way to Snow-mountain, that there were crags and huge boulders up there, chamois scampering, and great birds flying about. He often took her even high up above the tree-line, and they would gaze at the dry grass and stunted heather; but he led her back again in time, and they would have returned before the gloaming.

One winter, the day before Christmas, when in the valley of Gschaid early dawn had broadened into day, a faint clear-weather haze overspread the sky, so that the sun creeping up in the southeast could be seen only as an indistinct reddish ball; furthermore, the air was mild, almost warm in the valley and even in the upper reaches of the sky, as indicated by the unchanging forms of the motionless clouds. So the shoemaker's wife said to the children: "Since it is such a fine day and since it has not rained for a long time and the roads are hard, and since yesterday your father gave you permission, provided it was the right kind of day, you may go over to Millsdorf to see your grandmother; but first you must ask your father again."

The children, still in their night-clothes, ran into the adjoining room, where their father was talking with a customer, and begged him—since it was such a beautiful day—to give them his permission again. And as soon as they had his consent, they ran back to their mother, who then dressed them both with great care, or, rather, dressed the little girl, for the lad was able to dress by himself and was ready long before his mother had finished bundling up the little one in warm clothes.

Then, when everything was right, she said: "Now, Conrad, listen carefully. Since I am letting your sister go with you, you must start for home in plenty of time and you must not loiter on the way. As soon as dinner at your grandmother's is over, you must leave at once and come straight home. The days are short now, and the sun sets early."

"Yes, Mother, I know," said Conrad.

"And watch out for Sanna, so she doesn't fall or get herself overheated."

"Yes, Mother."

"Well, God protect you. Now go tell your father you are leaving."

The lad slung a calfskin pouch over his shoulder by a strap—a piece of his father's deft work, this little bag—and the children went into the next room to bid him farewell. They were soon back, and after their mother had made the sign of the cross over them in blessing, they skipped merrily off down the street.

They walked quickly along the square and the row of houses, past the picket fences of the orchards, and finally came into the open. The sun had already risen over the woodlands on the eastern heights, which were still shot with wefts of pale mist—the dull reddish ball keeping pace with them through the leafless branches of the crab-apple trees.

There was no snow anywhere in the valley; the higher mountains, which had been glistening for weeks, were covered with it; the lower ones stood snowless and silent in their pine mantle of green and fallow brown of bare branches. The ground was not yet frozen and would have been quite dry because of the long stretch without rain if the cold had not overlaid it with a faint moisture, which, instead of making it slippery, had made it all the safer and so resilient that walking was easy. The sparse grass still on the meadows, and particularly along the ditches, had an autumn look. There was no frost on the grass and, examined closely, not even any dew—all of which, interpreted locally, was a sign of imminent rain.

Down toward the far edge of the meadow was a mountain brook crossed by a high plank. The children walked along the plank and looked down. There was scarcely any water in the brook, a mere thread of intense blue on the stony bed, the dry pebbles having become perfectly white in the long weeks without rain, and the scantness as well as the color of the water meant bitter cold at the higher altitudes—cold that held the ground in a vise so it could not make the brook turbid with sediment, and freezing it hard till the core gave off only a few clear drops.

From the footbridge the children raced over the meadows, closer and closer to the woodland.

They came at last to the outskirts of the forest and went on into it.

When they had climbed into the higher woods of the col, the long ruts in the cart-road were not soft as they had been in the valley, but firm, because they were frozen. The children no longer kept to the smooth path by the road, but walked in the ruts, seeing which ridges would bear their weight. When in an hour they had reached the crest of the col, the ground was so hard their steps rang and the clods were like iron.

Sanna was the first to notice, at the shrine erected in memory of the baker, that the red post supporting the tablet was no longer there. They went closer and saw that it lay in the dry grass that stood up like pale straw, partly concealing it. They did not see why the post should be lying there—whether it had been thrown down or had fallen of itself—but they did see the wood rotted where it came out of the ground, and that it might have toppled over of itself; but as it lay there, they were glad to be able to have a closer look at the picture and the inscription. When they had studied it all—the basket with the rolls, the whitish hands of the baker, his closed eyes, his gray coat, and the pines about him—had spelled out the legend and then said it out loud, they proceeded on their way.

Another hour and the dark woods on both sides were dim behind them; thin-set trees, part single oaks, part birch and clusters of scrub, met the eye, continuing with them a distance, and shortly after, the children were running down through the meadows into the valley of Millsdorf.

Although this valley is considerably lower than that of Gschaid and is therefore so much warmer that harvest begins two weeks earlier than in Gschaid, the ground here was frozen too; and when the children came to their grandfather's tannery and fulling-mill, they found in the road, where the wheels scatter drops of water, thin sheets of cat's-ice, ever a delight to children.

Their grandmother had seen them and, coming out to meet them, took Sanna's little cold hands in hers and led the children inside.

She undid their wraps, had fresh wood put in the stove, and asked what had happened on the way over.

When they had answered, she said: "That's good, that's all right, I am glad you came, but this time you must be off very soon, the days are short and it is getting colder; nothing was frozen in Millsdorf this morning."

"Nor in Gschaid," said the lad.

"See? You must hurry, then, so you won't be too cold by evening," answered their grandmother.

Then she asked how their mother was, how was their father, and had anything happened in Gschaid.

After these inquiries she busied herself with the meal, made sure it would be on the table earlier than usual, and herself prepared little appetizing things for the children that she knew they liked. Then the dyer was called in, the children sat down at the table laid for them as for grown-ups, and ate with their grandfather and grandmother, the latter piling good things on their plates. After dinner she patted Sanna's cheek, quite rosy by this time. Then she bustled about here and there, packing to overflowing the lad's calfskin pouch, besides stuffing things into his pockets. She also put divers things into Sanna's little pockets, gave them each a piece of bread to eat on the way, and in the bag, she told them, were two rolls in case they became very hungry.

"For your mother," she said, "I am giving you some well-roasted coffee-beans, and in the very tightly wrapped bottle with the stopper is some black coffee extract better than your mother herself makes; she can use from it just as it is; it is a veritable tonic, so strong the merest sip warms the stomach so that you wouldn't be chilled even on the coldest of winter days. The other things in the bag, in the cardboard box wrapped with paper, you are to take home without opening."

After a word or two more with the children, she said they must go.

"Take good care, Sanna," she said, "not to get chilled; don't get overheated; and don't you run up over the meadows and under the trees. The wind may come up toward evening, and then you will have to go slower. Greetings to Father and Mother, and tell them we wish them a right merry Christmas." She kissed them each on the cheek, and hastened them forth. She accompanied them through the garden, let them out by the rear gate, shut it again, and came back into the house.

The children went past the thin sheets of cat's-ice beside their grandfather's mill, crossed the fields, and turned up toward the rising meadows.

When they had come to the heights covered with scattered trees and thickets of scrub, already mentioned, some few snow-flakes floated slowly down.

"See there, Sanna," said the lad. "I knew it would snow; remember when we left home, we could still see the sun, as red as the lamp over the holy sepulcher in church during Holy Week, and now we can't see even the faintest ray and there's only gray fog up there over the treetops. That always means snow."

The children walked on more briskly, and Sanna was delighted whenever she caught a falling flake on the sleeve of her dark coat and it did not melt for a long time. When finally they came to the farther fringe of the Millsdorf heights before entering the dark woods on the col, the serried wall of pines was already prettily flecked with the fast-falling snow. They now entered the deep woods, the longest part of the remaining way home. Up and up, from the fringe of the forest, the ground rises till one comes to the red post of the wayside shrine, from where, as we said before, the road turns off down to Gschaid. The ascent through the woods is so steep from the Millsdorf side that the road does not lead straight up, but in wide serpentines, west to east and east to west. At each side of the road, the whole way up to the shrine and down to the meadows of Gschaid, there are impenetrable, densely towering woods that thin only a little as one gains the valley level and comes out on the meadows in the valley of Gschaid. The col itself, though but a small link between two great ranges, would, if set on the floor of the valley, be a considerable mountain-chain.

The first thing that struck the children on entering the woods was that the frozen ground had a whitish look as though meal had been scattered; the heads of some of the grasses by the road and among the trees were drooping with the weight of snow, and the many green pine and fir ends, reaching out like hands, held up little thistledown pyramids.

"Is it snowing at home now, where Father is?" asked Sanna.

"Certainly," answered her brother, "getting colder, too, and you'll see tomorrow, the whole pond will be frozen over."

"Yes, Conrad," said the child.

She all but doubled her short steps to keep pace with the lad as he strode along.

They went steadily up the winding road, now west to east, now east to west. The wind predicted by their grandmother had not come up; the air, on the contrary, was so still not a twig or a branch stirred; in fact, it felt warmer in the woods, as is usual, in winter, among spaced objects like tree-trunks, and the flakes kept falling thicker and thicker so the ground was already white, and the woods began to take on a gray, dusty look, with snow settling upon the garments and hats of both the lad and his sister.

The children were delighted. They set their feet on the soft down and eagerly looked for places where it seemed thicker so they could make believe they were already deep in it. They did not shake the snow from their clothing. Peace had descended upon everything. Not the sound of a bird, though a few birds usually flit about the woods even in winter; and though the children on the way to Millsdorf had heard some twitter, they did not see any now, either flying or on branches. The whole forest was as though dead.

Since the footprints behind were their own and the snow ahead lay unbroken, it was evident that they were the only ones crossing the col that day.

They kept on in the same direction, now coming toward trees, now leaving them behind, and where the underbrush was thick they could even see the snow lying on the twigs.

Their spirits were still rising, for the flakes fell thicker and thicker and in a little while they did not have to look for snow to wade in, because it lay so thick it felt soft to the feet everywhere, and even came up around their shoes; and it was so still, it seemed as if they could almost hear the rustle of the flakes settling on the pine needles.

"Shall we see the baker's post, I wonder," asked little Sanna, "for it's fallen down and will be snowed on, so the red will be white."

"We'll see it, just the same," said the lad, "we'll see it lying there even if the snow does fall on it and make it white, for it's a good thick post and the black iron cross on top would always stick up."

"Yes, Conrad."

In the meantime, while they kept on, the snow became so thick they could see only the nearest trees.

They could not feel the hardness of the road or the ridges of the wheel-ruts; the road was an even softness everywhere because of the snow, and one could distinguish it only as it wound on through the forest smooth and white like a ribbon. Every bough was mantled in fairest white.

The children were walking now in the middle of the road, their little feet plowing through snow that slowed their steps, for the going was harder. The lad pulled his jacket together at the collar so the snow would not fall on the back of his neck, and shoved his hat farther down about his ears for protection. He also drew tighter the shawl that his mother had folded about his little sister, and pulled it out over her forehead in a little roof.

The wind predicted by their grandmother had not yet come up, but on the other hand the snowfall had by degrees become so heavy that after a while even the nearest trees were indistinct and stood in the blur like powdery sacks.

The children pushed on. They shrank down into their coats and pushed on.

Sanna took hold of the shoulder-strap by which Conrad's bag was suspended, and with her little hand clutching the strap, they wended their way.

They were still not as far as the wayside memorial. The lad could not be sure of the time, because there was no sun, and everything was the same monotonous gray.

"Will we be at the post soon?" asked Sanna.

"I don't know," answered her brother. "This time I can't make out the trees, or the road because it is so white. We may not see the post at all, because there is so much snow it will be covered up, and hardly a grass-blade or arm of the cross will stick out. But that's nothing. We'll just keep straight on; the road leads through the trees, and when it gets to the place where the post is, then it will start downhill and we keep right on it and when it comes out of the woods we are in Gschaid meadows; then comes the footbridge, and we're not far from home."

On they went, climbing the path. Their footprints did not show for long now, since the unusually heavy snow blotted them out at once. The quick-falling flakes no longer made even a ticking sound on the needles as they fell, but imperceptibly merged with the deep white already mantling the boughs.

The children drew their wraps still closer to keep the ever falling snow from working in on all sides.

They quickened their steps, and the road was still climbing.

After a great while they had not yet reached the place where the memorial post was supposed to be, from which the path to Gschaid turned off downhill.

At last they came to a tract with not a tree on it.

"I don't see any trees," said Sanna.

"Perhaps the road is so wide we can't see them because of the snow," said the lad.

"Yes, Conrad," said the little one.

After a time the lad came to a halt and said: "I don't see any trees myself now. We must be out of the forest. Yet the road is still going up. Let's stop a minute and look about. Perhaps we can see something."

But they did not see anything. They stared up through wan nothingness into the sky. As during a hailstorm, when leaden striations slant downward from the massed white or greenish cloudbanks, so here; and the mute downfall continued.

There was about them a great white space, nothing else.

"You know, Sanna," said the lad, "we are on that dry grass I have often brought you to in summer, where we used to sit and look at the grassy floor sloping up, where the beautiful herb-tufts grow. We shall turn right now and be going downhill."

"Yes, Conrad."

"The days are short, as Grandmother said and as you know yourself, so we must hurry."

"Yes, Conrad," said the little one.

"Wait a minute, I am going to snug you up a bit," said the lad.

He took off his hat, put it on Sanna, and tied the two ribbons under her chin. The kerchief she had been wearing was too slight protection, whereas the profusion of curls on his head was so thick, snow would rest on them a long time before the wet and cold could penetrate. Then he took off his little fur jacket and drew it on his sister up over her little arms. With only his shirt to protect him now, he tied about his shoulders the little shawl Sanna had been wearing. It would do for him, he thought, if they could just walk at a brisk pace.

He took his sister by the hand, and thus they started on again.

With trustful eyes the little thing gazed up at the prevailing gray all about them and accompanied him willingly; only that her small, hurrying feet could not keep up with him as he strove onward like someone bent on settling a thing once and for all.

They were going on now with the dogged endurance that children and animals have, not knowing what is ahead or when their reserves may give out.

As they went, however, they could not tell whether they were going down the mountain or not. They had soon turned downhill to the right, but then came to elevations leading up. Often they encountered sheer rises they had to avoid; and a hollow in which they were walking led them around in a curve. They climbed hummocks that became steeper under their feet than they expected; and what they had deemed a descent was level ground or a depression, or went on as an even stretch.

"But where are we, Conrad?" asked the child.

"I don't know," he answered. "If only my eyes could make out something and I could get my bearings."

But on every side was nothing but a blinding whiteness, white everywhere that none the less drew its ever narrowing circle about them, paling beyond into fog that came down in waves, devouring and shrouding everything till there was nothing but the voracious snow.

"Wait, Sanna," said the lad, "let's stand still a little and listen and see if we can't hear something—a sound from down there in the valley perhaps, a dog or a bell or the mill, or maybe someone calling; we ought to be able to hear something, at any rate; then we'll know which way to go."

They stood still, but heard nothing. They stood a little longer, but there was nothing to be heard, not a single sound, not the faintest except their breath; indeed, in the stillness reigning, it was as if they could hear the snow falling on their very eyelashes. Their grandmother's prediction had still not come true: the wind had not risen and, what was rare for those regions, not a breath stirred overhead, anywhere.

After waiting a considerable time, they went on again.

"Never mind, Sanna," said her brother, "don't be frightened, just follow me and I'll get you there yet. If it would only stop snowing."

She was not afraid, but lifted her feet as well as she could and followed him. He led her on through the all-pervading pearly opaqueness.

After a time rocks suddenly loomed up dark and indistinct in the white luminescence—they had almost run into them—rocks that rose so sheer scarcely any snow could cling to them.

"Sanna, Sanna," he said, "there are the rocks, let's go on, let's go on."

They went on, had to go on, between rocks and along the base. The rocks admitted of swerving neither to right nor to left, leading on in one narrow hollowed-out channel. After a time the children left them behind and could not see them any more. As unexpectedly as they had come in among them, as unexpectedly they came out. Again there was nothing about them but whiteness, with no dark obstructions looming up. It seemed one vast volume of light, and yet one could not see three feet ahead; everything was closed in, so to speak, by a mysterious white obscurity, and since there were no shadows it was impossible to judge the size of objects and the children did not know whether to step up or down until steepness raised the foot and compelled it to climb.

"My eyes hurt," said Sanna.

"Don't look at the snow," answered the lad, "but at the clouds. Mine have been hurting a good while, but it doesn't matter, I have to look at the snow anyhow, in order to watch the road. But don't be scared. I will get you down to Gschaid yet."

"Yes, Conrad."

They went on again; but however they went or however they turned, it didn't seem ever as if they were beginning to go downhill. At either side steep rooflike formations led upward, and they walked between, but always up. Whenever they went outside the "roofs" and turned downhill, it became so steep immediately that they had to come back; their little feet often encountered jagged objects, and they were constantly avoiding hummocks.

They noticed also that whenever their feet sank deeper in the fresh snow, they did not feel an earthly firmness beneath, but something different, like already frozen, older snow. But they kept on, walking fast and steadily. If they stopped, everything was silent, unbelievably silent; when they walked, they heard the shuffling of their feet, nothing else; for the pall of flakes descended without a sound, such heavy snow one could fairly see it wax deep. The children themselves were so thickly covered they did not stand out against the general whiteness and would not have been able to see each other if they had been more than a few steps apart.

It was a blessing the snow was dry as sand, so it shook off easily and slid from their feet and little mountain shoes and stockings without caking and soaking them.

At last they again came to something with form, immense shapes heaped in gigantic confusion, covered with snow that was sifting everywhere into the crevices; the children, moreover, had almost stumbled on them before they had seen them. They went close to look.

Ice—nothing but ice.

There were great slabs lying, covered with snow, but on the edges glassy green ice showed; there were mounds of what looked like pushed-up foam, the sides dull, but with inward glimmers as if crystals and splinters of precious stones had been jumbled together; there were, besides, great rounded bosses engulfed in snow, slabs and other shapes, slanting or upright—as high as the church steeple or houses in Gschaid. Some were eroded into cavities through which an arm, a head, a body, or a great cartload of hay, could pass. All these irregular shapes had been driven into one another or upright, and stood out in the form of roofs or eaves; and overlying and overlapping them were great white cat's-paws of snow. Even a fearsome black boulder huge as a house lay tilted up under the ice, resting on its point, so that snow could not cling to the sides. And not this stone merely, but others, and yet larger ones, locked in the ice, which one did not notice at first, formed a wall of Cyclopean debris along the ice rim.

"There must have been a great deal of water here, because there is so much ice," said Sanna.

"No, it wasn't made by water," answered her brother, "it's the ice of the mountain, and always here since God made it so."

"Yes, Conrad," said Sanna.

"We are as far as the ice now," said the lad, "we are on the mountain, you know, Sanna, the one that looks so white in the sun from the garden. Now think hard about this. Do you remember when we were sitting in our garden how pleasant it was, how the bees hummed round us, how sweet the lindens smelled, and how the sun was shining so bright on us?"

"Yes, Conrad, I remember."

"We would look at the mountain too. We saw how blue it was, blue as the gentle sky, we saw snow up there even though it was summer in the village and hot, and the wheat was getting ripe."

"Yes, Conrad."

"And down where the snow ends, you see all manner of colors if you look hard—green, blue, and a whitish color—that is the ice that looks so small from down below because you are so far away, and that, as Father said, is going to be there as long as the world lasts. And then I've often noticed that the blue color keeps on below the ice—probably stones, I've thought, or maybe plowed ground and pastures, and then come the pine woods that go down and down, and all kinds of rocks in between, then the green meadows, then the woods with leaves, and then our own meadows and fields in the valley of Gschaid. Now you see, Sanna, we are at the ice, and from here we will go down over the blue color and through the woods where the rocks are, then over the meadows and then through the woods with the leaves, and then we shall be in the valley of Gschaid and then it will be easy to find our village."

"Yes, Conrad," said the little one.

The children went on into the ice wherever they could find a place to step.

As they peered in beneath the projecting slabs, almost as if instinct were impelling them to seek shelter, they walked along in a broad, deeply scored channel that led straight out of the ice, like the bed of a stream, dried up now and covered with new-fallen snow. Where it emerged, it was vaulted over with ice, beautifully arched like a canopy. Following the channel, they went in—deeper and deeper. It was entirely dry, and they had smooth ice to walk on. But the whole cavern was blue, bluer than anything on earth, a blue deeper and finer than heaven itself, blue as azure glass with a faint light inside. There were massive ribs overhead, and more delicate ones, with pendant icicles, and tassels, the way leading farther still—they knew not how far—but they did not go on. It might even have been pleasant in the cave; it was warm, no snow was falling; but it was so fearsome a blue the children were frightened and ran out again. They walked on awhile in the hollowed bed of the stream and then climbed up over the side.

They kept along the edge of the ice as far as they could thread the detritus and creep between the great slabs.

"We have to get up over this and then we can run down, away from the ice," said Conrad.

"Yes," said Sanna, and clung tight to him.

They now struck a downward course through the snow, one that was to lead them into the valley. But they did not get far. Another river of ice, heaved up in a pile like a gigantic barricade, lay across the soft snow and seemed almost to be reaching out arms to the left and the right. Under the blanket of white that hid it there were greenish, bluish, leaden, black, even yellow and reddish glimmers from the sides.

They now had a better perspective since the unprecedented unwearying snow was thinning and flakes were coming down only as on ordinary snowy days. With the fortitude of ignorance they clambered up on the ice to cross the protruding tongue of the glacier and then descend on the farther side. They crept through slits, planted their feet on any snow-capped projection whether rock or ice, helped with their hands, crawled where they could not walk, their light bodies working on up until they had scaled the inside of the barrier and were on top.

They had intended to climb down the other side.

There was no other side.

As far as the eye could reach, there was only ice, pointed masses and irregular clumps thrusting up from the fearsome snow-encrusted ice. Instead of a barricade that could be surmounted, with snow beyond, as they had expected, yet other walls of ice rose from the buttress, cracked and fissured, with innumerable meandering blue veins, and beyond these walls, others like them; and beyond, others, until the falling snow blurred the distance in its veil of gray.

"Sanna, we cannot go over there," said the lad.

"No," said the little one.

"We shall just turn around and get down somewhere else."

"Yes, Conrad."

The children then tried to climb down at the place where they had clambered up, but were not able. There was nothing but ice, as if they had missed the direction from which they had come up. They turned this way and that and could not get away from the ice; it was as if they were clasped in it. They worked down and came to more ice. Finally when the lad went, as he thought, always in the direction from which they had come, they came to other scattered fragments, but larger and more intimidating, the kind usually found along the ice margin, and by crawling and clambering they managed to get out. At the edge of the moraine were gigantic boulders heaped up in a way the two children had never seen in all their lives. Many were shrouded in white; others on the undersides or where they slanted up had a smooth high-polished surface as if they had been shoved forward on it; some were tilted together like houses or the sides of a roof; some lay one upon another like misshapen clods. Not far from the children several were slanted together, and lying on them were great wide slabs like a roof. A little house had thus been formed, open at the front but closed at both sides and the back. It was dry inside since the snow had been falling straight down and not a flake had drifted in.

The children were thankful not to be in the midst of ice any longer, but to be standing on solid ground again.

By this time it had grown very dark.

"Sanna," said the lad, "we cannot go down any farther, because it's night, and we might fall, or even stumble into a crevasse. Let's go in under the stones where it's so dry and warm, and wait there. The sun will come up again and then we'll run down the mountain. Don't cry, please don't cry, you can have all the things to eat that Grandmother gave us to bring along."

She did not cry. But when they had both gone in under the projecting stone roof, where there was even room to sit, stand, or walk about, she sat down close to him and was still as a mouse.

"Mother is not going to be displeased with us," said Conrad. "We shall tell her all about the heavy snow that has kept us and she won't say anything; neither will Father. If we are cold, remember, slap your body with your hands the way the foresters do, and then you'll feel warmer."

"Yes, Conrad," said the little thing.

Sanna was not disheartened at not being able to go down the mountain and run home, as he might have expected, for the severe strain—the children had not realized how heavy it was—made it seem good to sit down, inexpressibly good, and they gladly gave in to their weariness.

But now hunger too made itself felt. At almost the same instant they took out their pieces of bread and ate them. They ate the other things too, bits of cake, almonds and nuts, and little things their grandmother had slipped into their pockets.

"Now, Sanna, we must get the snow off us," said the lad, "so we'll not be wet."

"Yes, Conrad," answered Sanna.

They went out in front of their little house, and Conrad first got the snow off his sister. He shook her things by the corners, removed his hat that he had put on her and emptied it of snow, and brushed off with his kerchief the snow that was left. Then he got off, as best he could, the snow collected on himself.

It had stopped snowing altogether by this time.

The children felt not a flake.

They went back into the stone house and sat down. Getting up had shown them how tired they really were, and they readily sat down again. Conrad took off his calfskin bag. He got out the cloth that had been wrapped by his grandmother around the cardboard box and paper-covered packages, and laid it about his shoulders for warmth. He also took the two rolls from the bag and gave them to Sanna. The child ate eagerly—one and then part of the second. But the rest she gave back to Conrad when she saw that he was not eating. He took it and ate it.

Then both sat and gazed straight ahead.

As far as they could see in the dusk, glimmering snow lay upon everything, separate tiny facets scintillating curiously here and there as if, after absorbing the light all day, they were now reflecting it again.

Darkness fell with the suddenness usual in high altitudes. Soon it was dark all around; only the snow continued to shine with its pallid glimmer. Not only had it stopped snowing, but the obscuring mist had begun to lift and was parting here and there, for the children caught the twinkle of a little star. Since the snow shed an actual radiance, as it were, and a veil no longer hung from the clouds, they could see from their refuge the mounds of snow sharply set off against the somber sky. They rested huddling close against each other, and even forgot to be afraid of the dark. Soon the stars came out in greater numbers, one here, one there, until it seemed not a cloud was left in the sky.

At this hour, in all the valleys, children were receiving gifts from the Christ-child; only these two sat alone by the glacier; and the finest gifts they might have received were lying in little sealed packages in the calfskin bag at the back of their shelter.

The cloudbanks had dropped behind the mountains on every side, and bending low about the children, the arch of heaven was an even blue, so dark it was almost black, spangled with stars blazing in countless array, and through their midst a broad luminous band was woven, pale as milk, which the children had indeed seen from the valley, but never before so distinctly. The night was progressing. The children did not know that the stars move westward and on; otherwise it might have been possible for them to tell the hour of night, as new stars appeared and others vanished; they supposed them, however, to be the same ones. The ground all about lay bright in the starlight, but they saw no valley, nothing familiar; nothing was to be seen anywhere but whiteness—all was pure white. Only a somber horn, a somber head, a somber arm, was discernible, looming up at this point or that from the shimmering waste. The moon was nowhere to be seen; perhaps it had gone down early with the sun or not risen at all.

After a great while Conrad said: "Sanna, you mustn't go to sleep; you know what Father said: 'If you fall asleep in the mountains you're sure to freeze,' the way the old ash-woodman went to sleep and was dead on a stone four long months and not a soul knew where he was."

"No, I'll not go to sleep," the little thing answered wearily.

Conrad had shaken her by the hem of her frock to rouse her and make her listen.

Then silence again.

Presently the lad was conscious of a gentle pressure on his arm, which grew heavier and heavier. Sanna had dropped off and settled down on him.

"Sanna, don't go to sleep, please don't," he said.

"No," she murmured drowsily, "I'm not asleep."

He moved a little way from her to rouse her, but she just dropped over and would have gone on sleeping on the ground. He grasped her shoulder and shook her. Although his motions were somewhat brisker, he found he was cold and that his arm was numb. He was alarmed and jumped up. He clutched his sister, shook her harder, and said: "Sanna, let's stand up awhile, so we'll feel better."

"I'm not cold, Conrad," she answered.

"Yes you are, Sanna; get up," he exclaimed.

"This fur jacket is nice and warm," she said.

"I'll help you up," he said.

"No," she said, and was silent again.

Then suddenly it came back to him. Grandmother had said: "Just a tiny sip warms the stomach, so that even on the coldest winter day you can't feel the cold."

He picked up the calfskin bag, opened it, and groped about till he had found the little flask in which his grandmother was sending his mother the black coffee extract, took the wrappings off, and with considerable effort pulled out the cork. Then he leaned down over Sanna and said: "Here is the coffee Grandmother is sending Mother; taste just a little, it will make you warm. Mother would give it to us if only she knew what we need it for."

The child—who only wanted to rest—said: "I am not cold."

"Just a little, then you may go to sleep."

This prospect tempted Sanna; she so nerved herself for the effort that she almost choked on the liquid. After her, Conrad too drank a little. The double-distilled strength of the decoction had an immediate effect, all the more powerful because the children had not tasted coffee before. Instead of going to sleep, Sanna became more animated, and herself admitted that she was cold, but said she felt quite warm inside now, and that her hands and feet were getting warm too. The children even chatted awhile.

As soon as the effect began to wear off, they took more and more of the extract in spite of the bitter taste, and their young nerves, unaccustomed to the stimulant, were strung to a pitch of excitement sufficient to overcome the dangerous drowsiness.

It was midnight by this time. Young as they were, they had always fallen asleep each Christmas Eve when it grew late, and had never heard the peal of the bells or the organ at midnight Mass though they lived close by the church. At this very moment all the bells were ringing, the bells in Millsdorf, the bells in Gschaid, and on the farther side of the mountain there was still another little church whose three clear-chiming bells were ringing out. In remote places beyond the valley there were innumerable churches with bells all ringing at this very hour; from village to village the waves of sound were floating, and in one village you could at times hear through the leafless branches the chiming of the bells in another. Away up by the ice, however, not a sound reached the children; nothing, for here nothing was being heralded. Along the winding paths of the mountain slopes lantern lights were moving, and on many a farmstead the bell was rousing the farm-hands—unseen here, and unheard. Only the twinkling stars shone down—steadily down.

Even though Conrad kept before his mind's eye the fate of the frozen woodman—even though the children had drunk all the black coffee in the little vial to keep their blood stirring—the reaction of fatigue would have been too much for them and they would never have been able to fight off sleep, whose seductiveness invariably gets the better of reason, had not Nature in all her grandeur befriended them and aroused in them a power strong enough to withstand it.

In the vast stillness that prevailed, a stillness in which not a snow-crystal seemed to stir, three times they heard the roar of the ice. What appears the most inert and is yet the most active and living of things, the glacier, had made the sounds. Three times they heard behind them the thundering as awesome as if the earth had broken asunder, a boom that reverberated through the ice in all directions and, as it seemed, through every smallest vein of it. The children sat, open-eyed, gazing up at the stars. Something now began to happen as they watched. While they sat thus, a faint light bloomed amid the stars, describing upon the heavens a delicate arc. The faint green luminescence traveled slowly downward. But the arc grew brighter and brighter until the stars paled away, while a shudder of light, invading other parts of the firmament—taking on an emerald tinge—vibrated and flooded the stellar spaces. Then from the highest point of the arc sheaves radiated like points of a crown, all aglow. Adjacent horizons caught the brightening flush; it flickered and spread in faint quivers through the vastness round about. Whether or not the electricity in the atmosphere had become so charged by the tremendous snowfall that it flashed forth in these silent magnificent shafts of light, or whether unfathomable Nature was to be explained in some other way, after a while the brightness paled, grew fainter and fainter, the sheaves dying down first, until imperceptible finally, and again there was nothing to be seen in the sky but thousands and thousands of familiar stars.

The children said not a word, the one to the other. They remained, on and on, never stirring from where they sat, gazing intently at the sky.

Nothing particular happened after that. The stars sparkled and fluctuated, crossed now and again by a shooting star.

At last, after the stars had been shining a great while and not even a glint of the moon had appeared, everything changed. The sky grew paler, then slowly but unmistakably it began to color, the fainter stars waned, and there were fewer of the bright ones. Finally the most brilliant had set, and the snow toward the heights could be seen more distinctly. The one horizon took on a yellow tinge, and along its edge a ribbon of cloud kindled to a glowing thread. Everything grew clear, and the distant snow-mounds stood out sharp in the frosty air.

"Sanna, it's almost day," said the lad.

"Yes, Conrad," answered the little one.

"When it's just a bit brighter, we shall leave the cave and run down off the mountain."

It grew brighter and there was not a star to be seen in the sky, and every object stood out clear in the dawn.

"Well, let's be going," said the lad.

"Yes, let's go," answered Sanna.

They stood up and tried their legs, which only now felt very tired. Although they had not been asleep all night long, they felt refreshed by the morning. The lad slung the calfskin pouch over his shoulder and drew Sanna's little fur jacket closer about her. Then he led her out of their stony retreat.

Since they thought they would only have to run down off the mountain, they gave no thought to food and did not explore the pouch for bits of bread or anything else that might be left.

The sky being clear, Conrad thought he would look down into the valley, recognize Gschaid, and climb down to it. But he saw no valley. They did not seem to be standing on a mountain from which one looks down, but rather on strange foreign ground full of unfamiliar sights. Today they saw towering up out of the snow great fearsome rocks in the distance, where they had not seen them the day before; they saw the glacier, snowy hills and slopes standing out boldly, and beyond them sky or the blue peak of some distant mountain above the snow-line. At this moment the sun came up.

A gigantic blood-red disk climbed the heavens above the skyline, and at the same instant the snow all around flushed as though bestrewn with thousands of roses. Summits and horns cast long, faint greenish shadows across the snowfields.

"Sanna, let's keep on till we get to the side of the mountain and can look down," said the lad.

They now started off through the snow. During the clear night it had become even drier and was easier to walk on. They plowed along briskly, their limbs becoming supple and strong as they went. But they came to no mountainside, and could not look down. Snowfield followed snowfield, and always, on the horizon of each, the sky.

Nevertheless they went on.

Then they found themselves on ice again. They did not know how the ice could have got there, but they felt the hard glaze underfoot, and though there was no such intimidating wreckage of mighty fragments as on the edge of the moraine where they had spent the night, yet they saw they were treading on solid ice.

Still they kept on, in the same direction.

Now they surmounted monstrous debris; now found themselves again on the icefield. Today, in the bright sun, they were able for the first time to see what it was like. In size it was stupendous, and beyond towered yet more somber rocks; wave after wave heaved up, as it were, and the snow-covered ice, compressed and buckling, seemed to be pushing down upon the children and threatening to flow over their very bodies. In the whiteness they saw countless meandering bluish lines. Between where ice-blocks stood up as if hurled together, there were straight lines like paths, but they were white, with solid ice beneath, where the ice-blocks had not been forced up by intense pressure. The children kept on these paths, since they wished to cross at least part of the glacier so as to reach the side of the mountain and be able to look down at last. They spoke not a word. The little one followed her brother. But again today there was ice, nothing but ice. Where they had meant to cross, it stretched on endlessly, farther and farther. Then they gave up and turned back. Where they could not set foot they crept forward on hands and knees along snowbanks that fell in before their very eyes and showed the dark blue of a crevasse—where just before all had been white; but paying no heed they struggled on till they had again come out of the ice.

"Sanna," said the lad, "we're not going out there on the ice again, because we get nowhere on it. And since we can't see down into our valley anyhow, let's go down the mountain in a straight line. We are bound to come into some valley, and shall tell the people we are from Gschaid. They will send a guide with us to show us our way home."

"Yes, Conrad," said the little one.

They started down through the snow in the direction that seemed most promising. The young lad took his sister by the hand. When they had worked down for a time, however, the slopes changed level and began to rise. They therefore altered their course and crept along a sort of gully. But it only led them to the ice again. So they clambered up the side of the gully to find a descent in some other direction. This brought them to a level stretch that by and by, however, became so steep again they could hardly find a foothold and were afraid of sliding down. After climbing through snow a great while and walking along an even ridge, it was again as before: either the slope was so steep they would have lost their footing, or it went on up so far they feared it would bring them to the mountaintop.

They now hoped to find the path by which they had first come up and make their way back to the red memorial post. Since it was not snowing and the sky was so bright, Conrad thought, they would easily recognize the place where the post ought to be, and then be able to find the way down to Gschaid.

He explained the plan to his sister and she followed him.

But the way to the col was not to be found either.

Shone the sun ever so bright, towered the heights ever so fair above the snowfields, there was no telling the place by which they had made their way up on the previous day. Then all had been so veiled by the terrifying snowfall they had scarcely been able to see a step ahead and everything was an intermingling of white and gray. Only the rocks beside and between which they passed had been visible. Today, too, they had seen many rocks, but all of them had looked just like the others. Today they left fresh footprints in the snow, but yesterday's had been all covered by the snow as it fell; they could not just by the look of things tell which way led to the col, for all places looked alike. Snow, nothing but snow. But still hoping, they pressed on. They avoided precipitous descents and did not climb any more steep gradients.

Today too they often stood and listened. But now, as yesterday, they could hear nothing, not the faintest sound. Again, nothing to be seen but snow—the white white snow, with somber horns and blackened ribs standing out in bold relief.

At length the lad thought he saw a fire. It seemed to him at last that on a far distant precipitous snowfield a flame was leaping up. It disappeared, went up, and died down. Now they saw it, now lost it. They stood and watched fixedly in that direction. The flame kept on leaping and seemed to be coming closer, for they saw it grow larger and saw its flaming more distinctly. It did not disappear so often now or for so long a time. After a while they heard faintly, very faintly, across the still, blue distance, something like the long-sustained note of an alpenhorn. Instinctively both shouted with all their might. After a while they heard the sound again and shouted again, staying where they were. The flame too was coming nearer. They caught the sound a third time, and this time more clearly. They answered again, with a loud shout. After considerable time they recognized the flame. It was not a flame. It was a red flag being waved. Meanwhile the horn sounded nearer, and again they answered.

"Sanna," exclaimed the lad, "people from Gschaid are coming. I know the flag. It is the red flag the foreign gentleman who climbed Gars with the young ash-woodman planted on top as a signal so the Reverend Father might see it with his spyglass and know they had reached the summit—the flag the foreign gentleman gave the Reverend Father afterward as a present. You were still very little then."

"Yes, Conrad."

After a while they saw people, too, around the flag, little black dots that seemed to be moving about. The call of the horn was repeated from time to time, steadily nearer. Each time the children would answer. Finally they saw several men coasting down the snowy slope on their alpenstocks, the flag in their midst. As they came nearer, the children recognized them. It was herdman Philip with his horn, his two sons, the young ash-woodman, and several men from Gschaid.

"Praised be God!" cried Philip, "there you are. We are scattered all over the mountain. Someone run down to the upland meadow and ring the bell so they will know we have found them; and someone get out on top of Crab Rock and set the flag up so they can see it from the valley and fire the mortars, to let the people searching Millsdorf forest know; and have them build smudge-fires that will smoke away up high to direct everyone on the mountain to the Sider Alp. What a Christmas!"

"I'll run down to the meadow," said one.

"I'll go up on Crab Rock with the flag," said another.

"And we shall bring the children down to the Sider Alp as best we may, pray God," said Philip.

One of his sons struck off downhill and the other set out through the snow with the flag.

The young ash-woodman took Sanna by the hand, and herdsman Philip, the lad; the others helping as best they could. Thus they started on their way. It had many a turning, now in this direction, now that. Now up, now down. Always through snow, always through snow they went, the look of the mountainside never changing. For the steepest inclines they fastened spikes to their shoes and carried the children. At last, after a great while, the tones of a little bell traveled up to them faint and clear—the first message to reach them from below. They had by this time, in fact, come down a long way, for as they looked, a snow-capped peak soared above them, lofty and blue. The little bell they had heard was the one being rung on the upland meadow, which had been agreed upon as meeting-place. When they had come farther down, they also heard, faintly through the still air, the booming of the mortars fired after the flag was hoisted, and later they saw columns of smoke rising tall and thin.

After a time, descending a gentle slope they caught sight of the alpine hut. They walked toward it. Inside, a fire was burning. The children's mother was there, and when she saw the children coming with the young ash-woodman, with a heart-rending cry she sank, faint, on the snow. Then she rushed to them, devoured them with her eyes, wanted to give them something to eat, wanted to make them warm, wanted them to lie down and rest on the hay, but soon satisfied herself that happiness had given them more strength than she had supposed. They needed only the warm food awaiting them, and rest, which also was afforded.

Presently they ran out with the others to see who was coming as a second group neared the hut, down through the snow, while the little bell kept on ringing. It was the shoemaker, the former mountaineer with his alpenstock and spiked shoes, accompanied by friends and fellow craftsmen.

"Sebastian, they are here," cried his wife.

Speechless and trembling, he ran toward them. His lips moved as if to say something, but no words came; he pressed the children to his heart, holding them close and long. Then he turned to his wife and locked her in his arms, crying: "Sanna, Sanna."

After a time he picked up his hat, fallen unnoticed on the snow, went over to the group of men intending to speak to them, but could only say: "Neighbors, friends, I thank you."

After waiting for a while until the children were somewhat recovered from their excitement, he said: "If we are all back now, let us start—and God be with us."

"Not quite all, I believe," said herdman Philip, "but those who are missing can tell by the smoke that we've found the children, and will go home when they do not find anyone in the hut."

Then everyone prepared to start.

The alpine hut was not far from Gschaid, and in summer one could see it plainly from the village, with its little bell-tower on the green of the upland pasture; but just below was a precipitous drop of many fathoms; it could be descended in summer, but only with spiked shoes, and in winter not at all. One had to take a roundabout way to the col and thence down to Gschaid from the memorial post. By that way, one crossed the meadow which is still nearer Gschaid and could, from there, almost imagine one saw the windows of the village.

Because of the commotion in Gschaid that morning, the priest had postponed High Mass, supposing the children would soon be found. But still no word came, so the rites must be observed, and when those crossing the Sider meadow heard the little bell that signified the Elevation of the Host, all sank on their knees in the snow and prayed. Then, when the sound of the bell died away, they rose and went on.

The shoemaker carried little Sanna most of the way, she telling him everything.

When they had almost reached the col-forest they came upon footprints, and the shoemaker said: "No work of mine ever made those marks."

It was soon explained. Attracted, no doubt, by the echoing of the many voices, another searching party was coming to join the one descending. It was headed by the dyer, chalk-white with fear, who had come down the mountain with his workmen, apprentices, and others from Millsdorf.

"They've been over the glacier and the crevasses without knowing it," the shoemaker called out to his father-in-law.

"Well, here they are—here they are—thank God," answered the dyer. "I knew they must be up there when your messenger came in the night, and we set out with lanterns and searched the whole woodland without finding anything; then as the gray of dawn broke, I noticed on the way from the memorial post, on the left up toward snow-mountain, just where you leave the post, fir-tips snapped off here and there—you know how children like to pull at things as they go along. Then I knew they would never be able to get back, for they would follow the trench and have the rocks on each side and get up on the ridge that has the sheer drop, and wouldn't be able to get down—would just have to go on up. When I saw that, I sent word at once to Gschaid. But when woodcutter Michael, who went for me, came back and rejoined us up near the ice, he told us you had found them, so we came down again."

"Yes," said Michael, "I knew it because from Gschaid they'd seen the red flag on Crab Rock, which was the signal. And I knew they would all come down this way since you can't come down the bluff."

"Upon your knees, thank God upon your knees, son-in-law," continued the dyer, "that there was no wind. Another hundred years and there may never be another tremendous snowfall like that, coming down straight as wet warp on a pole. If there had been wind, the children would have been lost."

"Ah, thanks be to God, thanks be to God," replied the shoemaker.

The dyer, who had never been in Gschaid since the marriage of his daughter, decided to accompany them all to the village.

When they drew near the red post where the timber-road began, a sleigh that the shoemaker had ordered on the chance of finding the children was waiting. Mother and children were helped in, well covered with rugs and furs already in the sleigh, and sent ahead to Gschaid.

The others followed, and reached the village by afternoon. Those still on the mountain, who had only learned by the smoke that they might turn back, arrived one by one. The last to appear, and not until evening, was herdman Philipp's son who had gone up Crab Rock with the red flag and planted it there.

Grandmother from Millsdorf had driven over and was waiting in Gschaid. "Never, never so long as they live," she declared, "shall they be allowed to cross the col in winter."

The children themselves were bewildered by all the commotion. They had been given something to eat and put to bed. Late in the evening, when they had somewhat recovered, and while neighbors and friends were congregated in the larger room talking about the events of the day, and in the little room adjoining Sanna's mother was sitting by the bed caressing her, the child said: "Mother, last night when we were up there on the mountain, I saw the Holy Christ-child."

"Oh, my brave long-suffering, my precious, my beloved child," answered her mother, "He has also sent you some presents and you are to have them now."

The cardboard boxes had been unpacked and the candles lit, the door into the big room was opened, and from their beds the children saw the belated, welcoming, brightly shining Christmas tree. Despite their fatigue they wanted to put on some clothes so that they could go into the other room; and there they received their presents, admired them, and then fell asleep over them.

Gschaid Inn that evening was livelier than usual. All who had not been in church were there; the others also. Each related what he had seen and heard, what he had done, what advised, what he had experienced, and all the risks he had run. And especially was it emphasized how everything could have been done differently and better.

A Christmas epoch-making in the history of Gschaid, the subject of conversation for a long time, it will be talked of for years to come, especially on clear days when the mountain is unusually distinct or when someone is describing its characteristics to strangers.

Only from that day on were the children really felt to belong to the village, and not to be outsiders. Thenceforth they were regarded as natives whom the people had brought back to themselves from the mountain.

Their mother Sanna was now a native of Gschaid too.

The children, however, can never forget the mountain, and earnestly fix their gaze upon it when in the garden, when as in times past the sun is out bright and warm, the linden diffuses its fragrance, the bees are humming, and the mountain looks down upon them as serene and blue as the sky above.

Translated by Elizabeth Mayer and Marianne Moore

THE BACHELOR'S DEATH

by Arthur Schnitzler

The knock at the door was very soft, but the doctor awoke instantly, switched on the light, and got out of bed. He glanced at his wife, who went on sleeping peacefully; then, slipping into his dressing-gown, he went out to the vestibule. He did not immediately recognize the old woman who stood there, a gray shawl around her head.

"Our gentleman's been taken very sick all of a sudden," she said. "Could you please come right away, doctor?"

Then the doctor recognized the voice. The woman was the housekeeper of his friend the bachelor. The doctor's first thought was: "My friend is fifty-five and his heart has been acting up these past two years—it may well be something serious." "I'll come at once," he said. "Would you mind waiting?"

"I beg your pardon, doctor, but I must drive over to fetch two other gentlemen right away." She mentioned the names of the businessman and the writer.

"Why do you have to go to *them*?"

"The master wants to see them once more."

"See them once more?"

"Yes, sir."

The Anatol *playlets, or* Light o' Love, *for which Arthur Schnitzler is best known in the English-speaking countries, do not do justice to the scope of his accomplishments. He was a wise critic of human nature, as well as of the Vienna society he was born into, in 1862, the son of a famous physician. After practicing as a doctor himself for some years, he devoted himself exclusively to writing. He was immensely successful as a dramatist* (The Lonely Way, Der junge Medardus, The Vast Domain, Professor Bernhardi)*. As a fiction writer, he was one of the few first-rate authors in the German language to master the genre of the short story. He died in 1931 in Vienna, where he had lived throughout his life.*

"He is sending for his friends," the doctor thought; "he must feel that death is very close." Aloud, he asked: "Is there some-one with your master?"

"Of course, doctor," the old woman answered. "Johann won't stir from his side." And she left.

The doctor went back to his bedroom. While he dressed as quickly and quietly as possible, an acrid feeling rose within him. It was caused less by sorrow that soon he might be losing a good old friend than by the painful sense that they were all coming close to it, all of them who had been young only a few years ago.

In an open carriage the doctor rode through the warm, pregnant spring night to the near-by suburb where the bachelor lived. He looked up at the bedroom window, which was wide open. From it a soft, dim light shimmered out into the night.

The doctor ascended the stairs. The servant opened the door, greeted him gravely, and sorrowfully let his left hand drop.

"What's that?" the doctor asked, his breath catching. "Have I come too late?"

"Yes, doctor," the servant replied. "The master died a quarter of an hour ago."

The doctor took a deep breath and entered the room. His dead friend lay on the bed, half-parted lips thin and bluish, arms outstretched on the white blanket. His sparse beard was disheveled; a few strands of gray hair had fallen over his pale, damp forehead. From the silken shade of the electric lamp on the night chest a russet shadow spread over the pillows. The doctor studied the dead man. "When was he at our house last?" he pondered. "I recall it was snowing that evening. So it must have been last winter. We've really seen little of each other lately."

From outside came the sound of horses' hoofs pawing the ground. The doctor turned away from the corpse and looked through the window at the slender branches stirring somewhat in the night air. The servant entered, and the doctor asked how it had all come about.

How well the doctor knew the story the servant told! It was the familiar pattern of sudden nausea, hard breathing, jumping out of bed, pacing the room, rushing to the desk and staggering back to bed, thirst and moans, a last starting up and sinking back upon the pillows. The doctor nodded as he listened, and his right hand touched the dead man's brow.

A carriage drove up. The doctor went to the window. He saw the businessman get out and cast a questioning look up at him. Involuntarily, the doctor dropped his hand as the servant had done before. The businessman threw back his head as though unwilling to believe it. The doctor shrugged, stepped away from the window, feeling suddenly exhausted, and sat down on a chair at the foot of the dead man's bed.

The businessman entered, wearing an unbuttoned tan overcoat. He laid his hat down on the small table near the door and shook hands with the doctor. "This is terrible," he said. "How did it happen?" And he stared apprehensively at the dead body.

The doctor told him what he knew, and added: "Even had I come in time, I would not have been able to help."

"Just think," the businessman said, "it's only a week since I last spoke to him at the theater. I wanted to dine with him afterward, but he had another of his mysterious engagements."

"Was he still having those?" the doctor asked with a wan smile.

Another carriage stopped. The businessman went to the window. When he saw the writer get out, he drew back; he did not want to be the one to impart the sad news, even by a look.

The doctor had taken a cigarette from his cigarette-case and was toying with it with an air of embarrassment. "It's an old habit from my hospital days," he remarked apologetically. "At night when I left a sickroom, the first thing I always did as soon as I got outside was to light a cigarette, no matter whether I had given only an injection of morphine or certified a death."

"You know how long it is since I've seen a dead man?" the businessman said. "Fourteen years—since my father lay on the bier."

"And—your wife?"

"I guess I saw my wife during the last few minutes, but not —afterward."

The writer came in. He shook hands with the others, his eyes glancing uneasily at the bed. Then he determinedly stepped closer and studied the corpse, gravely, but with a faint, contemptuous twitching of the lips. "So it's he," the writer thought. For he had often played with the question of which among his closer acquaintances would be the first to take the last road of all.

The housekeeper entered. Tears in her eyes, she fell to her knees by the bed, sobbed, and clasped her hands. The writer gently laid his hand in a consoling gesture upon her shoulder.

The businessman and the doctor stood at the window, the nocturnal spring air brushing their foreheads.

"It's really strange," the businessman said, "that he sent for all of us. Did he want to see us all assembled around his deathbed? Did he have something important to say to us?"

"As far as I am concerned," the doctor said with a tight laugh, "there isn't anything strange about it, since I am a doctor. And you probably gave him business advice now and then. Perhaps he had in mind some testamentary matters that he wanted to confide to you personally."

"That may be," the businessman said.

The housekeeper had left again; the friends could hear her in the anteroom, talking with the servant. The writer was still standing by the bed, holding a mysterious dialogue with the dead man.

"*He* saw a good deal more of him recently than either of us," the businessman said softly to the doctor. "Perhaps he can tell us why we were called." The writer continued to stand motionless, probing with his eyes the dead man's closed eyes. His hands, still holding his gray fedora, were crossed behind his back. The other two men grew impatient. The businessman went up closer to the writer and cleared his throat.

"Three days ago," the writer said, "I went for a two-hour walk with him, out among the vineyards. Would you like to know what he talked about? He spoke of his plans for a trip to Sweden this summer, of the new portfolio of Rembrandt prints that Watson's have brought out in London, and about Santos-Dumont. He gave me lengthy mechanical and mathematical explanations of the new dirigible balloon—to tell the truth, I couldn't get all of it through my head. One thing is sure: he was not thinking of death. But I suppose it may well be that at a certain age one again stops thinking about death."

The doctor had gone into the adjoining room. Here, he felt, he could venture to have his cigarette. Suddenly he noticed white ashes in the bronze tray on the desk, and that sight had a peculiar, weird effect upon him. "Why am I staying here?" he thought as he sat down in the armchair that stood before the desk. "I should really feel free to be the first to leave, since I was obviously called in only as a doctor. There was not much left of our friendship. At my age it's probably no longer possible for people of my sort to be a real friend of anyone who has no occupation—who never really had one, for that matter. What might he have done if he had not been wealthy? Probably he would have gone in for writing—he was very clever." And the doctor recalled a good many pointedly malicious remarks the bachelor had made, especially in regard to the works of their friend the writer.

The writer and the businessman came in. The writer, closing the door behind him, put on an offended expression when he saw the doctor sitting at the orphaned desk with a cigarette in his hand—though it was still unlighted.

"Have you any idea?" the businessman asked.

"About what?" the writer asked absently.

"What might have prompted him to send for us—us in particular."

The writer saw no point in looking for any special reason. "Our friend felt the approach of death," he said, "and though he lived in relative solitude—at least lately—at such a moment people whose basic bent is sociable probably feel the need to see around them those who were close to them."

"But he did have a sweetheart, you know," the businessman remarked.

"Sweetheart!" the writer said, raising his eyebrows scornfully.

The doctor now noticed that the middle drawer of the desk was half open. "I wonder whether his will is in here," he said.

"What concern is that of ours?" the businessman commented. "At least at this moment. Besides, there is a married sister of his living in London."

The servant entered. Would they mind advising him about the funeral arrangements, the announcement, and so on, he asked. As far as he knew, his master's last will and testament was in the care of his lawyer, but he doubted that the will contained any instructions on these matters.

The writer thought the air in the room was stale and sultry.

He drew the heavy red curtains aside from one window and opened both casements. The spring night flowed in, a broad, dark-blue band. The doctor asked the servant whether he perhaps knew the dead man's reason for sending for them—for now that he came to think of it, he had not been called to this house in his professional capacity for many years.

The servant welcomed the question as though he had expected it. He took an oversized wallet from his coat pocket, extracted a sheet of paper from it, and informed them that as far back as seven years ago his master had written down the names of the friends he wished to have assembled at his deathbed. For that reason, the servant said, even if his master had no longer been conscious, he would have taken it upon himself to send for the gentlemen.

The doctor took the sheet of paper from the servant's hand and saw that the list contained five names. In addition to those of the three who were here now, there was the name of another mutual friend who had died two years before, and a name none of them knew. The servant explained that this person had been a manufacturer whose home the bachelor had often visited nine or ten years ago. But the man's address was now lost.

The three looked at one another, bewildered and intrigued. "What can it mean?" the businessman asked. "Did he intend to make a speech in his last hour?"

"Perhaps his own funeral sermon," the writer added.

The doctor had been gazing at the open desk drawer. Suddenly he realized that three words, in large block letters, were staring him in the face: "To my friends."

"Oh," he exclaimed, picking up the envelope on which the words were printed. He held it up, showing it to the others. "This is for us," he said, turning to the servant and indicating by a nod that his presence was not necessary. The servant left.

"For us?" the writer exclaimed, wide-eyed.

"There can be no doubt that we have the right to open this," the doctor remarked.

"We're obligated to," said the businessman, buttoning his coat.

The doctor picked up a paperknife and opened the envelope. He took a letter from it, laid it down, and adjusted his glasses. The writer made use of the pause to take possession of the sheet of paper and unfold it. "Since it's for us all," he remarked lightly, and leaned forward on the desk so that the light of the chandelier fell directly upon the letter. The businessman posted himself at his side. The doctor remained in his seat. "Why not read it aloud?" the businessman said. The writer began reading:

"To my friends." He paused, smiling. "Yes, gentlemen, the words are repeated here." And then, with remarkable nonchalance he read on: "About a quarter of an hour ago I breathed my last. You are gathered at my deathbed and preparing to read this letter together—that is, I may add, if it is still extant at the hour of my death. For it may be that a better impulse will come over me."

"What's that?" the doctor asked.

"Better impulse will come over me," the writer repeated, and continued: "and that I will decide to destroy this letter, since it will not do me the slightest good and is likely to cause you all at least some unpleasant hours, or perhaps will actually poison the life of one or the other of you."

"Poison the life?" the doctor repeated inquiringly, wiping his glasses.

"Faster," the businessman said in a husky voice.

The writer read on: "And I ask myself what strange whim has made me go to my desk today and write down words whose effect I shall, after all, never be able to read in your faces. And even if I were able to, the satisfaction would be too small to justify this magnificent act of spite which I am now committing with the greatest pleasure."

"Ho!" the doctor exclaimed, and did not recognize his own voice.

The writer threw him a hasty look of anger and read on, faster and more tonelessly than before: "Yes, it is a whim, nothing more, for at bottom I have nothing against any of you. In fact, I like all of you, in my own fashion, as you like me in your fashion. I have considerable respect for you, and though I may often have made fun of you, I have never despised you. Not even—in fact, least of all—in those hours which will instantly arouse painful and vivid images in all your minds. What, then, is the source of this whim? Has it perhaps sprung from a profound and basically decent urge not to leave the world with too many lies on my conscience? So I might think if I had ever felt, even for a single moment, the slightest touch of what people call regret."

"For heaven's sake, read the end," the doctor commanded in his new voice.

The businessman rudely snatched the letter from the writer, who could feel a kind of paralysis creeping into his fingers, ran his eyes rapidly down the page to the bottom, and read the words: "It was fate, my friends, and I cannot alter it. I have gone to bed with all your wives. All of them." The businessman stopped abruptly and leafed back through the letter.

"What is it?" the doctor asked.

"The letter was written nine years ago," the businessman said.

"Go on," the writer said.

The businessman read: "The relationships, of course, varied greatly. With one of them I lived in what almost amounted to a marriage, for many months. With another it was pretty much what is generally termed a mad adventure. With the third it went so far that we were prepared to make a suicide pact. The fourth I threw down a flight of stairs because she was unfaithful to me with someone else. And one was my mistress only for a single time. Are you each breathing a sigh of relief, my dear fellows? Do not do so. For that was perhaps the most wonderful hour of my—and her—life. There you have it, my friends. I have no more to say to you. Now I shall fold this letter, lay it in my desk, and here it may wait until in some other mood I destroy it, or until it is given to you when I lie upon my deathbed. Farewell."

The doctor took the letter from the businessman's hand and read it carefully from beginning to end. Then he looked up at the businessman, who was standing with folded arms, surveying him with a, perhaps, patronizing air. "Even though your wife did die last year," the doctor said quietly, "it still remains true."

The writer was pacing back and forth in the room, tossing his head every so often as if he were suffering a fit. Suddenly he snarled between his teeth: "Dirty dog!" and looked up as if watching the words dissolving in the air. He tried to recall the image of the young wife whom he had once held in his arms.

The images of other women came to mind, some frequently remembered, some he thought he had forgotten; but he was unable to summon up the one he wanted. For his wife's body was withered and without any attraction for him now, and it had been a long while since she had stopped being his love-partner. But she had become something more and finer to him: a friend, a companion, full of pride in his successes, of sympathy for his disappointments, of knowledge of the depths of his being. It seemed to him not impossible that the old bachelor in his malice and secret envy had been trying to take away from him his dearest comrade. For at bottom what did all those other things mean? He thought of certain adventures, recent and of the distant past—for he had led the variegated life of an artist—and of how his wife had smiled or wept these incidents away. What was left of all that today? It was as faded as the distant hour when his wife had thrown herself into the arms of an insignificant person, without premeditation, unthinkingly perhaps—as faded, extinguished, almost, as the memory of that same hour in the lifeless head lying in the next room on a pillow rumpled by the last agonies. For all he knew, what the bachelor had written in this letter might even be a lie. The final revenge of a miserable mediocrity, who knew his destiny was eternal oblivion, and who wanted somehow to get back at a chosen spirit over whose works death had no power. There was much to be said for this view. But even if the letter told the truth, it remained an act of petty vengeance, and one that had misfired.

The doctor stared at the sheet of paper and thought of his aging, gentle, kind wife, who lay sleeping at home. He thought of his three children—the oldest, who was serving his twelve months in the army this year; their grown daughter, who was engaged to a lawyer; and the youngest girl, who was so graceful and charming that at a recent ball a famous artist had asked whether he might paint her. The doctor thought of his pleasant home—and all the emotions pulsing at him from the dead man's letter seemed to him not so much untrue as mysteriously and in fact sublimely unimportant. He scarcely felt that he had learned anything new at the moment. A strange period of his life came to his mind. It must have been fourteen or fifteen years ago, when he had run into certain troubles in his medical career; irritated at first and finally so outraged that he could no longer think straight, he had contemplated leaving the city, his wife, and his family. At that time he had begun leading a life of reckless dissipation in which a queer hysterical female had played a part—a woman who later committed suicide over another lover. He could no longer recall just how it was that his life had gradually returned to its former groove. But during that nasty period which had passed as it had come, like a disease—that must have been the time his wife had betrayed him. Of course, that was undoubtedly when it had happened—and he realized quite clearly that in his heart he had always known. Had she not at one time been on the point of confessing the affair to him? Had she not hinted at it? Thirteen or fourteen years ago? What was the occasion? . . . In the summertime, wasn't it—on a vacation trip—late one evening on the terrace of a hotel? . . . Vainly he tried to remember the forgotten phrases.

The businessman stood at the window and gazed out into the mild white night. He was determined to remember his dead wife. But much as he strained his mind, at first all he kept seeing was himself in the light of a gray morning standing in a doorway from which the door had been removed, wearing a black suit, receiving and returning sympathetic handclasps, his nostrils filled with the insipid odor of carbolic and flowers. It took a while before he succeeded in capturing the image of his wife. Even then, at first it was only the image of an image. For he saw only the large, gold-framed portrait that hung over the piano in the living-room at home; it showed a proud, fine lady of about thirty in ball dress. Then at last she herself appeared to him as the young girl who had listened, shy and pale, to his proposal, almost a quarter of a century ago. Then there rose to his mind the figure of a handsome woman sitting enthroned in the theater box beside him, her eyes fixed on the stage, miles away from him in her thoughts. Then he remembered a responsive wife who had received him with unexpected ardor when he returned from a long trip. Immediately afterward he thought of a nervous, tearful female with dulled greenish eyes whose many disagreeable moods had made life miserable for him. Then again he saw her in a pastel-colored morning gown, an anxious, solicitous mother watching by the bedside of a sick child—a child that had been doomed to die. Finally he saw a pallid creature, mouth curving with pain, drops of perspiration on the forehead, lying in a room smelling of ether, while he himself watched with tormenting pity. He knew that all these pictures, and a hundred others that with incredible rapidity flew past his mind's eye, represented one and the same being—the person who had been lowered into the grave two years ago. He had mourned her and nevertheless felt a sense of release after her death. It seemed to him that out of all these pictures he must choose one in order to arrive at some definite emotion. For now rage and shame vacillated, groping for an object. Irresolutely he stood gazing at the houses in their gardens across the way. They floated, yellow and russet in the moonlight, seeming to consist merely of pale painted walls with nothing but empty air behind them.

"Good night," the doctor said, getting up. "There is nothing more for me to do here." The businessman turned around. The writer had taken the letter and, unobserved, placed it in his pocket. Now he opened the door to the adjoining room. Slowly he went up to the deathbed, and the others saw him looking down at the corpse, hands clasped behind his back. Then they left.

In the anteroom the businessman said to the servant: "About the funeral—the will at the lawyer's may contain definite instructions after all."

"And don't forget to telegraph his sister in London," the doctor added.

"Certainly not," the servant replied, opening the door for them.

The writer caught up with them on the stairs. "I can give you both a lift," the doctor said, since his carriage was waiting for him.

"Thank you," the businessman said. "I'll walk." He shook hands with the other two and set off down the street toward town, letting the mildness of the spring night envelop him.

The writer got into the carriage with the doctor. In the gardens the birds began singing. The carriage passed the businessman, and all three men lifted their hats, each with the same expression and the same polite irony. "Will we be seeing anything of yours on the stage again before long?" the doctor asked the writer in his normal voice. The writer spoke of all the unusual obstacles standing in the way of the performance of his latest play—though of course he did have to admit, he said, that it contained almost outrageous attacks on everything people allegedly held sacred. The doctor nodded and paid no attention. For that matter, the writer was also paying no attention to what he was saying; the sentences he had framed so often fell from his lips as though he had learned them by heart.

In front of the doctor's house both men got out, and the carriage drove off.

The doctor rang the bell. Both men stood waiting in silence. When the footsteps of the concierge approached, the writer said: "Good night, my dear doctor." Then, nostrils twitching, he added slowly: "I shall not tell mine either." The doctor gazed past him and smiled sweetly. The door was opened; they shook hands and the doctor disappeared into the vestibule. The door shut behind him.

As he walked away, the writer felt in his breast pocket. Yes, the letter was there. Sealed and carefully preserved, his wife would find it among his posthumous papers. And with the peculiar power of imagination that was his, he could already hear her whispering at his grave: You great, you noble soul. . . .

Translated by Richard and Clara Winston

UNEXPECTED REUNION

by Johann Peter Hebel

A good fifty years ago or more, in Falun, which is in Sweden, a young miner kissed his pretty young fiancée and said to her: "On St. Lucy's Day our love will be blessed by the hand of the pastor, and then we shall be man and wife and we'll build a little nest of our own."

"And peace and love shall live there," said his pretty fiancée with an endearing smile, "for you are my one and all, and without you I'd rather be in the grave than anywhere else."

But before St. Lucy's Day had arrived, when the pastor called out for the second time in the church: "Does anyone know any reason why these two should not be joined together in marriage? . . ." Death spoke up. For though the youth had passed by her house the next morning in his black miner's outfit (miners always wear their death garb), and knocked at her window as always and bade her good-morning, he was never again to wish her good-night. He did not come back from the pit.

The same morning she happened to sew for him a black kerchief with a red border for the wedding day. But as he never came, she laid the kerchief aside and cried for him, and never forgot him.

Meanwhile the city of Lisbon, in Portugal, was destroyed in an earthquake, and the Seven Years' War ended, and the Emperor Francis I died, and Poland was divided up, and the Empress Maria Theresa passed away, and Struensee was decapitated, America became free, and the united French and Spanish might proved unable to subdue Gibraltar. The Turks locked General Stein up in the Veteran's Cave in Hungary, and the Emperor Joseph died, too. King Gustav of Sweden conquered Russian Finland, and the French Revolution and the Long War began, and Leopold II went also to his grave. The British bom-

---

See page 38.

barded Copenhagen, and the peasants sowed and reaped. The miller was grinding his meal, the smithies were hammering, and the people of the mines kept digging for metal ores in their underground workshop.

And when the miners of Falun, in the year 1809—in June, somewhere around St. John's Day—were about to make an opening between two shafts a good six hundred feet below the earth, they found in the diggings and vitriol-water the body of a young man, completely permeated with iron sulphate, but otherwise unimpaired and unaltered so that one could fully recognize his features and tell his age as if he had just died an hour before or dozed off a little at his job.

He was brought to the surface, and as his father, mother, friends, and acquaintances were all long dead, nobody recognized the sleeping youth or knew anything of his tragedy until the arrival at the place of the former fiancée of the miner who one day had gone on his shift and had never returned.

Gray and shriveled, she came on a crutch, and recognized her betrothed, and more with rapture than with sorrow she sank down upon the body of her beloved. And only after she had recovered from a long upheaval of emotions did she say: "It is my fiancé, for whom I've mourned these fifty years, and whom God has let me see once again before I die. A week before our wedding he went into the earth, and he never came back."

The hearts of all the bystanders were seized with grief, and they wept when they saw the fiancée of long ago, now a withered figure of spent old age, and her betrothed still in his youthful beauty, and how after fifty years the flame of young love once more awoke in her breast—but no longer did the beloved open his lips for a smile, nor his eyes for a glance of recognition—and how she had him carried at last to her little room, as the only one who belonged to him and had a right to him, while his grave was being prepared in the churchyard.

The next day, when the grave had been readied and the miners came to get him, she unlocked a little box, tied the black silk kerchief with the red border around his neck, and then accompanied him in her Sunday best, as if this were her wedding day and not the day of his interment.

Then as he was laid into his grave in the churchyard, she said: "Sleep well now for yet a day or ten in the cool wedding bed, and may time not be long for you. I have still only a few things to attend to, and shall come soon, and soon again it will be day. What the earth has relinquished once, it will not refuse to yield a second time," she said as she walked away, and, for the last time, looked back.

Translated by Paul Pratt

MONA LISA

by Alexander Lernet-Holenia

Toward the close of the year 1502, Louis XII, King of France, received Monsieur de La Trémouille, one of his marshals, and ordered him to betake himself at once to Milan, to raise an army there, and afterward to hasten to the aid of the two French governors in Naples, who had suffered a series of defeats at the hands of the Spanish.

"And I hope, monsieur," the King went on, "that you will manage to discharge this mission with your usual skill. You shall lack for nothing. Not only do I confer on you my own good wishes, but in addition I grant you leave on your march through Rome to request the blessing of the Holy Father. In the event, however, that the Pope should refuse to bless your arms, I give you my express permission to employ the same arms to compel His Holiness to do so. Select from among my noblemen as many as you may desire for your suite. For the flower of my nobility it will be an honor and a pleasure to serve under you, and those whom you single out will make themselves personally responsible for the arming and equipment of themselves and their retainers. A suitable number of clerics, whose expenses will be defrayed by the Church, will also be at

---

Alexander Lernet-Holenia's first novel, Abenteuer eines jungen Herrn in Polen, *published shortly after his return from army service in World War I, introduced a new tone to German twentieth-century fiction: a tongue-in-cheek romanticism that moves on the outermost edge of realistic storytelling. Of his novels, the dream story* Der Baron Bagge *is probably his most accomplished work. As an observer of the Austrian post-1918 gentry, he is the writer of the Lost Cause. A successful playwright and a poet of distinction, as well as a prolific novelist, Alexander Lernet-Holenia, born in 1897 in Carinthia, lives in Vienna and Sankt Wolfgang, Upper Austria.*

your disposal. Further, you have my consent to have cast in Milan the necessary cannon, to have embroidered such flags, standards, and pennons as you may require, and to procure an adequate supply of drums, trumpets, and kettledrums. The city will be held responsible for the cost of production. You have also my gracious permission to raise as many regiments of infantry and cavalry as you deem sufficient and as can be levied, paid, and fed from resources extracted from that country."

Here, as Louis appeared to be debating whether he should not also grant La Trémouille permission to employ for his purposes the sun, the water, the air, and the earth, for whose maintenance God Himself would be held responsible, he paused. Then, after gazing for a while into space with the expression of a man who is reluctant to make the slightest reference to money, he added: "So you can lack for nothing, monsieur. You will cover yourself with glory, will lead the army to victory, and will cause the fame of our arms to shine with renewed splendor. One thing further! I hope that you will also take this occasion to reimburse us for the heavy expenses incurred by this war. Do not fail, therefore, to exact suitable reparations from the countries for which we are making our sacrifice—either by way of direct payments or in the form of art treasures, jewelry, costly fabrics, and other such things. For this is my express wish and will. And now," concluded the King, "farewell and God be with you!"

So saying, he offered his hand to La Trémouille, laying it on the plumed hat that the Marshal held out to him, as though this were a cushion. La Trémouille, having bowed and kissed the King's hand, withdrew. But the King mounted his horse and rode off to hunt stag in the forest of Senlis.

This second Italian campaign of the French, then, was far less successful than the first, which nine years previously had been personally conducted by Charles VIII, the predecessor of Louis XII. Only a few lesser counts and insignificant nobles had been prevailed upon to join the retinue of La Trémouille. And instead of the millions in gold that the cities through which Charles VIII passed had paid out in order to be spared from pillage; instead of the loot of magnificent paintings, gems.

precious stones, brocades, and lapis lazuli with which Charles had loaded his six thousand pack horses; instead of all this, only paltry sums and a negligible amount of booty flowed in. In the course of his expedition, all that La Trémouille was able to get for his sovereign in Paris, either by appropriating them outright or by purchasing them with cash tributes, were one or two tolerably good pictures and a small collection of jewels, fabrics, alabaster statues, and the like.

As it was, it had taken the Marshal several months to raise and equip an army of sufficient size, and it was summer before he was able to get under way. He marched through Lombardy, crossed the Apennines, and pushed into Tuscany. While the army, its ostrich-plumed helmets and fluttering flags enveloped in dust, plodded on toward Romagna amid the rumble of ket-tledrums, he himself, accompanied by a few noblemen, ap-peared in Florence, where he planned to pass a few days before rejoining his forces.

In view of the greatly diminished strength of the French, he was glad even to have been admitted into the domain of the Republic. There could now be no question of the one hundred and twenty thousand pieces of gold that the city had formerly been required to pay to Charles VIII, nor of anything ap-proaching that sum. And the Marshal, who on his way to Florence had had to content himself with the bleeding of some smaller towns, now was eager at least to purchase some works of art in the city.

Da Vinci's studio in particular was recommended to him, and though, personally, La Trémouille found works of art ex-ceptionally boring and also had never so much as heard of Da Vinci, he resolved, because Louis's wish and will had been so emphatic on this score, to call on the painter.

Da Vinci was the natural son of a nobleman. A native of the little town of Vinci, he had later moved to Florence. After spending considerable time in Milan, Venice, and elsewhere, he was now back in Florence again, residing in the house of his father, who at this time was still living.

The morning hour that La Trémouille had chosen for his call was an early one, and the high towers of the houses of the no-bility, which could be seen by the hundreds above the rooftops, still cast long shadows.

La Trémouille was accompanied by several members of his suite. With him were also two Donatis, relatives of Dante and great art enthusiasts, though neither of them was too well informed on the subject, a Buondelmonte, an Alberighi, and a Calfucci—all young people from aristocratic Florentine families. A gaping throng followed the cavalcade. At the outset the young Florentine nobles had felt rather flattered to be seen in the company of the foreigners, but as the riders, with haughty mien, their hands on their hips, had slowly made their way through the crowd, the shouts that reached their ears sounded more nearly like curses than expressions of approval and admiration. For the constitution of the city had recently undergone a change and had again become extremely democratic. The Medici were in exile, and such was the temper of the times that people were inclined to be as distrustful of foreign nobles, no matter what their nationality, as of their own.

The cavalcade, having threaded its way through the clamor, the filth, and the press of the marketplaces, had entered the more quiet aristocratic quarter. As the visitors neared Leonardo's house, they were greeted with the sounds of wind and string instruments coming from within, as though some party was in progress. Clearly it was a dance tune that was being played and sung, but neither the laughter and shouting of the dancers nor the stamping of their feet could be heard, and as the procession came to a halt before the house, the music ceased.

The house, built of small, rough stones, was dominated by a fortified tower about one hundred and fifty feet in height. Below, in its embrasures, white doves were nesting; above, it was encircled with screaming falcons.

The Marshal and the gentlemen of his suite, after surveying the house and the tower, dismounted and were on the point of entering when they saw coming toward them several men with musical instruments tucked under their arms. It was they, apparently, who had been doing the playing. With them were also two persons in the garb of jugglers or tightrope walkers. They squeezed past the noblemen in the doorway and hurried out into the street.

The stillness that now prevailed in the house formed a curious contrast to the previous gaiety. But almost at once several servants came to receive the visitors, and Leonardo himself appeared on the steep wooden staircase.

He was a tall, handsome, though heavily bearded man of forty-five or fifty. His speech and manner were extremely urbane. Accustomed to the society of generals and princes, he came part way down the stairs to greet the callers with an air of ease and informality.

"Sir," said La Trémouille as he removed his hat and began to mount the staircase, "I am the Marshal of the King of France and I beg you to do me, and through me my sovereign, the honor of receiving me in your house."

Leonardo replied in grammatically faultless French, though with a marked Italian accent: "Sir, the honor is entirely mine, and I am uncommonly fortunate to have the privilege of greeting one of the most famous generals of chivalrous France. How is His Majesty?"

"The King, from what I hear, is well," answered La Trémouille, as he and his entourage stepped into the upper hall. He glanced approvingly at the openings in the floor, which were a typical feature of the houses of the Florentine nobility. Through them, in case of attack, hot pitch could be poured down upon the heads of the people below. "And you, sir?" he continued. "How are you?"

"In excellent health," replied Leonardo, opening the door into a small drawing-room. "After all, I am in the presence of the god of war himself, after whose health, as I hope, I may likewise be permitted to inquire."

"I, too," responded La Trémouille as he entered the room with his suite and noted with satisfaction the presence of pitch pots in the blue and white mosaic of the floor, "could not be in better health. After all, I have just had the good fortune to meet the artist who outshines not only a Zeuxis, a Protogenes, and an Apelles, but even the ingenious Vulcan himself!"

"Which I, however, in view of the proverbial sootiness of that gentleman, on whom Your Excellency has placed horns, must regard as a rather dubious honor," returned Leonardo.

The Marshal, who had had the compliments that he had just addressed to the painter drilled into him by one of his clerics, had never heard either of Vulcan's coating of dirt, or of the adultery of his wife, Aphrodite. He had not the slightest idea to what sooty husband and to what lady the artist alluded, nor did he know whether he should take the remark as flattery or whether Leonardo was making a fool of him. He therefore gave him a sharp look and replied: "My good sir, I don't know what you mean. And even if I did, I wouldn't say, for gentlemen don't tell tales. Let us rather converse on some other subject. But first let me present to you the noblemen who have done me the honor of following me into the field."

"I should like nothing better," said Leonardo.

"They are," the Marshal went on, "the Comtes de Villeneuve, de Goutaut-Biron, and de Jarnac; Messieurs Costé de Triquerville, du Plessis, de Chauvelin, and de Bridieu, the Vicomte de Châteaudun, and young Monsieur de Bougainville. With the Florentine noblemen who conducted me to your house you will already be acquainted."

Having assured one another that it was an honor and a pleasure to make one another's acquaintance, they all fell silent and for a while no one seemed to know what to say. At last, however, the servants came in bearing refreshments, and La Trémouille, who had been looking about the room, broke the silence. "Would you now grant us the privilege of inspecting your studio?" he asked.

"My studio?" inquired Leonardo. "You are in my studio, monseigneur."

This sparsely furnished room, the back of which was closed off by a curtain, was, in fact, the studio of Leonardo. Several empty chairs were disposed along the walls. On a chest were lying a few letters, poems, and drawings representing designs for fortifications, war machines, canals, and the like. That was all.

For not only was Leonardo one of the superior men of his time; he was also, and probably for this very reason, one of the most casual and the laziest. There are dozens of paintings that are generally ascribed to him to which, in reality, he contributed nothing but rough sketches. The execution he left to others. He tried his hand at all sorts of sculpture, using bronze, stone, and baked clay, but finished virtually nothing, and of the few things that he did manage to complete, the majority have been destroyed by time. He would begin a thing, then nearly always drop it and turn his attention to almost anything except his real work. Perhaps he had come to see that, in reality, nothing can be finished.

"What, sir," cried La Trémouille, "you say that this is your studio? It is quite different from what I had imagined, by my faith! When I leave a battlefield, which in a sense is my studio, you should see the lopped-off heads, arms, and legs strewn about over it. Where, then, are your paintings, your statues? Where are the sketches on which you are still at work?"

"For the moment I am not working on anything of that nature," replied Leonardo. "Or at least I have as yet had no opportunity to resume my artistic endeavors. For two years I served as engineer to the Duke de Valentinois, and have just recently returned from the camp outside of Pisa, where I was commissioned to draw plans for battering rams and other implements of war for the Florentine army. Since then I have been engaged in other things."

"What sort of things, if I may ask?"

"I have been devoting my time to music, to anatomy, to some extent to philosophy," replied Leonardo. "I have been attempting to describe in verse the essence of love, and in order to investigate the physical basis of it I have embarked on an experiment that has resulted in my studio, too, being littered with arms and legs. In other words, I was dissecting the bodies of two women. However, I discovered nothing of significance."

"That I could have foretold you, sir," said the Marshal. "How could you possibly expect to find anything where the only thing one can really hope to find is a lack of resistance! For if Parisian women are not prudish, what could you expect from two dead Italians! Well, and what did you do then?"

"I gave it up."

"You ought not to have done that, either," the Marshal observed. "You should have followed the example of all mankind, which has been conducting investigations of this sort since the days of Adam and Eve and still hasn't abandoned them. For if they are undertaken upon the proper object, they can afford no little pleasure! But what have you been doing instead?"

"I have been drawing a ship in which one can travel along the bottom of the sea, and another in which one can go up into the air."

"By my faith!" exclaimed the Marshal. "That makes more

sense, it seems to me! Not that I would prefer ships of that sort to a good horse, but one could make one's enemies travel in them, so that they would either drown under the water or fall out of the sky and break their necks."

"My researches into the density and the currents of water and air led me along rather different paths," said Leonardo. "One of the questions that came up was that concerning the weight of God, and it engaged my thoughts for several days."

"Well, and how much does He weigh?" asked the Marshal, who was beginning to get the impression that he was dealing with a man who wanted to make fun of him and was therefore determined to draw the conversation into the ridiculous. "At what conclusion did you arrive, Sir Wag?"

"At none, of course," replied Leonardo. "Nor did I wish to come to any conclusion. For who can arrive at conclusions concerning God! I was merely indulging in the pleasure of thinking about Him. That was all."

"And otherwise," inquired La Trémouille, raising his eyebrows, "otherwise you were doing nothing?"

"On the contrary. I was studying the nature of naiads, dryads, griffins, and dragons, as well as that of unicorns and other rare creatures."

"Well," said the Marshal, "that is all very fine and extremely useful! But the characteristics of the more common animals, did you investigate those as well?"

"No," replied Leonardo, "for they are already familiar to everyone."

"You think so? Then tell me, for example, how many legs a fly has."

"A fly?" returned Leonardo. "Four, of course!"

"No," said the Marshal, "six. I didn't think you'd know!"

"Monseigneur," contradicted Leonardo, "I am positively certain that the fly has four legs, and only four."

"And I," rejoined the Marshal, "can assure you that it has six, and I will not be argued out of a single one of them."

"In a book," persisted Leonardo, "which I myself wrote as an exercise in my youth and which deals with a great variety of animal species, I definitely described the fly as having four legs—"

"Six, sir! But in order not to give the world, whose eyes are upon us both, the impression that we are in disagreement on a point any schoolchild can verify, I will, with your permission, have a fly caught and give you the opportunity to count its legs. Monsieur de Bougainville! You are the youngest of my gentlemen. Do us the honor of catching a fly for us!"

The young man whom the Marshal had addressed appeared for a moment to be utterly astounded at this command. But he quickly regained his composure and replied laughingly: "No more, no less, monseigneur? It shall be done."

"On the shoulder of Monsieur de Bridieu," said the Marshal in a rather stern voice, for he could not tolerate it that an order of his should be taken lightly, "on Monsieur de Bridieu's shoulder I see one right now, a fly. Hold still, Monsieur de Bridieu!" And Monsieur de Bougainville approached Monsieur de Bridieu to catch the fly. The fly, however, perceiving Monsieur de Bougainville close by, flew off the shoulder of Monsieur de Bridieu and began to buzz about the room, pursued by Bougainville and the other gentlemen, who endeavored to swat it with their plumed hats. Suddenly the insect vanished behind the curtain that hung across the back of the room, and Bougainville thrust aside the drapery to continue the chase.

He was nearly blinded by a sudden burst of light. For a moment he thought it must be fire or the sparkle of jewels. But the shimmer came from the glazed surface of a picture that had been painted, apparently, on wood or metal in the new technique; that is to say, not only with egg white, but also with certain oils. The picture, which was propped slantwise in an upholstered armchair, was about three spans high and two wide, or perhaps a little more, and was surrounded by a temporary frame. It was the portrait of a young woman in a silvery blue dress with sleeves of Indian yellow. The eyes of the woman, who was facing the spectator, were turned slightly to the left, toward Bougainville, and she was smiling. She was smiling bewitchingly and enigmatically, but as if from behind some filmy shadow or veil. And yet it was this smile that produced the radiance which was so dazzling to the eye, though in the background of the picture too, where azure streams, like ribbons, wound their way among the lofty mountain ranges, the blue was more fabulous than the radiance of paradise.

Bougainville had but a moment to look at the woman. An

instant later he felt the artist's hand on his shoulder, and the curtain before him was drawn once more.

"What was that?" gasped the bewildered Frenchman.

"Nothing," replied Leonardo, putting his arm about the shoulders of the young man and leading him back to the center of the room. "A picture. That is all."

"A picture?" inquired the Marshal. "What kind of picture? May we see it?"

"It's unfinished," replied Leonardo. "I'm still working on it from time to time."

"But if we might have just one look—"

"Better not, monseigneur. It is quite imperfect. It is nothing."

"And would you sell it? It is the express wish and will of my King . . ."

"Perhaps. But I will not sell it until it is finished, and I don't know . . ."

"With the price," persisted the Marshal, "you would be quite satisfied. We could levy a small tribute from some city, and—"

"But who is this woman?" cried Bougainville. "What is her name?"

Leonardo hesitated for a moment, then he replied: "La Gioconda."

"And who is she?"

"Oh, no one of any consequence."

"Sir," insisted Bougainville, "if I may be allowed to ask one last question—"

"That you may not, sir!"

Thus ended this essentially fruitless, but, in the light of what was to follow, fateful visit. Of the fly and the number of its legs no further mention was made. The Marshal, after exchanging a few words with the artist on other matters, bade him farewell, left the house, and mounted his horse, and Bougainville had no choice but to follow him and the other gentlemen.

Philippe de Bougainville was twenty-three years of age. The picture of the unknown woman had made a very extraordinary impression upon him, and on the ride back he questioned the Florentines closely as to her identity. The young men said they had never heard of anyone called Gioconda, but that she must be the wife or a relative of some man whose name was

Giocondo; that there was only one such in Florence, a certain Francesco del Giocondo, who lived near the Bargello. He, however, was a widower. So if the picture—which, incidentally, they hadn't had a chance to see—was a portrait of his wife, or of one of his wives, for he had been married three times, she must be dead, and they knew of no other relatives of that name. The man himself was seldom seen. Though he was of the nobility and held several government posts, he rarely appeared in public.

It seemed quite improbable to young Bougainville that Leonardo would paint the portrait of a woman who was no longer living. But in the course of the day, which he devoted entirely to making inquiries, he learned from other sources as well that Giocondo's three wives were all dead, the last, Mona Lisa di Antonio Maria di Noldo Gherardini, having died two years previously during the plague of 1501, and that Giocondo had not remarried.

Bougainville then told himself that the picture (or rather the model), with which, as he himself admitted, he had fallen violently in love, must be that of some other woman, and as he had made up his mind to make her acquaintance, he went the next day, despite the ungracious manner in which Leonardo had cut short the conversation, once more to pay a call on the painter.

Oddly enough, once again as Bougainville neared the house of Da Vinci, the sound of music could be heard issuing from it, and again it was a dance tune that was being played and sung. But this time when the young man entered, the music did not cease. Probably because he was alone and on foot, his arrival had not been noticed. He gained the hall without encountering anyone, mounted the stairs, and stopped in the hall above.

The music was coming from the same room in which Leonardo had received the Marshal the day before. After a moment's hesitation Bougainville pushed open the door of the room. What he saw was this:

The curtain, which he himself had lifted the day before, was drawn aside. Leonardo, with his back to the door, a box filled with paints on the floor in front of him, and some brushes in his right hand, was sitting in a chair looking at the picture of

La Gioconda, which was propped up before him on a second chair. This manner of painting seemed extremely informal, and to add to that effect, several musicians, apparently the same who had been there the day before, were playing an accompaniment. The two jugglers were also present. They were dancing and turning somersaults.

The scene was all the more curious as they were not dancing in front of Leonardo, but behind his back, where they could be seen, as it were, only by the woman in the picture. Nor was he working. He was simply sitting there with an air of deep concentration and of almost regal impatience, motionless except for the fingers of his free left hand, with which he was beating time to the music.

Bougainville, struck once again by the fabulous radiance of the picture, also remained motionless until the musicians noticed him and broke off their song.

The painter spun quickly about and an instant later sprang to his feet. He seemed more than astonished to see Bougainville, and his face became flushed with annoyance. "Sir," he managed to say after a moment or two, "to what do I owe this repeated honor?" And he tossed his brushes into the paintbox and vigorously motioned to the musicians and the two jugglers to leave the room. "Please pardon the presence of these people," he added quickly. "But I was not expecting visitors. I have just begun to try my hand at painting again, but was getting bored with my work, and these men serve to divert me. *Via, via,*" he shouted, and the performers, who had by now gathered up their things, hurried out of the room. He was about to draw the curtain once more in front of the picture when Bougainville rushed up behind him and prevented him from doing so. So light and noiseless was the young man's step, one could almost hear the plumes of the hat that he held in his hand brushing against the floor like soft wings.

"Please don't!" he begged, with a gesture so full of natural charm and youthful passion that the artist was taken aback. "Allow me for a few minutes at least to gaze at this wonderful person who since yesterday has been constantly in my thoughts. I freely confess to you that it is really she who is the object of my visit. Otherwise I should never have ventured to impose on your valuable time again. You may think me childish, but it isn't given to me to distinguish between the beauty of a work of art and that of a model. Who is this model? I beg you, sir, to tell me! You said yesterday that she was the wife of Francesco del Giocondo, only—"

"What?" broke in Leonardo, amazed. "Did I say that this was Giocondo's wife?"

"Certainly! You gave her name as—"

"The wife of Ser Francesco?"

"That was it."

"Ah," cried Leonardo, "I did not say that he was her husband! I merely said that she was La Gioconda!"

"Exactly, exactly! But Mona Lisa is dead. She has been dead for two years, and the other two wives of Ser Francesco have also been dead for a long time."

"Do you mean to say that he had two wives before her?"

"Yes indeed. Mona Vanna and Mona Bice."

"Is that so? I didn't know that," murmured Leonardo. "But how did you find this out? And what do you want of me? Incidentally, won't you do me the honor to sit down?" And he drew up two chairs.

"Messer Leonardo," said Bougainville as he sat down and laid his plumed hat across his knees, "tell me who this woman is, I beg, I implore you! Is she the wife of someone other than Ser Francesco? Is she one of his relatives who lives in another city? Or is it because she is your own mistress that you are unwilling to have me know who she is?"

"My young sir," Leonardo said, magnanimously, "if I had a mistress I would be only too pleased to introduce you to her. You would make a handsome pair, and, even though it might mean a sacrifice on my part, I would give anything for the sight of such a couple. For on the whole one sees only very ill-matched couples. But I fear it will be impossible to bring about this meeting you seem to long for so much. You said yourself that Ser Francesco's wife was dead."

"So the picture is really that of La Gioconda?"

"Yes."

"And Mona Lisa is really dead?"

"Beyond a doubt."

"Then there is nothing left for me to do but to weep at her tomb!" exclaimed Bougainville in a heart-rending voice. "For

I thought that at last I had found her, and now it turns out that I lost her long ago. But you, sir, who knew her, who breathed the air that she breathed—tell me everything that you know about her, describe to me, I beg of you, everything down to the most minute, the most trivial details, and out of this flimsy substance I shall create a picture of my own more wonderful even than yours."

"Ah," said Leonardo, raising his eyebrows, "to tell you the truth, I knew her only quite casually, this woman, and the portrait here is neither hers nor that of any other woman. For, in reality, even had I wished to paint her, my picture would have become that of someone else. The only women one ever paints are women who don't exist, just as those that one loves do not really exist. But, of course, it is possible that this picture might still bear a kind of resemblance to her. It is perhaps conceivable that this Gioconda and the other—that because of their having the same name, certain memories— You see, I call her La Gioconda because she is smiling, for the word in Italian means 'the joyous one' or 'the smiling one.' Mona Lisa was someone else. But, in fact, it is not beyond the realm of possibility that, for this very reason, the memory of the other, the real woman found its way into the imaginary picture, asserted herself in the dream figure. . . . For, after all, none of us knows what it is that speaks from us, writes for us, guides our paintbrush, how much other, perhaps long dead life still haunts our own! In truth—"

Bougainville had risen. "If I didn't know," said he, going over a little farther to the right, so that the eyes of the woman in the portrait, which were turned to the left, were looking straight at him, "if I didn't know for a certainty that the woman whose portrait I thought this to be is dead, if it were not common knowledge in the city that she was buried years ago, I'd swear she is more alive than any living woman. It is almost inconceivable that these eyes no longer see, that this bosom no longer breathes, that the smile on those lips is no longer a living one, but is already immortal! I—"

"The smile," interrupted Leonardo, setting one foot on the paintbox and bending over to pick up a few of the brushes, which he then dropped back again one by one, "the smile is not immortal, it is unfinished, that is all."

"It is wonderful," said Bougainville.

"No, it is nothing. Women, to be sure, are the most perfect of creatures, and when they smile, it is their most perfect state. It is in fact the expression of perfection. Whenever anything is agitated it becomes distorted; in repose, it smiles. But there is nothing more ridiculous than the imperfect portrayal of the perfect. And I have not succeeded in really painting the smile of this woman. Every smile is enigmatical, not only in itself, but in every way. But I have not found the answer to the riddle. I do not know why she is smiling. You'll have been surprised to find musicians and jugglers here. Well, I conceived the notion that this woman might smile at the music and at the dancing of these people. It was their task, so to speak, to amuse the picture and to evoke a response in her which I myself have failed to evoke. For I find the expression of the figure in this picture meaningless. The smile of a real woman, of even the most ordinary one, is more nearly perfect than any attempt on the part of an artist, however great he may be, to paint it. There is no perfection in works of art. Only reality is perfect." And he added: "As long as the woman in this picture is not reality, she will never really smile."

"Well," murmured Bougainville, "she is real enough for me. The loss of the most entrancing mistress could cause me no greater pain than does the knowledge that she is no longer living."

"So you have actually fallen in love with this picture?"

"Not with the picture," replied Bougainville. "With the woman."

"That, in this case at least, is the same thing."

"Yes, for you, sir," said Bougainville. "But not for me." And he stared off into space. "However," he added at last, drawing himself up, "it is fruitless to discuss the irretrievable. What is more, I have already, I fear, imposed upon you outrageously. But you will pardon my intrusion, my questions, my folly, and forgive the dreams, yours and mine, for being so much more real than life." Then, without another glance at the picture, he bowed and left the room, hiding his deep emotion.

Mona Vanna and Mona Bice del Giocondo and a little daughter of Ser Francesco's were buried beside the outer wall of Santa Maria Novella. The tomb of Mona Lisa was in Santa Croce, and, because hers had been a family of great prominence, in the right aisle of the church proper. The tomb was in the wall between the so-called chapel of the Baroncelli and the entryway to the sacristy. A marble tablet had been placed there bearing a Latin inscription that Bougainville could not understand.

It must have been about noon when he entered the church, accompanied by a servant bearing a large wreath of dark-red roses. A fashionable Mass for late risers, however, was still in progress, a "perfumed Mass," as it was called in those days, attended for the most part by members of the aristocracy, richly attired and perfumed, who had come solely for the purpose of showing off their clothes, of criticizing others who were there for the same reason, and of chatting and joking with one another. To the priest and to what was taking place at the altar, no one paid the slightest attention.

The sight of the elegant, laughing, chattering crowd filled Bougainville with disgust. Ignoring the glances cast in his direction by the women, and shoving aside, heedless of their protests, the gentlemen who did not immediately make way for him, he asked to be led to Mona Lisa's grave.

He placed the roses on the tomb. Then he stood for a time staring at it. But suddenly, strange to say, he could no longer recall what had brought him there or what he had hoped to find.

Before the picture of Mona Lisa, it had seemed incredible to him that she was dead. Beside her tomb, it was no longer possible to think of her as being still alive for him, in any form. That he had placed a wreath of roses on the tomb of a perfect stranger now seemed to him an act of tactless presumption, an unpardonable intrusion upon the private affairs of others. Had he been discovered there by one of her relatives or by her husband, he would not have known in the least what to say. He turned away and let his eyes travel over the ornamented walls, the tapestries, and the long rows of triangular lindenwood shields, covered with brightly painted cowhide, which were suspended from the many-colored beams.

He cast a casual glance into the chapel of the Baroncelli. Here too were tombs, tapestries, shields. But as he turned back again, he was struck by the fact that the wall separating the chapel from the church was remarkably thin. To the left of the entrance, as he could see when he stepped back into the nave, there was no tomb in this thin wall. And yet to the right of the entrance was the tomb of Mona Lisa.

Still farther to the right and directly adjacent to the entryway leading to the sacristy, there was another tomb of a much earlier period—but it was embedded in the considerably deeper wall of the church proper. While the wall into which the memorial tablet of Ser Francesco's wife was inserted was no more than an ell and a half in depth!

Bougainville gazed at this wall and could not see how it could have been possible to bury a grown woman there except in an upright position, which, however, was very unlikely to have been the case and quite contrary to custom. On the other hand, the grave itself might be under the church floor while only the tablet had been set into the wall. But this, too, seemed unlikely, for if she were buried there, the memorial tablet would certainly have been set into the floor as well.

He became alarmed. He took two steps into the chapel, faced about, and studied the wall from the opposite side. He was right. To contain a human body the wall would have to have been more than an arm's length thicker. But if she had not been buried here, where was she?

It can only be supposed that, being in a state of mind which from the outset had made it impossible for him to accept the fact that this woman was dead, he immediately dismissed every other possible explanation and jumped to the conclusion that she was still alive.

"If a person is not in the tomb that is supposed to be his," cried a voice within him, "if the tomb is so narrow that he *can't* be in it, then he isn't dead! If a painter is still at work on the portrait of a woman, the sight of which is as breathtaking as if the woman herself were only two steps away, it cannot be a picture from the realm of dreams, even if the artist were a Leonardo twice over. It is impossible that this woman should have died two years ago! If he says he is no longer using her as his model, he is lying, and if Giocondo put up a tablet to her memory, he is deceiving the whole world! I don't know what reason these two can have for concealing the existence of this wonderful being, I don't know why her husband is hiding her, or where. Probably in some secret room in his house, most probably in a state of degrading and harrowing imprisonment. Why? She must have betrayed him. Once she saw him for what he was and realized that he was the kind of man who, instead of killing his unfaithful wife, would bury her alive, as it were, and, too cowardly to admit his shame and hers, would take it out on her by torturing her in secret, she could not help deceiving him. She had no choice. And he, the monster, is now revenging himself on this bewitching creature for the despair into which he himself has plunged her!"

Bougainville resolved at once to do everything in his power to bring about her liberation. To confide his discovery to the city authorities seemed unwise. Those people would never believe that anything so appalling could have taken place right before their eyes, and would laugh in his face. And having already been tricked by the painter, he had no desire to make himself ridiculous before the whole world. To take into his confidence Monsieur de La Trémouille, who was endeavoring to maneuver his way through the political mazes of Italy, also appeared inadvisable. It seemed best to him simply to appeal to a few of his friends, with their help and with that of their servants to force his way into Giocondo's house, to search it, and set free the unfortunate woman.

But he told himself that before taking this step, he must first be quite sure of his ground, surer at least than he was at the moment. There was still a shred of possibility that La Gioconda was really buried in the tomb supposed to be hers. He therefore determined to verify his suspicions for himself and to open the tomb that night.

He spent the afternoon alternately tortured by pictures of the pitiable plight of his beloved and transported with joy at the thought that she was alive after all and that he would soon be able to see and talk to her. Then again he would be seized with fear lest he might have been mistaken and that the tomb might really be hers.

Long before dusk he was in Santa Croce, accompanied by two of his retainers, who were carrying the necessary tools concealed beneath their cloaks. The three men hid behind one of the side altars until the church was closed; then they came out and set about opening the grave.

By the light of a few candle ends they had taken from one of the altars, they pried out the tablet and found behind it a sealed-up grave. They chipped away the masonry, opened up the aperture, and shone a light inside. Bougainville had not been mistaken: the tomb was empty.

It was not more than an ell in depth and probably at some previous time had contained the body of a stillborn infant or of some child that had died at birth. Ser Francesco must have purchased the tomb and have managed to make all the world believe that he had interred his wife in it. Because of the general confusion which, owing to the plague, prevailed at that particular time, and because scarcely anyone would have dared attend the funeral, the fraud had not been detected. Even later on, no one had become suspicious.

But Bougainville wanted to make quite sure. He ordered his men to take up the stone slabs in the floor in front of the tomb as well, and to poke about in the dirt. But there was nothing to be found.

After he had everything restored to its proper place, he went to one of the church doors and his two servants applied themselves to the task of prying it open. Men of their station at that time, and quite justifiably, enjoyed the reputation of being born burglars, and in fact it was not long before the lock yielded to their efforts.

As Bougainville emerged into the purple night and stepped out on the big square in front of the church, it must have been about ten o'clock. He set off at once for Leonardo's house.

The house was already closed up for the night. He had to knock for some time before it was opened. The artist had already gone to bed. Leonardo's father, his stepmother Lucretia, his half-brothers and their wives, all of them awakened from their first sleep by the clamor, appeared half-clothed on the landing, accompanied by servants with tapers in their hands. Seeing Bougainville dash past without paying the slightest attention to them and burst into Leonardo's room, they thought him a madman.

This impression was shared by Leonardo when Bougainville disclosed to him that he, Leonardo, was as much of a scoundrel as Ser Francesco, for Mona Lisa was not dead at all, but was being held prisoner. Leonardo, sitting up in bed, stared at the young man in utter bewilderment and kept asking him what had caused him to arrive at this curious conclusion.

"The evidence of my own eyes!" cried Bougainville. "Evidence that I myself have uncovered! You're a rogue, Ser Leonardo, and a liar into the bargain! You tried to make me believe that Mona Lisa was dead. But she's not! Far from it!"

"She isn't dead?" exclaimed Leonardo. "What is she, then?"

"She's alive!" shouted Bougainville. "What else could she be? She isn't in her grave!"

"Isn't she?" exclaimed Leonardo. "She isn't in her grave! What makes you think so?"

"I opened the grave!" cried Bougainville.

"What?" roared Leonardo. "You opened her grave?"

"Yes indeed! And it was empty. So tell me where she is! Explain to me this abominable conspiracy of which she is the victim! Tell me everything, or, by God," he shouted, drawing his sword, "I'll run you through this instant right in your bed!"

Leonardo, after a moment, flung back the blanket, stood up, and, without once taking his eyes off Bougainville, walked up to him. It being customary in those days to sleep without nightclothes, he was naked. While his enormous beard concealed his chest, it was obvious from the muscles elsewhere that he was a man of great strength. Instinctively Bougainville retreated a step.

"One moment, my young sir," said Leonardo. And with a quick, very deft movement he pushed up Bougainville's eyelid.

"What's the meaning of this?" shouted Bougainville.

"Nothing," replied Leonardo, reaching for a coat that was lying on a chair and wrapping it about him. "Nothing, young man. Put your sword back in its sheath. So you claim in all seriousness to know that Ser Francesco's wife is not in her tomb? Where else would she be?"

"That is what I am asking you!" cried Bougainville. "Where is she? You know! You must know, for you've been painting her since she vanished from the world! Is she still in Ser Francesco's house? Why is he keeping her concealed? Or has she perhaps gone into hiding of her own accord? That I will never believe! So why is Giocondo making a secret of the fact that she is alive? Did she betray him, and he didn't dare kill her but incarcerated her instead? Who was her lover? Out with it! Out with it!"

Leonardo gazed at the young man for a few moments in silence. Finally he said: "Sir, because you are standing before me with a sword in your hand, you think you can force me to speak. Let me tell you that it would be quite easy for me to wrest your weapon from you and to fling you down the stairs. Only your agitation, not to say the mental aberration to which you have fallen prey, in a sense excuses you. So I could answer your questions as if you had the right to ask them. Only there is no need for me to answer them. You answer them yourself, and I, even if I wanted to, could never set you straight. Let me briefly recapitulate. You call on me in the company of your marshal. You see, by chance, the picture of a woman who doesn't exist, but with whom you fall in love. You think that this woman is the wife of Ser Francesco del Giocondo who died two years ago. But you cannot bear to think she is dead. You imagine that you have searched her tomb and found it empty. From this you conclude that she is still living. You ask questions about her whereabouts which plainly show that in your delusion you have already formed your own ideas also about what is to happen next. What sense would there be in my trying to make it clear to you that Mona Lisa is really dead? That Giocondo is not hiding her? That I did not paint her? That she did not betray him? For that matter, she may very well have betrayed him. There are rumors that her lover was Amerigo Capponi, the son of Ser Piero, to whom Florence owes so much. When your King Charles marched into our city and dictated humiliating terms, Ser Piero tore up the treaty and compelled him to agree to more favorable ones. But this too, I fear, is only grist for your mill. For you will, of course, think it only natural that the, in your opinion, most beautiful woman in Florence should have had as her lover the son of the most distinguished of Etruscan noblemen. But when all is said and done, what good does it do you? It all happened years ago. But you won't believe that any more than the rest of the story. So, in my opinion, you might as well stick to your notion that she is alive, that her husband, to whom she has been unfaithful, is keeping her concealed, and that I painted her portrait. Now are you satisfied?"

"The subterfuges," replied Bougainville, who had been listening to him with glittering eyes, "the subterfuges you must use to confirm my conjectures—what am I saying, my convictions! —are a matter of total indifference to me. Whatever you may think of the state of my sanity, you do admit, then, that Mona Lisa is still alive?"

"What would be the point of my saying anything else?" asked Leonardo.

"And this Signor Capponi is still her lover?"

"I shouldn't have mentioned it," replied Leonardo with a shrug of his shoulders. "But if you think it feasible for a woman incarcerated by her husband to continue to have a lover—go ahead and think so. Women, as you doubtless know, are very often clever and will resort to all sorts of cunning to achieve their ends; and the lovers of unhappy women, if only out of common decency, are, for the most part, extraordinarily faithful. So the two still love each other. And now, if you will be so kind as to leave me, I shall be grateful. It is my intention to get a few more hours of sleep. In any event I shall soon have the pleasure of another visit from you. Pester me if you must, but don't on any account pester Giocondo and Capponi—to whom, by the way, I am in debt—or anyone else. I, on the other hand, am already used to being pestered. Meanwhile, farewell!"

Bougainville, who had thrust his sword under his arm, stood silent for a moment longer and seemed about to make some reply. "More," he finally murmured to himself, however, "I didn't hope to learn." And without a word he turned and left the house.

Several of La Trémouille's noblemen were still out when Bougainville returned home. He found them gathered in the house of a certain Fifante, drinking with some girls and singing at the top of their lungs.

"Gentlemen," said Bougainville as he came in, "forgive me for disturbing your gaiety. I need your assistance in an important matter."

The songsters fell silent. One of the wenches, who was being tickled by Monsieur de Pierredon, who had not noticed Bougainville's entrance, let out a squeal. Perceiving, in the silence, that all eyes were upon him, Pierredon switched abruptly from tenderness to severity and slapped the girl's face. She leaped up indignantly and raced out.

Bougainville looked from one to the other.

"Well, sir," finally inquired the Vicomte de Châteaudun, "what is it all about? I hope you will do us the honor to tell us."

"A lady—" began Bougainville.

"A lady, of course!" shouted Monsieur de Chauvelin. "But what about this lady?"

"She is being held prisoner in a house in this city. Do not ask me to describe to you the circumstances that led me to the discovery of her lamentable plight. Suffice it to say that this lady is very young, very beautiful, and very unhappy. I consider it my duty to hasten to her aid, and I am counting on your assistance, gentlemen. Let us break into the house, search it, and set the lady free!"

Bougainville's proposal was greeted with shouts of joy. For some time it had galled these noblemen not a little to be merely tolerated in the city instead of being able to lord it over the Florentines as had the men of Charles VIII nine years before. Bougainville's request provided a most welcome opportunity to remedy this situation. They did not inquire further into the facts of the matter, nor did they ask the name of the lady on whom they were to bestow their services, but straightway called for horses and arms, and shortly thereafter the cavalcade, with Bougainville at its head and a handful of retainers bringing up the rear, was on its way, blustering and shouting, to the house of Ser Francesco.

There they pelted the entryway of the house and all the window shutters within reach with cobblestones, and it was not long before the door had been broken down. Tumult and shouting arose throughout the entire neighborhood. Terrified sleepers peered out of all the windows to find out what was going on. A bell began to ring frantically.

On the second floor the intruders came face to face with Ser Francesco. He was an aristocratic-looking man between forty and forty-five years of age, slightly gray, but still retaining the vestiges of youthful handsomeness. Half-clad, he was carrying in his hand a naked sword. Arrayed behind him, and armed with cudgels, meat axes, and spits, were his servants.

"Gentlemen of France," said he, "what right have you to break into my house? How dare you break down the doors? What do you want here?"

"That, Sir Scoundrel, you shall soon learn!" cried one of the nobles. Not being entirely sure himself, he could say no more.

Bougainville, however, planted himself in front of Giocondo and shouted: "Where is your wife?"

Ser Francesco stared at him dumbfounded.

"Yes indeed!" cried Bougainville. "Your wife! Where is she? We want to know!"

"Sir," answered Ser Francesco, "who are you that you feel called upon to inquire about her? I no longer have a wife. I have had three, but they are all dead."

"That is not true!" shouted Bougainville. "That is to say: Mona Vanna *is* dead and so is Mona Bice, but Mona Lisa is not!"

"How do you know that?" cried Giocondo. "Or rather, what makes you think so? Did you know her? And how do you happen to be so well informed about my family affairs?"

"I am very well informed about them!" said Bougainville. "But I have also discovered things unknown to others—for example, that your wife is not buried in Santa Croce. What do you say to that, my gentleman of Italy?"

Giocondo fell back a step or two and turned pale. "What does this mean?" he gasped.

"It means what it means," Bougainville shouted.

"But how do you come to make such a statement?"

"Because I have convinced myself of its truth!"

"What?" cried Giocondo. "You could have—"

"Yes indeed! I not only could have, but I have! So tell me where she is, your wife! Tell me at once if you don't want me to ferret your secret out of you with the point of this blade, blackguard, who has the temerity to shut away from the world so ravishing a creature, to torment her, and to have her portrait painted, to boot!"

For a moment Giocondo stood there motionless; then, all of a sudden, instead of replying, he thrust Bougainville aside, elbowed his way through the group of noblemen who stood in his path, and shot down the stairs.

"Stop!" cried Bougainville.

But Giocondo had already reached the gate and was hurrying down the street, and by the time that Bougainville, who had raced after him down the stairs, arrived at the gate, Ser Francesco had vanished into the throng that had assembled before the house, which greeted Bougainville with menacing shouts.

Meanwhile the French noblemen had shoved aside the servants of Ser Francesco and had begun to ransack the house from top to bottom. But they found no trace of Mona Lisa. All that they managed to unearth in the way of females were two pretty young maids, whom they dragged naked from their beds and carried about in triumph, heedless of their kicks and screams, until it turned out that neither of them was the lady in question —whereupon the poor girls, wringing their hands, darted about hither and thither like terrified hens, pursued by the bare swords of the noblemen. But this pandemonium was soon brought to an end. Giocondo returned at the head of a troop of armed Florentine nobles. They made their way into the house, and it was all the French could do to run for their lives. There was a brief skirmish during which several shots were fired. Luckily, however, no one suffered anything more serious than a few scratches. The French fought their way to the door and beat a retreat amid a shower of stones, garbage, and rotten fruit, hurled at them by the irate populace, which was now jamming all the streets.

When Monsieur de La Trémouille learned of the outrage committed by his cavaliers, he flew into a towering rage, for his relations with the city government, already none of the best, were now strained to the breaking-point by this incident. He was forced to go that very night to the *signoria*, which had also been alerted, to offer his apologies, and he promised to castigate the instigators of the scandalous affair.

Upon his return he berated his men in the most abusive language. He tried his best to discover what had occasioned the fracas, but everyone pretended to have forgotten completely, and they all excused themselves on the grounds of inebriation; as they had not found the woman for whom Bougainville was looking, they had begun to doubt her existence, and in any case thought it better not to mention her. In the end, Monsieur de La Trémouille, having learned nothing from them, had no choice but to put them under detention in their quarters. As Giocondo too, quite naturally, was careful to say nothing about the real cause of the broil, it was finally concluded that the whole affair was simply a case of disorderly conduct on the part of intoxicated gentlemen.

Bougainville, confined within his four walls, was in despair over the failure of his undertaking. He could not explain the fact that he had been unable to find his beloved. At the same time he became more and more fearful that Giocondo, seeing that people had found out about his wife and actually were searching for her, might imprison her even more closely and subject her to yet worse tortures.

In his desperation Bougainville finally made up his mind to confide in Monsieur de La Trémouille. He dispatched a servant to him with a note entreating the Marshal to call on him for the purpose of discussing a very important matter.

When La Trémouille appeared, Bougainville began by thanking the Marshal in the most courteous language for giving him the pleasure of a visit.

"The pleasure, sir," replied La Trémouille, plunking his hat down on the table, "the pleasure is certainly not on my side, believe me!"

"Then I beg you, monseigneur, to let me express my regret," said Bougainville. "I do not know why I have again incurred your displeasure. But I hope that you will do me the honor of telling me."

La Trémouille had sunk into an armchair. He tapped the calves of his legs with his riding crop. "On my way here," he said, "the crowd was not only hurling insults at me and my suite, it was also cursing France and the King. The aristocracy of the town is extremely provoked with us, and the populace is like a swarm of angry bees. Assassins are trying to fire at us from ambush; the *signoria* was loath to accept the apologies that I was compelled to present to these gentlemen. Last night in the stables a patriot chopped the tail of my dapple-gray horse right off, and in the general furor all of us are constantly in danger of being thrown into prison. What do you say to that? Had I dreamed, sir, that you would be the author of such irresponsible pranks, I would have ordered one of our regiments to remain in the vicinity. As it is, however, the army, as you know, is far to the south, and we are at the mercy of the Republic. I can't even leave this confounded city as soon as I would like to without arousing suspicion. And all this because of your idiotic escapade! If, sir, you would only tell me what was behind it!" And he began angrily to tie the laces of his breeches.

"Monseigneur," replied Bougainville, "I should like nothing better than to have your permission to tell you everything! It was for this very reason that I requested the honor of your—"

"Then tell me!" interrupted the Marshal.

As Bougainville related his story, La Trémouille listened first with a scowl, then with raised eyebrows and eyes wide with amazement, finally with an air of uneasiness natural in one who finds himself shut up in a room with a lunatic. At the conclusion Bougainville, to top it all, urged the Marshal to undertake personally to free Mona Lisa.

"Sir," said La Trémouille rising, and beginning to grope for his hat without taking his eyes off the young man, "sir! Not only do I refuse to stick my nose into this crazy business, I also strictly forbid you to go in for any more of this tomfoolery. If you make any attempt to pursue this matter further, I shall have your sword taken away from you. Your detention will, of course, remain in force. Nor are you to receive any visitors, but are to employ the time and leisure provided you by your confinement to examine your conscience, and to wait quietly for the doctor whom I shall send to bleed you. And so farewell!" Thereupon, disregarding the protests and protestations that Bougainville attempted to make, he hurriedly left the room.

The young man was thrown into a state of extreme agitation. Had he not seen with his own eyes that the grave of his beloved was empty, had he not been able to swear by the sacrament that he had not been mistaken, he too, like the others, would now have been forced to doubt his sanity. What is more, the obstacles that stood in his path, the inaccessibility of the object of his passion, and the ill fortune that seemed to attend his enterprises intensified his bewilderment and his love to such a degree that he thought he must really be on the verge of madness. Above all, it seemed to him utterly intolerable to have to remain shut up in his room any longer. After some reflection he decided to disobey La Trémouille's orders and to set forth once more in search of the missing woman. Once he had found her—and he still had no doubt he would—he believed that he could readily obtain the Marshal's pardon.

In the course of the afternoon he explored, in the burning August heat, on horse, and followed by his servants, two country estates pointed out to him as belonging to Giocondo; but without success. Nor did he in reality have any hope of finding her there: even if the woman he was searching for had been hidden there previously, Ser Francesco, after what had happened the night before, was more than likely to have carried her elsewhere to safety.

Toward evening, having spoken not a single word for the past two or three hours, his heart aching at the memory of his beloved's smile, he rode back to the city. A desperate plan had taken shape within his breast. He had made up his mind to go once more to Ser Francesco and to force him to reveal his secret at the point of the sword.

Delicate dove-gray and flamingo-red cloud strips hung motionless in the silvery air.

As ill luck would have it, just as Bougainville was about to dismount in front of Giocondo's house, he espied in the dusky street the figure of a nobleman who, with two servants, was on the point of entering the house. Bougainville hastily sprang down from his horse and ran up to him.

"One word, sir!" he shouted in French, barring the man's way.

"Sir," replied, also in French, the noble, a handsome, if rather arrogant-looking young man with dark-blue eyes, and eyebrows that formed a continuous line, "what can I do for you?" And he shot a quick glance at Bougainville and at the group of servants and horses standing behind him.

"Are you," asked Bougainville, "acquainted with Ser Francesco del Giocondo? May I also inquire, because I should like to get further information from you, whether you know him well?"

"So well, in fact," was the reply of the nobleman, "that it

is my purpose just now to call upon him to express my regret at certain incidents that occurred in his house last night."

"And what was the nature of these incidents?" asked Bougainville, frowning.

"A madman," replied the aristocrat, accentuating each word, "a madman, accompanied by several other members of the suite of Monsieur de La Trémouille, broke into the house and insisted upon being told where Ser Francesco was keeping his long-dead wife. As I not only am a friend of Ser Francesco, but also was close to his late wife, I consider it my duty to tell him how shocked I am to hear of this insult to the memory of the dead." And at these words he gave the Frenchman a cold, haughty stare.

"Sir *gentiluomo*," said Bougainville, placing his hands on his hips, the blood rising to his face, "will you be so kind as to tell me who you are and I shall then, for a purpose you'll learn at once, tell you who I am!"

"This favor I can grant you," the noble replied. "For your information, then: I am Amerigo Capponi."

"And I," cried Bougainville, "Monsieur Capponi, who not only betray Ser Francesco, but also have the poor taste to call upon him in his own house, I am no other than that madman who broke in yesterday. And now you will fight with me!"

"I wouldn't think of it!" shouted Capponi. "You are, as everyone in the city knows, a crazy fool, and I have no intention of putting myself at the disposal of every imbecile who happens to come my way. Don't hold me up any longer! Off with you!"

"You are a coward!" cried Bougainville, reaching for his sword and moving in on him. "But you are mistaken if you think you can get away with that kind of talk! Draw, if you don't want me to spear an unarmed man against the wall like a rat!"

"Enough!" shouted Capponi. "Don't plague me any further with your idiocies! Step aside! Ho there, men!" he called in Italian, clapping his hands. "Get this booby out of my way!"

At this command Capponi's servants rushed forward and fell upon Bougainville with their sticks. So violent was the assault, he barely could hold them at bay. But at the same instant his own retainers also dashed up to pitch into the fray. They were followed in turn by various passers-by eager to join in the attack on the French. A tumult arose and shouts of "To arms!" and there was a general scuffle. In the scrimmage Capponi was finally forced to draw his sword. But scarcely had he got it out of its sheath when one of Bougainville's men, who had stolen up on him from behind, leaped on his neck. Capponi dropped the sword, fell forward under the weight of the assailant, and drove the blade right through his own body.

When they turned him over, his eyes were already closed. Only the lids, with their long, almost feminine lashes, were still quivering, and little bubbles of bloody foam had formed on his lips.

He died as he was being carried into Giocondo's house.

After the death of Capponi, La Trémouille was no longer able to answer for Bougainville's life. Before the Marshal's quarters the crowd gathered so threateningly that he would have brought up his artillery had not the cannon, which he had had made by the bell-casters at the expense of the Milanese, long since rumbled down through Umbria. It appeared that it would be impossible to leave the city without making some redress. It seemed only a matter of time before La Trémouille's quarters would be stormed. Thus the Marshal found himself compelled to sacrifice Bougainville, and he sentenced him to death by the sword.

Before his execution, the young man expressed only one last wish: to see Giocondo's wife.

In her stead he received in his room, before which a strong guard had been stationed—not so much to prevent his escaping as to protect him from the populace, who would have rent him limb from limb—a visit from Leonardo da Vinci.

"Poor, unhappy man!" the artist exclaimed. "So you still don't believe that she has been dead all this time!"

"Who?" asked Bougainville.

"La Gioconda, of course! The wife of Ser Francesco! The object of your ill-starred passion. Are you really insane, then?"

Bougainville did not reply at once. He clenched his teeth. "So she really no longer exists, this woman?" he said at last. "I must assume that you are speaking the truth, sir. For one doesn't lie to a dying man."

"Of course I am speaking the truth!" cried Leonardo. "And I have always told you the truth. But you, in your madness, wouldn't believe me, unfortunate man!"

Bougainville shrugged his shoulders and stared at the floor. Finally he said: "Why, in that case, do you call me unfortunate, Messer Leonardo? I would be unhappy only if I had to go on living. For as long as I lived I should never have found Mona Lisa. But as it is, I shall see her soon."

"Sir," said Leonardo, "one should not deprive a man who, after all, is facing a perhaps overestimated but nevertheless generally very much feared event, of his belief in certain pleasures that will follow this accident which we call death. The Turks and Moors, to be sure, are of the opinion that in heaven they will have the opportunity for the first time to enjoy to the full a pleasure usually thought to exist only on earth, which, when it comes down to it, was the thing you yourself labored so hard to attain—to your ruin, be it said. As one nobleman to another, however, I am bound to speak out frankly and boldly, and as one man of parts to another, though your recent behavior has not shown you to be such, I tell you that I fear that you will not possess your beloved in death any more than you could in life. I need have no anxiety that you, a condemned man, will accuse me of heresy. So I can freely confess to you that I think very little of those two fantasies of dying or timid mortals, heaven and hell. We should be sustained in life neither by the hope of bliss in the other world nor by the hope of some sort of physical raptures in an earthly paradise. The only thing that can give us strength is the pleasure we feel in truth and beauty, in honor and morality."

"You may be right in your contention that the hereafter is not so easy of access as the Church has thought proper to represent it," replied Bougainville after a few moments. "But you are wrong in rejecting it altogether. During these last remaining hours that have been vouchsafed me, I have had the opportunity to reflect on these matters, and I tell you that there are some things which are eternal and immortal. Above all, love. Nothing is more indestructible than love, where the souls of lovers are locked in a far tighter embrace than their bodies can ever be. But it is not even necessary to divide love into two sorts, a physical and a spiritual, an earthly and a heavenly. There is only one love. For it is the only thing that unites everything in itself. Nothing is capable of tearing asunder a double constellation of two lovers, two stars revolving about one another to eternity, not even God. Anyone who has really loved knows that, in comparison with this, everything else, even heaven and hell, is quite ephemeral. Nor is there any real death. There is, in reality, only one thing, love. Don't you agree with me?"

Leonardo made no reply. He gazed in silence at this young nobleman whom all this time he had regarded as insane, and who now had put him to shame by the greatness of his feeling.

"And now," went on Bougainville, "now tell me only how it could have been possible for me to have supposed that Giocondo's wife was still alive, that she was not in her grave. Why was it impossible for me to believe that she had died?"

"The explanation," replied Leonardo, "the explanation is quite simple. You loved her. And then, I have made inquiries and have discovered that she really wasn't buried in the tomb in Santa Croce. She died during the plague. She was buried somewhere with dozens of other corpses. But Giocondo, because of the prominence of his family and hers, did not want it known that she had been cast into a collective grave, and gave it out that she was buried in Santa Croce. That is the secret of which you were the victim. But I have one consolation to offer you. Didn't I once tell you that the woman one paints is never a real one? By the same token, one loves in truth only the woman who doesn't exist."

"Why should I console myself?" asked Bougainville. "Love needs no consolation. It doesn't even need to be requited. It needs only itself."

And a few moments later he was taken from the prison, led to the Old Market, and beheaded.

The execution took place before the entire populace. The Marshal was present, together with his suite, as were also several members of the *signoria*, the greater part of the nobility, and Da Vinci himself.

The spectacle of the milling crowd, of the harnesses glittering in the sun, of the horses, the scarlet cloak of the headsman, the flash of his sword, of all the many shapes and colors, was a splendid and imposing one. But Leonardo looked on with unseeing eyes.

He returned home immediately after the execution and with a few strokes of his brush altered the smile of La Gioconda. As he did so, he stood a little to the right of the picture at the very spot where Bougainville had stood when he looked at it, and the eyes of the woman, which were turned to the left, gazed at Leonardo as they had gazed at Philippe de Bougainville. After Leonardo had been painting for a few moments, the smile became completely transformed and the artist told himself that it was now perfect. It was utterly enchanting, mysterious, and enigmatical. It was impossible to tell whether the beauty was smiling about Bougainville or beckoning him with her smile to high heavens of rapture. No one knew what she was smiling about.

The next day the Marshal departed from Florence and went on to Naples. In December 1503 he was crushingly defeated by the Spaniards.

It is said that Leonardo worked for four more years on the picture of La Gioconda. But the truth of the matter is that he simply sat and stared at it.

When he went to Milan, he took it with him. Later he carried it to France and sold it to King Francis I for a very large sum in gold.

Ever since then it has remained in Paris and has been considered one of the most famous paintings in the world. There, too, countless people have fallen in love with it—among them, an idiot who painted it over, and a certain Vincenzo Peruggia, a glazier, who stole it and later, in Florence, returned it, no one knows quite why. People have tried to link the theft with a dreary love story in which a real woman was supposed to have figured. But the true explanation has never been discovered. Nor can it be known. The real reasons for anything can never be known.

It has also been contended that the picture in the Louvre is not genuine, but a forgery. But no one could entertain such a thought who had any real understanding either of the greatness of a true artist or of love.

Translated by Jane B. Greene

THE PICNIC OF MORES THE CAT
(as told by a Croatian nobleman)

by Clemens Brentano

My estate is situated in a lonely spot, a half-hour from the Turkish border, in a swampy wood where there is a most glorious and exasperating profusion of everything, including nightingales, which always wake you out of your sleep before dawn. Last summer the creatures had the effrontery to come so close and in such numbers that once, in a towering rage, I hurled my chamberpot at them. But I was soon to acquire a housemate who knew how to deal with them and who delivered me from the pests.

It was three years ago today, in the morning, that I set out for my fowling preserve, armed with a broadsword, a good double-barreled rifle, and a pair of double pistols, for I was on the lookout for a Turkish poacher and game-dealer to whom, for some time, I had been losing a lot of valuable game. When I warned him to keep out, he had replied insolently that I couldn't stop him from coming into my wood and that he meant to go on hunting right under my very nose.

When I reached the fowling preserve, I found all the springes and snares I had set emptied and realized that the rogue must

---

The son of an Italian-Swiss merchant who had settled in the Rhineland, Clemens Brentano was born in 1778. He joined the circle of the romanticists when still a student, and soon began to publish polemical essays, poetry, satirical stories, and dramas. He also wrote a novel and several longer stories. His place in German literature is secured through his joint editorship of Des Knaben Wunderhorn, *a collection of old German folk poems. His was a restless, thoroughly unhappy life. Married to a hysterical woman, he divorced her, thus thwarting his subsequent ambition to become a priest. He resided in various west German cities, in Vienna, and also for some years in a monastery. He died in 1842.*

have got there ahead of me. As I was resetting my traps, seething with rage, a big black cat strolled out of the bushes. It came up to me purring and behaved in so ingratiating a fashion that its fur caught my eye and I began to stroke it in the hopes of making a pet of it and perhaps of getting a cap for myself out of its winter coat.

In summer I always have a kind of live winter wardrobe in my hunting grounds. Four pairs of stout leather breeches are always running about the place in the form of live billy-goats, and among them is a magnificent bagpipe which, even now as a live billy-goat, is displaying such musical talents that the candidates for the various trouser legs, the moment he comes bleating into their midst, begin dancing and keeping step with one another, as though they were already aware that they were destined one day to dance with my legs in Hungarian fashion to this same bagpipe.

I had designs of a similar nature upon the black cat and, partly because he was as black as a Moor, partly because he had the most superb mores or manners, I gave him the name of Mores. The cat followed me home and proved himself so proficient at mouse-catching and at getting along with my dogs that I soon abandoned the idea of turning him out of his skin. Mores was my constant companion and slept at night on a leather chair beside my bed. Several things struck me as particularly odd about the animal. Every now and then I would try, for the fun of it, to get him to drink some wine from my glass, only to meet with the most strenuous resistance. But once I caught him in the cellar dangling his tail in the bunghole and afterward licking it with the greatest gusto. Mores also differed from other cats in that, whereas his kind usually has an aversion to water, he was very fond of taking a bath. All these eccentricities made Mores famous in my neighborhood. I allowed him the run of the place. He hunted on his own and cost me nothing but coffee, which he guzzled with inordinate pleasure.

So I had had him as my constant companion and roommate for some time when for the last two days and nights before Christmas he failed to appear. It had already occurred to me that some poacher, perhaps even my neighbor at the Turkish border, might have shot Mores down or caught him, and for this reason I sent one of my men over to the game-dealer to see if he could find out anything about the matter. But the man came back with the news that the game-dealer knew nothing about my cat, that he had just returned from a trip to Constantinople, bringing his wife a collection of handsome cats; that, as it happened, he was glad to have heard about my fine animal and would try his best to get his hands on it, as he was in need of a pasha for his seraglio.

Great was my annoyance when I received this news on Christmas Eve, and I longed all the more to recover my Mores since I did not care to lose him to the Turkish rogue. I went to bed early that evening because at midnight I planned to attend Mass at the church an hour's ride away. My servant awakened me at the proper time. I strapped on my pistols and sword and slung my double-barreled rifle, loaded with buckshot, over my shoulder. Then I set out. It was the coldest winter night I have ever experienced. I was all bundled up like Father Christmas himself. My smoldering tobacco pipe froze up several times, the fur around my neck stiffened from my frosty breath like a porcupine, and the hard snow crackled under my boots. The wolves were howling all around my property and I ordered my men to go out after them.

I had come out on the open field beneath a starlit sky and could already see in the distance an oak tree that stood on an island in the middle of a frozen pond and marked the halfway point of my expedition to the village where the church was situated. Suddenly I heard an extraordinary music. For a moment I thought it must be some band of peasants who were whiling away the time on their way to church by playing a bagpipe. So I quickened my pace a little in order to catch up with them. But the closer I got, the wilder this curious music became, until finally it dissolved into a wail. I had nearly reached the tree before I realized that the sounds were coming from out of its branches.

I took my gun in hand, cocked it, and crept across the solid pond to the oak. And what did I see? What did I hear? My hair stood on end. The whole tree was alive with howling cats, and at the very top was enthroned my cat Mores, his back arched, playing in the most wretched fashion on a bagpipe, while the other cats, uttering bloodcurdling cries, were dancing about him in the branches.

For a while I stood there transfixed with horror. But soon the sound of the bagpipe produced such a curious twitching in my legs that I too began to dance and very nearly tumbled into a hole that had been cut in the ice by some fishermen. But just then the church bell rang out through the starry night and I came to my senses. Seizing my rifle, I fired the entire load into the midst of the infamous dancing chorus, and instantly the whole crew shot down from the oak like hail and swept over me like a swarm of bees. So violent was the impact, I slipped on the ice and fell flat on my back. When I picked myself up, the field was clear, and I was amazed to find not a single cat, wounded or dead, under the tree.

I was so terrified and addled by the episode that I gave up all idea of going to church. I hurried home and fired my pistols several times to summon my servants. At this signal they quickly appeared and I related to them my adventure. "Your lordship can set his mind at rest," said one of them, an experienced old fellow, "we shall soon find the cats that your lordship shot."

Greatly disquieted, I went into the house, and after drinking some warm wine to calm myself after my terrifying experience, I retired to bed.

Toward morning, becoming aware of a noise, I awakened out of an uneasy sleep, and saw lying there beside me as usual, on the leather chair, my confounded cat, Mores—with his fur all singed. A black rage came over me and I began to tremble in every limb. "*Passavanélkiterémentete!*" I screamed, "infamous witch's scum, are you back again?" And I reached for a new pitchfork that was standing beside my bed, but the beast lunged at my throat and tried to strangle me—I shouted for help. My servants came rushing to my assistance with drawn sabers and slashed out at my Mores in no uncertain fashion. He shot up one wall and down the other, finally broke open a windowpane and plunged down into the wood below, where it would have been futile to try to pursue him. But we were quite sure that Sir Mores had received a sufficient number of saber wounds to keep him from ever again blowing the bagpipe.

I was horribly scratched, and my neck and face swelled up in a hideous fashion. I sent for the Slavonian dairymaid, who worked for me, to have her cook me a poultice, but she was nowhere to be found and I was forced to drive to the village, where there was an army surgeon.

When we reached the oak where the nocturnal concert had taken place, we saw a figure up in the branches crying piteously for help. I soon recognized Mladka, the Slavonian maid. She was hanging half frozen by her skirt, which had been caught in the branches, and her blood was dripping down on the snow. We also saw bloody tracks leading away from the tree into the woods. I knew then how matters stood with the Slavonian girl. I had her carried to the wagon, so that her body would not touch the ground, and securely bound. Then we drove off at top speed to the village with the witch.

As soon as I arrived at the surgeon's house, the vice-governor and the local priest were summoned immediately. All the evidence was taken down, and the maid, Mladka, was cast into prison.

Luckily for her, she died of the bullet wound she had received; otherwise she would certainly have been burned at the stake. She was a beautiful figure of a woman, and her skeleton was sent to Budapest and placed in a natural-history cabinet as a specimen of fine bone structure.

She repented sincerely and died weeping bitterly. On her testimony several other females in the district were to have been arrested, but two of them were found dead in their beds, and the rest had fled.

After I recovered, I had to make an expedition across the Turkish border with a district commission. We reported to the authorities our complaints against the wild-game-dealer, only to find that we had stepped out of the frying-pan into the fire. We were told that the game-dealer, together with his wife and various Turkish, Serbian, and Slavonian girls, had returned home with bullet and saber wounds and soon after had died, stating on his deathbed that on his way back from a wedding he had been attacked by me at the border and brought to this sorry pass. While we were listening to this accusation, a crowd of people gathered about, and the wife of the game-dealer, with several women and girls bandaged from head to foot, raised a loud outcry against us. The judge told us that he could not protect us, that we must make our getaway as best we could. We dashed out into the courtyard and leaped on our horses. The district commissioner was put in the middle, I placed myself at the head of the six hussars who had accompanied us, and we galloped out of the village at such a pace that we got off with nothing worse than a few stones, a few wild shots, and a volley of Turkish curses. The Turks pursued us over the frontier, but were dealt with by the hussars so effectively that a few of them at least will have given a report of the outcome to the game-dealer in Mohammed's paradise.

When I arrived home, the first thing I did was to examine my bagpipe, which I found lying under my bed. It was punctured with three bullet holes. So it was Mores who had been playing on my own bagpipe and had been protected by it from my shot!

Nor was this the end of my troubles over this miserable affair. Again and again I was called in to give evidence. One commissioner after another came out to my estate and had to be entertained in fine style. The Turks complained of frontier violation, and before the legal fuss finally died down, I had to pay out several more pieces of game and a considerable sum of money, and my servants and I were made to testify once more under oath.

To add to this, I was examined several times by the county doctor to determine the state of my sanity, and he could not be persuaded to make up his mind until after I had sent him a couple of pairs of double pistols and his wife a strip of black fox fur and several excellent game roasts. Then at last the matter was dropped.

Translated by Jane B. Greene

ZERLINE, THE OLD SERVANT GIRL

by Hermann Broch

The church clocks of the city had just struck two—a confused medley of sounds in which only the quaint, chime-like tones issuing from the castle church up on the little hill overlooking the town were clearly distinguishable. The summer Sunday moved toward its decline, more tediously and indeed more slowly than any weekday, and A., reclining on his living-room sofa, observed that the boredom of Sunday is atmospheric: the suspension of mass activity has been communicated to the air, and anyone who does not wish to be affected by it must fill up his Sunday with twice or three times as much work. On weekdays, even when one is completely idle, one does not hear any church clocks.

Work? A. thought of the office that he had set up for himself in the business section of the town. At times he displayed there a positively brisk activity, but often he merely passed the days in idleness, though actually his thoughts never ceased to revolve about money and money-making. This annoyed him. There was something uncanny about his natural flair for money-making. To be sure, he liked to eat, he liked to drink, and he

---

A native of Vienna (1886), Hermann Broch was trained as a mathematician. Not before his late thirties did he take up the systematic study of philosophy, at the same time abandoning a conventional business career. His novel trilogy, The Sleepwalkers *(translated by Willa and Edwin Muir), established him as one of the important authors of his times. Imprisoned by the Nazis in 1938, he went, upon his release, to the United States. Living in Princeton, New Jersey, he finished his vast prose poem,* The Death of Virgil *(translated by Jean Starr Untermeyer), and under the auspices of the Rockefeller Foundation embarked on psychological and epistemological research. He died, an American citizen, in 1951 in New Haven, Connecticut, where he had been connected with Yale University.*

enjoyed a more or less comfortable life. But he did not like money as such. On the contrary, he took pleasure in giving it away. Why, then, this uncanny facility for attracting money far beyond his needs? The problem of making good solid investments had always been more difficult for him than that of acquiring money in the first place. Now he was buying up real estate and houses. Purchased with devalued marks, they cost him virtually nothing. And yet he took no pleasure in it: it was like some burdensome obligation.

Because of the morning sun, the jalousies had been lowered, and he had been too lazy, despite the shade of the afternoon, to raise them again. Actually, it made little difference. Darkened, the room would stay cooler, and in the evening the windows would be opened. Again and again this indolence of his had worked to his advantage. In reality, however, he was not lazy; he was merely decision-shy. He was unable to wrest anything from fate by open defiance. He left it to fate to make his decisions for him, and in these he would acquiesce, not, however, without exercising a certain watchfulness, a cunning all the more necessary because this court of decision had contrived a remarkable system for his guidance. It would encompass him with dangers from which he was forced to take flight, and the flight would then bring in money. His insane fear of being examined, his fear of the examining professors (in whose hands fate has placed that fear-inspiring weapon, a knowledge of the most intimate secrets of the examinee, which makes him as empty of knowledge as if he had never possessed any)—this insane fear of being cross-questioned had caused him fifteen years before to flee to Africa. Without a cent—his father, infuriated by his son's conduct, had paid his passage and nothing more—he had landed on the East African coast, decision-shy and penniless, but happy, because, entering upon the unknown, he felt no dread of an examiner, but only a trust in fate.

A truster in fate he became at that time. It came about in the form of a watchful dreaminess, and for that very reason, perhaps as a result of the watchfulness, perhaps as a result of the dreaminess, he had never again, from this time forth, lacked for money. Whether as gardener's boy, waiter, or clerk (in the beginning he took a whole series of jobs of this sort), he discharged his duties satisfactorily as long as no one inquired into his qualifications and previous experience. The moment he was questioned, he would quit the position, each time, to be sure, with a somewhat larger sum in his pocket, because each time there had been an opportunity, as there always is in the colonies, for all sorts of business on the side, and before long the business on the side became the main business. It took him to Capetown, it took him to Kimberley, it took him into a diamond syndicate in which he became a partner, and always it was his fate that took him from one place to another, his avoidance of unpleasantnesses, his avoidance of the interrogations that he would have had to face somewhere else. He could not remember ever having taken a step of his own free will; rather, his inability to make a decision always had induced a certain laziness, that industrious laziness which was his trust in fate and which had brought him success. "Lazy digestion of life, lazy digestion of fate," said something within him, and this brought him, well pleased with himself, back to the present. Let the Sunday slip away, trickle away; let the jalousies remain closed. It would all turn out for the best.

Then—perhaps after a timid knock—the door opened a crack and through it, craning its neck like a bird, appeared the old crone's head of Zerline, the servant girl.

"Are you sleeping?"

"No, no—come right in."

"She's sleeping."

"Who?" That was a stupid question. Zerline could only have meant the old Baroness.

A look of contempt, like a breeze of scorn, flitted across the wrinkles: "The one in there—she's sleeping soundly." And, partly by way of explanation for the quiet of the afternoon, partly as the first number on her program, she added at once: "Hildegard has gone out—the bastard."

"What?"

She had now come all the way into the room, and while maintaining a respectful distance, she placed one hand, because of her arthritic knee, on the edge of the chest of drawers in order to steady herself. "She got another man to make the girl for her," she confided. "Hildegard is a bastard."

Much as he would have liked to hear more, he couldn't allow

this. "See here, Zerline, I am a boarder here and such things are none of my business—I can't even listen to them."

She gazed down at him shaking her head: "But you're thinking about it—what are you thinking about?"

Her searching glance annoyed and discomfited him. Weren't his trousers properly buttoned? He had the unpleasant feeling of being trapped and would have liked to tell her that he was thinking about his financial affairs. But what had come over her to make her cross-question him? He remained silent.

She perceived his embarrassment, but refused to give in. "It will become your business once she crawls into your bed."

"Tell me, Zerline, what has come over you?"

Unperturbed, she continued: "She is always running off, and if she had a proper lover, one she slept with, it would be all right. Then she'd be a real woman. . . . But she's a humbug if ever I saw one—she plays the real woman who runs secretly to her lover and covers up, because she doesn't know any better, with clumsy lies. . . . The clumsiness is part of the act too. She takes along her prayer book as though she were going to church, because everyone knows just when the church services really are and everyone sees through her transparent subterfuge, is supposed to see through it. . . . What comes out of her mouth is sham lies, double lies at that, and back of them there's something horrible. . . . I'd better not think about what she might be doing with the prayer book in bed, yet I'll find out—I find out everything."

She paused a moment, and as A., who had closed his eyes in an effort to discourage her, made no reply, she came a few steps closer, sliding one hand along the edge of the bureau and letting the other hang down rather stiffly. "I find out everything, and I also found out how El—how the Baroness had the child made to her back in those days—and I found out very quickly too. I wasn't so young or so dumb even then, though that was a long time ago, more than thirty years. Then, yes then, I was still with the Frau General—that was the Frau Baroness's blessed mother. There was a fine house. I was first lady's maid, and the second was what you might call my A.D.C., and we had a cook and a scullery girl besides. And as long as His Excellency, the Herr General, was still alive, there was an orderly there for the heavy work in the house and to help with the waiting on table too. But by this time His Excellency had already died, and one fine day, it was February and I remember as though it were yesterday how the damp snow stuck to the windowpanes, her ladyship rang for me, and when I came up she said: 'Zerlin',' she said, 'Zerlin', we shall have to cut down our household here, but I don't want to lose you entirely.' Yes, yes, that's just how she put it. 'Wouldn't you like to go to my daughter? She's expecting a child, and I'd rather have you in the house with my grandchild than some strange nursemaid.' Yes, that's what she said, and I went obediently. Though with a heavy heart. I was no longer as young as I might have been and, God knows, would rather have had children of my own to take care of. But when a girl goes into service, she has to put such thoughts out of her head. For a girl to go into service means giving up all that, and a child is a calamity one's afraid of. Too bad—I would have been good for a dozen children. When I went to work for her ladyship, I was just a young thing. . . ." She made a bold gesture with her arm that was probably supposed to suggest a shout of joy, but was almost Goya-like in its grotesqueness. "You should have seen me then. Everything about me was firm and round, and my breasts stood out so that everyone wanted to get his hands on them. Even the Herr Baron, who at that time was not yet a presiding judge, but only a judge of the lower court, couldn't restrain himself. You think he shouldn't have done it because he was a young married man and it wasn't seemly for someone like him? Dear no, it wasn't that. It was that he was one of those people who are way above lust and can't allow themselves, for their souls' sake, to desire any woman. Probably he never even desired her." She pointed her thumb back toward the door. "No, she wasn't made to give him much fun. As for me, now, I could have given him the fun and yet I didn't want to, though he was a handsome man. It would have hurt his soul. Instead I played about with the orderlies of His Excellency, and though I nearly always enjoyed it, it still wasn't much good. Almost never the proper way in bed. Always with your clothes on and hurry-up-quick in the dark room, in the parlor when the master and the mistress were at the theater. That's what it's like for a girl who comes to the city to go into service. The fellows had their girls at home in the village, and though they might have had more fun with me and I might have been prettier than the one back home, it made no difference to them. The one that waits has the better right. And so it went. The years of youth's flower"—this apparently was a quotation—"they passed away. For more than twelve years I was with Her Excellency, and then that one"—again she pointed her thumb behind her—"not I, got pregnant. Though I was much better-looking than she. She won. And I took the job with her and her bastard."

She paused long enough to heave a deep sigh. Then, paying very little attention to her listener, who by now had pulled himself up to a sitting position, she continued:

"By the time the child, Hildegard, was born, the Herr Baron was nearly fifty and had just become presiding judge. Perhaps he didn't much like my coming into the house, because I doubt if he'd forgotten any more than I had that he once put his hands on my breasts. Such things have no date, they last forever. Now though, no matter how well I carried myself or how good I was to look at, he had no more eyes for me. He had become what he certainly had been destined to become, a man who no longer desires any woman. And even if he hadn't been able to any more, there are plenty who really aren't able to and therefore want to all the more. Those are the ugliest. With him, though, the not-being-able-to came out of the not-wanting-to, and that's why he became more and more handsome. If Hildegard had been his, she would have been a beautiful woman."

A. now felt called upon to contradict: "She is a beautiful woman, and the first time I saw the portrait of the judge there in the dining-room, I was immediately struck by the likeness."

Zerline snickered: "It was I and no one else who made them alike. Again and again I would take the child up to the picture and teach her to look as he is looking there—the look is everything."

This was certainly surprising. A. became thoughtful. "Along with his look she should also have acquired his spirit."

"That's just what I wanted, just that. . . . But she's a woman and has the blood of the other."

"Who was the other?" Something far stronger than mere curiosity impelled him, in spite of himself, to ask this question.

"The other?" Zerline smiled. "Oh, the other, he used to

come to tea at Her Excellency's from time to time, and at first I didn't notice how often the Frau Baroness was there, too, and without her husband. But that the other, Herr von Juna, was also very handsome, that struck me right off. A rusty brown goatee, he had, rusty-brown curls, a skin like darkened meerschaum, and he carried himself as if he were off to a ball. Yes, you had to hand it to her, she knew how to pick them. Only with this one, if you really looked at him, behind the fine goatee and even behind the handsome mouth, you could spot the ugliness in his face, the not-being-able-to and still-wanting-to, the ugly lechery that has weakness in it. One like that is easy to get, and if I'd wanted him I could have had him from the first moment as easy as that." She snapped her fingers as though she were crushing an imaginary flea. "Her Excellency told me he was someone who was always traveling, in the diplomatic service, what they call a diplomat. So far so good. He'd settled down in the old hunting-box out there in the wood"—she made a gesture with her arm to indicate some distant spot. "Not on account of the hunting, but on account of the women he always had with him. Of course, people didn't have much to go on except rumors, but he did everything to make them curious with his sudden appearances and disappearances and all those women of his. I was curious too. And I couldn't get a thing out of the forester's wife who looked after the house for him. She kept her mouth shut. I doubt if he passed that one over, she more or less filled the bill. That's how he lived, and the child looked like him from the start. But how was it going to be introduced to him, this child? I was anxious to see. Well, she thought up a good scheme. The grandchild was to pay a visit to its grandmamma the day it was two years old. So that was it. We drove over to Her Excellency's. The child was put down to sleep in the guest-room, and wild horses couldn't have dragged me out of there, for I knew he would show up as if by chance. And I had pictured, too, just exactly how *she* would give herself away. I didn't have to wait very long and I almost burst out laughing when she brought him up so promptly, and I had an even harder time to keep from laughing at the way he bent over the bed, the papa, and she couldn't hide her feelings and reached for his hand. It was real feeling, and yet there was something phony about it. He, on the other hand, was more cagey. He saw that I had been watching her, and as he went out, as though to rid himself of his fatherhood, he shot me a look that told me that I and not she was the right one for him. And I, not to be caught napping, let him see I had understood."

The answering smile that she had then given him appeared once more on her face, as though summoned back by some enchantment from out of the past, and shimmered there now as an echo of itself, wrinkled with age, faded with age. And, because of its very witheredness, it had become something abiding, an answer that abides forever.

"I let him feel it and I felt it myself, saw how it went right into him and took away his peace of mind, so that he would never find peace until he had slept with me. That's how I wanted it to be. I was just as much shaken by it myself, though neither he nor I had meant it that way. Man is cheap. And it's not only the poor servant girl from the country that's cheap, it's everyone. It's only the saint that has the wisdom and the strength not to have to be cheap. But even for lust, no matter how cheap, it takes strength, and the ones who want to deny their cheapness out of sheer weakness, out of sheer inability to lust, are the worst of all. They want to have it dear and they're even cheaper, the ones that look down their noses, that lie out of squeamishness, that lie out of weakness; all the ones that try to drown out lust with a great soul-clamor because it isn't fine enough for their souls, or even more often because they don't know a thing about it and think that it can be coaxed out and held with the clamor. They want to snare the lust with their souls, but at the same time it's supposed to be drowned out.

"And the Frau Baroness? Voice never raised by day! But at night, I'll wager, nothing but soul-clamor! Of course you have to make allowances for her because she was never a real woman, and could never learn to be one with that stern saintliness of the Baron's. So it was only natural that she should fall for the other, the lecher. The child she managed to get with him on their last trip to the baths. That checked to the exact day. But then? Why didn't she go the whole way with him? Why didn't she run out to him in the hunting-box? Oh dear no. Her lust was too small for that, her fear too great. She was far too weak and dishonest. You might just as well have suggested that she lie down with him in the public marketplace. But still I wanted to help her, all jealousy aside and at the cost, so to speak, of my own lust, but I couldn't get it across to her.

"Finally, once when the judge had gone to Berlin, I came right out with it. 'Frau Baroness,' I said, 'Frau Baroness, you should invite guests in now and then.' 'Guests?' she answered stupidly. 'Who?' To which I replied sort of casually: 'Well, for example, Herr von Juna.' Then she looked at me suspiciously out of the corner of her eye and said: 'Oh no, not him.' 'Leave well enough alone, if that's how it is,' I thought to myself. But meanwhile my words had sunk in, and after a few days she asked him for dinner. At that time we still had the fine villa, and parlors and dining-room were on the ground floor. There was no such clutter of furniture as we have here where you bump into things all the time and the work's never done, especially when you don't even get any help from Hildegard. So it was a regular dining-room and the Frau Baroness and he sat there at a proper distance from each other. I waited on table and didn't return his glances either, and afterward asked permission to retire. My room in the attic there was a lot finer, of course, than my room here. But when I crept down later to see how things were going, it was the same as before, and they were calmly sitting side by side, this time in the parlor. There was a bored look in his beautiful, wistful eyes, and even when she got up to pour him a fresh cup of coffee, even then he never once tried to touch her hand, let alone to fondle it. 'She's thrown that one away too,' I thought to myself. When people have nothing but love in bed and never drum out lust with their legs, it's bad. When all was said and done, they'd missed out on everything, and deep down I felt sorry for them, for him especially, since, after all, they were bound to each other on account of the child. To be sure, still deeper down I was pleased, and that's why I was ready waiting for him among the bushes in the front garden, so that he was hardly out of the house when, without a moment's hesitation, without a single word, we plunged like lightning into our kiss. I clung to his mouth so hard with my lips, with my teeth, with my tongue, that I all but fainted away, and yet I resisted him. I couldn't understand in the least why I didn't simply tumble over onto the grass with him, and still less why I didn't drag him up to my room as he begged me to, his voice all hoarse, but had to answer instead: 'In the hunting-box.' But when at these words the look of wild panic came into his eyes, the panic of madness, such as you see in an animal, which told me plainly that he had a woman sitting out there and that therefore I had asked for the impossible, then it dawned on me that what I was really after when I resisted was this impossible thing and the forcing of the impossible. What had been itching me was not so much my lust as this obstinate and relentless curiosity about the hunting-box. And yet I realized that this too is a part of lust, its bitterness and its misery."

The agitation that all this could still arouse in her forced her to sit down, and she was silent for a while, her elbows propped on the table and her head between her fists. When she again resumed her story, it was in a completely altered voice. It was a whisper, a whispered singsong, and it was as though quite another person were speaking.

"Man is cheap, and his memory is full of holes that he can never patch up. How much of what you forget forever you have to do in order for what you have done to be able to carry the little that you keep forever. Everyone forgets his everyday life. With me it was all the furniture that I dusted day after day, all the plates that had to be wiped, and like everyone else, I sat down every day to eat. But as with everyone, it's only a knowing about it, not a real remembering, as though it had all happened without any weather, good or bad. Even the lust that I enjoyed has become a space without weather, and though my gratitude for what was alive has remained, the names and features that once meant lust and even love to me have vanished more and more from my mind, vanished into a glass gratitude that has no content any more. Empty glasses, empty glasses. And yet if it weren't for the emptiness, if it weren't for the forgotten, the unforgettable wouldn't have been able to grow. The forgotten carries empty-handed the unforgettable, and we are carried by the unforgettable. With the forgotten we feed time, we feed death, but the unforgettable is death's gift to us, and while at the moment when we receive it we are, to be sure, still here, right where we're standing, we are at the same time back there where the world plunges into darkness. For the unforgettable is a bit of the future, is the bit of timelessness given us in advance, which carries us and makes our plunge into the dark so gentle that it is as if we were floating down. And everything that happened between me and Herr von Juna was one of those dark-gentle, timeless gifts of death, and one day it will help to carry me down gently, itself carried by the complete memory. People will say that that was love, love unto death. No, it has nothing to do with love, still less with soul-clamor. Much can become unforgettable, can carry us as it stays with us, can stay with us as it carries us, without ever having been love, with no possibility of becoming love. The unforgettable is a moment of ripeness produced by an infinite number of previous moments, previous similarities; and carried by them, the moment when we perceive that shaping, we are being shaped, have become shaped. It is dangerous to confuse that with love."

That is how A. heard it, but there's no certainty that Zerline had really spoken these words. Elderly people occasionally break into a kind of mumbling chant, and it is easy to imagine something into it, particularly on a hot summer Sunday afternoon behind closed jalousies. A. wanted to make certain that he had heard aright and waited to see whether the singsong would begin again, but Zerline had returned to her ordinary old woman's speech.

"It goes without saying that he could have overcome my resistance there among the bushes in the garden. Had he done so, I would doubtless have forgotten him, as I have forgotten so many others. But he didn't. The weak, as often as not, are crafty, and it makes no difference anyway whether he allowed himself to be sent away out of weakness or out of craftiness. In any case his leaving threw me into a frenzy. Scarcely had he gone when I fell into a state of frenzied impatience, and, given my nature, it was a miracle that I was able to restrain myself, that I didn't write him to come right to my room. But a good miracle. For before the week was up, there was a letter there from him. Then I had to laugh. He had written the address in block letters on a business envelope, so that the Frau Baroness wouldn't see that he was corresponding with me too. Inside, it said that he would be waiting for me the very next evening out near the tramway terminus to go for a ride in the trap. And though the Frau Baroness downstairs might also have had a letter from him and read it, it was still a kind of victory over her.

"While he said not a word about the hunting-box in my letter, which meant that he still had the woman out there, for that very reason I was right there on the spot the next day, and before I climbed up on the seat with him, I told him everything straight out to his face. He wouldn't give any answer, and since that was in itself like an admission of guilt, I kissed him and said: 'Let's be off, drive me anywhere at all, only not to the hunting-box, more's the pity.' Then he said: 'The next time in the hunting-box.' I asked whether that was a promise, and he said yes. 'Will you really send her away?' I asked, and again he said yes. And to make quite sure, I asked whether she had manicured hands. 'Yes,' he replied, greatly surprised. 'Why?' Then I pulled off my gloves and laid my two red hands on the fine carriage robe that was spread over our knees and I said: 'Washerwoman's hands.' He looked down at the hands and didn't let on whether he was shocked or not, but said: 'Every man needs a good strong hand to wash away his guilt.' Then he took my hands and kissed them, but on the wrists and not where they were red, and then I knew how things stood, and all I could manage to say was: 'Drive on.' Otherwise I would have burst into tears. So we drove along the narrow road between the harvest fields and I gazed out across them and then glanced down at the little strip of turf between the two dusty carriage tracks on which our horses were planting fresh hoofprints and here and there a fresh horse-dropping. It was like being back home in the village. Only I didn't like his black horses. Peasants don't plow with black horses. Black horses are supposed to carry men into the great darkness. But when I told him that, he laughed and said: 'You are my field and my darkness.' That made me so happy that I slid over close to him. Even today, old as I am, I can still feel the heat of the desire that welled up in me, I can feel the desire for the child that he should have made for me, more and more of them, many children. Don't say I loved him. I wanted to take him on, take him in, but not to love him. He was dark and strange, an unholy one. And even then, at the cool edge of the forest where you already felt the night, though it still hung suspended in invisibility between the tree-trunks, I didn't give in to my desire. He stopped the carriage, but I didn't get out, and to hurt us both I reminded him that his child was waiting for me and that I shouldn't stay away any longer. 'Nonsense!' he cried, and because it was no nonsense, I heartlessly bored still deeper: 'If you make my own children for me I won't need this one any more.' He stared at me in utter dismay, again with that wild panic in his eyes, this time, no doubt, because it had suddenly dawned on him that he had saddled himself with yet a third woman, a new woman with new demands, though a chambermaid is not supposed to make any. In order to put Herr von Juna and the chambermaid back on an equal footing, and because his desire was in such bitter conflict with his terror, I kissed him, as though in farewell, with all the passion of which I was capable. Meekly and without a word of protest, he then drove me back to the trolley, and though it had been left that his next letter was to call me to the hunting-box, and though I burned with longing to go there, I didn't for a moment believe I would."

Apparently the time had come to introduce another dramatic silence, during which she moistened her weary lips before resuming her tale.

"And because I never hoped to get that letter, I was doubly vexed that the Frau Baroness, to whom the hunting-box was an object of terror rather than of desire, should get letters from him. And out of jealous vexation I wanted to get hold of them. They were, of course, sent poste restante, but perhaps I could find an envelope with the password on it. Well, so I rummaged through the Frau Baroness's wastebasket every day, and in no time I had the password. Timid, yes, but cautious, no, the Frau Baroness! And to make it really transparent, they had simply turned Elvire, the Christian name of the Frau Baroness, into 'Ilvere'; that was the password. So from then on, whenever I went out shopping or with the baby-carriage, I collected most of the letters at the postoffice window, carefully steamed them open, and after reading them, dropped them back in the box with fresh stamps. A few I stole. But with rubbish like that it was no robbery. Such rubbish! Such soul-clamor! Besides the 'elf queen,' which is what the Elvire queen had turned into, there was just a lot of whimpering about saintliness and chaste motherhood and about the 'elf baby' and 'God's baby,' and, to make it worse, God's elf baby was howling beside me to get me to change its diapers. But the worst was the endless complaining and carrying on about the woman out in the hunting-box. I made careful note of that, and the most disgusting parts I stole. This woman was a 'clinging bur,' a 'burden of fate,' someone 'who refuses to clear out of the picture,' a 'blackmailer who is taking advantage of my criminal weakness.' And then he threatened that he would 'find a way to do away with the evil, root and branch.' Yes, he wrote that, and finally he wrote that he wished that she—'you, my love'—'could deal in like manner' with her 'tyrannical husband.' Of course he knew what he was about. Only with soul-clamor could he fulfill his obligation to a person like the Frau Baroness and at the same time hold her at bay; and that he should have wished the one out there in the hunting-box in Jericho, since because of her he couldn't sleep with me, I was quite willing to believe. But it made me sick anyway. This disgusting eating-your-cake-and-having-it-too. Yes, I, a village girl who had never had any schooling, felt ashamed to the depths of my soul for this educated gentleman who had written all these lies, and I was all the more ashamed since this was the man for whom all my senses yearned. I was almost glad that I was not fine enough in his eyes for such fibbing letters, and that I didn't get any.

"But then the letter came, was suddenly there, just two lines in which he asked when I wanted to come to the hunting-box. God knows what joy I felt then. He had kept his word. And coming right on top of all that rotten nonsense of his that I had been reading during those weeks, this was important. It was so important to me to be able to respect him and not to be disappointed again that I had to restrain the wild impatience that broke out in me and impose on myself another three days of waiting. What I really wanted was to intercept his next letter to the Frau Baroness. If he had boasted in it that it was for her sake that he had sent the woman away from the hunting-box, I would never have wanted to see him again. I was trembling as I took the letter at the window. I nearly dropped it into the boiling water as I was opening it, and when there was really nothing in it about sending the woman away—I couldn't believe my eyes. Finally I did believe them and raced up to the

Frau Baroness to ask for time off to go home. Four weeks I asked for. She gave me three."

Suddenly she came back from out of the past and realized where she was. And with great vehemence she began to smooth out the creton cover under the vase on the table in front of her, as though there were some hidden wrinkle that had to be conjured up in order to give meaning to this meaningless activity. But she had not wholly emerged from the dream of the past. "It sustains me through the years, and the years pass, and it would stay with me even if I were to tell it a thousand times. Try as I may, I can't get rid of it." And as A. was about to make some reply she motioned him to be silent. "Will I ever get rid of it?" she laughed, and began once more.

"You won't believe me when I tell you that I was sorry for the Frau Baroness. That had begun a long time back when I used to listen at the bedroom door and there was not a sound to be heard. And though I was glad that the Herr Baron, with his strictness, wanted it that way, still she had let him down as well as herself, and there was something pitiful and indecent about it that made me sorry for her. But when later I set eyes on that lying scribble, much as it pained me that he had to write her and had to write her in just that way, I became even sorrier, because she didn't know any better and because her answers, which, of course, I should also have liked to read, must have been full of even uglier falsehoods. Wasn't I downright rich beside her?" She gazed triumphantly at A.

And A. perceived that what she was recounting was the greatest victory of her life. But he also perceived that the letters of Herr von Juna were not quite as mendacious as old Zerline had represented them. For in the dæmonic lust by which this man was possessed, there is on the one hand, and this is its best part, the deep seriousness in which the lust is enacted, its unerring honesty; on the other hand, however, there is the sense of guilt which is inseparable from any kind of the dæmonic, the eclipsing of the ego. Thus while the man who succumbs to lust may with perfect justification recoil from the mendaciousness of the lustless woman, yet to him, in the dark night of his ego, her very lack of lust, and especially if this incompleteness has been converted into motherhood, becomes something brighter that he cannot grasp, becomes something more mysterious and magical and elfin which his own earthliness is compelled to serve. This is not confined to the voluptuary alone, but exists, to some degree, in every man, and it was his realization of this that gave A. a feeling of sympathy for Herr von Juna, a feeling of secret complicity. It was not that he doubted for a moment the veracity of Zerline's account, but for him too an elfin-queen aura was woven about the figure of the Baroness. But now the tale of victory had been taken up once more.

"He kept his word and I was rich, though I went out with nothing but a little servant girl's grip. I could have left in the morning, but I wanted to get there at night and so it was already quite dark. He was waiting there again at the tram terminus with the black horses. We were both solemn. Riches make you solemn. With me it was the riches and I wished it would be the same for him. But who knows what makes other people solemn? And in my distrust I announced, as I sat down beside him on the seat, that I had only ten days off. 'It will be lovely,' I thought to myself, 'if I can ever let him know that there are ten more days and, if God is gracious, the eternity of a whole lifetime.' But just then he was so silent and solemn that I quickly swallowed my disappointment at his not showing any regret about the shortness of the ten days. 'Go by a roundabout way,' I begged him.

"So we drove at an even pace down into the wood and up onto the hill. It was a woodmen's road, and it was cool and pitch-dark there, and he didn't reach out to take hold of me, nor I of him. Up there on the hilltop it was still dusky-light. For a moment or so we could still make out the bluebells with which the glade was covered, and then only the sky was light, and at the same time you could see the first stars. The piles of logs soon vanished also into the blackness, leaving behind them only their odor, as though it had been taken prisoner by the chirping of the crickets. For each thing there, cricket chirp, bluebell, and star, carried the other without ever touching it. In the midst of all this we drew rein, and everything that was there I have retained and shall retain forever, because it has carried me and never ceases to carry me. And everything there shared in our desire. His was linked with mine and mine with his, and his hand never touched mine nor mine his. Then I said:

'Drive home.' It was still darker now as we drove down. The black horses trod cautiously, and when their hoofs struck a bit of rock, there were sparks. The brakes were on hard, and the wheels scraped. Sometimes there was sound of crunching stone. Sometimes a twig with moist leaves would strike me across the face. Nothing of that can I ever forget. And suddenly he released the brakes and we were on level ground, standing before the house, in which not a single light was burning. Its own blackness was hung suspended in the blackness of the night. But in me was burning the heavy light of richness. He helped me down and then led the horses to the stall. Had I not heard the hoofbeats on the stable floor, I would have thought he wasn't coming back, it was so dark even there. He came back and we lit no light in the house. Nor did we speak a single word, out of sheer seriousness."

Her voice had become hoarse with excitement, and now once again the monotonous singsong returned.

"He was the most wonderful lover; no other could ever compare with him. Like a person cautiously feeling his way he was, as he felt out my lust. He was full of impatience for me. His impatience made him tremble as though with a fever, and yet it did not overpower him and he did not overpower me, but waited until I had been swept down to the abyss, to where a man can feel that he is about to take the final plunge. If it was a current that was carrying me, he discovered the current and listened to it. I was naked and he made me still more naked, as though even nakedness had garments to be shed. For shame itself is like a garment. And so carefully did he strip from me the last vestiges of shame that aloneness, even in its most hidden recesses, could become a twoness. In the cautiousness with which he handled me he was like a doctor, but to my lust he was like a teacher. He urged my body to express wishes and to give orders, crude as well as tender, because lust has many fine shades of desire and each has its rights. He was doctor and teacher and at the same time the servant of my lust. Actually, for his own part, he scarcely knew any lust but mine. If I screamed with lust, this was the praise he required, which his desire required in order to be stimulated anew. He was strong and powerful out of weakness. And we were lifted higher and higher until we became a single being. At the verge of the abyss we stood together as a single being, through those nights and days. And yet I knew that it was wrong. For it should be the woman who serves the man's lust and not the other way round, and the fellows who, without consulting my lust, had simply flung me down to gratify their own had been more nearly right. Yes, even their talk about loving was more real. To be real his talk needed my coarse, naked lustfulness, the coarser my words, the realer became his love. From this I learned just why women clung to him and why they didn't want to let him go, but I learned too that I was not one of them, and that I had to get away, great as was my desire for him.

"I was clever," said she, nodding to herself and to her listener. But she did not wait for him to reply. The story was sweeping her onward.

"I never got a look at the forester's wife. But when I choose to I can sleep lightly. She came to the house at five o'clock in the morning to do the cleaning, and then she would also lay out for me on the kitchen table the cooking utensils for the day. What bothered me most was that she always was in the house the moment we left to go out for a walk. Because I had tidied up the bedroom myself, I was all the more aware of where she had picked up after me. What kind of an arrangement did he have with her? It was too neat, it had been drilled in too well from all the women visitors, and with such an occupation no woman can help becoming a spy. It wasn't hard for *me*. The house was old and the furniture was old. The rickety locks in the cupboards and desks were simple enough to pry open. What is more, any man who allows himself to be expended so unstintingly sleeps heavily. And I didn't spare him at all. Only I hated to leave him. In sleep his face was without lustfulness, handsome and faultless, and I would often sit there on the edge of the bed and gaze at it for a long time before going about my spying business. It was a sad and angry business. The woman, as a sign that this was her permanent home, had left all her clothes in the closets, and I was certain that all his rage at her would not prevent him from doing her will, might even goad him into it, if ever she were to order him to obey her lust again.

"Curious as I had been before about the letters from the Frau Baroness, I now felt only disgust. They were lying about in a jumble in the drawers with letters from his other women, and because he would never miss them, I took with me all that I could get my hands on. Wait, I'll read you one."

Pulling out of the pocket of her smock her glasses and a few crumpled letters, she went over to the window. "Just listen to this and see the kind of empty, worthless soul-clamor with which people fill up their empty lives and their empty boredom. Just see how poor she is, the Frau Baroness. Just see what poor, empty wickedness there is in this. Just see!

" 'My sweet beloved, every day our relationship is growing richer, even when you are far away. In our little child you are always present, and for me it is the pledge of our eternal union which, sooner or later, is bound to begin. Have faith. Heaven is kind to lovers, and it will help you to get free of that infamous woman who has so cruelly buried her talons in you. May I, oh may I achieve the same liberation in my marriage! Although my husband is really a very noble man, he has never had the slightest understanding of my wounded heart! It will be painful to have to tell him, but I shall find the strength. Your love for me, mine for you, which is constantly with me, give me this faith in the future. In this confident certainty, I kiss your dear, lovely eyes.

Yours
Elvire-Elf'

"Did you hear that? She spewed out rot like that by the yard, the old windbag, and he put up with it. Probably it annoyed and disgusted him, but he put up with it none the less. I almost hated him for it. Why did he put up with it? Only because he was one of those men who have both too high and too low an opinion of women and who, therefore, must serve them with his body since he can give them no consideration with his soul? He cannot love, he can only serve, and in every woman that he meets he serves someone who doesn't exist and whom he could love if she did exist, but who, as she is, is nothing but an evil spirit that enslaves him. And because I knew that I was powerless to rescue him from this hell and that I had to run away, my hatred dissolved into tenderness and I got back into bed with him to clasp him about with my arms and legs, merciless out of hatred, merciless out of tenderness. But perhaps, too, I hoped that exhaustion would make our parting easier for us both. Nevertheless I asked him after ten days whether I should stay any longer, saying that I could arrange it. And scarcely had I spoken when the sudden wild panic which I had seen that night in the garden reappeared in his eyes, and he stammered: 'Better later, in a few weeks, as soon as I am back from my trip.' This was a lie, and in my fury I screamed at him: 'You'll never see me here until that woman's clothes are out of the house!' And then for the first time he was a man, though it was cowardice that had made him one. He flung me down and, without consulting my lust, he took me so wildly that I kissed him the way I had that time in the garden. But it was no use. The hate was there. And that evening we drove down to the tramway in silence, my servant girl's grip in the back of the carriage."

Was this the end of the story? It seemed to be only just beginning, for Zerline's voice now became quite firm and clear.

"It may be that the hatred was all on my side. It may be that my threat never to come back really struck home because he realized quite well that it was no soul-clamor. It may be that he really did want to get rid of the person who certainly returned to her clothes the very next day and in the kitchen heated the food meant for me.

"In any event, a few weeks later the whole town was in an uproar because the mysterious mistress of Herr von Juna had suddenly died in the hunting-box. Now, things like that have often happened before, and yet right away there were rumors that he had poisoned her. Certainly it was not I who started the rumors. I was glad to be left out of it and not to have to say anything about the letters or about all the bottles and flasks that he had had out there and that had made me feel none too comfortable. But gossip is always quick to grow and quick to spread. Of course I couldn't refrain from telling the Frau Baroness about the wild fire. White as snow she became and could only murmur: 'Impossible!' I shrugged my shoulders and replied: 'Anything is possible.' That Hildegard might have murderer's blood in her brought out something harsh and wild in me. Meanwhile more and more people were saying that Herr von Juna should be brought to trial, and a few days later, in fact, he was arrested. And the more I brooded over the matter, the surer I became that he had killed the woman. Yes, today I am, if possible, even surer than I was then. And since he had done it on account of me, for which reason, for all my hatred, I didn't want to have him under the guillotine, I was glad when people began to whisper that the evidence against him was not strong enough for a death sentence. It had turned out, you see, that the woman, who was a Munich actress, was a morphine addict and had only kept herself alive with her drug and strong sleeping-pills. A body like that easily breaks down, and even with an overdose of sleeping-pills it might have been an accident, it might have been suicide, and it would be hard to prove that it was murder.

"The only really incriminating material would have been the letters, and I had stolen them. What luck for him! What luck for the Frau Baroness! For a while I was pretty proud of what I had done, until it suddenly occurred to me that he hadn't needed me at all, that he had probably burned up all his correspondence before his arrest, and that he was probably tearing his hair because the most dangerous ones were missing. And I could see so clearly the wild panic in his eyes that it gripped me too. So I did what I ought to have done before. I took the letters and rushed with them to his two lawyers, one of whom was from Berlin, so that they could deliver him from his torment and uncertainty. They offered me a lot of money, but I refused it, for I had begun to dream. I imagined how he would now have to marry me out of gratitude after he had been acquitted, and, God knows, it would have been a blow to his pride and an even worse one to the Frau Baroness, who would then have had to wish her maid happiness. And for that reason I kept a few letters, the most incriminating of all, for myself. No one was in a position to check whether they were all there, least of all Herr von Juna himself. What I handed over was more than enough to relieve his mind. The rest I needed for my marriage dream. If you want to get married, it's a good idea to have on hand some means of putting on a little pressure, and even after marriage it can be quite useful."

"It was very fine of you to rescue Herr von Juna," interjected A., "only you shouldn't have been so hard on the poor Frau Baroness."

Zerline did not like interruptions. "I am just getting to the most important part," said she firmly, and she was right. For now as her story became filled with lamentations, accusations, self-accusations, it quite changed its character.

"The marriage dream was great wickedness, but I'd only made it up in order to divert myself from still greater wickedness, and for this I also needed the letters. I was utterly lost and I didn't know it. Who was the cause of my being lost? Juna, because he had got into my blood though I didn't love him? The Frau Baroness with the bastard that was his child? Or perhaps the judge himself, because I couldn't bear to have him be a cuckold who, in his saintliness, had become stupid and blind and ignorant of what had happened to him. I alone could have revealed it to him, and when it began to be noised about that the judge himself would take the Juna trial, then I was really lost. Was he to acquit with his own lips the man who had entered his house by stealth and planted the bastard in it? I couldn't bear it and I couldn't bear my secret knowledge. It was almost like sharing in the guilt, and behind the guilt was something still worse, and that was wickedness. And it was not the knowledge, not the guilt, no, but the wickedness that I wanted to shout out so as to find my way back out of my lostness. I had to go still deeper into wickedness in order to become whole again in the light of day, along with all my wickedness. And yet I shall never understand it.

"As though I had been commanded to do it, I suddenly wrapped up all the remaining letters, Juna's, as well as those of the Frau Baroness, where they both threatened murder, and sent them anonymously, with the address printed in block letters, to the judge. Something made me do it, and yet I was quite aware of what I was doing. Actually the letters were intended for the public prosecutor, so that the judge, because of the scandal about the Frau Baroness, would have to resign from his position, while Juna would simply get his head chopped off. And perhaps I wished that the judge, out of sheer despair, would kill himself and the Frau Baroness and the bastard. And because I wanted to confess everything—my own guilt and the stealing of the letters in the hunting-box and in the Frau Baroness's bedroom—it would have been all right with me if he had killed me as well. That would have been real justice, since it was for me and not for the Frau Baroness that the woman in the hunting-box had been murdered, and it was for this higher justice that I wanted to admire the judge. It was a terrible test to which I put him and which he had to meet for the sake of justice, so that I would be able to believe twice over in his greatness and in his saintliness. For this I was willing to pay with my life, and yet it was wickedness that I still don't understand."

She gave a deep sigh. This indeed was the most important part. It was the great confession of her life, and obviously it was as a confession, not as an account of a victory over the Frau Baroness, though this too had been one aspect of it and could not be ignored, that the story had been told. And, in fact, Zerline seemed relieved. Ever since she had read the letter, she had remained by the window, and now it was to become apparent that she had done so intentionally. With great ceremony she once more placed the glasses on her nose, brought another slip of paper out of her pocket; and after another heavy sigh her voice regained its strength and firmness.

"The packet of letters was sent off to the judge, and I expected, feared, hoped, that now a lot of dreadful things would happen. The days passed without anything happening. He never once questioned me, though the anonymous sender could scarcely have been anyone but me. Then a feeling of great disappointment came over me because the judge too was turning out to be a coward to whom justice meant less than his position and his reputation, and who, for the sake of these things, was even willing to put up with a murderer's bastard in his house. But I was soon set straight, and thoroughly so. For he, who usually talked so little, suddenly began at dinner, while I was waiting on table, to speak in a loud voice, so that I couldn't help hearing, about crime and punishment. I took in every word and wrote it all down right afterward. Now I shall read it, so that you can see for yourself. So listen carefully.

" 'Our trial by jury is a very important and at the same time dangerous institution; dangerous because the judge can easily be swayed by emotional motives. And particularly in very serious cases, where a jury is required—above all, that is, in murder cases—the desire for revenge, which, in the last analysis, is always present whenever a judgment is pronounced, can creep in unnoticed and gain the upper hand. Once this has happened, people tend to lose sight of the fact that a legal error can also be murder, and they forget that the death sentence is a terrible thing. They become reckless, irresponsible, and, all too frequently, evaluate incorrectly certain evidence out of a lust for revenge. The judge, therefore, must be doubly and triply on his guard, when it comes to the admission and treatment of evidence, to see that nothing of the sort creeps in. Even documents written or signed by the defendant himself are open to misinterpretation. When, for example, a person writes that he would like to "do away with" a person or to "get rid of him," it is far from being undeniable evidence of the intent to kill. Only the lust for revenge will see it as proof positive of the will to murder, the lust for revenge which clamors for the executioner's ax and thirsts for the blood of the victim.'

"That's what he said, and I understood, understood so well that my hands began to shake and I nearly dropped the meat platter. He was even greater, even more saintly than I had imagined, stupid woman that I was. He had guessed that I had wanted to move him to revenge, to an executioner's revenge, and he refused to be moved. He knew everything.

"But did the Frau Baroness also understand, or was she too empty even for that? Even if she only half remembered the letters she had received, she must have been struck by expressions like 'do away with' and 'get rid of.' The judge looked at her, too, all kindliness, and I should not have been surprised to see her fling herself down on her knees before him. But she didn't stir, no, she didn't stir. Only her lips went a little white. 'Oh, the guillotine,' she said, 'capital punishment, a dreadful institution!' That was all, and the judge stared down at his plate as I brought in the dessert. That's how she was, that empty. And what followed afterward held no further surprises for me. Just before Christmas the trial took place, and the defense had an easy time of it since the judge helped out by holding the public prosecutor in check. Not a single letter was produced. The jury's verdict of not guilty was almost unanimous, eleven to one, and the one dissenting voice might have been mine. Yet I was glad that he was acquitted, that Herr von Juna, and even more glad that he cleared out at once without thanking me and without saying good-by, to look for a permanent home abroad, in Spain, I think."

That was the end of the story, and Zerline breathed a long

sigh. "Yes, that is the story of me and Herr von Juna, and I shall never forget it. He escaped the guillotine, and he escaped from me, and the second was even luckier for him than the first. For had he been noble and had he married me, I would have made it a hell on earth for him, and if he were still alive he would still have me, old woman that I am. Just look at me!"

But before A. could make a reply, she had begun again:

"After the verdict there was a great deal of uproar. The papers attacked the judge, especially the red ones, which accused him of class discrimination. As was to be expected, he withdrew more and more into solitude. He hardly ever came out of his study any more, and before long I had to make his bed there. A year later he handed in his resignation on grounds of health. But in reality it was on grounds of death. He wasn't yet sixty when it overtook him, and, whatever the doctors said, he died of a broken heart. She, on the other hand, was permitted to go on living along with the bastard. And it was because of this, on account of this injustice, that I brought up Hildegard as I did. She was to become the real daughter of the judge, so that his home should be respectable and shouldn't harbor a murderer's bastard. Actually, I was never able to rid her of her murderer's blood, but for that very reason she had to learn to be worthy of her daughterhood. Had she been a Catholic, I would have put her in a convent; but as it was, I could only keep the pure saintliness of the departed before her eyes and urge her to imitate it. The more like him I have made her, the more she has expiated her guilt, the more her mother's has been expiated, though hers will never be atoned for to eternity. Her daughter has taken it on. That is, the more she has entered into her father's spirit, the more the will to revenge has entered into her, the revenge that he himself refused to exact out of saintly severity with himself. She too enslaves herself through imitation. I enslaved her for that. But no one could implant the saintliness in her, and without the saintliness she must hand on the slavery, so that the silent, sham revenge that is in all this training will force her mother to atone. One is linked with the other, and that's how I wanted it. That's how I brought her up: to atone for the guilt. Actually she rebels against it with her lecherous murderer's blood, which refuses to take on any atonement. But it doesn't do her no good."

"For heaven's sake," cried A., "what must she atone for? Wherein is she guilty? You can't make her responsible for her parents, especially since the love of the Frau Baroness for Herr von Juna can't necessarily be regarded as a crime!"

She gave him a reproachful look, less perhaps because of what he had said, though this must not have been to Zerline's liking either, than because he had interrupted her.

"Are you falling for her lechery? I warn you. Better take a real girl with whom you like to sleep and who likes to sleep with you, and even hands that are a little red are better than manicured soul-clamor. Do you know why she didn't want you as a boarder? Well, there hasn't been a single boarder here before whose door"—and she gestured toward the door behind her—"she hasn't stood night after night. And night after night the command of her father, who is not her father, has paralyzed her, and she has never got beyond the threshold. And if you don't believe it, scatter some flour in the hall tonight, as I've done often enough, so that tomorrow you can see her faltering footsteps. That's her guilt torment. Don't let yourself get tangled up in it. For our responsibility as well as our wickedness is always greater than we are, and the deeper a person has to go into his wickedness in order to find himself, the more responsibility he has to assume for crimes that he didn't commit. That goes for everyone, for you as well as for me, as well as for Hildegard, and it is up to her to atone for the sins of her parents. But she, the Frau Baroness, who is the prisoner of us both, would like to escape from the enslavement, and she implores every boarder to help her. They're full of soul-clamor, those two, and I've stirred it up into a hell clamor, so that their ears would ring with it, and this house is a hell indeed in its quiet gentility. The saint and the devil, the judge and Herr von Juna, who must also be dead by now, two menacing shadows who never budge from their sides, and who tear them to pieces. Me too, perhaps.

"And it didn't make it any better that after Herr von Juna I took other lovers, if only so as not to be faithful to him. It made matters even worse when before long I saw how I was driven to find younger and younger ones, in the end mere boys that I rocked on my breast so that they would lose their fear of women and would learn lust, that human peace. When I realized that, I gave it up for good. Only for that reason? No. No. I ought to have given it up long ago. And if it hadn't been for the Frau Baroness, quite possibly I might never have had anything to do with Herr von Juna, either. The image of the judge was in me, forever indelible, and it grew and grew. . . . Who was his widow after he died? Who if not I? It's been more than forty years since he put his hands on my breast, and I have loved him all my life, with my whole soul."

This, of course, was really the natural end of the story, and A. wondered a little why he hadn't realized it all along. Zerline, for her part, rather spent as was natural at her age, gazed for a while into space before saying with her customary maid's politeness and in her maid's voice: "But now I've robbed you of your whole afternoon nap with my chatter, Herr A. I hope you'll make up for it now." And, her back bent with age, she hobbled out of the room, closing the door gently and cautiously behind her as though someone was sleeping within.

A. had sunk back on the couch. Yes, she was right. He should get a little more sleep. After all, it wasn't so late. The tower clocks had just struck four. So it was quite proper that the sleep-entangled thoughts that had been broken off by Zerline's entrance should resume their train once more. But once again, to his annoyance, the subject of money thrust itself into the foreground. And again he had to tell himself how the money-making had started back there in Cape Colony, and how since then he had been led by money, with his scarcely lifting a finger, from continent to continent, from stock exchange to stock exchange, and if you counted South America as a separate continent, there had been six in fifteen years. That made two and a half per continent. And it had all been pure accident. As a boy, he had longed to have the triangular Cape of Good Hope stamp for his collection, longed in vain, and this had been the source of his longing for South Africa. Stamps might not have been a bad investment, but the collecting urge had died out. What did he really want? A home, wife, children? It was only grandmothers who got any real pleasure out of children. Children were disturbing to comfortable life, and love-affairs even more so; they were, in fact, incomprehensible. What the Baroness did was simply stupid. Had he known her then—but he had scarcely been born then—he would have summoned her to Cape Town and rescued her from that fellow and his bad treatment. Of course women didn't like to go down there. Herr von Juna would never have been able to make any collection of women there. He had led an uncomfortable life, that man. Was the judge any more to be envied? If those two had at least made a son for the cuckold. But a son would also have escaped to Africa despite the futility of any escape; for the widow remains at home, remains a prisoner. One should always be one's own son. Hadn't he tried to take his mother with him to Cape Town after his father's death to build her a house there? Had she come, she would probably still be alive; at any rate she would have grandchildren. For children you should start a stamp collection. He should get the triangular Cape of Good Hope too. Though the Sunday slips away, trickles away, that is a good plan for life.

Yes, yes, that is how one ought to plan life, A. knew for a certainty. What he did not know was that he had already dropped off to sleep.

Translated by Jane B. Greene

THE FRIEND IN THE CLOSET

by Hermann Kesten

Sitting in his room, Anton Laufer meditated upon his life. Now and then he glanced up at the old-fashioned wall clock and observed how quietly his last day in Munich was passing. Soon it would be time for him to leave for Berlin. Yesterday he had already said his good-bys to the Pflaum family, in whose flat he rented this single room. Already he felt like a guest in his room.

The Pflaum family were extremely fond of their lodger. Yesterday, when Laufer had surprised them by turning up once more after his emotional farewell, the family had invited him to supper and had given him back his room for one more night without exhibiting that mingled resentment and disappointment which people generally feel when someone violates all expectations by failing to depart or to die.

Laufer sat on the squeaking red sofa, whose battered splendor gave it a melancholy look, and started to hum. His own voice comforted him, helping him to overcome his disconsolate mood.

There was a knock. Laufer opened the door and found the entire Pflaum family there. Herr Pflaum was holding a carafe of red wine, Frau Pflaum a tray of sandwiches, and the three blonde daughters were carrying glasses and plates. They all smiled in their nice ingratiating way, and Herr Pflaum asked whether they might join him.

Hermann Kesten, born in 1900 in Nuremberg, is a moralist who writes satire. He is the author of several historical novels (Ferdinand and Isabella, I the King) *and of others dealing with the historical events of his own time* (The Children of Guernica, The Twins of Nuremberg). *He has also published a number of biographies* (Copernicus, Casanova) *and some anthologies of European literature. He is an American citizen and, when not traveling, lives in New York City.*

They wished to have a second farewell celebration—an altogether unofficial one this time, Herr Pflaum assured Laufer.

And so Laufer sat once more on the squeaking red sofa, and the sweet, vivacious girls, ranging in age from twenty to twenty-five, sat on both sides of him.

Opposite him sat Herr and Frau Pflaum. The mother, still erect and pretty, made them finish up their meat sandwiches as though they would have to fast for the next month. Herr Arthur Pflaum smiled sadly and filled their glasses with the Tyrolean wine. He seemed to be gloating over the sight of his daughters and his embarrassed lodger.

"We shall miss you, my dear Herr Laufer," he said. "We do not have a better friend."

The compliment made Laufer uncomfortable. If it was true, he could only feel sorry for the man. For Laufer was no friend of Chief Magistrate Pflaum. He had long since passed his verdict on the judge.

Pflaum seemed to read Laufer's thoughts. He had a prepossessing appearance, Herr Arthur Pflaum. And he also had a dignified manner of speech, the articulateness of a university professor. His hair was white, though he was only forty-seven; he had the red cheeks of the wine-drinker and the sharp eyes of a hunter. He had risen to the chief magistracy of the superior court, but after the war he had been demoted to county-court judge because in 1939 he had joined the National Socialist Party. Now he was waiting eagerly for his trial in the denazification court, for he hoped to be able to explain his action satisfactorily.

Herr Pflaum filled the glasses again, took a drink of wine himself, put down his glass, and declared suddenly: "I must justify myself to you, Herr Laufer. You are a noble person. I am certain you do not wholly condemn me; otherwise you would not have moved in with us after the war. Ever since you did move in I have wanted to tell you our story, but I have not had the courage. I don't know whether what I have to tell you will make you think better or worse of me and my family. But this story, untold, hurts me deeply. And perhaps you will be able to say whether I am a bad man—yes, to some extent a murderer—or whether I am morally entitled to go on being a judge in high position. Help me, Herr Laufer. You are well disposed toward me, I know. But you do not respect me. Don't say it is not so."

Frau Pflaum said it was not so, in Laufer's stead. "I know far better than you what Herr Laufer thinks. He thinks just as I do. Don't you, Herr Laufer?" She offered him a sandwich, and Laufer covered his embarrassment by eating.

Bella Pflaum was a good woman and often made a point of it. She loved her daughters, her husband, her lodger, and the good Lord. With all of them she stood on a familiar footing. Her husband had given her and their daughters the strictest orders not to discuss "the old story." And so now that he was about to tell it himself she shook her finger at him and said: "Don't talk about it, Arthur. You know . . ."

Arthur could not be checked. "After all, it's your fault that we put up Siegfried in your dressing-room." He turned to Laufer and began his story.

"I had a school friend named Siegfried Rosen. In after years he went to Kassel and became director of the municipal art gallery there. A bald-headed, skinny, and fanatical fellow, he looked like a waiter in a vegetarian restaurant. He'd published a sound work on the sixteenth-century painter Altdorfer. One evening in January 1939 he turned up at our apartment. He was in bad shape. He had lost his job long since—I had read about that in the papers. Now he told me that in November 1938 he had been arrested in his apartment and sent to a concentration camp on account of the murder of Herr vom Rath, an official of the German Embassy at Paris. A Jew had assassinated vom Rath, and my old school friend Siegfried Rosen was a Jew. Therefore he was being punished.

"At first he was unwilling to tell me anything about the camp. He said he had been forbidden to speak on pain of death. Later I learned that they had tortured him, and released him only because he promised to leave Germany and emigrate to Peru. His wife had obtained a visa from the Peruvian consulate for him. She was Christian, and had meanwhile divorced him because she could not be expected to go on living with a Jew.

"Rosen had picked up his Peruvian visa in Berlin, and in Kassel he had obtained all his emigration papers and tickets. But instead of boarding the ship in Hamburg, he had now come to Munich, to our apartment, to tell me that he could not leave

Germany. Twenty generations of his ancestors were buried here, he said, and here he wanted to die. Except that he did not care to die right off.

" 'What do you want me to do?' I asked.

" 'You are not in the party,' he said.

" 'But I have my profession,' I said. 'I have my family to think of, and I am a German.'

" 'So am I,' he said. 'Give me advice.'

" 'I will have to sleep on that,' I said.

" 'Good,' he replied. 'I'll come back tomorrow evening.'

" 'Where will you stay the night?' I asked.

"He shrugged.

" 'Let's ask Bella,' I suggested.

"With her happy gift for striking at the heart of a matter my wife at once asked: 'Are you involved in the murder?'

" 'What murder?' Rosen and I asked together.

" 'Of that councilor of the Embassy in Paris?'

" 'Not at all!' Rosen and I assured her.

" 'Then you are innocent,' Bella declared with surprisingly sound logic. 'You will sleep in Marianne's, our eldest daughter's, room.'

" 'Out of the question,' Rosen declared at once.

" 'Don't you understand the consequences?' I asked my wife under my breath.

"She answered loudly: 'Do we fear men more than God? Herr Rosen is your old friend. Didn't you say yourself that he is innocent? Can he sleep out in the rain?'

"To make it brief, he slept in our eldest daughter's bed, and Marianne slept on the sofa in her sister Edith's room. We were well aware of the danger. It took warm friendship and a lot of courage to shelter a Jew in a Christian home in the city of Munich in 1939.

"Next morning I made up my mind to persuade him to leave Germany. Then we saw an item in the day's newspaper that in Hamburg the Gestapo had taken many Jews off a ship and sent them to concentration camps.

" 'These excesses will happen,' I told my school friend.

"Rosen looked much better that morning. He had slept well. In the evening, he said, he would leave us; he would find another place to stay.

" 'Where?' my wife asked.

"I would have let him go. My wife would not permit it. 'Excesses pass,' she said. 'In the long run the German people will not permit innocent persons to be punished.'

"And so Rosen stayed. We got used to him. It was evident that he was continually making up his mind to leave us the next day. He used to insist that he could not accept this terrible sacrifice on our part. 'You have a wife; you have children,' he said. 'They will kill me. Very well. But what will they do to all of you?'

"We forbade him to speak of it. We also forbade him, for safety's sake, to leave his room. He was allowed into the bathroom only at night. He must never put on the light in his room. We had no ration cards for him. And he had no money with which we could buy him food on the black market. If he were discovered, he would be killed—that was clear. Would we then be tried, tortured, beheaded?

"Siegfried Rosen was a good sort, a German patriot. His former wife had meanwhile married a major in the SS. Siegfried kept repeating that to his mind life in exile was worse than death. My wife and my daughters admired him. For my part, I often wished that a life in Basel or Zurich had not seemed so inconceivable to him. Though of course the Swiss would not have admitted him.

"Being unable to move around made poor Siegfried nervous. He wrote a book on the painter Grünewald and would read aloud to my daughters from the manuscript. Later we were afraid to keep the manuscript, and burned it.

"Naturally Siegfried fell in love with my wife and daughters. That was inevitable. Of course you could rely on him; he was a man of principle. Still, with teen-age girls in the house and the national laws against the Jews, especially the law against miscegenation, it was doubly dangerous. But I suppose it was already so dangerous it didn't matter.

"A month after Siegfried had settled on us, I joined the party. Even Siegfried could not dissuade me. As a party member I would be above suspicion, I thought. Then I would be able to shield Siegfried. I also wanted to keep my position—so that entering the party was done for my children's sake as well.

"When the war began, we worried more. Once the house

warden came to inspect the apartment for fire hazards during bombings. Bella hid poor Siegfried among the clothes in her dressing-room, back of our bedroom. It's a narrow, windowless room, really no more than a closet. The warden did not notice anything amiss. That evening I asked Siegfried whether he would not try after all to escape into Switzerland. He promptly asked me for poison. That was the day Hitler marched into Paris. We almost came to blows, Siegfried and I. And right after our quarrel we almost wept.

"Throughout this period our girls used to have friends of both sexes visiting them quite often. Naturally, Siegfried's room was always locked. Once we were in deadly peril. A young man who had fought in Russia and developed heart trouble was studying art history at our university. He courted all three of the girls and asked each for her hand in a perfectly old-fashioned way. He started with our youngest, but Gusti quickly made it clear that she wanted a husband with a sound heart. Poor girls—nowadays there are hardly any young men left in Germany! Edith, too, refused him in the end. Then he went at Marianne. She was quite fond of him, but could not make up her mind.

"One evening he came to dinner and told us he had at last hit on a subject for his doctoral thesis. He was going to write on Altdorfer, and in particular he intended to tear to pieces a book on Altdorfer by a Jew, a person named Siegfried Rosen. We, of course, said nothing. He gave us a queer look and asked several times whether we were acquainted with the book or the author.

"My heart beat faster, and Bella turned pale. The girls tried to change the subject. But he came back to Altdorfer and Siegfried Rosen again. He was going to annihilate the man, he said; he hated that book. 'You really don't know the book?' he asked me mockingly.

"I murmured that I did not, and that Altdorfer was a great painter.

"Then the student went up to our bookshelves and took out a volume. We were all terrified when we saw that he was holding Rosen's book. Rosen had sent it to me in 1930, with the inscription: 'For my dear friend Arthur Pflaum.'

"The student laid the book on the sideboard, as if absent-mindedly, excused himself, and left the room. We thought he was going to the bathroom.

"My wife asked: 'Marianne, did you say no to him?'

" 'This afternoon,' she replied. 'But he refused to take my refusal as final. He said I must take three days to think it over. To make it easier, I finally agreed.'

" 'So we have three days' time,' my wife said.

"Then, from the hallway, we heard a pounding on one of the doors and shouts of 'Open up. Open at once! Open or we will fire!'

"We all ran out into the hall. There stood our student in front of the locked room, pounding on the door with his fist and shouting.

"We rushed up to him and got him away from the door. He was not very strong—a frail, fair-haired fellow with big horn-rimmed glasses and a tiny mustache.

" 'What's the matter with you?' I asked him.

" 'There's someone in there,' he shouted. 'A man in there sneezed.'

" 'I sneezed,' I said. 'In the dining-room. Do you suffer from auditory hallucinations?'

"Marianne and Gusti each took one of his arms and led him with gentle insistence into our dining-room.

" 'Why is that room always locked?' the student asked my wife. Before she could reply, he asked whether I could lend him Rosen's book on Altdorfer.

"You know, my dear Herr Laufer, I am a magistrate in a high position. But at that moment I seriously considered how I could get rid of that young man without leaving any traces. Luckily I had no weapon on me and I was still able to consider the difficulties of removing a corpse from an apartment. I imagined that the young man wanted to take Siegfried's book with him in order to denounce me for having kept a Jew's book, with author's dedication, in my library. But I did not care. I believed he knew who was in our locked room.

"At that moment the doorbell rang. We all jumped up. Gusti cried out: 'Don't open the door!'

" 'Shall I go to the door?' the student asked. Have I mentioned his name—Fritz von Strachow?

" 'I will,' I said. There at the door were three of our daughters' friends—a student from the Technical High School, an SS lieutenant, and a young surgeon from the Municipal Hospital. Gusti had invited them and quite forgotten about it.

"I prepared a bowl of punch and we had a pleasant evening. The surgeon played the piano—Schumann. Then we turned on our phonograph and the young people danced. Even I danced a waltz with Gusti while Fritz von Strachow waltzed with my wife. When the others left, he left also. He did not mention again the book on Altdorfer or the locked room.

"We spent a sleepless night. I made my will. All night we sorted over letters and papers and burned them. We argued for a long time whether we ought to burn Rosen's book, but couldn't make up our minds. When dawn came, we waited for the notorious ring. It was well known that the Gestapo came shortly after daybreak.

"For three days we lived in hell. Naturally we had to tell Siegfried all about it. We had been afraid that Strachow's shouts and pounding on the door might have given Rosen a heart attack. But certain fugitives can be killed only by brute force.

"Of course, Siegfried asked us to get poison for him. We were all furious with him. In one breath my daughter Edith and I cried out: 'What about your dead body?'

" 'My body?' Siegfried asked, gaping idiotically at us. He looked at us and realized that we all hated him. 'What do you want with my body? What do you need it for?'

" 'That's just it!' Marianne cried. 'We don't need it, don't want it.'

"He goggled at us, each of us in turn, his eyes filled with horror. It was unendurable.

"Marianne hated him most of all, for obvious reasons. 'Can't you go away, dear Herr Rosen?' she asked, giving him a friendly smile.

" 'Go away?' he repeated uncomprehendingly.

" 'Clear out!' Marianne burst out. 'Out of the way, you murderer, you conscienceless—' She hesitated, then completed the phrase: 'you conscienceless art historian, you!' But we all knew that she had meant to say: 'You conscienceless Jew!'

" 'That's enough!' Bella said. She is a resolute woman. 'Considering the gravity of these times, we will invite no more than twelve guests to dinner next Sunday to celebrate the engagement.'

" 'I won't allow that!' I said.

" 'An engagement isn't a marriage,' my wife said. 'And Marianne is a brave and clever girl.'

" 'Strachow is the kind to take liberties with his fiancée,' I said. 'He will kiss her and—'

" 'Under the present circumstances even I would kiss Herr von Strachow,' my wife declared. 'I would even kiss a crocodile. And Siegfried must move.'

" 'I must move?' the poor fellow asked, trembling in every limb.

" 'Why not?' I asked, not understanding Bella's meaning. 'You will move, my dear Siegfried.' With the same expression I might have said: 'You will be a ring-tailed monkey, my dear Siegfried.'

"Finally Bella came out with what she had in mind—to move Siegfried into her dressing-room. This room can be reached only through our bedroom, and the door looks just like a closet door. Bella had thought of everything. We pushed the big chiffonier in front of the door to this dressing-room, hiding it completely.

"Naturally we had to push the chiffonier aside for a short time every night in order to permit Siegfried to empty his chamberpot, to give him food and drink for the next twenty-four hours, and to ask whether he needed anything. The only light in his room was electric, and he had little fresh air. We had placed hangings over the inside of the door to stifle all sounds. Naturally, Siegfried could leave his room only when we pushed away the heavy chiffonier. It was not a pleasant thought, while we were in our shelters during air raids, to know that he was a captive there, and that no one was in the apartment to hear if he cried for help.

"What was I to do? I don't mean to harp on his being my friend and innocent. By that time I already hated him. But what were we to do? We had become involved. And even if it had been possible to inform on him without getting into trouble ourselves, we still did not want to hand a living human being over to the executioner.

"You will ask me whether I was not, in my capacity of

superior-court justice, bound to act according to the laws of our country. Professionally I was, of course. But in private one lives by other principles than the publicly accepted ones. Isn't that true of everyone? After all, I could not simply send Siegfried out into the streets. He would have killed himself, or he would have been killed, slowly and inexorably. And even if he did not want to inform on us, they would have tortured him until in the end he confessed everything. But, above all, we had already invested too much suffering, anxiety, and sacrifice in him; for this reason we all believed we must now hold out to the end at any cost, come what might.

"We had to restrict ourselves, for Siegfried's sake. Of course he had no ration cards and we saved his food out of our own meals. And there was this always having a person in the closet, for the locked room was no more than a big closet. Always having our guilty conscience in the closet, fear back of our beds.

"I began to be afraid of him. I could not go to bed without thinking of him. I started up out of nightmares crying: 'Siegfried!' When I touched my wife, I thought: 'Can he hear us?' By day, in court or in the street, I would find myself imagining the five minutes at night when we let him out as one lets a wild animal out of its cage. He always smelled unaired or sickish. His appearance was unhealthy also, but of course that was to be expected. He did not look at us; we gazed past him.

"Perhaps you will ask me what Siegfried thought about it all. For he must have had thoughts, during all those years. But I no longer came to the point of asking him.

"Fritz von Strachow had actually been no problem. In the course of the engagement party Marianne found a pretext to show her fiancé through the whole apartment, including the formerly locked room and even our bedroom. Strachow made no comment. He kissed Marianne in all the rooms of our apartment. He was tactful enough never to mention Siegfried Rosen's book again. We had placed the book in Rosen's hide-out, so he could read his own work if he wished.

"One day something happened that we had not dared imagine. Siegfried fell ill. He had fevers, chills, aching limbs, a sore throat; he became delirious. We felt like furniture-movers—we were pushing that heavy chiffonier back and forth all the time.

"In his fever Siegfried heaped violent reproaches upon us. It was obvious that he hated us, despised us. He called us Nazis and anti-Semites, reproached us for having set up a private concentration camp in our apartment. When we gave him aspirin he asked us scornfully whether we were trying to save a doctor's fee. He asked us what we intended to do with his dead body. It would not be easy to get a corpse out of the house unseen, he remarked. He refused to eat or drink. And day by day he grew weaker. His fever rose. We were desperate, helpless. We discussed every doctor we knew, wondering whether we dared risk calling any of them.

"Finally we made up our minds to let the young surgeon of the Municipal Hospital in on our secret. Edith took it upon herself to tell him; the young doctor was running after her. 'What Marianne has done with Fritz I can do with Erich,' Edith said, and next morning she came to our house with the young man, Dr. Erich Kolbe.

"We had placed Siegfried in Marianne's room, the room we had formerly kept locked, and figured out a story to tell the doctor. We would say Siegfried had come to our apartment the day before, deathly ill as he was now; that he had been living in Berlin on false papers all these years.

"We told this story to Siegfried and asked him to keep it in mind and to think up plausible details to fit in, and not to betray us under any circumstances. He stared at us blankly, without replying. We did not know whether he understood us at all. He looked as though he would not live another forty-eight hours.

"Dr. Kolbe came, gave Siegfried a quick examination, and said we were to dress him after dark. He himself would come in his car that evening and drive the patient to his hospital. He would leave Siegfried off at one of the side entrances. Then Siegfried was to go in, ask his way to the admission desk, and then request that Dr. Kolbe be called. The doctor would then admit him, examine him, and operate at once. The operation was required less for medical reasons than to throw the police off the track. Siegfried was to claim that he was a refugee bombed out of Hamburg and give some name that sounded Christian. The rest was in the hands of God. . . . 'Have you understood me?' Dr. Kolbe asked Siegfried.

"Siegfried nodded. Dr. Kolbe gave him an injection and a few tablets.

"Siegfried slept for several hours. In the evening we dressed him and turned him over to Dr. Kolbe. We were lucky. Nobody saw Siegfried leave the house.

"We were very lucky. Dr. Kolbe was a competent medical man and very much in love with our Edith. He made Siegfried well—with the help of God, so to speak.

"For five weeks Siegfried lay in Dr. Kolbe's ward. The first day he was allowed out, he visited us. He stayed only ten minutes. It was not a very pleasant visit. He had come for his manuscript, his study of Grünewald. We had burned it, along with all of Siegfried's other things.

" 'Burned it so fast?' he asked. 'Then I'll go.' And he stood up.

"Naturally we said nothing. In fact, all of us remained sitting. We did not even look at him. You understand—we were treating him like a shadow. It was fear, above all, that made us do that. If we pretended we did not see him, perhaps no one else would.

" 'Oh yes,' he said, 'I still owe you my thanks.'

"We, of course, said nothing.

" 'Well then, thanks,' he said, 'and no hard feelings.'

"We remained sitting mute for a long time after he had left. He was to be discharged from the hospital as cured in four days. Neither he nor we had mentioned the problem of where he was to go afterward.

"But his discharge never came. The day after his visit to us the Gestapo came to the hospital—two young officials. They greeted him very courteously, waited until he had changed his clothes, and took him with them for interrogation. Dr. Kolbe telephoned Edith that same day to come to the hospital. He advised her to warn us.

"That night the Gestapo brought Rosen back to the hospital, on a stretcher. He screamed all night, until Dr. Kolbe arrived in the morning. The night nurse called Dr. Kolbe to the patient's bed and whispered to him that the Gestapo was guarding closely all exits from the hospital.

"Dr. Kolbe sent the nurse away and stayed alone with the patient for a while. Then he gave him morphine.

"That evening the doctor came to see us. We all sat around him. Since Rosen's interrogation we had been waiting for our arrest to come any minute. But by now I didn't care. If only we could get it over with, I thought.

" 'Well?' I asked Dr. Kolbe.

"Dr. Kolbe was silent. At last he gathered courage and said: 'I respect this Jew. A brave man. He asked me for poison. They beat him up brutally. He swore he did not betray me or your family. And I do believe they got nothing out of him. For this afternoon they telephoned me to get my patient in Room 77 ready for another interrogation as soon as possible. I said I needed at least a week before he'd be fit to get up. They haggled with me like—like Jews. We agreed on five days.'

" 'And then?' I asked.

"Dr. Kolbe only looked at us.

" 'I have a family,' I said despairingly. 'I am a government official.'

" 'A government official?' the doctor said. 'Do you also do your duty as a judge? What sentence would you pass on me?'

" 'Death,' I said.

" 'Death?' he asked, turning pale as though I had told him something new.

" 'Of course,' I said. 'The law requires it.'

" 'This Jew in Number 77 is very ill,' he said. 'I am considering a second operation. You people, as his closest friends—perhaps his relatives or in-laws—'

" 'How dare you!' I exclaimed.

" 'I beg your pardon," he replied. 'I thought that perhaps this man Rosen is your son-in-law, in secret. Nowadays people don't make such sacrifices for a friend.'

" 'He was a schoolmate of mine.'

" 'That's ridiculous. Well, then, you would have no objections to a second operation? That is all I wanted to know. That is why I came here.'

" 'A second operation?' I asked. 'What prospects do you think he has?'

" 'What!' Dr. Kolbe cried out, standing up. 'What prospects? For Christ's sake—'

" 'You don't mean to say that this second operation will undoubtedly—'

"Dr. Kolbe did not reply. We had understood him only too well. I felt the perspiration starting on my brow. I said: 'After all, doctor, you have taken the Hippocratic Oath. If you consider the operation necessary, we as the patient's closest friends must be grateful to you.'

"Dr. Kolbe asked: 'Do you wish to send the patient any message?'

"I shook my head.

"Siegfried Rosen did not survive the second operation.

"The two Gestapo officials afterward came to the hospital and questioned Dr. Kolbe about the deceased patient. Dr. Kolbe said he knew nothing about the man. The officials informed him that this patient allegedly named Friedrich Bartscher had been in reality an art historian from Kassel by the name of Siegfried Rosen. But Dr. Kolbe was a party member of long standing.

"In spite of our warnings, Edith broke off all relations with Dr. Kolbe immediately after Siegfried Rosen died from his alleged heart attack. The explanation she gave was that she could not stand the way Kolbe's feet perspired.

"Tell me, Herr Laufer, am I guilty of the murder of Rosen? Am I his murderer?"

"Good heavens," Laufer exclaimed, jumping up. "It's almost four o'clock. I must run or I'll miss the Berlin train. Please excuse me, Herr Pflaum, I really must hurry!"

"Well, do you condemn me?"

"Do I?" Laufer asked. "I thank God that He has not made me a judge."

In a trice Laufer was gone. The family sat still, disconcerted. At last Herr Pflaum got up, finished his glass, and remarked: "We shall have to look around for a new lodger." He was already at the door, but turned once more, threw a reproachful look at his daughters, sighed heavily, and said: "And here I have been hoping right along that one of you would marry Laufer. He's such a decent fellow."

Translated by Richard and Clara Winston

THE METAMORPHOSIS

by Franz Kafka

I

As Gregor Samsa awoke one morning from uneasy dreams, he found himself transformed in his bed into a gigantic insect. He was lying on his hard—as it were, armor-plated—back, and when he lifted his head a little, he could see his dome-like brown belly divided into stiff arched segments, on top of which the bedquilt could hardly keep in position and was about to slide off completely. His numerous legs, which were pitifully thin compared to the rest of his bulk, waved helplessly before his eyes.

"What has happened to me?" he thought. It was no dream. His room, a regular human bedroom, only rather too small, lay quite inside the four familiar walls. Above the table, on which a collection of cloth samples was unpacked and spread out—Samsa was a commercial traveler—hung the picture that he had recently cut out of an illustrated magazine and put into a pretty gilt frame. It showed a lady, with a fur cap and a fur stole, sitting upright and holding out to the spectator a huge fur muff into which the whole of her forearm had vanished.

This is one of the few stories that Franz Kafka allowed to be published during his lifetime. He was born, in 1883, into the German-speaking Jewish community of Prague, then the capital of the Austrian-ruled Kingdom of Bohemia. For many years after winning a law degree in 1906, Kafka held a position with the Workmen's Compensation Division of the Labor Office in his native town. When he died of tuberculosis in 1924—after a life whose loneliness, inner conflicts, and quest for faith have become a legend—he had enjoined his closest friend, Max Brod, to destroy all his manuscripts. Brod, happily, disobeyed Kafka's wish and undertook their publication. The Trial, The Castle, *and* Amerika *are the most widely known of Kafka's books.*

Gregor's eyes turned next to the window, and the overcast sky—one could hear raindrops beating on the window gutter—made him quite melancholy. "What about sleeping a little longer and forgetting all this nonsense?" he thought; but it could not be done, for he was accustomed to sleep on his right side, and in his present condition he could not turn himself over. However violently he forced himself toward his right side, he always rolled onto his back again. He tried it at least one hundred times, shutting his eyes to keep from seeing his struggling legs, and only desisted when he began to feel in his side a faint dull ache that he had never experienced before.

"Oh God," he thought, "what an exhausting job I've picked on! Traveling about, day in, day out. It's much more irritating work than doing the actual business in the office, and on top of that there's the trouble of constant traveling, of worrying about train connections, the bed and irregular meals, casual acquaintances who are always new and never become intimate friends. The devil take it all!" He felt a slight itching up on his belly; slowly pushed himself on his back nearer to the top of the bed so that he could lift his head more easily; identified the itching place, which was surrounded by many small white spots, the nature of which he could not understand, and made to touch it with a leg, but drew the leg back immediately, for the contact made a cold shiver run through him.

He slid down again into his former position. "This getting up early," he thought, "makes one quite stupid. A man needs his sleep. Other commercials live like harem women. For instance, when I come back to the hotel of a morning to write up the orders I've got, these others are only sitting down to breakfast. Let me just try that with my chief; I'd be sacked on the spot. Anyhow, that might be quite a good thing for me, who can tell? If I didn't have to hold my hand because of my parents, I'd have given notice long ago, I'd have gone to the chief and told him exactly what I think of him. That would knock him endways from his desk! It's a queer way of doing, too, this sitting on high at a desk and talking down to employees, especially when they have to come quite near because the chief is hard of hearing. Well, there's still hope; once I've saved enough money to pay back my parents' debts to him—that should take another five or six years—I'll do it without fail. I'll cut myself completely loose then. For the moment, though, I'd better get up, for my train goes at five."

He looked at the alarm clock ticking on the chest. "Heavenly Father!" he thought. It was half past six o'clock and the hands were quietly moving on. It was even past the half-hour; it was getting on toward a quarter to seven. Had the alarm clock not gone off? From the bed one could see that it had been properly set for four o'clock; of course it must have gone off. Yes, but was it possible to sleep quietly through that ear-splitting noise? Well, he had not slept quietly, yet apparently all the more soundly for that. But what was he to do now? The next train went at seven o'clock; to catch that he would need to hurry like mad, and his samples weren't even packed up, and he himself wasn't feeling particularly fresh and active. And even if he did catch the train he wouldn't avoid a row with the chief, for the firm's porter would have been waiting for the five-o'clock train and long since would have reported his failure to turn up. The porter was a creature of the chief's, spineless and stupid. Well, supposing he were to say he was sick? But that would be most unpleasant and would look suspicious, as during his five years' employment he had not been ill once. The chief himself would be sure to come with the sick-insurance doctor, would reproach his parents with their son's laziness, and would cut all excuses short by referring to the insurance doctor, who of course regarded all mankind as perfectly healthy malingerers. And would he be so far wrong on this occasion? Gregor really felt quite well, apart from a drowsiness that was utterly superfluous after such a long sleep, and he was even unusually hungry.

As all this was running through his mind at top speed without his being able to decide to leave his bed—the alarm clock had just struck a quarter to seven—there came a cautious tap at the door behind the head of his bed. "Gregor," said a voice —it was his mother's—"it's a quarter to seven. Hadn't you a train to catch?" That gentle voice! Gregor had a shock as he heard his own voice answering hers, unmistakably his own voice, it was true, but with a persistent horrible twittering squeak behind it like an undertone, leaving the words in their clear shape only for the first moment and then rising up reverberating around them to destroy their sense, so that one could not be sure one had heard them rightly. Gregor wanted to answer at length and explain everything, but in the circumstances he confined himself to saying: "Yes, yes, thank you, Mother, I'm getting up now." The wooden door between them must have kept the change in his voice from being noticeable outside, for his mother contented herself with this statement and shuffled away. Yet this brief exchange of words had made the other members of the family aware that Gregor was still in the house, as they had not expected, and at one of the side doors his father was already knocking, gently, yet with his fist. "Gregor, Gregor," he called, "what's the matter with you?" And after a little while he called again in a deeper voice: "Gregor! Gregor!"

At the other side door his sister was saying in a low, plaintive tone: "Gregor? Aren't you well? Are you needing anything?"

He answered them both at once: "I'm just ready," and did his best to make his voice sound as normal as possible by enunciating the words very clearly and leaving long pauses between them. So his father went back to his breakfast, but his sister whispered: "Gregor, open the door, do." However, he was not thinking of opening the door, and felt thankful for the prudent habit he had acquired in traveling of locking all doors during the night, even at home.

His immediate intention was to get up quietly without being disturbed, to put on his clothes and above all eat his breakfast, and only then to consider what else was to be done, as in bed, he was well aware, his meditations would come to no sensible conclusion. He remembered that often enough in bed he had felt small aches and pains, probably caused by awkward postures, which had proved purely imaginary once he was up, and he looked forward eagerly to seeing this morning's delusions gradually fall away. That the change in his voice was nothing but the precursor of a severe chill, a standing ailment of commercial travelers, he had not the least possible doubt.

To get rid of the quilt was quite easy; he had only to inflate himself a little and it fell off by itself. But the next move was difficult, especially because he was so uncommonly broad. He would have needed arms and hands to hoist himself up; instead he had only the numerous little legs, which never stopped waving in all directions, and which he could not control in the least. When he tried to bend one of them, it was the first to stretch itself straight; and did he succeed at last in making it do what he wanted, all the other legs meanwhile waved the more wildly in a high degree of unpleasant agitation. "But what's the use of lying idle in bed?" said Gregor to himself.

He thought that he might get out of bed with the lower part of his body first, but this lower part, which he had not yet seen and of which he could form no clear conception, proved too difficult to move because it shifted so slowly; and when finally, almost wild with annoyance, he gathered his forces together and thrust out recklessly, he had miscalculated the direction and bumped heavily against the lower end of the bed, and the stinging pain he felt informed him that precisely this lower part of his body was at the moment probably the most sensitive.

So he tried to get the top part of himself out first, and cautiously moved his head toward the edge of the bed. That proved easy enough, and despite its breadth and mass the bulk of his body at last slowly followed the movement of his head. Still, when he finally got his head free over the edge of the bed he felt too scared to go on advancing, for after all if he let himself fall in this way it would take a miracle to keep his head from being injured. And at all costs he must not lose consciousness now, precisely now; he would rather stay in bed.

But when after a repetition of the same efforts he lay in his former position again, sighing, and watched his little legs struggling against one another more wildly than ever, if that were possible, and saw no way of bringing any order into this arbitrary confusion, he told himself again that it was impossible to stay in bed and that the most sensible course was to risk everything for the smallest hope of getting away from it. At the same time he did not forget meanwhile to remind himself that cool reflection, the coolest possible, was much better than desperate resolves. In such moments he focused his eyes as sharply as possible on the window, but, unfortunately, the prospect of the morning fog, which muffled even the other side of the narrow street, brought him little encouragement and comfort. "Seven o'clock already," he said to himself when the alarm clock chimed again, "seven o'clock already, and still such a thick fog." And for a little while he lay quiet, breathing lightly, as if perhaps expecting such complete repose to restore all things to their real and normal condition.

But then he said to himself: "Before it strikes a quarter past seven I must be quite out of this bed, without fail. Anyhow, by that time someone will have come from the office to ask for me, since it opens before seven." And he set himself to rocking his whole body at once in a regular rhythm, with the idea of swinging it out of the bed. If he tipped himself out in that way, he could keep his head from injury by lifting it at an acute angle when he fell. His back seemed to be hard and was not likely to suffer from a fall on the carpet. His biggest worry was the loud crash he would not be able to help making, which would probably cause anxiety, if not terror, behind all the doors. Still, he must take the risk.

When he was already half out of the bed—the new method was more a game than an effort, for he needed only to hitch himself across by rocking to and fro—it struck him how simple it would be if he could get help. Two strong people—he thought of his father and the servant girl—would be amply sufficient; they would only have to thrust their arms under his convex back, lever him out of the bed, bend down with their burden, and then be patient enough to let him turn himself right over onto the floor, where it was to be hoped his legs would then find their proper function. Well, ignoring the fact that the doors were all locked, ought he really to call for help? In spite of his misery, he could not suppress a smile at the very idea of it.

He had got so far that he could barely keep his equilibrium when he rocked himself strongly, and he would have to nerve himself very soon for the final decision, for in five minutes' time it would be a quarter past seven—when the front door-bell rang. "That's someone from the office," he said to himself, and grew almost rigid, while his little legs only jigged about all the faster. For a moment everything stayed quiet. "They're not going to open the door," said Gregor to himself, catching at some kind of irrational hope. But then of course the servant girl went as usual to the door with her heavy tread and opened it. Gregor needed only to hear the first good-morning of the visitor to know immediately who it was—the chief clerk himself. What a fate, to be condemned to work for a firm where the smallest omission at once gave rise to the gravest suspicion! Were all employees in a body nothing but scoundrels, was there not among them one single loyal, devoted man who, had he wasted only an hour or so of the firm's time in a morning, was so tormented by conscience as to be driven out of his mind and actually incapable of leaving his bed? Wouldn't it really have been sufficient to send an apprentice to inquire—if any inquiry were necessary at all? Did the chief clerk himself have to come, and thus indicate to the entire family, an innocent family, that this suspicious circumstance could be investigated by no one less versed in affairs than himself? And more through the agitation caused by these reflections than through any act of will Gregor swung himself out of bed with all his strength. There was a loud thump, but it was not really a crash. His fall was broken to some extent by the carpet; also, his back was less stiff than he had thought, and so there was merely a dull thud, not so very startling. Only he had not lifted his head carefully enough and had hit it; he turned it and rubbed it on the carpet in pain and irritation.

"That was something falling down in there," said the chief clerk in the next room to the left. Gregor tried to suppose to himself that something like what had happened to him today might some day happen to the chief clerk; one really could not deny that it was possible. But as if in brusque reply to this supposition the chief clerk took a couple of firm steps in the next room, and his patent-leather boots creaked. From the right-hand room his sister was whispering to inform him of the situation: "Gregor, the chief clerk's here."

"I know," muttered Gregor to himself; but he didn't dare to make his voice loud enough for his sister to hear it.

"Gregor," said his father now from the left-hand room, "the chief clerk has come and wants to know why you didn't catch the early train. We don't know what to say to him. Besides, he wants to talk to you in person. So open the door, please. He will be good enough to excuse the untidiness of your room."

"Good morning, Mr. Samsa," the chief clerk was calling amiably meanwhile.

"He's not well," said his mother to the visitor, while his father was still speaking through the door, "he's not well, sir, believe me. What else would make him miss a train! The boy thinks about nothing but his work. It makes me almost cross the way he never goes out in the evenings. He's been here the last eight days and has stayed at home every single evening. He just sits there quietly at the table reading a newspaper or looking through railway timetables. The only amusement he gets is doing fretwork. For instance, he spent two or three evenings cutting out a little picture frame; you would be surprised to see how pretty it is; it's hanging in his room; you'll see it in a minute when Gregor opens the door. I must say I'm glad you've come, sir; we should never have got him to unlock the door by ourselves, he's so obstinate; and I'm sure he's unwell, though he wouldn't have it to be so this morning."

"I'm just coming," said Gregor slowly and carefully, not moving an inch for fear of losing one word of the conversation.

"I can't think of any other explanation, madam," said the chief clerk, "I hope it's nothing serious. Although on the other hand I must say that we men of business—fortunately or unfortunately—very often simply have to ignore any slight indisposition, since business must be attended to."

"Well, can the chief clerk come in now?" asked Gregor's father impatiently, again knocking on the door.

"No," said Gregor. In the left-hand room a painful silence followed this refusal; in the right-hand room his sister began to sob.

Why didn't his sister join the others? She was probably newly out of bed and hadn't even begun to put on her clothes yet. Well, why was she crying? Because he wouldn't get up and let the chief clerk in, because he was in danger of losing his job, and because the chief would begin dunning his parents again for the old debts? Surely these were things one didn't need to worry about for the present. Gregor was still at home, and not in the least thinking of deserting the family. At the moment, true, he was lying on the carpet and no one who knew the condition he was in could seriously expect him to admit the chief clerk. But for such a small discourtesy, which could plausibly be explained away somehow later on, Gregor could hardly be dismissed on the spot. And it seemed to Gregor that it would be much more sensible to leave him in peace for the present than to trouble him with tears and entreaties. Still, of course, their uncertainty bewildered them all and excused their behavior.

"Mr. Samsa," the chief clerk called now in a louder voice, "what's the matter with you? Here you are, barricading yourself in your room, giving only 'yes' and 'no' for answers, causing your parents a lot of unnecessary trouble, and neglecting—I mention this only in passing—neglecting your business duties in an incredible fashion. I am speaking here in the name of your parents and of your chief, and I beg you quite seriously to give me an immediate and precise explanation. You amaze me, you amaze me. I thought you were a quiet, dependable person, and now all at once you seem bent on making a disgraceful exhibition of yourself. The chief did hint to me early this morning a possible explanation for your disappearance—with reference to the cash payments that were entrusted to you recently—but I almost pledged my solemn word of honor that this could not be so. But now that I see how incredibly obstinate you are, I no longer have the slightest desire to take your part at all. And your position in the firm is not so unassailable. I came with the intention of telling you all this in private, but since you are wasting my time so needlessly, I don't see why your parents shouldn't hear it too. For some time past your work has been most unsatisfactory; this is not the season of the year for a business boom, of course, we admit that, but a season of the year for doing no business at all, that does not exist, Mr. Samsa, must not exist."

"But, sir," cried Gregor, beside himself and in his agitation forgetting everything else, "I'm just going to open the door this very minute. A slight illness, an attack of giddiness, has kept me from getting up. I'm still lying in bed. But I feel all right again. I'm getting out of bed now. Just give me a moment or two longer! I'm not quite so well as I thought. But I'm all right, really. How a thing like that can suddenly strike one down! Only last night I was quite well, my parents can tell you, or rather I did have a slight presentiment. I must have showed some sign of it. Why didn't I report it at the office! But one always thinks that an indisposition can be got over without staying in the house. Oh, sir, do spare my parents! All that you're reproaching me with now has no foundation; no one has ever said a word to me about it. Perhaps you haven't looked at the last orders I sent in. Anyhow, I can still catch the eight-o'clock train, I'm much the better for my few hours' rest. Don't let me detain you here, sir; I'll be attending to business very soon, and do be good enough to tell the chief so and to make my excuses to him!"

And while all this was tumbling out pell-mell and Gregor hardly knew what he was saying, he had reached the chest quite easily, perhaps because of the practice he had had in bed, and was now trying to lever himself upright by means of it. He meant actually to open the door, actually to show himself and speak to the chief clerk; he was eager to find out what the others, after all their insistence, would say at the sight of him. If they were horrified, then the responsibility was no longer his and he could stay quiet. But if they took it calmly, then he had no reason, either, to be upset, and could really get to the station for the eight-o'clock train if he hurried. At first he slipped down a few times from the polished surface of the chest, but at length with a last heave he stood upright; he paid no more attention to the pains in the lower part of his body, however they smarted. Then he let himself fall against the back of a near-by chair and clung with his little legs to the edges of it. That brought him into control of himself again, and he stopped speaking, for now he could listen to what the chief clerk was saying.

"Did you understand a word of it?" the chief clerk was asking. "Surely he can't be trying to make fools of us?"

"Oh dear," cried his mother, in tears, "perhaps he's terribly ill and we're tormenting him. Grete! Grete!" she called out then.

"Yes, Mother?" called his sister from the other side. They were calling to each other across Gregor's room.

"You must go this minute for the doctor. Gregor is ill. Go for the doctor, quick. Did you hear how he was speaking?"

"That was no human voice," said the chief clerk in a voice noticeably low beside the shrillness of the mother's.

"Anna! Anna!" his father was calling through the hall to the kitchen, clapping his hands, "get a locksmith at once!" And the two girls were already running through the hall with a swish of skirts—how could his sister have got dressed so quickly?—and were tearing the front door open. There was no sound of its closing again; they had evidently left it open, as one does in houses where some great misfortune has happened.

But Gregor was now much calmer. The words he uttered were no longer understandable, apparently, although they seemed clear enough to him, even clearer than before, perhaps because his ear had grown accustomed to the sound of them. Yet at any rate people now believed that something was wrong with him, and were ready to help him. The positive certainty with which these first measures had been taken comforted him. He felt himself drawn once more into the human circle and hoped for great and remarkable results from both the doctor and the locksmith, without really distinguishing precisely between them. To make his voice as clear as possible for the decisive conversation that was now imminent he coughed a little, as quietly as he could, of course, since this noise too might not sound like a human cough, for all he was able to judge. In the next room meanwhile there was complete silence. Perhaps his parents were sitting at the table with the chief clerk, whispering; perhaps they were all leaning against the door and listening.

Slowly Gregor pushed the chair toward the door, then let go of it, caught hold of the door for support—the soles at the end of his little legs were somewhat sticky—and rested against it for a moment after his efforts. Then he set himself to turning the key in the lock with his mouth. It seemed, unhappily, that he hadn't really any teeth—what could he grip the key with?—but on the other hand his jaws were certainly very strong; with their help he did manage to set the key in motion, heedless of the fact that he was undoubtedly damaging them somewhere, since a brown fluid issued from his mouth, flowed over the key, and dripped on the floor.

"Just listen to that," said the chief clerk next door; "he's turning the key." That was a great encouragement to Gregor; but they should all have shouted encouragement to him, his father and mother too: "Go on, Gregor," they should have called out, "keep going, hold on to that key!"

And in the belief that they were all following his efforts intently, he clenched his jaws recklessly on the key with all the force at his command. As the turning of the key progressed he circled round the lock, holding on now only with his mouth, pushing on the key, as required, or pulling it down again with all the weight of his body. The louder click of the finally yielding lock literally quickened Gregor. With a deep breath of relief he said to himself: "So I didn't need the locksmith," and laid his head on the handle to open the door wide.

Since he had to pull the door toward him, he was still invisible when it was really wide open. He had to edge himself slowly round the near half of the double door, and to do it very carefully if he was not to fall plump upon his back just on the threshold. He was still carrying out this difficult maneuver, with no time to observe anything else, when he heard the chief clerk utter a loud "Oh!"—it sounded like a gust of wind—and now he could see the man, standing, as he was, nearest to the door, clapping one hand before his open mouth and slowly backing away as if driven by some invisible steady pressure. His mother—in spite of the chief clerk's being there her hair was still undone and sticking up in all directions—first clasped her hands and looked at his father, then took two steps toward Gregor and fell on the floor among her outspread skirts, her face quite hidden on her breast. His father knotted his fist with a fierce expression on his face as if he meant to knock Gregor back into his room, then looked uncertainly around the living-room, covered his eyes with his hands, and wept till his great chest heaved.

Gregor did not go now into the living-room, but leaned against the inside of the firmly shut wing of the door, so that only half his body was visible and his head above it bending sideways to look at the others. The light had meanwhile strengthened; on the other side of the street one could see clearly a section of the endlessly long, dark-gray building opposite—it was a hospital—abruptly punctuated by its row of regular windows; the rain was still falling, but only in large singly discernible and literally singly splashing drops. The breakfast dishes were set out on the table lavishly, for breakfast was the most important meal of the day to Gregor's father, who lingered it out for hours over various newspapers. Right opposite Gregor on the wall hung a photograph of himself in military service, as a lieutenant, hand on sword, a carefree smile on his face, inviting one to respect his uniform and military bearing. The door leading to the hall was open, and one could see that the front door stood open too, showing the landing beyond and the beginning of the stairs going down.

"Well," said Gregor, knowing perfectly that he was the only one who had retained any composure, "I'll put my clothes on at once, pack up my samples, and start off. Will you only let me go? You see, sir, I'm not obstinate, and I'm willing to work; traveling is a hard life, but I couldn't live without it. Where are you going, sir? To the office? Yes? Will you give a true account of all this? One can be temporarily incapacitated, but that's just the moment for remembering former services and bearing in mind that later on, when the incapacity has been got over, one will certainly work with all the more industry and concentration. I'm loyally bound to serve the chief, you know that very well. Besides, I have to provide for my parents and my sister. I'm in great difficulties, but I'll get out of them again. Don't make things any worse for me than they are. Stand up for me in the firm. Travelers are not popular there, I know. People think they earn sacks of money and just have a good time. A prejudice there's no particular reason for revising. But you, sir, have a more comprehensive view of affairs than the rest of the staff, yes, let me tell you in confidence, a more comprehensive view than the chief himself, who, being the owner, lets his judgment easily be swayed against one of his employees. And you know very well that the traveler, who is never seen in the office almost the whole year round, can so easily fall a victim to gossip and ill luck and unfounded complaints, which he mostly knows nothing about, except when he comes back exhausted from his rounds, and only then suffers in person from their evil consequences, which he can no longer trace back to the original causes. Sir, sir, don't go away without a word to me to show that you think me in the right at least to some extent!"

But at Gregor's very first words the chief clerk had already backed away, merely staring at him with parted lips over one twitching shoulder. And while Gregor was speaking he did not stand still one moment, but stole away toward the door without taking his eyes off Gregor, yet only an inch at a time, as if obeying some secret injunction to leave the room. He was already at the hall, and the suddenness with which he took his last step out of the living-room would have made one believe he had burned the sole of his foot. Once in the hall, he stretched his right arm before him toward the staircase, as if some supernatural power were waiting there to deliver him.

Gregor perceived that the chief clerk must on no account be allowed to go away in this frame of mind if his position in the firm were not to be endangered to the utmost. His parents did not understand this so well; they had convinced themselves in the course of years that Gregor was settled for life in this firm, and besides they were so preoccupied with their immediate troubles that all foresight had forsaken them. Yet Gregor had this foresight. The chief clerk must be detained, soothed, persuaded, and finally won over; the whole future of Gregor and his family depended on it! If only his sister had been there! She was intelligent; she had begun to cry while Gregor was still lying quietly on his back. And no doubt the chief clerk, so partial to ladies, would have been guided by her; she would have shut the door of the flat and in the hall talked him out of his horror. But she was not there, and Gregor would have to handle the situation himself. And without remembering that he was still unaware what powers of movement he possessed, without even remembering that his words in all possibility, indeed in all likelihood, would again be unintelligible, he let go the wing of the door, pushed himself through the opening, started to walk toward the chief clerk, who was already ridiculously clinging with both hands to the railing on the landing; but immediately, as he was feeling for a support, he fell down with a little cry upon all his numerous legs. Hardly was he down when he experienced for the first time this morning a sense of physical comfort; his legs had firm ground under them; they were completely obedient, as he noted with joy; they even strove to carry him forward in whatever direction he chose; and he was inclined to believe that a final relief from all his sufferings was at hand. But at the moment when he found himself on the floor, rocking with suppressed eagerness to move, not far from his mother—indeed, just in front of her—she, who had seemed so completely crushed, sprang all at once to her feet, her arms and fingers outspread, cried: "Help, for God's sake, help!" bent her head down as if to see Gregor better, yet on the contrary kept backing senselessly away; had quite forgotten that the laden table stood behind her; sat upon it hastily, as if in absence of mind, when she bumped into it; and seemed altogether unaware that the big coffeepot beside her was upset and pouring coffee in a flood over the carpet.

"Mother, Mother," said Gregor in a low voice, and looked up at her. The chief clerk, for the moment, had quite slipped from his mind; instead, he could not resist snapping his jaws together at the sight of the streaming coffee. That made his mother scream again. She fled from the table and fell into the arms of his father, who hastened to catch her. But Gregor had now no time to spare for his parents; the chief clerk was already on the stairs; with his chin on the banisters he was taking one last backward look. Gregor made a spring, to be as sure as possible of overtaking him. The chief clerk must have divined his intention, for he leaped down several steps and vanished; he was still yelling "Ugh!" and it echoed through the whole staircase.

Unfortunately, the flight of the chief clerk seemed completely to upset Gregor's father, who had remained relatively calm until now, for instead of running after the man himself, or at least not hindering Gregor in his pursuit, he seized in his right hand the walking-stick that the chief clerk had left behind on a chair, together with a hat and greatcoat, snatched in his left hand a large newspaper from the table, and began stamping his feet and flourishing the stick and the newspaper to drive Gregor back into his room. No entreaty of Gregor's availed; indeed, no entreaty was even understood; however humbly he bent his head, his father only stamped on the floor the more loudly. Behind his father, his mother had torn open a window despite the cold weather and was leaning far out of it with her face in her hands. A strong draft set in from the street to the staircase, the window curtains blew in, the newspapers on the table fluttered, stray pages whisked over the floor. Pitilessly Gregor's father drove him back, hissing and crying "Shoo!" like a savage. But Gregor was quite unpracticed in walking backwards, it really was a slow business. If he only had a chance to turn round he could get back to his room at once, but he was afraid of exasperating his father by the slowness of such a rotation and at any moment the stick in his father's hand might hit him a fatal blow on the back or on the head.

In the end, however, nothing else was left for him to do since to his horror he observed that in moving backwards he could not even control the direction he took; and so, keeping an anxious eye on his father all the time over his shoulder, he began to turn round as quickly as he could, which was in reality very slowly. Perhaps his father noted his good intentions, for he did not interfere except every now and then to help him in the maneuver from a distance with the point of the stick. If only he would have stopped making that unbearable hissing noise! It made Gregor quite lose his head. He had turned almost completely round when the hissing noise so distracted him that he even turned a little the wrong way again. But when at last his head was fortunately right in front of the doorway, it appeared that his body was too broad simply to get through the opening. His father, of course, in his present mood was far from thinking of such a thing as opening the other half of the door, to let Gregor have enough space. He had merely the fixed idea of driving Gregor back into his room as quickly as possible. He would never have suffered Gregor to make the circumstantial preparations for standing up on end and perhaps slipping his way through the door. Maybe he was now making more noise than ever to urge Gregor forward, as if no obstacle impeded him; to Gregor, anyhow, the noise in his rear sounded no longer like the voice of one single father; this was really no joke, and Gregor thrust himself—come what might—into the doorway. One side of his body rose up, he was tilted at an angle in the doorway. His flank was quite bruised; horrid blotches stained the white door; soon he was stuck fast and, left to himself, could not have moved at all. His legs on one side fluttered trembling in the air; those on the other were crushed painfully to the floor—when, from behind, his father gave him a strong push, which was literally a deliverance, and he flew far into the room, bleeding freely. The door was slammed behind him with the stick, and then at last there was silence.

II

Not until it was twilight did Gregor awake out of a deep sleep, more like a swoon than a sleep. He would certainly have waked up of his own accord not much later, for he felt himself sufficiently rested and well-slept, but it seemed to him as if a fleeting step and a cautious shutting of the door leading into the hall had aroused him. The electric lights in the street cast a pale sheen here and there on the ceiling and the upper surfaces of the furniture, but down below, where he lay, it was dark. Slowly, awkwardly trying out his feelers, which he now first learned to appreciate, he pushed his way to the door to see what had been happening there. His left side felt like one single long, unpleasantly tense scar, and he had actually to limp on his two rows of legs. One little leg, moreover, had been severely damaged in the course of that morning's events—it was almost a miracle that only one had been damaged—and trailed uselessly behind him.

He had reached the door before he discovered what had really drawn him to it: the smell of food. For there stood a basin filled with fresh milk in which floated little sops of white bread. He could almost have laughed with joy, since he was now still hungrier than in the morning, and he dipped his head almost over the eyes straight into the milk. But soon in disappointment he withdrew it again; not only did he find it difficult to feed because of his tender left side—and he could only feed with the palpitating collaboration of his whole body—he did not like the milk either, though milk had been his favorite drink and that was certainly why his sister had set it there for him. Indeed, it was almost with repulsion that he turned away from the basin and crawled back to the middle of the room.

He could see through the crack of the door that the gas was turned on in the living-room, but while usually at this time his father made a habit of reading the afternoon newspaper in a loud voice to his mother and occasionally to his sister as well, not a sound was now to be heard. Well, perhaps his father had recently given up this habit of reading aloud, which his sister had mentioned so often in conversation and in her letters. But there was the same silence all around, though the flat was certainly not empty of occupants. "What a quiet life our family has been leading!" said Gregor to himself, and as he sat there motionless, staring into the darkness, he felt great pride in the fact that he had been able to provide such a life for his parents and sister in such a fine flat. But what if all the quiet, the comfort, the contentment were now to end in horror? To keep himself from being lost in such thoughts Gregor took refuge in movement and crawled up and down the room.

Once during the long evening one of the side doors was opened a little and quickly shut again, later the other side door too; someone had apparently wanted to come in and then thought better of it. Gregor now stationed himself immediately before the living-room door, determined to persuade any hesitating visitor to come in, or at least to discover who it might be; but the door was not opened again, and he waited in vain. In the early morning, when the doors were locked, they had all wanted to come in; now that he had opened one door, and the other had apparently been opened during the day, no one came in and even the keys were on the other side of the doors.

It was late at night before the gas went out in the living-room, and Gregor could easily tell that his parents and his sister had all stayed awake until then, for he could clearly hear the three of them stealing away on tiptoe. No one was likely to visit him, not until the morning, that was certain; so he had plenty of time to meditate at his leisure on how he was to arrange his life afresh. But the lofty, empty room in which he had to lie flat on the floor filled him with an apprehension he could not account for: it had been his very own room for the past five years—and with a half-unconscious action, not without a slight feeling of shame, he scuttled under the sofa, where he felt comfortable at once, though his back was a little cramped and he could not lift his head up, and his only regret was that his body was too broad to get the whole of it under the sofa.

He stayed there all night, spending the time partly in a light slumber, from which his hunger kept waking him up with a start, and partly in worrying and sketching vague hopes, which all led to the same conclusion, that he must lie low for the present and, by exercising patience and the utmost consideration, help the family to bear the inconvenience he was bound to cause them in his present condition.

Very early in the morning—it was still almost night—Gregor had the chance to test the strength of his new resolutions, for his sister, nearly fully dressed, opened the door from the hall and peered in. She did not see him at once, yet when she caught sight of him under the sofa—well, he had to be somewhere, he couldn't have flown away, could he?—she was so startled that without being able to help it she slammed the door shut again. But as if regretting her behavior she opened the door again immediately and came in on tiptoe, as if she were visiting an invalid or even a stranger. Gregor had pushed his head forward to the very edge of the sofa and watched her. Would she notice that he had left the milk standing, and not for lack of hunger, and would she bring in some other kind of food more to his taste? If she did not do it of her own accord, he would rather starve than draw her attention to the fact, though he felt a wild impulse to dart out from under the sofa, throw himself at her feet, and beg her for something to eat. But his sister at once noticed, with surprise, that the basin was still full, except for a little milk that had been spilt all around it; she lifted it immediately, not with her bare hands, true, but with a cloth, and carried it away. Gregor was wildly curious to know what she would bring instead, and made various speculations about it. Yet what she actually did next, in the goodness of her heart, he could never have guessed at. To find out what he liked, she brought him a whole selection of food, all set out on an old newspaper. There were old, half-decayed vegetables, bones from last night's supper covered with a white sauce that had thickened; some raisins and almonds; a piece of cheese that Gregor would have called uneatable two days ago; a dry roll, a buttered roll, and a roll both buttered and salted. Besides all that, she set down again the same basin, into which she had poured some water, and which was apparently to be reserved for his exclusive use. And with fine tact, knowing that Gregor would not eat in her presence, she withdrew quickly and even turned the key, to let him understand that he could take his ease as much as he liked.

Gregor's legs all whizzed toward the food. His wounds must have healed completely, moreover, for he felt no disability, which amazed him and made him reflect how more than a month ago he had cut one finger a little with a knife and had still suffered pain from the wound only the day before yesterday. "Am I less sensitive now?" he thought, and sucked greedily at the cheese, which above all the other edibles attracted him at once and strongly. One after another and with tears of satisfaction in his eyes he quickly devoured the cheese, the vegetables, and the sauce; the fresh food, on the other hand, had no charms for him; he could not even stand the smell of it and actually dragged away to some little distance the things he could eat.

He had long finished his meal and was only lying lazily on the same spot when his sister turned the key slowly as a sign for him to retreat. That roused him at once, though he was nearly asleep, and he hurried under the sofa again. But it took considerable self-control for him to stay under the sofa, even for the short time his sister was in the room, for the large meal had swollen his body somewhat and he was so cramped he could hardly breathe. Slight attacks of breathlessness afflicted him, and his eyes were starting a little out of his head as he watched his unsuspecting sister sweeping together with a broom not only the remains of what he had eaten but even the things he had not touched, as if these were now of no use to anyone, and hastily shoveling it all into a bucket, which she covered with a wooden lid and carried away. Hardly had she turned her back when Gregor came from under the sofa and stretched and puffed himself out.

In this manner Gregor was fed, once in the early morning while his parents and the servant girl were still asleep, and a second time after they had all had their midday dinner, for then his parents took a short nap and the servant girl could be sent out on some errand or other by his sister. Not that they would have wanted him to starve, of course, but perhaps they could not have borne to know more about his feeding than from hearsay; perhaps too his sister wanted to spare them such little anxieties wherever possible, they having quite enough to bear as it was.

Under what pretext the doctor and the locksmith had been got rid of on that first morning Gregor could not discover, for since what he said was not understood by the others, it never struck any of them, not even his sister, that he could understand what they said, and so whenever his sister came into his room he had to content himself with hearing her utter only a sigh now and then and an occasional appeal to the saints. Later on, when she had got a little used to the situation—of course she could never get completely used to it—she sometimes threw out a remark that was kindly meant or could be so interpreted.

"Well, he liked his dinner today," she would say when Gregor had made a good clearance of his food; and when he had not eaten, which gradually happened more and more often, she would say almost sadly: "Everything's been left standing again."

But although Gregor could get no news directly, he overheard a lot from the neighboring rooms, and as soon as voices were audible, he would run to the door of the room concerned and press his whole body against it. In the first few days especially there was no conversation that did not refer to him somehow, even if only indirectly. For two whole days there were family consultations at every mealtime about what should be done; but also between meals the same subject was discussed, for there were always at least two members of the family at home because no one wanted to be alone in the flat and to leave it quite empty was unthinkable. And on the very first of these days the household cook—it was not quite clear what and how much she knew of the situation—went down on her knees to his mother and begged leave to go, and when she departed, a quarter of an hour later, gave thanks for her dismissal with tears in her eyes as if for the greatest benefit that could have been conferred on her, and without any prompting swore a solemn oath that she would never say a single word to anyone about what had happened.

Now Gregor's sister had to cook too, helping her mother; true, the cooking did not amount to much, for they ate scarcely anything. Gregor was always hearing one of the family vainly urging another to eat and getting no answer but: "Thanks, I've had all I want," or something similar. Perhaps they drank nothing either. Time and again his sister kept asking his father if he wouldn't like some beer and offering kindly to go and fetch it herself, and when he made no answer suggesting that she could ask the concierge to fetch it, so that he need feel no sense of obligation, but then a round "No" came from his father and no more was said about it.

In the course of that very first day Gregor's father explained the family's financial position and prospects to both his mother and his sister. Now and then he rose from the table to get some voucher or memorandum out of the small safe he had rescued from the collapse of his business five years earlier. One could hear him opening the complicated lock and rustling papers out and shutting it again. This statement made by his father was the first cheerful information Gregor had heard since his imprisonment. He had been of the opinion that nothing at all was left over from his father's business; at least his father had never said anything to the contrary, and of course he had not asked him directly. At that time Gregor's sole desire was to do his utmost to help the family to forget as soon as possible the catastrophe that had overwhelmed the business and thrown them all into a state of complete despair. And so he had set to work with unusual ardor and almost overnight had become a commercial traveler instead of a little clerk, with of course much greater chances of earning money, and his success was immediately translated into good round coin that he could lay on the table for his amazed and happy family. These had been fine times, and they had never recurred, at least not with the same sense of glory, though later on Gregor had earned so much money that he was able to meet the expenses of the whole household, and did so. They had simply got used to it, both the family and Gregor; the money was gratefully accepted and gladly given, but there was no special uprush of warm feeling. With his sister alone had he remained intimate, and it was a secret plan of his that she, who loved music, unlike himself, and could play movingly on the violin, should be sent next year to study at the Conservatorium, despite the great expense that would entail, which must be made up in some other way. During his brief visits home the Conservatorium was often mentioned in the talks he had with his sister, but always merely as a beautiful dream that could never come true, and his parents discouraged even these innocent references to it; yet Gregor had made up his mind firmly about it and meant to announce the fact with due solemnity on Christmas Day.

Such were the thoughts, completely futile in his present condition, that went through his head as he stood clinging upright to the door and listening. Sometimes out of sheer weariness he had to give up listening and let his head fall negligently against the door, but he always had to pull himself together again at once, for even the slight sound his head made was audible next door and brought all conversation to a stop. "What can he be doing now?" his father would say after a while, obviously turning toward the door, and only then would the interrupted conversation gradually be set going again.

Gregor was now informed as amply as he could wish—for his father tended to repeat himself in his explanations, partly because it was a long time since he had handled such matters and partly because his mother could not always grasp things at once—that a certain amount of investments, a very small amount it was true, had survived the wreck of their fortunes and had even increased a little because the dividends had not been touched meanwhile. And besides that, the money Gregor brought home every month—he had kept only a few dollars for himself—had never been quite used up, and now amounted to a small capital sum. Behind the door Gregor nodded his head eagerly, rejoiced at this evidence of unexpected thrift and foresight. True, he could really have paid off some more of his father's debts to the chief with this extra money, and so brought much nearer the day on which he could quit his job, but doubtless it was better the way his father had arranged it.

Yet this capital was by no means sufficient to let the family live on the interest of it; for one year, perhaps, or at the most two, they could live on the principal, that was all. It was simply a sum that ought not to be touched and should be kept for a rainy day; money for living expenses would have to be earned. Now his father was still hale enough, but an old man, and he had done no work for the past five years and could not be expected to do much; during these five years, the first years of leisure in his laborious though unsuccessful life, he had grown rather fat and become sluggish. And Gregor's old mother—how was she to earn a living with her asthma, which troubled her even when she walked through the flat, and kept her lying on a sofa every other day, panting for breath beside an open window? And was his sister to earn her bread, she who was still a child of seventeen and whose life hitherto had been so pleasant, consisting as it did in dressing herself nicely, sleeping long, helping in the housekeeping, going out to a few modest entertainments, and above all playing the violin? At first whenever the need for earning money was mentioned, Gregor let go his hold on the door and threw himself down on the cool leather sofa beside it because he felt so hot with shame and grief.

Often he just lay there the long nights through without sleeping at all, scrabbling for hours on the leather. Or he nerved himself to the great effort of pushing an armchair to the window, then crawled up over the window-sill and, braced against the chair, leaned against the windowpanes, obviously in some recollection of the sense of freedom that looking out of a window always used to give him. For in reality day by day things that were even a little way off were growing dimmer to his sight; the hospital across the street, which he had used to execrate for being all too often before his eyes, was now quite beyond his range of vision, and if he had not known that he lived in Charlotte Street, a quiet street but still a city street, he might have believed that his window gave on a desert waste where gray sky and gray land blended indistinguishably into each other. His quick-witted sister only needed to observe twice that the armchair stood by the window; after that whenever she had tidied the room she always pushed the chair back to the same place at the window and even left the inner casements open.

If he could have spoken to her and thanked her for all she had to do for him, he could have borne her ministrations better; as it was, they oppressed him. She certainly tried to make as light as possible of whatever was disagreeable in her task, and as time went on she succeeded, of course, more and more, but time brought more enlightenment to Gregor too. The very way she came in distressed him. Hardly was she in the room when she rushed to the window, without even taking time to shut the door, careful as she was usually to shield the sight of Gregor's room from the others, and, as if she were almost suffocating, tore the casements open with hasty fingers, standing then in the open draft for a while even in the bitterest cold and drawing deep breaths. This noisy scurry of hers upset Gregor twice a day; he would crouch trembling under the sofa all the time, knowing quite well that she would certainly have spared him such a disturbance had she found it at all possible to stay in his presence without opening the window.

On one occasion, about a month after Gregor's metamorphosis, when there was surely no reason for her to be still startled at his appearance, she came a little earlier than usual and found him gazing out of the window, quite motionless, and thus well placed to look like a bogy. Gregor would not have been surprised had she not come in at all, for she could not immediately open the window while he was there; but not only did she retreat, she jumped back as if in alarm and banged the door shut; a stranger might well have thought that he had been lying in wait for her there meaning to bite her. Of course he hid himself under the sofa at once, but he had to wait until midday before she came again, and she seemed more ill at ease than usual. This made him realize how repulsive the sight of him still was to her, and that it was bound to go on being repulsive, and what an effort it must cost her not to run away even from the sight of the small portion of his body that stuck out from under the sofa. In order to spare her that, therefore, one day he carried a sheet on his back to the sofa—it cost him four hours' labor—and arranged it there in such a way as to hide him completely, so that even if she were to bend down she could not see him. Had she considered the sheet unnecessary, she would certainly have stripped it off the sofa again, for it was clear enough that this curtaining and confining of himself was not likely to conduce to Gregor's comfort, but she left it were it was, and Gregor even fancied that he caught a thankful glance from her eye when he lifted the sheet carefully a very little with his head to see how she was taking the new arrangement.

For the first fortnight his parents could not bring themselves to the point of entering his room, and he often heard them expressing their appreciation of his sister's activities, whereas formerly they had frequently scolded her for being as they thought a somewhat useless daughter. But now both of them often waited outside the door, his father and his mother, while his sister tidied his room, and as soon as she came out she had to tell them exactly how things were in the room, what Gregor had eaten, how he had conducted himself this time, and whether there was not perhaps some slight improvement in his condition. His mother, moreover, began relatively soon to want to visit him, but his father and sister dissuaded her at first with arguments that Gregor listened to very attentively and altogether approved. Later, however, she had to be held back by main force, and when she cried out: "Do let me in to Gregor, he is my unfortunate son! Can't you understand that I must go to him?" Gregor thought that it might be well to have her come in, not every day, of course, but perhaps once a week; she understood things, after all, much better than his sister, who was only a child despite the efforts she was making and who had perhaps taken on so difficult a task merely out of childish thoughtlessness.

Gregor's desire to see his mother was soon fulfilled. During the daytime he did not want to show himself at the window, out of consideration for his parents, but he could not crawl very far around the few square yards of floor space he had, nor could he bear lying quietly at rest all during the night, while he was fast losing any interest he had ever taken in food, so that for mere recreation he had formed the habit of crawling crisscross over the walls and ceiling. He especially enjoyed hanging suspended from the ceiling; it was much better than lying on the floor; one could breathe more freely; one's body swung and rocked lightly; and in the almost blissful absorption induced by this suspension it could happen to his own surprise that he let go and fell plump on the floor. Yet he now had his body much better under control than formerly, and even such a big fall did him no harm.

His sister at once remarked the new distraction Gregor had found for himself—he left traces behind him of the sticky stuff on his soles wherever he crawled—and she got the idea in her head of giving him as wide a field as possible to crawl in and of removing the pieces of furniture that hindered him—above all, the chest of drawers and the writing desk. But that was more than she could manage all by herself; she did not dare ask her father to help her; and as for the servant girl, a young creature of sixteen who had had the courage to stay on after the cook's departure, she could not be asked to help, for she had begged as an especial favor that she might keep the kitchen door locked and open it only on a definite summons; so there was nothing left but to apply to her mother at an hour when her father was out.

And the old lady did come, with exclamations of joyful eagerness, which, however, died away at the door of Gregor's room. Gregor's sister, of course, went in first, to see that everything was in order before letting his mother enter. In great haste Gregor pulled the sheet lower and rucked it more in folds so that it really looked as if it had been thrown accidentally over the sofa. And this time he did not peer out from under it; he renounced the pleasure of seeing his mother on this occasion and was only glad that she had come at all. "Come in, he's out of sight," said his sister, obviously leading her mother in by the hand. Gregor could now hear the two women struggling to shift the heavy old chest from its place, and his sister claiming the greater part of the labor for herself, without listening to the admonitions of her mother, who feared she might overstrain herself. It took a long time. After at least a quarter of an hour's tugging his mother objected that the chest had better be left where it was, for in the first place it was too heavy and could never be got out before his father came home, and standing in the middle of the room like that it would only hamper Gregor's movements; while in the second place it was not at all certain that removing the furniture would be doing a service to Gregor. She was inclined to think to the contrary; the sight of the naked walls made her own heart heavy, and why shouldn't Gregor have the same feeling, considering that he had been used to his furniture for so long and might feel forlorn without it. "And doesn't it look," she concluded in a low voice—in fact, she had been almost whispering all the time as if to avoid letting Gregor, whose exact whereabouts she did not know, hear even the tones of her voice, for she was convinced that he could not understand her words—"doesn't it look as if we were showing him, by taking away his furniture, that we have given up hope of his ever getting better and are just leaving him coldly to himself? I think it would be best to keep his room exactly as it has always been, so that when he comes back to us he will find everything unchanged and be able all the more easily to forget what has happened in between."

On hearing these words from his mother Gregor realized that the lack of all direct human speech for the past two months, together with the monotony of family life, must have confused his mind; otherwise he could not account for the fact that he had quite earnestly looked forward to having his room emptied of furnishing. Did he really want his warm room, so comfortably fitted with old family furniture, to be turned into a naked den in which he would certainly be able to crawl unhampered in all directions but at the price of shedding simultaneously all recollection of his human background? He had indeed been so near the brink of forgetfulness that only the voice of his mother, which he had not heard for so long, had drawn him back from it. Nothing should be taken out of his room; everything must stay as it was; he could not dispense with the good influence of the furniture on his state of mind; and even if the furniture did hamper him in his senseless crawling round and round, that was no drawback but a great advantage.

Unfortunately his sister was of the contrary opinion; she had grown accustomed, and not without reason, to consider herself an expert in Gregor's affairs as against her parents, and so her mother's advice was now enough to make her determined on the removal not only of the chest and the writing desk, which had been her first intention, but of all the furniture except the indispensable sofa. This determination was not, of course, merely the outcome of childish recalcitrance and of the self-confidence she had recently developed so unexpectedly and at such cost; she had in fact perceived that Gregor needed a lot of space to crawl about in, while on the other hand he never used the furniture at all, so far as could be seen. Another factor might have been also the enthusiastic temperament of an adolescent girl, which seeks to indulge itself on every opportunity and which now tempted Grete to exaggerate the horror of her brother's circumstances in order that she might do all the more for him. In a room where Gregor lorded it all alone over empty walls no one save herself was likely ever to set foot.

And so she was not to be moved from her resolve by her mother, who seemed moreover to be ill at ease in Gregor's room and therefore unsure of herself, and who was soon reduced to silence and helped her daughter as best she could to push the chest outside. Now, Gregor could do without the chest, if need be, but the writing desk he must retain. As soon as the two women had got the chest out of his room, groaning as they pushed it, Gregor stuck his head out from under the sofa to see how he might intervene as kindly and cautiously as possible. But as bad luck would have it, his mother was the first to return, leaving Grete clasping the chest in the room next door, where she was trying to shift it all by herself, without of course moving it from the spot. His mother, however, was not accustomed to the sight of him, it might sicken her, and so in alarm Gregor backed quickly to the other end of the sofa, yet could not prevent the sheet from swaying a little in front. That was enough to put her on the alert. She paused, stood still for a moment, and then went back to Grete.

Although Gregor kept reassuring himself that nothing out of the way was happening, that only a few bits of furniture were being changed round, he soon had to admit that all this trotting to and fro of the two women, their little ejaculations, and the scraping of furniture along the floor affected him like a vast disturbance coming from all sides at once, and however much he tucked in his head and legs and cowered to the very floor, he was bound to confess that he would not be able to stand it for long. They were clearing his room out, taking away everything he loved; the chest in which he kept his fret saw and other tools was already dragged off; they were now loosening the writing desk, which had almost sunk into the floor, the desk at which he had done all his homework when he was at the commercial academy, at the grammar school before that, and, yes, even at the primary school—he had no more time to waste in weighing the good intentions of the two women, whose existence he had by now almost forgotten, for they were so exhausted that they were laboring in silence and nothing could be heard but the heavy scuffling of their feet.

And so he rushed out—the women were just leaning against the writing desk in the next room to give themselves a breather—and four times changed his direction, since he really did not know what to rescue first; then on the wall opposite, which was already otherwise cleared, he was struck by the picture of the lady muffled in so much fur and quickly crawled up to it and pressed himself to the glass, which was a good surface to hold on to and comforted his hot belly. This picture at least, which was entirely hidden beneath him, was going to be removed by nobody. He turned his head toward the door of the living-room so as to observe the women when they came back.

They had not allowed themselves much of a rest, and were already coming; Grete had twined her arm round her mother and was almost supporting her. "Well, what shall we take now?" said Grete, looking around. Her eyes met Gregor's from the wall. She kept her composure, presumably because of her mother, bent her head down to her mother, to keep her from looking up, and said, though in a fluttering, unpremeditated voice: "Come, hadn't we better go back to the living-room for a moment?" Her intentions were clear enough to Gregor; she wanted to bestow her mother in safety and then chase him down from the wall. Well, just let her try it! He clung to his picture and would not give it up. He would rather fly in Grete's face.

But Grete's words had succeeded in disquieting her mother, who took a step to one side, caught sight of the huge brown mass on the flowered wallpaper, and before she was really conscious that what she saw was Gregor, screamed in a loud, hoarse voice: "Oh God, oh God!" fell with outspread arms over the sofa as if giving up, and did not move.

"Gregor!" cried his sister, shaking her fist and glaring at him. This was the first time she had directly addressed him since his metamorphosis. She ran into the next room for some aromatic essence with which to rouse her mother from her fainting fit. Gregor wanted to help too—there was still time to rescue the picture—but he was stuck fast to the glass and had to tear himself loose; he then ran after his sister into the next room as if he could advise her, as he had used to do; but then had to stand helplessly behind her. She meanwhile searched among various small bottles and, when she turned round, started in alarm at the sight of him; one bottle fell on the floor and broke; a splinter of glass cut Gregor's face, and some kind of corrosive medicine splashed him. Without pausing a moment longer Grete gathered up all the bottles she could carry and ran to her mother with them; she banged the door shut with her foot. Gregor was now cut off from his mother, who was perhaps nearly dying because of him; he dared not open the door for fear of frightening away his sister, who had to stay with her mother; there was nothing he could do but wait; and harassed by self-reproach and worry, he began now to crawl to and fro, over everything, walls, furniture, and ceiling, and finally in his despair, when the whole room seemed to be reeling round him, fell down onto the middle of the big table.

A little while elapsed. Gregor was still lying there feebly, and all around was quiet; perhaps that was a good omen. Then the doorbell rang. The servant girl was of course locked in her kitchen, and Grete would have to open the door. It was his father. "What's been happening?" were his first words.

Grete's face must have told him everything. Grete answered

in a muffled voice, apparently hiding her head on his breast: "Mother has been fainting, but she's better now. Gregor's broken loose."

"Just what I expected," said his father, "just what I've been telling you, but you women would never listen." It was clear to Gregor that his father had taken the worst interpretation of Grete's all too brief statement and was assuming that Gregor had been guilty of some violent act. Therefore, Gregor must now try to propitiate his father, as he had neither time nor means for an explanation. And so he fled to the door of his own room and crouched against it, to let his father see as soon as he came in from the hall that his son had the good intention of getting back into his room immediately and that it was not necessary to drive him there, but that if only the door were opened he would disappear at once.

Yet his father was not in the mood to perceive such fine distinctions. "Ah!" he cried as soon as he appeared, in a tone that sounded at once angry and exultant. Gregor drew his head back from the door and lifted it to look at his father. Truly, this was not the father he had imagined to himself; admittedly he had been too absorbed of late in his new recreation of crawling over the ceiling to take the same interest as before in what was happening elsewhere in the flat, and he ought really to be prepared for some changes. And yet, and yet, could that be his father? The man who used to lie wearily sunk in bed whenever Gregor set out on a business journey; who welcomed him back of an evening lying in a long chair in a dressing-gown; who could not really rise to his feet but only lifted his arms in greeting, and on the rare occasions when he did go out with his family, on one or two Sundays a year and on high holidays, walked between Gregor and his mother, who were slow walkers anyhow, even more slowly than they did, muffled in his old greatcoat, shuffling laboriously forward with the help of his crook-handled stick, which he set down most cautiously at every step, and, whenever he wanted to say anything, nearly always came to a full stop and gathered his escort around him?

Now he was standing there in fine shape, dressed in a smart blue uniform with gold buttons, such as bank messengers wear; his strong double chin bulged over the stiff high collar of his jacket; from under his bushy eyebrows his black eyes darted fresh and penetrating glances; his onetime tangled white hair had been combed flat on either side of a shining and carefully exact parting. He pitched his cap, which bore a gold monogram, probably the badge of some bank, in a wide sweep across the whole room onto a sofa and with the tail ends of his jacket thrown back, his hands in his trouser pockets, advanced with a grim visage toward Gregor. Likely enough he did not himself know what he meant to do; at any rate he lifted his feet uncommonly high, and Gregor was dumbfounded at the enormous size of his shoe soles. But Gregor could not risk standing up to him, aware as he had been from the very first day of his new life that his father believed only the severest measures suitable for dealing with him. And so he ran before his father, stoppng when he stopped and scuttling forward again when his father made any kind of move. In this way they circled the room several times without anything decisive happening. Indeed, the whole operation did not even look like a pursuit because it was carried out so slowly. And so Gregor did not leave the floor, for he feared that his father might take as a piece of peculiar wickedness any excursion of his over the walls or the ceiling. All the same, he could not stay this course much longer, for while his father took one step he had to carry out a whole series of movements. He was already beginning to feel breathless, just as in his former life his lungs had not been very dependable. As he was staggering along, trying to concentrate his energy on running, hardly keeping his eyes open; in his dazed state never even thinking of any other escape than simply going forward; and having almost forgotten that the walls were free to him, which in this room were well provided with finely carved pieces of furniture full of knobs and crevices—suddenly something lightly flung landed close behind him and rolled before him. It was an apple; a second apple followed immediately; Gregor came to stop in alarm; there was no point in running on, for his father was determined to bombard him. He had filled his pockets with fruit from the dish on the sideboard and was now shying apple after apple, without taking particularly good aim for the moment. The small red apples rolled about the floor as if magnetized, and cannoned into each other. An apple thrown without much force grazed Gregor's back and glanced off harmlessly. But another following immediately landed right on his back and sank in; Gregor wanted to drag himself forward, as if this startling, incredible pain could be left behind; but he felt as if nailed to the spot, and flattened himself out in a complete derangement of all his senses.

With his last conscious look he saw the door of his room being torn open and his mother rushing out ahead of his screaming sister, in her underbodice, for her daughter had loosened her clothing to let her breathe more freely and recover from her swoon; he saw his mother rushing toward his father, leaving one after another behind her on the floor her loosened petticoats, stumbling over her petticoats straight to his father and embracing him, in complete union with him—but here Gregor's sight began to fail—with her hands clasped round his father's neck as she begged for her son's life.

III

The serious injury done to Gregor, which disabled him for more than a month—the apple went on sticking in his body as a visible reminder, for no one ventured to remove it—seemed to have made even his father recollect that Gregor was a member of the family, despite his present unfortunate and repulsive shape, and ought not to be treated as an enemy; that, on the contrary, family duty required the suppression of disgust and the exercise of patience, nothing but patience.

And although his injury had impaired, probably forever, his powers of movement, and for the time being it took him long, long minutes to creep across his room like an old invalid—there was no question now of crawling up the wall—yet in his own opinion he was sufficiently compensated for this worsening of his condition by the fact that toward evening the living-room door, which he used to watch intently for an hour or two beforehand, was always thrown open, so that lying in the darkness of his room, invisible to the family, he could see them all at the lamplit table and listen to their talk, by general consent as it were, very different from his earlier eavesdropping.

True, their intercourse lacked the lively character of former times, which he had always called to mind with a certain wistfulness in the small hotel bedrooms where he had been wont to throw himself down, tired out, on damp bedding. They were now mostly very silent. Soon after supper his father would fall asleep in his armchair; his mother and sister would admonish each other to be silent; his mother, bending low over the lamp, stitched at fine sewing for an underwear firm; his sister, who had taken a job as a salesgirl, was learning shorthand and French in the evenings on the chance of bettering herself. Sometimes his father woke up and, as if quite unaware that he had been sleeping, said to his mother: "What a lot of sewing you're doing today!" and at once fell asleep again, while the two women exchanged a tired smile.

With a kind of mulishness his father persisted in keeping his uniform on even in the house; his dressing-gown hung uselessly on its peg, and he slept fully dressed where he sat, as if he were ready for service at any moment and even here only at the beck and call of his superior. As a result, his uniform, which was not brand-new to start with, began to look dirty despite all the loving care of the mother and sister to keep it clean, and Gregor often spent whole evenings gazing at the many greasy spots on the garment, gleaming with gold buttons always in a high state of polish, in which the old man sat sleeping in extreme discomfort and yet quite peacefully.

As soon as the clock struck ten, his mother tried to rouse his father with gentle words and to persuade him after that to get into bed, for sitting there he could not have a proper sleep and that was what he needed most, as he had to go on duty at six. But with the mulishness that had obsessed him since he became a bank messenger he always insisted on staying longer at the table, though he regularly fell asleep again and in the end only with the greatest trouble could be got out of his armchair and into his bed. However insistently Gregor's mother and sister kept urging him with gentle reminders, he would go on slowly shaking his head for a quarter of an hour, keeping his eyes shut, and refuse to get to his feet. The mother plucked at his sleeve, whispering endearments in his ear, the sister left her lessons to come to her mother's help, but Gregor's father was not to be caught. He would only sink down deeper in his chair. Not until the two women hoisted him up by the armpits did he open his eyes and look at them both, one after the other, usually with the remark: "This is a life. This is the peace and quiet of my old age." And leaning on the two of them he would heave himself up, with difficulty, as if he were a great burden to himself, suffer them to lead him as far as the door, and then wave them off and go on alone, while the mother abandoned her needlework and the sister her pen in order to run after him and help him farther.

Who could find time, in this overworked and tired-out family, to bother about Gregor more than was absolutely needful? The household was reduced more and more; the servant girl was turned off; a gigantic bony charwoman with white hair flying round her head came in morning and evening to do the rough work; everything else was done by Gregor's mother, as well as great piles of sewing. Even various family adornments, which his mother and sister used to wear with pride at parties and celebrations, had to be sold, as Gregor discovered of an evening from hearing them all discuss the prices obtained. But what they lamented most was the fact that they could not leave the flat, which was much too big for their present circumstances, because they could not think of any way to shift Gregor. Yet Gregor saw well enough that consideration for him was not the main difficulty preventing the removal, for they could have easily shifted him in some suitable box with a few air holes in it. What really kept them from moving into another flat was rather their own complete hopelessness and the belief that they had been singled out for a misfortune such as had never happened to any of their relations or acquaintances. They fulfilled to the uttermost all that the world demands of poor people. The father fetched breakfast for the small clerks in the bank; the mother devoted her energy to making underwear for strangers; the sister trotted to and fro behind the counter at the behest of customers. But more than this they had not the strength to do. And the wound in Gregor's back began to nag at him afresh when his mother and sister, after getting his father into bed, came back again, left their work lying, drew close to each other, and sat cheek by cheek; when his mother, pointing toward his room, said: "Shut that door now, Grete," and he was left again in darkness, while next door the women mingled their tears or perhaps sat dry-eyed staring at the table.

Gregor hardly slept at all by night or by day. He was often haunted by the idea that next time the door opened he would take the family's affairs in hand again just as he used to do;

once more, after this long interval, there appeared in his thoughts the figures of the chief and the chief clerk, the commercial travelers and the apprentices, the porter who was so dull-witted, two or three friends in other firms, a chambermaid in one of the rural hotels, a sweet and fleeting memory, a cashier in a milliner's shop, whom he had wooed earnestly but too slowly—they all appeared, together with strangers or people he had quite forgotten, but instead of helping him and his family they were one and all unapproachable, and he was glad when they vanished. At other times he would not be in the mood to bother about his family, but was only filled with rage at the way they were neglecting him, and though he had no clear idea of what he might care to eat, he would make plans for getting into the larder to take the food that was after all his due, even if he was not hungry. His sister no longer took thought to bring him what might especially please him, but in the morning and at noon before she went to business hurriedly pushed into his room with her foot any food that was available, and in the evening cleared it out again with one sweep of the broom, heedless of whether it had been merely tasted or—as most frequently happened—left untouched. The cleaning of his room, which she now did always in the evenings, could not have been more hastily done. Streaks of dirt stretched along the walls, here and there lay balls of dust and filth. At first Gregor used to station himself in some particularly filthy corner when his sister arrived, in order to reproach her with it, so to speak. But he could have sat there for weeks without getting her to make any improvement; she could see the dirt as well as he did, but she had simply made up her mind to leave it alone. And yet, with a touchiness that was new to her, which seemed anyhow to have infected the whole family, she jealously guarded her claim to be the sole caretaker of Gregor's room.

His mother once subjected his room to a thorough cleaning, which was achieved only by means of several buckets of water—all this dampness of course upset Gregor too and he lay widespread, sulky, and motionless on the sofa—but she was well punished for it. Hardly had his sister noticed the changed aspect of his room that evening when she rushed in high dudgeon into the living-room and, despite the imploringly raised hands of her mother, burst into a storm of weeping, while her parents—her father had of course been startled out of his chair—looked on at first in helpless amazement; then they too began to go into action. The father reproached the mother on his right for not having left the cleaning of Gregor's room to his sister; shrieked at the sister on his left that never again was she to be allowed to clean Gregor's room; while the mother tried to pull the father into his bedroom, for he was beyond himself with agitation; the sister, shaken with sobs, then beat upon the table with her small fists; and Gregor hissed loudly with rage because not one of them thought of shutting the door to spare him such a spectacle and so much noise.

Still, even if the sister, exhausted by her daily work, had grown tired of looking after Gregor as she did formerly, there was no need for his mother's intervention or for Gregor's being neglected at all. The charwoman was there. This old widow, whose strong bony frame had enabled her to survive the worst a long life could offer, by no means recoiled from Gregor. Without being in the least curious she had once by chance opened the door of his room and at the sight of Gregor, who, taken by surprise, began to rush to and fro though no one was chasing him, merely stood there with her arms folded. From that time she never failed to open his door a little for a moment, morning and evening, to have a look at him. At first she even used to call him to her, with words that apparently she took to be friendly, such as: "Come along, then, you old dung beetle!" or "Look at the old dung beetle, then!" To such allocutions Gregor made no answer, but stayed motionless where he was, as if the door had never been opened. Instead of being allowed to disturb him so senselessly whenever the whim took her, she should rather have been ordered to clean out his room daily, that charwoman! Once, early in the morning—heavy rain was lashing on the windowpanes, perhaps a sign that spring was on the way—Gregor was so exasperated when she began addressing him again that he ran at her, as if to attack her, though slowly and feebly enough. But the charwoman instead of showing fright merely lifted high a chair that happened to be beside the door; and as she stood there with her mouth wide open, it was clear that she meant to shut it only when she brought the chair down on Gregor's back. "So you're not coming any nearer?" she asked, as Gregor turned away again, and quietly put the chair back in the corner.

Gregor was now eating hardly anything. Only when he happened to pass the food laid out for him did he take a bit of something in his mouth as a pastime, kept it there for an hour at a time, and usually spat it out again. At first he thought it was chagrin over the state of his room that prevented him from eating, yet he soon got used to the various changes in his room. It had become a habit in the family to push into his room things there was no space for elsewhere, and there were plenty of these now, since one of the rooms had been let to three lodgers. These serious gentlemen—all three of them with full beards, as Gregor once observed through a crack in the door—had a passion for order, not only in their own room but, since they were now members of the household, in all its arrangements, especially in the kitchen. Superfluous, not to say dirty, objects they could not bear. Besides, they had brought with them most of the furnishings they needed. For this reason many things could be dispensed with that it was no use trying to sell but that should not be thrown away either. All of them found their way into Gregor's room. The ash can likewise and the kitchen garbage can. Anything that was not needed for the moment was simply flung into Gregor's room by the charwoman, who did everything in a hurry; fortunately Gregor usually saw only the object, whatever it was, and the hand that held it. Perhaps she intended to take the things away again as time and opportunity offered, or to collect them until she could throw them all out in a heap, but in fact they just lay wherever she happened to throw them, except when Gregor pushed his way through the junk heap and shifted it somewhat, at first out of necessity, because he had not room enough to crawl, but later with increasing enjoyment, though after such excursions, being sad and weary to death, he would lie motionless for hours. And because the lodgers often ate their supper at home in the common living-room, the living-room door stayed shut many an evening.

Yet Gregor reconciled himself quite easily to the shutting of the door, for often enough on evenings when it was opened he had disregarded it entirely and lain in the darkest corner of his room, quite unnoticed by the family. But on one occasion the charwoman left the door open a little, and it stayed ajar even when the lodgers came in for supper and the lamp was lit. They set themselves at the top end of the table where formerly Gregor and his father and mother had eaten their meals, unfolded their napkins, and took knife and fork in hand. At once his mother appeared in the other doorway with a dish of meat and close behind her his sister with a dish of potatoes piled high. The food steamed with a thick vapor. The lodgers bent over the food set before them as if to scrutinize it before eating; in fact, the man in the middle, who seemed to pass for an authority with the other two, cut a piece of meat as it lay on the dish, obviously to discover if it was tender or should be sent back to the kitchen. He showed satisfaction, and Gregor's mother and sister, who had been watching anxiously, breathed freely and began to smile.

The family itself took its meals in the kitchen. None the less, Gregor's father came into the living-room before going into the kitchen and with one prolonged bow, cap in hand, made a round of the table. The lodgers all stood up and murmured something in their beards. When they were alone again, they ate their food in almost complete silence. It seemed remarkable to Gregor that among the various noises coming from the table he could always distinguish the sound of their masticating teeth, as if this were a sign to Gregor that one needed teeth in order to eat, and that with toothless jaws even of the finest make one could do nothing. "I'm hungry enough," said Gregor sadly to himself, "but not for that kind of food. How these lodgers are stuffing themselves, and here am I dying of starvation!"

On that very evening—during the whole of his time there Gregor could not remember ever having heard the violin—the sound of violin-playing came from the kitchen. The lodgers had already finished their supper. The one in the middle had brought out a newspaper and given the other two a page apiece, and now they were leaning back at ease reading and smoking. When the violin began to play they pricked up their ears, got to their feet, and went on tiptoe to the hall door, where they stood huddled together.

Their movements must have been heard in the kitchen, for Gregor's father called out: "Is the violin-playing disturbing you, gentlemen? It can be stopped at once."

"On the contrary," said the middle lodger, "could not Fräulein Samsa come and play in this room, beside us, where it is much more convenient and comfortable?"

"Oh certainly," cried Gregor's father, as if he were the violin-player. The lodgers came back into the living-room and waited. Presently Gregor's father arrived with the music stand, his mother carrying the music and his sister with the violin. His sister quietly made everything ready to start playing; his parents, who had never let rooms before and so had an exaggerated idea of the courtesy due to lodgers, did not venture to sit down on their own chairs; his father leaned against the door, the right hand thrust between two buttons of his livery coat, which was formally buttoned up; but his mother was offered a chair by one of the lodgers and, as she left the chair just where he had happened to put it, she sat down in a corner to one side.

Gregor's sister began to play; the father and mother, from either side, intently watched the movements of her hands. Gregor, attracted by the playing, ventured to move forward a little until his head was actually inside the living-room. He felt hardly any surprise at his growing lack of consideration for the others; there had been a time when he prided himself on being considerate. And yet just on this occasion he had more reason than ever to hide himself, for owing to the amount of dust that lay thick in his room and rose into the air at the slightest movement, he too was covered with dust; fluff and hair and remnants of food trailed with him, caught on his back and along his sides; his indifference to everything was much too great for him to turn on his back and scrape himself clean on the carpet, as once he had done several times a day. And in spite of his condition, no shame deterred him from advancing a little over the spotless floor of the living-room.

To be sure, no one was aware of him. The family was entirely absorbed in the violin-playing; the lodgers, however, who first of all had stationed themselves, hands in pockets, much too close behind the music stand so that they could all have read the music, which must have bothered his sister, had soon retreated to the window, half-whispering with downbent heads, and stayed there while his father turned an anxious eye on them. Indeed, they were making it more than obvious that they had been disappointed in their expectation of hearing good or enjoyable violin-playing, that they had had more than enough of the performance and only out of courtesy suffered a continued disturbance of their peace. From the way they all kept blowing the smoke of their cigars high in the air through nose and mouth one could divine their irritation. And yet Gregor's sister was playing so beautifully. Her faced leaned sideways, intently and sadly her eyes followed the notes of music. Gregor crawled a little farther forward and lowered his head to the ground so that it might be possible for his eyes to meet hers. Was he an animal, that music had such an effect upon him? He felt as if the way was opening before him to the unknown nourishment he craved. He was determined to push forward till he reached his sister, to pull at her skirt and so let her know that she was to come into his room with her violin, for no one here appreciated her playing as he would appreciate it. He would never let her out of his room, at least not so long as he lived; his frightful appearance would become, for the first time, useful to him; he would watch all the doors of his room at once and spit at intruders; but his sister should need no constraint, she should stay with him of her own free will; she should sit beside him on the sofa, bend down her ear to him, and hear him confide that he had had the firm intention of sending her to the Conservatorium, and that, but for his mishap, last Christmas—surely Christmas was long past?—he would have announced it to everybody without allowing a single objection. After this confession his sister would be so touched that she would burst into tears, and Gregor would then raise himself to her shoulder and kiss her on the neck, which, now that she went to business, she kept free of any ribbon or collar.

"Mr. Samsa!" cried the middle lodger to Gregor's father, and pointed, without wasting any more words, at Gregor, now working himself slowly forwards. The violin fell silent; the middle lodger first smiled to his friends with a shake of the head and then looked at Gregor again. Instead of driving Gregor out, his father seemed to think it more needful to begin by soothing the lodgers, though they were not at all agitated and apparently found Gregor more entertaining than the violin-playing. He hurried toward them and, spreading out his arms, tried to urge them back into their own room and at the same time to block their view of Gregor. They now began to be really a little angry, one could not tell whether because of the old man's behavior or because it had just dawned on them that all unwittingly they had such a neighbor as Gregor next door. They demanded explanations of his father, they waved their arms like him, tugged uneasily at their beards, and only with reluctance backed toward their room. Meanwhile Gregor's sister, who stood there as if lost when her playing was so abruptly broken off, came to life again, pulled herself together all at once after standing for a while holding violin and bow in nervelessly hanging hands and staring at her music, pushed her violin into the lap of her mother, who was still sitting in her chair fighting asthmatically for breath, and ran into the lodgers' room, to which they were now being shepherded by her father rather more quickly than before. One could see the pillows and blankets on the beds flying under her accustomed fingers and being laid in order. Before the lodgers had actually reached their room she had finished making the beds and slipped out.

The old man seemed once more to be so possessed by his mulish self-assertiveness that he was forgetting all the respect he should show to his lodgers. He kept driving them on and driving them on until in the very door of the bedroom the middle lodger stamped his foot loudly on the floor and so brought him to a halt. "I beg to announce," said the lodger, lifting one hand and looking also at Gregor's mother and sister, "that because of the disgusting conditions prevailing in this household and family"—here he spat on the floor with emphatic brevity—"I give you notice on the spot. Naturally, I won't pay you a penny for the days I have lived here; on the contrary, I shall consider bringing an action for damages against you, based on claims—believe me—that will be easily susceptible of proof." He ceased and stared straight in front of him, as if he expected something. In fact, his two friends at once rushed into the breach with these words: "And we too give notice on the spot." On that he seized the door-handle and shut the door with a slam.

Gregor's father, groping with his hands, staggered forward and fell into his chair; it looked as if he were stretching himself there for his ordinary evening nap, but the marked jerkings of his head, which was as if uncontrollable, showed that he was far from asleep. Gregor had simply stayed quietly all the time on the spot where the lodgers had espied him. Disappointment at the failure of his plan, perhaps also the weakness arising from extreme hunger, made it impossible for him to move. He feared, with a fair degree of certainty, that at any moment the general tension would discharge itself in a combined attack upon him, and he lay waiting. He did not react even to the noise made by the violin as it fell off his mother's lap from under her trembling fingers and gave out a resonant note.

"My dear parents," said his sister, slapping her hand on the table by way of introduction, "things can't go on like this. Perhaps you don't realize that, but I do. I won't utter my brother's name in the presence of this creature, and so all I say is: we must try to get rid of it. We've tried to look after it and to put up with it as far as is humanly possible, and I don't think anyone could reproach us in the slightest."

"She is more than right," said Gregor's father to himself. His mother, who was still choking for lack of breath, began to cough hollowly into her hand with a wild look in her eyes.

His sister rushed over to her and held her forehead. His father's thoughts seemed to have lost their vagueness at Grete's words. He sat more upright, fingering his service cap, which lay among the plates still lying on the table from the lodgers' supper, and from time to time looked at the still form of Gregor.

"We must try to get rid of it," his sister now said explicitly to her father, for her mother was coughing too much to hear a word; "it will be the death of both of you, I can see that coming. When one has to work as hard as we do, all of us, one can't stand this continual torment at home on top of it. At least I can't stand it any longer." And she burst into such a passion of sobbing that her tears dropped on her mother's face, where she wiped them off mechanically.

"My dear," said the old man sympathetically, and with evident understanding, "but what can we do?"

Gregor's sister merely shrugged her shoulders to indicate the feeling of helplessness that had now overmastered her during her weeping fit, in contrast to her former confidence.

"If he could understand us," said her father, half questioningly; Grete, still sobbing, vehemently waved a hand to show how unthinkable that was. "If he could understand us," repeated the old man, shutting his eyes to consider his daughter's conviction that understanding was impossible, "then perhaps we might come to some agreement with him. But as it is—"

"He must go," cried Gregor's sister, "that's the only solution, Father. You must just try to get rid of the idea that this is Gregor. The fact that we've believed it for so long is the root of all our trouble. But how can it be Gregor? If this were Gregor, he would have realized long ago that human beings can't live with such a creature, and he'd have gone away of his own accord. Then we wouldn't have any brother, but we'd be able to go on living and keep his memory in honor. As it is, this creature persecutes us, drives away our lodgers, obviously wants the whole apartment to himself, and would have us all sleep in the gutter. Just look, Father," she shrieked all at once, "he's at it again!" And in an access of panic that was quite incomprehensible to Gregor she even quitted her mother, literally thrusting the chair from her as if she would rather sacrifice her mother than stay so near to Gregor, and rushed behind her father, who also rose up, being simply upset by her agitation, and half-spread his arms out as if to protect her.

Yet Gregor had not the slightest intention of frightening anyone, far less his sister. He had only begun to turn round in order to crawl back to his room, but it was certainly a startling operation to watch, since because of his disabled condition he could not execute the difficult turning movements except by lifting his head and then bracing it against the floor over and over again. He paused and looked round. His good intentions seemed to have been recognized; the alarm had only been momentary. Now they were all watching him in melancholy silence. His mother lay in her chair, her legs stiffly outstretched and pressed together, her eyes almost closing for sheer weariness; his father and his sister were sitting beside each other, his sister's arm around the old man's neck.

"Perhaps I can go on turning round now," thought Gregor, and began his labors again. He could not stop himself from panting with the effort and had to pause now and then to take breath. Nor did anyone harass him; he was left entirely to himself. When he had completed the turn-round he began at once to crawl straight back. He was amazed at the distance separating him from his room and could not understand how in his weak state he had managed to accomplish the same journey so recently, almost without remarking it. Intent on crawling as fast as possible, he barely noticed that not a single word, not an ejaculation from his family, interfered with his progress. Only when he was already in the doorway did he turn his head round, not completely, for his neck muscles were getting stiff, but enough to see that nothing had changed behind him except that his sister had risen to her feet. His last glance fell on his mother, who was not quite overcome by sleep.

Hardly was he well inside his room when the door was hastily pushed shut, bolted, and locked. The sudden noise in his rear startled him so much that his little legs gave beneath him. It was his sister who had shown such haste. She had been standing ready waiting and had made a light spring forward—Gregor had not even heard her coming—and she cried: "At last!" to her parents as she turned the key in the lock.

"And what now?" said Gregor to himself, looking round in the darkness. Soon he made the discovery that he was now unable to stir a limb. This did not surprise him; rather it seemed unnatural that he should ever actually have been able to move on these feeble little legs. Otherwise he felt relatively comfortable. True, his whole body was aching, but it seemed that the pain was gradually growing less and would finally pass away. The rotting apple in his back and the inflamed area around it, all covered with soft dust, already hardly troubled him. He thought of his family with tenderness and love. The decision that he must disappear was one that he held to even more strongly than his sister, if that was possible. In this state of vacant and peaceful meditation he remained until the tower clock struck three in the morning. The first broadening of light in the world outside the window entered his consciousness once more. Then his head sank to the floor of its own accord and from his nostrils came the last faint flicker of his breath.

When the charwoman arrived early in the morning—what between her strength and her impatience she slammed all the doors so loudly, never mind how often she had been begged not to do so, that no one in the whole apartment could enjoy any quiet sleep after her arrival—she noticed nothing unusual as she took her customary peep into Gregor's room. She thought he was lying motionless on purpose, pretending to be in the sulks; she credited him with every kind of intelligence. Since she happened to have the long-handled broom in her hand, she tried to tickle him up with it from the doorway. When that too produced no reaction, she felt provoked and poked at him a little harder, and only when she had pushed him along the floor without meeting any resistance was her attention aroused. It did not take her long to establish the truth of the matter. Her eyes widened and she let out a whistle, yet did not waste much time over it, but tore open the door of the Samsas' bedroom and yelled into the darkness at the top of her voice: "Just look at this, it's dead; it's lying here dead and done for!"

Mr. and Mrs. Samsa started up in their double bed and before they realized the nature of the charwoman's announcement had some difficulty in overcoming the shock of it. But then they got out of bed quickly, one on either side, Mr. Samsa throwing a blanket over his shoulders, Mrs. Samsa in nothing but her nightgown; in this array they entered Gregor's room. Meanwhile the door of the living-room opened, too, where Grete had been sleeping since the advent of the lodgers; she was completely dressed as if she had not been to bed, which seemed to be confirmed also by the paleness of her face.

"Dead?" said Mrs. Samsa, looking questioningly at the charwoman, though she could have investigated for herself, and the fact was obvious enough without investigation.

"I should say so," said the charwoman, proving her words by pushing Gregor's corpse a long way to one side with her broomstick. Mrs. Samsa made a movement as if to stop her, but checked it.

"Well," said Mr. Samsa, "now thanks be to God." He crossed himself, and the three women followed his example.

Grete, whose eyes never left the corpse, said: "Just see how thin he was. It's such a long time since he's eaten anything. The food came out again just as it went in." Indeed, Gregor's body was completely flat and dry, as could only now be seen when it was no longer supported by the legs and nothing prevented one from looking closely at it.

"Come in with us, Grete, for a little while," said Mrs. Samsa with a tremulous smile, and Grete, not without looking back at the corpse, followed her parents into their bedroom. The charwoman shut the door and opened the window wide. Although it was so early in the morning, a certain softness was perceptible in the fresh air. After all, it was already the end of March.

The three lodgers emerged from their room and were surprised to see no breakfast; they had been forgotten. "Where's our breakfast?" said the middle lodger peevishly to the charwoman. But she put her finger to her lips and hastily, without a word, indicated by gestures that they should go into Gregor's room. They did so and stood, their hands in the pockets of their somewhat shabby coats, around Gregor's corpse in the room, where it was now fully light.

At that the door of the Samsas' bedroom opened and Mr. Samsa appeared in his uniform, his wife on one arm, his daughter on the other. They all looked a little as if they had been crying; from time to time Grete hid her face on her father's arm.

"Leave my house at once!" said Mr. Samsa, and pointed to the door without disengaging himself from the women.

"What do you mean by that?" said the middle lodger, taken somewhat aback, with a feeble smile. The two others put their hands behind them and kept rubbing them together, as if in gleeful expectation of a fine set-to in which they were bound to come off the winners.

"I mean just what I say," answered Mr. Samsa, and advanced in a straight line with his two companions toward the lodger.

He stood his ground at first quietly, looking at the floor as if his thoughts were taking a new pattern in his head. "Then let us go, by all means," he said, and looked up at Mr. Samsa as if in a sudden access of humility he were expecting some renewed sanction for this decision. Mr. Samsa merely nodded briefly once or twice with meaning eyes. Upon that the lodger really did go with long strides into the hall. His two friends had been listening, and had quite stopped rubbing their hands for some moments, and now went scuttling after him as if afraid that Mr. Samsa might get into the hall before them and cut them off from their leader.

In the hall they all three took their hats from the rack, their sticks from the umbrella stand, bowed in silence, and quitted the apartment. With a suspiciousness that proved quite unfounded Mr. Samsa and the two women followed them out to the landing; leaning over the banister, they watched the three figures slowly but surely going down the long stairs, vanishing from sight at a certain turn of the staircase on every floor and coming into view again after a moment or so. The more they dwindled, the more the Samsa family's interest in them dwindled, and when a butcher's boy met them and passed them on the stairs coming up proudly with a tray on his head, Mr. Samsa and the two women soon left the landing and as if a burden had been lifted from them went back into their apartment.

They decided to spend this day in resting and going for a stroll; they had not only deserved such a respite from work, but absolutely needed it. And so they sat down at the table and wrote three notes of excuse, Mr. Samsa to his board of management, Mrs. Samsa to her employer, and Grete to the head of her firm. While they were writing, the charwoman came in to say that she was going now, since her morning's work was finished. At first they only nodded without looking up, but as she kept hovering there, they eyed her irritably. "Well?" said Mr. Samsa. The charwoman stood grinning in the doorway as if she had good news to impart to the family but meant not to say a word unless properly questioned. The small ostrich feather standing upright on her hat, which had annoyed Mr. Samsa ever since she had been engaged, was waving gaily in all directions.

"Well, what is it then?" asked Mrs. Samsa, who obtained more respect from the charwoman than the others.

"Oh," said the charwoman, giggling so amiably that she could not at once continue, "just this: you don't need to bother about how to get rid of the thing next door. It's been seen to already." Mrs. Samsa and Grete bent over their letters again, as if preoccupied; Mr. Samsa, who perceived that she was eager to begin describing it all in detail, stopped her with a decisive hand. But since she was not allowed to tell her story, she remembered the great hurry she was in, being obviously deeply huffed: "Bye, everybody," she said, whirling off violently, and departed with a frightful slamming of doors.

"She'll be given notice tonight," said Mr. Samsa, but neither from his wife nor from his daughter did he get any answer, for the charwoman seemed to have shattered again the composure they had barely achieved. They rose, went to the window, and stayed there, clasping each other tight. Mr. Samsa turned in his chair to look at them and quietly observed them for a little. Then he called out: "Come along, now, do. Let bygones be bygones. And you might have some consideration for me." The two of them complied at once, hastened to him, caressed him, and quickly finished their letters.

Then they all three left the apartment together, which was more than they had done for months, and went by tram into the open country outside the town. The tram, in which they were the only passengers, was filled with warm sunshine. Leaning comfortably back in their seats they canvassed their prospects for the future, and it appeared on closer inspection that these were not at all bad, for the jobs they had got, which so far they had never really discussed with each other, were all three admirable and likely to lead to better things later on. The greatest immediate improvement in their condition would of course arise from moving to another house; they wanted to take a smaller and cheaper, but also better-situated and more easily run, apartment than the one they had, which Gregor had selected. While they were thus conversing, it struck both Mr. and Mrs. Samsa, almost at the same moment, as they became aware of their daughter's increasing vivacity, that in spite of all the sorrow of recent times, which had made her cheeks pale, she had bloomed into a pretty girl with a good figure. They grew quieter, and half unconsciously exchanged glances of complete agreement, having come to the conclusion that it would soon be time to find a good husband for her. And it was like a confirmation of their new dreams and excellent intentions that at the end of their journey their daughter sprang to her feet first and stretched her young body.

Translated by Willa and Edwin Muir

A LITTLE LEGEND OF THE DANCE

by Gottfried Keller

Saint Gregory relates in his tales that Musa was the dancer among the saints. She was the child of good folk, and a graceful little maiden, who diligently served the Mother of God and knew only one passion: namely, a love of dancing so uncontrollable that if the girl was not praying, then she was assuredly dancing. And she danced in every conceivable way. Musa danced with her playmates, with the children, with the young men, and even alone. She danced in her little chamber, in the great hall, in the gardens, and over the meadows, and even when she approached the altar she seemed to be dancing a delicious measure rather than walking. And on the smooth marble flags at the church door she never forgot to try a few hasty steps.

Indeed, one day, when she happened to be alone in church, she could not refrain from dancing a few figures in front of the altar and, so to speak, dancing a pretty prayer to the Virgin. She forgot herself so utterly that she fancied she was dreaming when an elderly but handsome gentleman came dancing toward

---

Gottfried Keller—to this day the most representative author of Switzerland—was born in Zurich in 1819. He studied in Heidelberg and then lived in Berlin, where he wrote the first version of the four-volume "educational novel" Der grüne Heinrich, *a work that ranks with Goethe's* Wilhelm Meister. *In 1855 he returned to his native town, where for fifteen years he worked as the secretary to the cantonal government. His* novellas, *short stories, "legends" (collected in* Die Leute von Seldwyla, Züricher Novellen, *and* Sieben Legenden), *and poetry show this great storyteller also as a great Christian humanist. His last novel,* Martin Salander, *is significant of Gottfried Keller's final appraisal of modern democracy—whose problems occupied him throughout his life. He remained unmarried, and died in 1890 in Zurich.*

her and supplemented her figures so deftly that the two between them performed the most finished *pas de deux.* The gentleman wore a royal robe of purple and a golden crown on his head, and had a glossy black beard lightly silvered with age as by distant starlight. And music sounded from the choir, for there half a dozen cherubs were sitting or standing on the top of the screen, swinging their chubby little legs over it while they played or blew divers instruments. And the urchins made themselves quite comfortable, for each propped his music against one of the stone angels that adorned the choir screen. But the smallest, a round-cheeked piper, was an exception, for he crossed his legs and contrived to hold his music in his rosy toes. And he was the most zealous of all. The others swung their feet, stretched their rustling wings till they shimmered like the breasts of doves, and teased each other as they played.

Musa found no time to wonder at all this until the dance, which lasted some time, was over, and the merry gentleman seemed to enjoy it as much as the maiden, who, for her part, might have been tripping about in heaven. But when the music stopped and Musa stood there panting, she began to be really afraid and looked at the old gentleman in amazement, for he was neither out of breath nor hot and now began to speak. He introduced himself as David, the royal ancestor of Mary the Virgin, and her messenger. And he asked her whether she would like to pass an eternity of bliss in an endless dance of joy, a dance compared with which the one they had just ended could only be called a dismal crawl.

Whereupon she promptly replied that she could wish for nothing better. Whereupon the blessed King David rejoined that all she had to do was to give up all dancing and all joy for the rest of her earthly days and dedicate herself to penitence and spiritual exercises, and that without faltering or relapse.

At this the maiden was somewhat taken aback, and asked whether she must give up dancing altogether. She doubted whether there really was dancing in heaven, for there was a time for everything. Solid earth seemed a good and suitable place for dancing; therefore heaven must have other things to offer, otherwise death would simply be superfluous.

But David explained to her how sorely she was in error, and proved by many passages from the Bible, as by his own example, that dancing was certainly a blessed occupation for the blessed. But now she must make up her mind quickly, yes or no, whether by temporal renunciation she wished to enter into eternal bliss or not; if not, he must be getting along, as heaven was in need of a few dancers.

Musa still stood there irresolute, her fingertips playing anxiously about her mouth. It seemed too hard never to dance again just for the sake of an unknown reward.

Then David made a sign and suddenly the musicians played a few bars of a dance, so incredibly blissful and unearthly that the maiden's soul leaped in her body and she twitched in every limb; but she could not move one of them to the measure, and she saw that her body was too stiff and heavy for that music. Full of longing, she struck her hand into the King's and gave her promise.

Forthwith he vanished and the cherub musicians whirred and fluttered and crowded away through an open window in the church, but first they rolled up their music sheets and, like mischievous children, slapped the patient angels' faces till the church re-echoed.

But Musa walked home with devout steps, the heavenly melody in her ears. She had a coarse garment made, laid aside all her fine raiment, and put it on. Then she built a cell in the back of her parents' garden, where the shadows of the trees lay thick, made a little bed of moss in it, and lived thenceforth apart from her companions as a penitent and a saint. She passed all her time in prayer, and often scourged herself; but her hardest penance was to keep her limbs still and rigid. As soon as there was a single sound in the air, the twittering of a bird or the rustling of the leaves in the trees, her feet twitched and felt that they must dance. As this involuntary twitching would not disappear and sometimes, before she was even aware of it, she could not suppress a little pirouette, she had her frail feet bound together with a light chain. Her relatives and friends marveled day and night at the change, but rejoiced in the possession of such a saint and guarded the hermitage under the trees as the apple of their eye. Many came for counsel and intercession. Above all, young maidens were brought to her who were a little heavy on their feet, for it had been noticed that any she touched became light and graceful of movement.

So she passed three years in her solitude, and toward the end of the third year Musa had become almost as thin and transparent as a summer cloud. She no longer moved from her little bed of moss, and lay looking longingly up to heaven, and she thought that she could see the golden soles of the blessed dancing and gliding through the blue.

One raw autumn day the news went round that the saint was lying at the point of death. She had had her dark penitential robe taken from her and was clad in dazzling white bridal garments. So she lay with folded hands and smilingly awaited the hour of death. The whole garden was filled with pious people, the breezes whispered, and the leaves were falling from the trees on every hand. But imperceptibly the whispering of the trees passed into music, which seemed to sound in every treetop, and when the people looked up, lo! everything was clothed in tender green, the myrtles and pomegranates bloomed in fragrance, the earth was decked with flowers, and a rose-colored light lay on the frail form of the dying maiden.

At that moment she gave up the ghost. The chain on her feet sprang asunder with a clear ringing sound, heaven opened far and wide, full of infinite splendor, and all might look in. Then there could be seen host upon host of lovely maidens and youths in the utmost glory, dancing in endless circles. A splendid King, enthroned on a cloud with a little separate band of six cherubs sitting on its edge, descended a little toward earth and received the form of the blessed Musa before the eyes of all those who filled the garden. They saw how she was borne up to heaven, and forthwith danced out of sight amid the singing and shining hosts.

In heaven it was high festival. On festal days, however—this is contested by Saint Gregory of Nyssa, but maintained by his namesake of Nazianzus—it was the custom to invite the Muses, who were sitting in hell, into heaven to lend a hand. They were well entertained, but when their work was done, they had to go back to the other place.

When the dances and all the ceremonies were at an end, and the heavenly hosts sat down to table, Musa was led to the table where the nine Muses were sitting. They sat huddled together, half-intimidated, staring round them with their fiery black or deep blue eyes. Busy Martha from the Gospel served them with her own hands. She had put on her best kitchen apron and had a dainty little smudge on her white chin, and she kindly pressed the good things on the Muses. But it was only when Musa and Saint Cecilia and other women famed in art came along and cheerily greeted the shy Pierians and sat down beside them that they brightened up and grew confidential, while a charming gaiety spread over the whole circle of the women. Musa sat beside Terpsichore, and Cecilia between Polyhymnia and Euterpe, and they all held one another's hands. Then the little cherub musicians came up and made much of the beautiful women, hoping to get some of the shining fruit on the ambrosial table. King David came too in person and brought a golden goblet, from which all drank. He passed kindly round the table, not forgetting to pat the lovely Erato's chin as he passed. As things were going so merrily at the Muses' table, our dear Lady herself appeared in all her beauty and goodness, to sit with the Muses awhile, and she tenderly kissed the august Urania on the mouth under her starry coronal, and, as she said good-by, whispered that she would not rest until the Muses should again sit in paradise forever.

But it did not turn out so. To show their gratitude for the kindness shown them, the Muses took counsel together and, in a distant corner of the underworld, practiced a hymn of praise, to which they tried to give the form of the solemn chorales usual in heaven. They divided into two groups of four voices each, with Urania singing a kind of descant, and so produced a remarkable piece of music.

But when the next festival was celebrated in heaven, and the Muses were again on duty, they took advantage of a moment that seemed favorable, grouped themselves, and softly began their song, which soon swelled into a mighty chorus. But in those spaces it sounded so somber—nay, defiant and harsh—so heavy with longing, and so complaining, that at first a terrified silence reigned; but the whole assembly was seized by earthly suffering and the yearning for earth, and a general weeping broke out.

Endless sighs throbbed through heaven: all the Elders and Prophets started up, terrified and dismayed, while the Muses, with the best intentions, sang ever louder and more sadly, and all paradise, with the Patriarchs, the Elders, and the Prophets, all who had ever walked or lain on green pastures, were quite beside themselves. But at last the Holy Trinity itself came up to set things right, and silenced the zealous Muses with a long rolling peal of thunder.

Then peace and serenity returned to heaven, but the poor sisters had to depart; they have never been allowed to return since.

Translated by M. D. Hottinger

DEATH IN VENICE

by Thomas Mann

Gustave Aschenbach—or von Aschenbach, as he had been known officially since his fiftieth birthday—had set out alone from his house in Prince Regent Street, Munich, for an extended walk. It was a spring afternoon in that year of grace 19—, when Europe sat upon the anxious seat beneath a menace that hung over its head for months. Aschenbach had sought the open soon after tea. He was overwrought by a morning of hard, nerve-taxing work, work that had not ceased to exact his uttermost in the way of sustained concentration, conscientiousness, and tact; and after the noon meal found himself powerless to check the onward sweep of the productive mechanism within him, that *motus animi continuus* in which, according to Cicero, eloquence resides. He had sought but not found relaxation in sleep—though the wear and tear upon his system had come to make a daily nap more and more imperative—and now undertook a walk, in the hope that air and exercise might send him back refreshed to a good evening's work.

May had begun, and after weeks of cold and wet a mock summer had set in. The English Gardens, though in tenderest

---

Thomas Mann was born in 1875, the son of a senator of the Free City of Lübeck and of a half-Brazilian mother. After his father's death he took up residence in Munich. In 1929 he was awarded the Nobel Prize in Literature. He left Germany in 1933, came to the United States in 1938, and became an American citizen. His principal works of fiction are: Buddenbrooks (*1900*), Tonio Kröger (*1903*), Royal Highness (*1909*), Death in Venice (*1913*), The Magic Mountain (*1924*), Disorder and Early Sorrow (*1925*), Mario and the Magician (*1931*), Joseph and His Brothers (*1933–44*), The Beloved Returns (*1940*), Doctor Faustus (*1947*), *and* The Holy Sinner (*1951*). *His nonfictional work includes literary and historical essays and numerous critical comments on the political scene.*

leaf, felt as sultry as in August and were full of vehicles and pedestrians near the city. But toward Aumeister the paths were solitary and still, and Aschenbach strolled thither, stopping awhile to watch the lively crowds in the restaurant garden with its fringe of carriages and cabs. Thence he took his homeward way outside the park and across the sunset fields. By the time he reached the North Cemetery, however, he felt tired, and a storm was brewing above Föhring; so he waited at the stopping-place for a tram to carry him back to the city.

He found the neighborhood quite empty. Not a wagon in sight, either on the paved Ungererstrasse, with its gleaming tramlines stretching off toward Schwabing, nor on the Föhring highway. Nothing stirred behind the hedge in the stonemason's yard, where crosses, monuments, and commemorative tablets made a supernumerary and untenanted graveyard opposite the real one. The mortuary chapel, a structure in Byzantine style, stood facing it, silent in the gleam of the ebbing day. Its façade was adorned with Greek crosses and tinted hieratic designs, and displayed a symmetrically arranged selection of scriptural texts in gilded letters, all of them with a bearing upon the future life, such as: "They are entering into the House of the Lord" and "May the Light Everlasting shine upon them." Aschenbach beguiled some minutes of his waiting with reading these formulas and letting his mind's eye lose itself in their mystical meaning. He was brought back to reality by the sight of a man standing in the portico, above the two apocalyptic beasts that guarded the staircase, and something not quite usual in this man's appearance gave his thoughts a fresh turn.

Whether he had come out of the hall through the bronze doors or mounted unnoticed from outside, it was impossible to tell. Aschenbach casually inclined to the first idea. He was of medium height, thin, beardless, and strikingly snub-nosed; he belonged to the red-haired type and possessed its milky, freckled skin. He was obviously not Bavarian; and the broad, straight-brimmed straw hat he had on even made him look distinctly exotic. True, he had the indigenous rucksack buckled on his back, wore a belted suit of yellowish woolen stuff, apparently frieze, and carried a gray mackintosh cape across his left forearm, which was propped against his waist. In his right hand, slantwise to the ground, he held an iron-shod stick, and braced himself against its crook, with his legs crossed. His chin was up, so that the Adam's apple looked very bald in the lean neck rising from the loose shirt; and he stood there sharply peering up into space out of colorless, red-lashed eyes, while two pronounced perpendicular furrows showed on his forehead in curious contrast to his little turned-up nose. Perhaps his heightened and heightening position helped out the impression Aschenbach received. At any rate, standing there as though at survey, the man had a bold and domineering, even a ruthless, air, and his lips completed the picture by seeming to curl back, either by reason of some deformity or else because he grimaced, being blinded by the sun in his face; they laid bare the long, white, glistening teeth to the gums.

Aschenbach's gaze, though unawares, had very likely been inquisitive and tactless; for he became suddenly conscious that the stranger was returning it, and indeed so directly, with such hostility, such plain intent to force the withdrawal of the other's eyes, that Aschenbach felt an unpleasant twinge and, turning his back, began to walk along the hedge, hastily resolving to give the man no further heed. He had forgotten him the next minute. Yet whether the pilgrim air the stranger wore kindled his fantasy or whether some other physical or psychical influence came in play, he could not tell; but he felt the most surprising consciousness of a widening of inward barriers, a kind of vaulting unrest, a youthfully ardent thirst for distant scenes —a feeling so lively and so new, or at least so long ago outgrown and forgot, that he stood there rooted to the spot, his eyes on the ground and his hands clasped behind him, exploring these sentiments of his, their bearing and scope.

True, what he felt was no more than a longing to travel; yet coming upon him with such suddenness and passion as to resemble a seizure, almost a hallucination. Desire projected itself visually: his fancy, not quite yet lulled since morning, imaged the marvels and terrors of the manifold earth. He saw. He beheld a landscape, a tropical marshland, beneath a reeking sky, steaming, monstrous, rank—a kind of primeval wilderness-world of islands, morasses, and alluvial channels. Hairy palm-trunks rose near and far out of lush brakes of fern, out of bottoms of crass vegetation, fat, swollen, thick with incredible bloom. There were trees, misshapen as a dream, that dropped their naked roots straight through the air into the ground or into water that was stagnant and shadowy and glassy-green, where mammoth milk-white blossoms floated, and strange high-shouldered birds with curious bills stood gazing sidewise without sound or stir. Among the knotted joints of a bamboo thicket the eyes of a crouching tiger gleamed—and he felt his heart throb with terror, yet with a longing inexplicable. Then the vision vanished. Aschenbach, shaking his head, took up his march once more along the hedge of the stonemason's yard.

He had, at least ever since he commanded means to get about the world at will, regarded travel as a necessary evil, to be endured now and again willy-nilly for the sake of one's health. Too busy with the tasks imposed upon him by his own ego and the European soul, too laden with the care and duty to create, too preoccupied to be an amateur of the gay outer world, he had been content to know as much of the earth's surface as he could without stirring far outside his own sphere—had, indeed, never even been tempted to leave Europe. Now more than ever, since his life was on the wane, since he could no longer brush aside as fanciful his artist fear of not having done, of not being finished before the works ran down, he had confined himself to close range, had hardly stepped outside the charming city that he had made his home and the rude country house he had built in the mountains, whither he went to spend the rainy summers.

And so the new impulse that thus late and suddenly swept over him was speedily made to conform to the pattern of self-discipline he had followed from his youth up. He had meant to bring his work, for which he lived, to a certain point before leaving for the country, and the thought of a leisurely ramble across the globe, which should take him away from his desk for months, was too fantastic and upsetting to be seriously entertained. Yet the source of the unexpected contagion was known to him only too well. This yearning for new and distant scenes, this craving for freedom, release, forgetfulness—they were, he admitted to himself, an impulse toward flight, flight from the spot that was the daily theater of a rigid, cold, and passionate service. That service he loved, had even almost come to love the enervating daily struggle between a proud, tenacious, well-tried will and this growing fatigue, which no one must suspect, nor the finished product betray by any faintest sign that his inspiration could ever flag or miss fire. On the other hand, it seemed the part of common sense not to span the bow too far, not to suppress summarily a need that so unequivocally asserted itself. He thought of his work, and the place where yesterday and again today he had been forced to lay it down, since it would not yield either to patient effort or to a swift *coup de main.* Again and again he had tried to break or untie the knot—only to retire at last from the attack with a shiver of repugnance. Yet the difficulty was actually not a great one; what sapped his strength was distaste for the task, betrayed by a fastidiousness he could no longer satisfy. In his youth, indeed, the nature and inmost essence of the literary gift had been, to him, this very scrupulosity; for it he had bridled and tempered his sensibilities, knowing full well that feeling is prone to be content with easy gains and blithe half-perfection. So now, perhaps, feeling, thus tyrannized, avenged itself by leaving him, refusing from now on to carry and wing his art and taking away with it all the ecstasy he had known in form and expression. Not that he was doing bad work. So much, at least, the years had brought him, that at any moment he might feel tranquilly assured of mastery. But he got no joy of it—not though a nation paid it homage. To him it seemed his work had ceased to be marked by that fiery play of fancy which is the product of joy, and more, and more potently, than any intrinsic content, forms in turn the joy of the receiving world. He dreaded the summer in the country, alone with the maid who prepared his food and the man who served him; dreaded to see the familiar mountain peaks and walls that would shut him up again with his heavy discontent. What he needed was a break, an interim existence, a means of passing time, other air and a new stock of blood, to make the summer tolerable and productive. Good, then, he would go a journey. Not far—not all the way to the tigers. A night in a *wagon-lit,* three or four weeks of lotus-eating at some one of the gay world's playgrounds in the lovely south. . . .

So ran his thoughts, while the clang of the electric tram drew nearer down the Ungererstrasse; and as he mounted the platform he decided to devote the evening to a study of maps and railway guides. Once in, he bethought him to look back after the man in the straw hat, the companion of this brief interval which had after all been so fruitful. But he was not in his former place, nor in the tram itself, nor yet at the next stop; in short, his whereabouts remained a mystery.

Gustave Aschenbach was born at L—, a country town in the province of Silesia. He was the son of an upper official in the judicature, and his forebears had all been officers, judges, departmental functionaries—men who lived their strict, decent, sparing lives in the service of king and state. Only once before had a livelier mentality—in the quality of a clergyman—turned up among them; but swifter, more perceptive blood had in the generation before the poet's flowed into the stock from the mother's side, she being the daughter of a Bohemian musical conductor. It was from her he had the foreign traits that betrayed themselves in his appearance. The union of dry, conscientious officialdom and ardent, obscure impulse produced an artist—and this particular artist: author of the lucid and vigorous prose epic on the life of Frederick the Great; careful, tireless weaver of the richly patterned tapestry entitled *Maia*, a novel that gathers up the threads of many human destinies in the warp of a single idea; creator of that powerful narrative *The Abject*, which taught a whole grateful generation that a man can still be capable of moral resolution even after he has plumbed the depths of knowledge; and lastly—to complete the tale of works of his mature period—the writer of that impassioned discourse on the theme of Mind and Art whose ordered force and antithetic eloquence led serious critics to rank it with Schiller's *Simple and Sentimental Poetry*.

Aschenbach's whole soul, from the very beginning, was bent on fame—and thus, while not precisely precocious, yet thanks to the unmistakable trenchancy of his personal accent he was early ripe and ready for a career. Almost before he was out of high school he had a name. Ten years later he had learned to sit at his desk and sustain and live up to his growing reputation, to write gracious and pregnant phrases in letters that must needs be brief, for many claims press upon the solid and successful man. At forty, worn down by the strains and stresses of his actual task, he had to deal with a daily post heavy with tributes from his own and foreign countries.

Remote on one hand from the banal, on the other from the

eccentric, his genius was calculated to win at once the adhesion of the general public and the admiration, both sympathetic and stimulating, of the connoisseur. From childhood up he was pushed on every side to achievement, and achievement of no ordinary kind; and so his young days never knew the sweet idleness and blithe *laissez aller* that belong to youth. A nice observer once said of him in company—it was at the time when he fell ill in Vienna in his thirty-fifth year: "You see, Aschenbach has always lived like this"—here the speaker closed the fingers of his left hand to a fist—"never like this"—and he let his open hand hang relaxed from the back of his chair. It was apt. And this attitude was the more morally valiant in that Aschenbach was not by nature robust—he was only called to the constant tension of his career, not actually born to it.

By medical advice he had been kept from school and educated at home. He had grown up solitary, without comradeship; yet had early been driven to see that he belonged to those whose talent is not so much out of the common as is the physical basis on which talent relies for its fulfillment. It is a seed that gives early of its fruit, whose powers seldom reach a ripe old age. But his favorite motto was "Hold fast"; indeed, in his novel on the life of Frederick the Great he envisaged nothing else than the apotheosis of the old hero's word of command, "*Durchhalten*," which seemed to him the epitome of fortitude under suffering. Besides, he deeply desired to live to a good old age, for it was his conviction that only the artist to whom it has been granted to be fruitful on all stages of our human scene can be truly great, or universal, or worthy of honor.

Bearing the burden of his genius, then, upon such slender shoulders and resolved to go so far, he had the more need of discipline—and discipline, fortunately, was his native inheritance from the father's side. At forty, at fifty, he was still living as he had commenced to live in the years when others are prone to waste and revel, dream high thoughts and postpone fulfillment. He began his day with a cold shower over chest and back; then, setting a pair of tall wax candles in silver holders at the head of his manuscript, he sacrificed to art, in two or three hours of almost religious fervor, the powers he had assembled in sleep. Outsiders might be pardoned for believing that his *Maia* world and the epic amplitude revealed by the life of Frederick were a manifestation of great power working under high pressure, that they came forth, as it were, all in one breath. It was the more triumph for his morale; for the truth was that they were heaped up to greatness in layer after layer, in long days of work, out of hundreds and hundreds of single inspirations; they owed their excellence, of both mass and detail, to one thing and one alone: that their creator could hold out for years under the strain of the same piece of work, with an endurance and a tenacity of purpose like that which had conquered his native province of Silesia, devoting to actual composition none but his best and freshest hours.

For an intellectual product of any value to exert an immediate influence which shall also be deep and lasting, it must rest on an inner harmony, yes, an affinity, between the personal destiny of its author and that of his contemporaries in general. Men do not know why they award fame to one work of art rather than another. Without being in the faintest connoisseurs, they think to justify the warmth of their commendations by discovering in it a hundred virtues, whereas the real ground of their applause is inexplicable—it is sympathy. Aschenbach had once given direct expression—though in an unobtrusive place —to the idea that almost everything conspicuously great is great in despite: has come into being in defiance of affliction and pain, poverty, destitution, bodily weakness, vice, passion, and a thousand other obstructions. And that was more than observation—it was the fruit of experience, it was precisely the formula of his life and fame, it was the key to his work. What wonder, then, if it was also the fixed character, the outward gesture, of his most individual figures?

The new type of hero favored by Aschenbach, and recurring many times in his works, had early been analyzed by a shrewd critic: "The conception of an intellectual and virginal manliness, which clenches its teeth and stands in modest defiance of the swords and spears that pierce its side." That was beautiful, it was *spirituel,* it was exact, despite the suggestion of too great passivity it held. Forbearance in the face of fate, beauty constant under torture, are not merely passive. They are a positive achievement, an explicit triumph; and the figure of Sebastian is the most beautiful symbol, if not of art as a whole, yet certainly of the art we speak of here. Within that world of Aschenbach's creation were exhibited many phases of this theme: there was the aristocratic self-command that is eaten out within and for as long as it can conceals its biologic decline from the eyes of the world; the sere and ugly outside, hiding the embers of smoldering fire—and having power to fan them to so pure a flame as to challenge supremacy in the domain of beauty itself; the pallid languors of the flesh, contrasted with the fiery ardors of the spirit within, which can fling a whole proud people down at the foot of the Cross, at the feet of its own sheer self-abnegation; the gracious bearing preserved in the stern, stark service of form; the unreal, precarious existence of the born intrigant with its swiftly enervating alternation of schemes and desires—all these human fates and many more of their like one read in Aschenbach's pages, and reading them might doubt the existence of any other kind of heroism than the heroism born of weakness. And, after all, what kind could be truer to the spirit of the times? Gustave Aschenbach was the poet-spokesman of all those who labor at the edge of exhaustion; of the overburdened, of those who are already worn out but still hold themselves upright; of all our modern moralizers of accomplishment, with stunted growth and scanty resources, who yet contrive by skillful husbanding and prodigious spasms of will to produce, at least for a while, the effect of greatness. There are many such, they are the heroes of the age. And in Aschenbach's pages they saw themselves; he justified, he exalted them, he sang their praise—and they, they were grateful, they heralded his fame.

He had been young and crude with the times and by them badly counseled. He had taken false steps, blundered, exposed himself, offended in speech and writing against tact and good sense. But he had attained to honor, and honor, he used to say, is the natural goal toward which every considerable talent presses with whip and spur. Yes, one might put it that his whole career had been one conscious and overweening ascent to honor, which left in the rear all the misgivings or self-derogation which might have hampered him.

What pleases the public is lively and vivid delineation which makes no demands on the intellect; but passionate and absolutist youth can only be enthralled by a problem. And Aschenbach was as absolute, as problematist, as any youth of them all. He had done homage to intellect, had overworked the soil of knowledge and ground up her seed-corn; had turned his back on the "mysteries," called genius itself in question, held up art to scorn—yes, even while his faithful following reveled in the characters he created, he, the young artist, was taking away the breath of the twenty-year-olds with his cynic utterances on the nature of art and the artist life.

But it seems that a noble and active mind blunts itself against nothing so quickly as the sharp and bitter irritant of knowledge. And certain it is that the youth's constancy of purpose, no matter how painfully conscientious, was shallow beside the mature resolution of the master of his craft, who made a right-about-face, turned his back on the realm of knowledge, and passed it by with averted face, lest it lame his will or power of action, paralyze his feelings or his passions, deprive any of these of their conviction or utility. How else interpret the oft-cited story of *The Abject* than as a rebuke to the excesses of a psychology-ridden age, embodied in the delineation of the weak and silly fool who manages to lead fate by the nose; driving his wife, out of sheer innate pusillanimity, into the arms of a beardless youth, and making this disaster an excuse for trifling away the rest of his life?

With rage the author here rejects the rejected, casts out the outcast—and the measure of his fury is the measure of his condemnation of all moral shilly-shallying. Explicitly he renounces sympathy with the abyss, explicitly he refutes the flabby humanitarianism of the phrase: "*Tout comprendre c'est tout pardonner.*" What was here unfolding, or rather was already in full bloom, was the "miracle of regained detachment," which a little later became the theme of one of the author's dialogues, dwelt upon not without a certain oracular emphasis. Strange sequence of thought! Was it perhaps an intellectual consequence of this rebirth, this new austerity, that from now on his style showed an almost exaggerated sense of beauty, a lofty purity, symmetry, and simplicity, which gave his productions a stamp of the classic, of conscious and deliberate mastery? And yet: this moral fiber, surviving the hampering and disintegrating effect of knowledge, does it not result in its turn in a dangerous simplification, in a tendency to equate the world and the human soul, and thus to strengthen the hold of the evil, the forbidden, and the ethically impossible? And has not form two aspects? Is it not moral and immoral at once: moral in so far as it is the expression and result of discipline, immoral—yes, actually hostile to morality—in that of its very essence it is indifferent to good and evil, and deliberately concerned to make the moral world stoop beneath its proud and undivided scepter?

Be that as it may. Development is destiny; and why should a career attended by the applause and adulation of the masses necessarily take the same course as one that does not share the glamour and the obligations of fame? Only the incorrigible bohemian smiles or scoffs when a man of transcendent gifts outgrows his carefree prentice stage, recognizes his own worth, and forces the world to recognize it too and pay it homage, though he puts on a courtly bearing to hide his bitter struggles and his loneliness. Again, the play of a developing talent must give its possessor joy, if of a willful, defiant kind. With time, an official note, something almost expository, crept into Gustave Aschenbach's method. His later style gave up the old sheer audacities, the fresh and subtle nuances—it became fixed and exemplary, conservative, formal, even formulated. Like Louis XIV—or as tradition has it of him—Aschenbach, as he went on in years, banished from his style every common word. It was at this time that the school authorities adopted selections from his works into their textbooks. And he found it only fitting—and had no thought but to accept—when a German prince signalized his accession to the throne by conferring upon the poet-author of the life of Frederick the Great on his fiftieth birthday the letters-patent of nobility.

He had roved about for a few years, trying this place and that as a place of residence, before choosing, as he soon did, the city of Munich for his permanent home. And there he lived, enjoying among his fellow citizens the honor which is in rare cases the reward of intellectual eminence. He married young, the daughter of a university family; but after a brief term of wedded happiness his wife had died. A daughter, already married, remained to him. A son he never had.

Gustave von Aschenbach was somewhat below middle height, dark and smooth-shaven, with a head that looked rather too large for his almost delicate figure. He wore his hair brushed back; it was thin at the parting, bushy and gray on the temples, framing a lofty, rugged, knotty brow—if one may so characterize it. The nose-piece of his rimless gold spectacles cut into the base of his thick, aristocratically hooked nose. The mouth was large, often lax, often suddenly narrow and tense; the cheeks lean and furrowed, the pronounced chin slightly cleft. The vicissitudes of fate, it seemed, must have passed over this head, for he held it, plaintively, rather on one side; yet it was art, not the stern discipline of an active career, that had taken over the office of modeling these features. Behind this brow were born the flashing thrust and parry of the dialogue between Frederick and Voltaire on the theme of war; these eyes, weary and sunken, gazing through their glasses, had beheld the bloodstained inferno of the hospitals in the Seven Years' War. Yes, personally speaking too, art heightens life. She gives deeper joy, she consumes more swiftly. She engraves adventures of the spirit and the mind in the faces of her votaries; let them lead outwardly a life of the most cloistered calm, she will in the end produce in them a fastidiousness, an over-refinement, a nervous fever and exhaustion, such as a career of extravagant passions and pleasures can hardly show.

Eager though he was to be off, Aschenbach was kept in Munich by affairs both literary and practical for some two weeks after that walk of his. But at length he ordered his country home put ready against his return within the next few weeks, and on a day between the middle and the end of May took the evening train for Trieste, where he stopped only twenty-four hours, embarking for Pola the next morning but one.

What he sought was a fresh scene, without associations, which should yet be not too out-of-the-way; and accordingly he chose an island in the Adriatic, not far off the Istrian coast. It had been well known some years, for its splendidly rugged cliff formations on the side next the open sea, and its population, clad in a bright flutter of rags and speaking an outlandish tongue. But there was rain and heavy air; the society at the hotel was provincial Austrian, and limited; besides, it annoyed him not to be able to get at the sea—he missed the close and soothing contact which only a gentle sandy slope affords. He could not feel this was the place he sought; an inner impulse made him wretched, urging him on he knew not whither; he racked his brains, he looked up boats, then all at once his goal stood plain before his eyes. But of course! When one wanted to arrive overnight at the incomparable, the fabulous, the like-nothing-else-in-the-world, where was it one went? Why, obviously; he had intended to go there, what ever was he doing here? A blunder. He made all haste to correct it, announcing his departure at once. Ten days after his arrival on the island a swift motorboat bore him and his luggage in the misty dawning back across the water to the naval station, where he landed only to pass over the landing-stage and on to the wet decks of a ship lying there with steam up for the passage to Venice.

It was an ancient hulk belonging to an Italian line, obsolete, dingy, grimed with soot. A dirty hunchbacked sailor, smirkingly polite, conducted him at once belowships to a cavernous, lamplit cabin. There behind a table sat a man with a beard like a goat's; he had his hat on the back of his head, a cigar-stump in the corner of his mouth; he reminded Aschenbach of an old-fashioned circus-director. This person put the usual questions and wrote out a ticket to Venice, which he issued to the traveler with many commercial flourishes.

"A ticket for Venice," repeated he, stretching out his arm to dip the pen into the thick ink in a tilted inkstand. "One first-class to Venice! Here you are, *signore mio*." He made some scrawls on the paper, strewed bluish sand on it out of a box, thereafter letting the sand run off into an earthen vessel, folded the paper with bony yellow fingers, and wrote on the outside. "An excellent choice," he rattled on. "Ah, Venice! What a glorious city! Irresistibly attractive to the cultured man for her past history as well as her present charm." His copious gesturings and empty phrases gave the odd impression that he feared the traveler might alter his mind. He changed Aschenbach's note, laying the money on the spotted table-cover with the glibness of a croupier. "A pleasant visit to you, signore," he said, with a melodramatic bow. "Delighted to serve you." Then he beckoned and called out: "Next" as though a stream of passengers stood waiting to be served, though in point of fact there was not one. Aschenbach returned to the upper deck.

He leaned an arm on the railing and looked at the idlers lounging along the quay to watch the boat go out. Then he turned his attention to his fellow passengers. Those of the second class, both men and women, were squatted on their bundles of luggage on the forward deck. The first cabin consisted of a group of lively youths, clerks from Pola, evidently, who had made up a pleasure excursion to Italy and were not a little thrilled at the prospect, bustling about and laughing with satisfaction at the stir they made. They leaned over the railings and shouted, with a glib command of epithet, derisory remarks at such of their fellow clerks as they saw going to business along the quay; and these in turn shook their sticks and shouted as good back again. One of the party, in a dandified buff suit, a rakish panama with a colored scarf, and a red cravat, was loudest of the loud: he outcrowed all the rest. Aschenbach's eye dwelt on him, and he was shocked to see that the apparent youth was no youth at all. He was an old man, beyond a doubt, with wrinkles and crow's-feet round eyes and mouth; the dull carmine of the cheeks was rouge, the brown hair a wig. His neck was shrunken and sinewy, his turned-up mustaches and small imperial were dyed, and the unbroken double row of yellow teeth he showed when he laughed were but too obviously a cheapish false set. He wore a seal ring on each forefinger, but the hands were those of an old man. Aschenbach was moved to shudder as he watched the creature and his association with the rest of the group. Could they not see he was old, that he had no right to wear the clothes they wore or pretend to be one of them? But they were used to him, it seemed; they suffered him among them, they paid back his jokes in kind and the playful pokes in the ribs he gave them. How could they? Aschenbach put his hand to his brow, he covered his eyes, for he had slept little, and they smarted. He felt not quite canny, as though the world were suffering a dreamlike distortion of perspective which he might arrest by shutting it all out for a few minutes and then looking at it afresh. But instead he felt a floating sensation, and opened his eyes with unreasoning alarm to find that the ship's dark sluggish bulk was slowly leaving the jetty. Inch by inch, with the to-and-fro motion of her machinery, the strip of iridescent dirty water widened, the boat maneuvered clumsily and turned her bow to the open sea. Aschenbach moved over to the starboard side, where the hunchbacked sailor had set up a deck-chair for him, and a steward in a greasy dress-coat asked for orders.

The sky was gray, the wind humid. Harbor and island dropped behind, all sight of land soon vanished in mist. Flakes of sodden, clammy soot fell upon the still undried deck. Before the boat was an hour out a canvas had to be spread as a shelter from the rain.

Wrapped in his cloak, a book in his lap, our traveler rested; the hours slipped by unawares. It stopped raining, the canvas was taken down. The horizon was visible right round: beneath the somber dome of the sky stretched the vast plain of empty sea. But immeasurable unarticulated space weakens our power to measure time as well: the time-sense falters and grows dim. Strange, shadowy figures passed and repassed—the elderly coxcomb, the goat-bearded man from the bowels of the ship—with vague gesturings and mutterings through the traveler's mind as he lay. He fell asleep.

At midday he was summoned to luncheon in a corridor-like saloon with the sleeping-cabins giving off it. He ate at the head of the long table; the party of clerks, including the old man, sat with the jolly captain at the other end, where they had been carousing since ten o'clock. The meal was wretched, and soon done. Aschenbach was driven to seek the open and look at the sky—perhaps it would lighten presently above Venice.

He had not dreamed it could be otherwise, for the city had ever given him a brilliant welcome. But sky and sea remained leaden, with spurts of fine, mistlike rain; he reconciled himself to the idea of seeing a different Venice from that he had always approached on the landward side. He stood by the foremast, his gaze on the distance, alert for the first glimpse of the coast. And he thought of the melancholy and susceptible poet who had once seen the towers and turrets of his dreams rise out of these waves; repeated the rhythms born of his awe, his mingled emotions of joy and suffering—and easily susceptible to a prescience already shaped within him, he asked his own sober, weary heart if a new enthusiasm, a new preoccupation, some late adventure of the feelings could still be in store for the idle traveler.

The flat coast showed on the right, the sea was soon populous with fishing-boats. The Lido appeared and was left behind as the ship glided at half speed through the narrow harbor of the same name, coming to a full stop on the lagoon in sight of garish, badly built houses. Here it waited for the boat bringing the sanitary inspector.

An hour passed. One had arrived—and yet not. There was no conceivable haste—yet one felt harried. The youths from Pola were on deck, drawn hither by the martial sound of horns coming across the water from the direction of the Public Gardens. They had drunk a good deal of Asti and were moved to shout and hurrah at the drilling *bersaglieri.* But the young-old man was a truly repulsive sight in the condition to which his company with youth had brought him. He could not carry his wine like them: he was pitiably drunk. He swayed as he stood—watery-eyed, a cigarette between his shaking fingers, keeping upright with difficulty. He could not have taken a step without falling and knew better than to stir, but his spirits were deplorably high. He buttonholed anyone who came within reach, he stuttered, he giggled, he leered, he fatuously shook his beringed old forefinger; his tongue kept seeking the corner of his mouth in a suggestive motion ugly to behold. Aschenbach's brow darkened as he looked, and there came over him once more a dazed sense, as though things about him were just slightly losing their ordinary perspective, beginning to show a distortion that might merge into the grotesque. He was prevented from dwelling on the feeling, for now the machinery began to thud again, and the ship took up its passage through the Canale di San Marco which had been interrupted so near the goal.

He saw it once more, that landing-place that takes the breath away, that amazing group of incredible structures the Republic set up to meet the awe-struck eye of the approaching seafarer: the airy splendor of the palace and Bridge of Sighs, the columns of lion and saint on the shore, the glory of the projecting flank of the fairy temple, the vista of gateway and clock. Looking, he thought that to come to Venice by the station is like entering a palace by the back door. No one should approach save by the high seas, as he was doing now, this most improbable of cities.

The engines stopped. Gondolas pressed alongside, the landing-stairs were let down, customs officials came on board and did their office, people began to go ashore. Aschenbach ordered a gondola. He meant to take up his abode by the sea and needed to be conveyed with his luggage to the landing-stage of the little steamers that ply between the city and the Lido. They called down his order to the surface of the water where the gondoliers were quarreling in dialect. Then came another delay while his trunk was worried down the ladder-like stairs. Thus he was forced to endure the importunities of the ghastly young-old man, whose drunken state obscurely urged him to pay the stranger the honor of a formal farewell. "We wish you a very pleasant sojourn," he babbled, bowing and scraping. "Pray keep us in mind. *Au revoir, excusez et bon jour, votre Excellence.*" He drooled, he blinked, he licked the corner of his mouth, the little imperial bristled on his elderly chin. He put the tips of two fingers to his mouth and said thickly: "Give her our love, will you, the p-pretty little dear"—here his upper plate came away and fell down on the lower one. . . . Aschenbach escaped. "Little sweety-sweety-sweetheart" he heard behind him, gurgled and stuttered, as he climbed down the rope stair into the boat.

Is there anyone but must repress a secret thrill on arriving in Venice for the first time—or returning thither after long absence—and stepping into a Venetian gondola? That singular conveyance, come down unchanged from ballad times, black as nothing else on earth except a coffin—what pictures it calls up of lawless, silent adventures in the plashing night; or even more, what visions of death itself, the bier and solemn rites and last soundless voyage! And has anyone remarked that the seat in such a bark, the armchair lacquered in coffin-black and dully black-upholstered, is the softest, most luxurious, most relaxing seat in the world? Aschenbach realized it when he had let himself down at the gondolier's feet, opposite his luggage, which lay neatly composed on the vessel's beak. The rowers still gestured fiercely; he heard their harsh, incoherent tones. But the strange stillness of the water-city seemed to take up their voices gently, to disembody and scatter them over the sea. It was warm here in the harbor. The lukewarm air of the sirocco breathed upon him, he leaned back among his cushions and gave himself to the yielding element, closing his eyes for very pleasure in an indolence as unaccustomed as sweet. "The trip will be short," he thought, and wished it might last forever. They gently swayed away from the boat with its bustle and clamor of voices.

It grew still and stiller all about. No sound but the splash of the oars, the hollow slap of the wave against the steep, black, halbert-shaped beak of the vessel, and one sound more—a muttering by fits and starts, expressed as it were by the motion of his arms, from the lips of the gondolier. He was talking to himself, between his teeth. Aschenbach glanced up and saw with surprise that the lagoon was widening, his vessel was headed for the open sea. Evidently it would not do to give himself up to sweet *far niente;* he must see his wishes carried out.

"You are to take me to the steamboat landing, you know," he said, half turning round toward it. The muttering stopped. There was no reply.

"Take me to the steamboat landing," he repeated, and this time turned quite round and looked up into the face of the gondolier as he stood there on his little elevated deck, high against the pale gray sky. The man had an unpleasing, even brutish face, and wore blue clothes like a sailor's, with a yellow sash; a shapeless straw hat with the braid torn at the brim perched rakishly on his head. His facial structure, as well as the curling blond mustache under the short snub nose, showed him to be of non-Italian stock. Physically rather undersized, so that one would not have expected him to be very muscular, he pulled vigorously at the oar, putting all his body-weight behind each stroke. Now and then the effort he made curled back his lips and bared his white teeth to the gums. He spoke in a decided, almost curt voice, looking out to sea over his fare's head: "The signore is going to the Lido."

Aschenbach answered: "Yes, I am. But I only took the gondola to cross over to San Marco. I am using the *vaporetto* from there."

"But the signore cannot use the *vaporetto.*"

"And why not?"

"Because the *vaporetto* does not take luggage."

It was true. Aschenbach remembered it. He made no answer. But the man's gruff, overbearing manner, so unlike the usual courtesy of his countrymen toward the stranger, was intolerable.

Aschenbach spoke again: "That is my own affair. I may want to give my luggage in deposit. You will turn round."

No answer. The oar splashed, the wave struck dull against the prow. And the muttering began anew, the gondolier talked to himself, between his teeth.

What should the traveler do? Alone on the water with this tongue-tied, obstinate, uncanny man, he saw no way of enforcing his will. And if only he did not excite himself, how pleasantly he might rest! Had he not wished the voyage might last forever? The wisest thing—and how much the pleasantest!—was to let matters take their own course. A spell of indolence was upon him; it came from the chair he sat in—this low, black-upholstered armchair, so gently rocked at the hands of the despotic boatman in his rear. The thought passed dreamily through Aschenbach's brain that perhaps he had fallen into the clutches of a criminal; it had not power to rouse him to action. More annoying was the simpler explanation: that the man was only trying to extort money. A sense of duty, a recollection, as it were, that this ought to be prevented, made him collect himself to say:

"How much do you ask for the trip?"

And the gondolier, gazing out over his head, replied: "The signore will pay."

There was an established reply to this; Aschenbach made it, mechanically:

"I will pay nothing whatever if you do not take me where I want to go."

"The signore wants to go to the Lido."

"But not with you."

"I am a good rower, signore. I will row you well."

"So much is true," thought Aschenbach, and again he relaxed. "That is true, you row me well. Even if you mean to rob me, even if you hit me in the back with your oar, and send me down to the kingdom of Hades, even then you will have rowed me well."

But nothing of the sort happened. Instead, they fell in with company: a boat came alongside and waylaid them, full of men and women singing to guitar and mandolin. They rowed persistently bow for bow with the gondola and filled the silence that had rested on the waters with their lyric love of gain.

Aschenbach tossed money into the hat they held out. The music stopped at once, they rowed away. And once more the gondolier's mutter became audible as he talked to himself in fits and snatches.

Thus they rowed on, rocked by the wash of a steamer returning citywards. At the landing two municipal officials were walking up and down with their hands behind their backs and their faces turned toward the lagoon. Aschenbach was helped on shore by the old man with a boat-hook who is the permanent feature of every landing-stage in Venice; and having no small change to pay the boatman, crossed over into the hotel opposite. His wants were supplied in the lobby; but when he came back, his possessions were already on a hand-car on the quay, and gondola and gondolier were gone.

"He ran away, signore," said the old boatman. "A bad lot, a man without a license. He is the only gondolier without one. The others telephoned over, and he knew we were on the look-out, so he made off."

Aschenbach shrugged.

"The signore has had a ride for nothing," said the old man, and held out his hat. Aschenbach dropped some coins. He directed that his luggage be taken to the Hôtel des Bains and followed the hand-car through the avenue, that white-blossoming avenue with taverns, booths, and pensions on either side it, which runs across the island diagonally to the beach.

He entered the hotel from the garden terrace at the back and passed through the vestibule and hall into the office. His arrival was expected, and he was served with courtesy and dispatch. The manager, a small, soft, dapper man with a black mustache and a caressing way with him, wearing a French frock-coat, himself took him up in the lift and showed him his room. It was a pleasant chamber, furnished in cherry-wood, with lofty windows looking out to sea. It was decorated with strong-scented flowers. Aschenbach, as soon as he was alone, and while they brought in his trunk and bags and disposed them in the room, went up to one of the windows and stood looking out upon the beach in its afternoon emptiness, and at the sunless sea, now full and sending long, low waves with rhythmic beat upon the sand.

A solitary, unused to speaking of what he sees and feels, has mental experiences that are at once more intense and less articulate than those of a gregarious man. They are sluggish, yet more wayward, and never without a melancholy tinge. Sights and impressions which others brush aside with a glance, a light comment, a smile, occupy him more than their due; they sink silently in, they take on meaning, they become experience, emotion, adventure. Solitude gives birth to the original in us, to beauty unfamiliar and perilous—to poetry. But also it gives birth to the opposite: to the perverse, the illicit, the absurd. Thus the traveler's mind still dwelt with disquiet on the episodes of his journey hither: on the horrible old fop with his drivel about a mistress, on the outlaw boatman and his lost tip. They did not offend his reason, they hardly afforded food for thought; yet they seemed by their very nature fundamentally strange, and thereby vaguely disquieting. Yet here was the sea; even in the midst of such thoughts he saluted it with his eyes, exulting that Venice was near and accessible. At length he turned round, disposed his personal belongings and made certain arrangements with the chambermaid for his comfort, washed up, and was conveyed to the ground floor by the green-uniformed Swiss who ran the lift.

He took tea on the terrace facing the sea and afterwards went down and walked some distance along the shore promenade in the direction of Hôtel Excelsior. When he came back, it seemed to be time to change for dinner. He did so, slowly and methodically as his way was, for he was accustomed to work while he dressed; but even so found himself a little early when he entered the hall, where a large number of guests had collected—strangers to each other and affecting mutual indifference, yet united in expectancy of the meal. He picked up a paper, sat down in a leather armchair, and took stock of the company, which compared most favorably with that he had just left.

This was a broad and tolerant atmosphere, of wide horizons. Subdued voices were speaking most of the principal European tongues. That uniform of civilization, the conventional evening dress, gave outward conformity to the varied types. There were long, dry Americans, large-familied Russians, English ladies, German children with French *bonnes*. The Slavic element predominated, it seemed. In Aschenbach's neighborhood Polish was being spoken.

Round a wicker table next him was gathered a group of young folk in charge of a governess or companion—three young girls, perhaps fifteen to seventeen years old, and a long-haired boy of about fourteen. Aschenbach noticed with astonishment the lad's perfect beauty. His face recalled the noblest moment of Greek sculpture—pale, with a sweet reserve, with clustering honey-colored ringlets, the brow and nose descending in one line, the winning mouth, the expression of pure and godlike serenity. Yet with all this chaste perfection of form it was of such unique personal charm that the observer thought he had never seen, either in nature or in art, anything so utterly happy and consummate. What struck him further was the strange contrast the group afforded, a difference in educational method, so to speak, shown in the way the brother and sisters were clothed and treated. The girls, the eldest of whom was practically grown up, were dressed with an almost disfiguring austerity. All three wore half-length slate-colored frocks of cloister-like plainness, arbitrarily unbecoming in cut, with white turnover collars as their only adornment. Every grace of outline was willfully suppressed; their hair lay smoothly plastered to their heads, giving them a vacant expression, like a nun's. All this could only be by the mother's orders; but there was no trace of the same pedagogic severity in the case of the boy. Tenderness and softness, it was plain, conditioned his existence. No scissors had been put to the lovely hair that (like the Spinnario's) curled about his brows, above his ears, longer still in the neck. He wore an English sailor suit, with quilted sleeves that narrowed round the delicate wrists of his long and slender though still childish hands. And this suit, with its breast-knot, lacings, and embroideries, lent the slight figure something "rich and strange," a spoilt, exquisite air. The observer saw him in half profile, with one foot in its black patent leather advanced, one elbow resting on the arm of his basket-chair, the cheek nestled into the closed hand in a pose of easy grace, quite unlike the stiff subservient mien that was evidently habitual to his sisters. Was he delicate? His facial tint was ivory-white against the golden darkness of his clustering locks. Or was he simply a pampered darling, the object of a self-willed and partial love? Aschenbach inclined to think the latter. For in almost every artist nature is inborn a wanton and treacherous proneness to side with the beauty that breaks hearts, to single out aristocratic pretensions and pay them homage.

A waiter announced, in English, that dinner was served. Gradually the company dispersed through the glass doors into the dining-room. Late-comers entered from the vestibule or the lifts. Inside, dinner was being served; but the young Poles still sat and waited about their wicker table. Aschenbach felt comfortable in his deep armchair, he enjoyed the beauty before his eyes, he waited with them.

The governess, a short, stout, red-faced person, at length gave the signal. With lifted brows she pushed back her chair and made a bow to the tall woman, dressed in palest gray, who now entered the hall. This lady's abundant jewels were pearls, her manner was cool and measured; the fashion of her gown and the arrangement of her lightly powdered hair had the simplicity prescribed in certain circles whose piety and aristocracy are equally marked. She might have been, in Germany, the wife of some high official. But there was something faintly fabulous, after all, in her appearance, though lent it solely by the pearls she wore: they were well-nigh priceless, and consisted of ear-rings and a three-stranded necklace, very long, with gems the size of cherries.

The brother and sisters had risen briskly. They bowed over their mother's hand to kiss it, she turning away from them, with a slight smile on her face, which was carefully preserved but rather sharp-nosed and worn. She addressed a few words in French to the governess, then moved toward the glass door. The children followed, the girls in order of age, then the governess, and last the boy. He chanced to turn before he crossed the threshold, and as there was no one else in the room, his strange, twilit gray eyes met Aschenbach's, as our traveler sat there with the paper on his knee, absorbed in looking after the group.

There was nothing singular, of course, in what he had seen. They had not gone in to dinner before their mother, they had waited, given her a respectful salute, and but observed the right and proper forms on entering the room. Yet they had done all this so expressly, with such self-respecting dignity, discipline, and sense of duty that Aschenbach was impressed. He lingered still a few minutes, then he, too, went into the dining-room, where he was shown a table far away from the Polish family, as he noted at once, with a stirring of regret.

Tired, yet mentally alert, he beguiled the long, tedious meal with abstract, even with transcendent matters: pondered the mysterious harmony that must come to subsist between the individual human being and the universal law, in order that human beauty may result; passed on to general problems of form and art, and came at length to the conclusion that what seemed to him fresh and happy thoughts were like the flattering inventions of a dream, which the waking sense proves worthless and insubstantial. He spent the evening in the park, which was sweet with the odors of evening—sitting, smoking, wandering about; went to bed betimes, and passed the night in deep, unbroken sleep, visited, however, by varied and lively dreams.

The weather next day was no more promising. A land breeze blew. Beneath a colorless, overcast sky the sea lay sluggish, and as it were shrunken, so far withdrawn as to leave bare several rows of long sandbanks. The horizon looked close and prosaic. When Aschenbach opened his window he thought he smelt the stagnant odor of the lagoons.

He felt suddenly out of sorts and already began to think of leaving. Once, years before, after weeks of bright spring weather, this wind had found him out; it had been so bad as to force him to flee from the city like a fugitive. And now it seemed beginning again—the same feverish distaste, the pressure on his temples, the heavy eyelids. It would be a nuisance to change again; but if the wind did not turn, this was no place for him. To be on the safe side, he did not entirely unpack. At nine o'clock he went down to the buffet, which lay between the hall and the dining-room and served as breakfast-room.

A solemn stillness reigned here, such as it is the ambition of all large hotels to achieve. The waiters moved on noiseless feet. A rattling of tea-things, a whispered word—and no other sounds. In a corner diagonally to the door, two tables from his own, Aschenbach saw the Polish girls with their governess. They sat there very straight, in their stiff blue linen frocks with little turnover collars and cuffs, their ash-blond hair newly brushed flat, their eyelids red from sleep; and handed each other the marmalade. They had nearly finished their meal. The boy was not there.

Aschenbach smiled. "Aha, little Phæax," he thought. "It seems you are privileged to sleep yourself out." With sudden gaiety he quoted:

"*Oft veränderten Schmuck und warme Bäder und Ruhe.*"

He took a leisurely breakfast. The porter came up with his braided cap in his hand, to deliver some letters that had been sent on. Aschenbach lighted a cigarette and opened a few letters and thus was still seated to witness the arrival of the sluggard.

He entered through the glass doors and passed diagonally across the room to his sisters at their table. He walked with extraordinary grace—the carriage of the body, the action of the knee, the way he set down his foot in its white shoe—it was all so light, it was at once dainty and proud, it wore an added charm in the childish shyness that made him twice turn his head as he crossed the room, made him give a quick glance and then drop his eyes. He took his seat, with a smile and a murmured word in his soft and blurry tongue; and Aschenbach, sitting so that he could see him in profile, was astonished anew, yes, startled, at the godlike beauty of the human being. The lad had on a light sailor suit of blue and white striped cotton, with a red silk breast-knot and a simple white standing collar round the neck—a not very elegant effect—yet above this collar the head was poised like a flower, in incomparable loveliness. It was the head of Eros, with the yellowish bloom of Parian marble, with fine serious brows, and dusky clustering ringlets standing out in soft plenteousness over temples and ears.

"Good, oh, very good indeed!" thought Aschenbach, assuming the patronizing air of the connoisseur to hide, as artists will, their ravishment over a masterpiece. "Yes," he went on to himself, "if it were not that sea and beach were waiting for me, I should sit here as long as you do." But he went out on that, passing through the hall, beneath the watchful eye of the functionaries, down the steps and directly across the board walk to the section of the beach reserved for the guests of the hotel. The bathing-master, a barefoot old man in linen trousers and sailor blouse, with a straw hat, showed him the cabin that had been rented for him, and Aschenbach had him set up table and chair on the sandy platform before it. Then he dragged the reclining-chair through the pale yellow sand, closer to the sea, sat down, and composed himself.

He delighted, as always, in the scene on the beach, the sight of sophisticated society giving itself over to a simple life at the edge of the element. The shallow gray sea was already gay with children wading, with swimmers, with figures in bright colors lying on the sandbanks with arms behind their heads. Some were rowing in little keelless boats painted red and blue, and laughing when they capsized. A long row of *capanne* ran down the beach, with platforms, where people sat as on verandas, and there was social life, with bustle and with indolent repose; visits were paid, amid much chatter, punctilious morning toilettes hobnobbed with comfortable and privileged dishabille. On the hard wet sand close to the sea, figures in white bathrobes or loose wrappings in garish colors strolled up and down. A mammoth sand-hill had been built up on Aschenbach's right, the work of children, who had stuck it full of tiny flags. Vendors of sea-shells, fruit, and cakes knelt beside their wares spread out on the sand. A row of cabins on the left stood obliquely to the others and to the sea, thus forming the boundary of the enclosure on this side; and on the little veranda in front of one of these a Russian family was encamped; bearded men with strong white teeth, ripe, indolent women, a Fräulein from the Baltic Provinces, who sat at an easel painting the sea and tearing her hair in despair; two ugly but good-natured children and an old maidservant in a head-cloth, with the caressing, servile manner of the born dependent. There they sat together in grateful enjoyment of their blessings: constantly shouting at their romping children, who paid not the slightest heed; making jokes in broken Italian to the funny old man who sold them sweetmeats, kissing one another on the cheeks—no jot concerned that their domesticity was overlooked.

"I'll stay," thought Aschenbach. "Where could it be better than here?" With his hands clasped in his lap he let his eyes swim in the wideness of the sea, his gaze lose focus, blur, and grow vague in the misty immensity of space. His love of the ocean had profound sources: the hard-worked artist's longing for rest, his yearning to seek refuge from the thronging manifold shapes of his fancy in the bosom of the simple and vast; and another yearning, opposed to his art and perhaps for that very reason a lure, for the unorganized, the immeasurable, the eternal—in short, for nothingness. He whose preoccupation is with excellence longs fervently to find rest in perfection; and is not nothingness a form of perfection? As he sat there dreaming thus, deep, deep into the void, suddenly the margin line of the shore was cut by a human form. He gathered up his gaze and withdrew it from the illimitable, and lo, it was the lovely boy who crossed his vision coming from the left along the sand. He was barefoot, ready for wading, the slender legs uncovered above the knee, and moved slowly, yet with such a proud, light tread as to make it seem he had never worn shoes. He looked toward the diagonal row of cabins; and the sight of the Russian family, leading their lives there in joyous simplicity, distorted his features in a spasm of angry disgust. His brow darkened, his lips curled, one corner of the mouth was drawn down in a harsh line that marred the curve of the cheek, his frown was so heavy that the eyes seemed to sink in as beneath they uttered the black and vicious language of hate. He looked down, looked threateningly back once more; then giving it up with a violent and contemptuous shoulder-shrug, he left his enemies in the rear.

A feeling of delicacy, a qualm, almost like a sense of shame, made Aschenbach turn away as though he had not seen; he felt unwilling to take advantage of having been, by chance, privy to this passionate reaction. But he was in truth both moved and exhilarated—that is to say, he was delighted. This childish exhibition of fanaticism, directed against the good-naturedest simplicity in the world—it gave to the godlike and inexpressive the final human touch. The figure of the half-grown lad, a masterpiece from nature's own hand, had been significant enough when it gratified the eye alone; and now it evoked sympathy as well—the little episode had set it off, lent it a dignity in the onlooker's eyes that was beyond its years.

Aschenbach listened with still averted head to the boy's voice announcing his coming to his companions at the sand-heap. The voice was clear, though a little weak, but they answered, shouting his name—or his nickname—again and again. Aschenbach was not without curiosity to learn it, but could make out nothing more exact than two musical syllables, something like Adgio—or, oftener still, Adjiu, with a long-drawn-out *u* at the end. He liked the melodious sound, and found it fitting; said it over to himself a few times and turned back with satisfaction to his papers.

Holding his traveling-pad on his knees, he took his fountain-pen and began to answer various items of his correspondence. But presently he felt it too great a pity to turn his back, and the eyes of his mind, for the sake of mere commonplace correspondence, to this scene which was, after all, the most rewarding one he knew. He put aside his papers and swung round to the sea; in no long time, beguiled by the voices of the children at play, he had turned his head and sat resting it against the chair-back, while he gave himself up to contemplating the activities of the exquisite Adgio.

His eye found him out at once, the red breast-knot was unmistakable. With some nine or ten companions, boys and girls of his own age and younger, he was busy putting in place an old plank to serve as a bridge across the ditches between the sand-piles. He directed the work by shouting and motioning with his head, and they were all chattering in many tongues—French, Polish, and even some of the Balkan languages. But his was the name oftenest on their lips, he was plainly sought after, wooed, admired. One lad in particular, a Pole like himself, with a name that sounded something like Jaschiu, a sturdy lad with brilliantined black hair, in a belted linen suit, was his particular liegeman and friend. Operations at the sand-pile being ended for the time, they two walked away along the beach, with their arms round each other's waists, and once the lad Jaschiu gave Adgio a kiss.

Aschenbach felt like shaking a finger at him. "But you, Critobulus," he thought with a smile, "you I advise to take a year's leave. That long, at least, you will need for complete recovery." A vendor came by with strawberries, and Aschenbach made his second breakfast of the great luscious, dead-ripe fruit. It had grown very warm, though the sun had not availed to pierce the heavy layer of mist. His mind felt relaxed, his senses reveled in this vast and soothing communion with the silence of the sea. The grave and serious man found sufficient occupation in speculating what name it could be that sounded like Adgio. And with the help of a few Polish memories he at length fixed on Tadzio, a shortened form of Thaddeus, which sounded, when called, like Tadziu or Adziu.

Tadzio was bathing. Aschenbach had lost sight of him for a moment, then descried him far out in the water, which was shallow a very long way—saw his head, and his arm striking out like an oar. But his watchful family were already on the alert; the mother and governess called from the veranda in front of their bathing-cabin, until the lad's name, with its softened consonants and long-drawn *u*-sound, seemed to possess the beach like a rallying-cry; the cadence had something sweet and wild: "Tadziu! Tadziu!" He turned and ran back against the water, churning the waves to a foam, his head flung high. The sight of this living figure, virginally pure and austere, with dripping locks, beautiful as a tender young god, emerging from the depths of the sea and sky, outrunning the element—it conjured up mythologies, it was like a primeval legend, handed down from the beginning of time, of the birth of form, of the origin of the gods. With closed lids Aschenbach listened to this poesy hymning itself silently within him, and anon he thought it was good to be here and that he would stay awhile.

Afterwards Tadzio lay on the sand and rested from his bathe, wrapped in his white sheet, which he wore drawn underneath the right shoulder, so that his head was cradled on his bare right arm. And even when Aschenbach read, without looking up, he was conscious that the lad was there; that it would cost him but the slightest turn of the head to have the rewarding vision once more in his purview. Indeed, it was almost as though he sat there to guard the youth's repose; occupied, of course, with his own affairs, yet alive to the presence of that noble human creature close at hand. And his heart was stirred, it felt a father's kindness: such an emotion as the possessor of beauty can inspire in one who has offered himself up in spirit to create beauty.

At midday he left the beach, returned to the hotel, and was carried up in the lift to his room. There he lingered a little time before the glass and looked at his own gray hair, his keen and weary face. And he thought of his fame, and how people gazed respectfully at him in the streets, on account of his unerring gift of words and their power to charm. He called up all the worldly successes his genius had reaped, all he could remember, even his patent of nobility. Then went to luncheon down in the dining-room, sat at his little table, and ate. Afterwards he mounted again in the lift, and a group of young folk, Tadzio among them, pressed with him into the little compartment. It was the first time Aschenbach had seen him close at hand, not merely in perspective, and could see and take account of the details of his humanity. Someone spoke to the lad, and he, answering, with indescribably lovely smile, stepped out again, as they had come to the first floor, backwards, with his eyes cast down. "Beauty makes people self-conscious," Aschenbach thought, and considered within himself imperatively why this should be. He had noted, further, that Tadzio's teeth were imperfect, rather jagged and bluish, without a healthy glaze, and of that peculiar brittle transparency which the teeth of chlorotic people often show. "He is delicate, he is sickly," Aschenbach thought. "He will most likely not live to grow old." He did not try to account for the pleasure the idea gave him.

In the afternoon he spent two hours in his room, then took the *vaporetto* to Venice, across the foul-smelling lagoon. He got out at San Marco, had his tea in the Piazza, and then, as his custom was, took a walk through the streets. But this walk of his brought about nothing less than a revolution in his mood and an entire change in all his plans.

There was a hateful sultriness in the narrow streets. The air was so heavy that all the manifold smells wafted out of houses, shops, and cook-shops—smells of oil, perfumery, and so forth—hung low, like exhalations, not dissipating. Cigarette smoke seemed to stand in the air, it drifted so slowly away. Today the crowd in these narrow lanes oppressed the stroller instead of diverting him. The longer he walked, the more was he in tortures under that state, which is the product of the sea air and the sirocco and which excites and enervates at once. He perspired painfully. His eyes rebelled, his chest was heavy, he felt feverish, the blood throbbed in his temples. He fled from the huddled, narrow streets of the commercial city, crossed many bridges, and came into the poor quarter of Venice. Beggars waylaid him, the canals sickened him with their evil exhalations. He reached a quiet square, one of those that exist at the city's heart, forsaken of God and man; there he rested awhile on the margin of a fountain, wiped his brow, and admitted to himself that he must be gone.

For the second time, and now quite definitely, the city proved that in certain weathers it could be directly inimical to his health. Nothing but sheer unreasoning obstinacy would linger on, hoping for an unprophesiable change in the wind. A quick decision was in place. He could not go home at this stage, neither summer nor winter quarters would be ready. But Venice had not a monopoly of sea and shore: there were other spots where these were to be had without the evil concomitants of lagoon and fever-breeding vapors. He remembered a little bathing-place not far from Trieste of which he had had a good report. Why not go thither? At once, of course, in order that this second change might be worth the making. He resolved, he rose to his feet and sought the nearest gondola-landing, where he took a boat and was conveyed to San Marco through the gloomy windings of many canals, beneath balconies of delicate marble traceries flanked by carven lions; round slippery corners of wall, past melancholy façades with ancient business shields reflected in the rocking water. It was not too easy to arrive at his destination, for his gondolier, being in league with various lace-makers and glass-blowers, did his best to persuade his fare to pause, look, and be tempted to buy. Thus the charm of this bizarre passage through the heart of Venice, even while it played upon his spirit, yet was sensibly cooled by the predatory commercial spirit of the fallen queen of the seas.

Once back in his hotel, he announced at the office, even before dinner, that circumstances unforeseen obliged him to leave early next morning. The management expressed its regret, it changed his money and receipted his bill. He dined, and spent the lukewarm evening in a rocking-chair on the rear terrace, reading the newspapers. Before he went to bed, he made his luggage ready against the morning.

His sleep was not of the best, for the prospect of another journey made him restless. When he opened his window next morning, the sky was still overcast, but the air seemed fresher —and there and then his rue began. Had he not given notice too soon? Had he not let himself be swayed by a slight and momentary indisposition? If he had only been patient, not lost heart so quickly, tried to adapt himself to the climate, or even waited for a change in the weather before deciding! Then, instead of the hurry and flurry of departure, he would have before him now a morning like yesterday's on the beach. Too late! He must go on wanting what he had wanted yesterday. He dressed and at eight o'clock went down to breakfast.

When he entered the breakfast-room it was empty. Guests came in while he sat waiting for his order to be filled. As he sipped his tea he saw the Polish girls enter with their governess, chaste and morning-fresh, with sleep-reddened eyelids. They crossed the room and sat down at their table in the window. Behind them came the porter, cap in hand, to announce that it was time for him to go. The car was waiting to convey him and other travelers to the Hôtel Excelsior, whence they would go by motorboat through the company's private canal to the station. Time pressed. But Aschenbach found it did nothing of the sort. There still lacked more than an hour of train-time. He felt irritated at the hotel habit of getting the guests out of the house earlier than necessary; and requested the porter to let him breakfast in peace. The man hesitated and withdrew, only to come back again five minutes later. The car could wait no longer. Good, then it might go, and take his trunk with it, Aschenbach answered with some heat. He would use the public conveyance, in his own time; he begged them to leave the choice of it to him. The functionary bowed. Aschenbach, pleased to be rid of him, made a leisurely meal, and even had a newspaper of the waiter. When at length he rose, the time was grown very short. And it so happened that at that moment Tadzio came through the glass doors into the room.

To reach his own table he crossed the traveler's path, and modestly cast down his eyes before the gray-haired man of the lofty brows—only to lift them again in that sweet way he had and direct his full soft gaze upon Aschenbach's face. Then he was past. "For the last time, Tadzio," thought the elder man. "It was all too brief!" Quite unusually for him, he shaped a farewell with his lips, he actually uttered it, and added: "May God bless you!" Then he went out, distributed tips, exchanged farewells with the mild little manager in the frock-coat, and, followed by the porter with his hand-luggage, left the hotel. On foot as he had come, he passed through the white-blossoming avenue, diagonally across the island to the boat-landing. He went on board at once—but the tale of his journey across the lagoon was a tale of woe, a passage through the very valley of regrets.

It was the well-known route: through the lagoon, past San Marco, up the Grand Canal. Aschenbach sat on the circular bench in the bows, with his elbow on the railing, one hand shading his eyes. They passed the Public Gardens, once more the princely charm of the Piazzetta rose up before him and then dropped behind, next came the great row of palaces, the canal curved, and the splendid marble arches of the Rialto came in sight. The traveler gazed—and his bosom was torn. The atmosphere of the city, the faintly rotten scent of swamp and sea, which had driven him to leave—in what deep, tender, almost painful drafts he breathed it in! How was it he had not known, had not thought, how much his heart was set upon it all! What this morning had been slight regret, some little doubt of his own wisdom, turned now to grief, to actual wretchedness, a mental agony so sharp that it repeatedly brought tears to his eyes, while he questioned himself how he could have foreseen it. The hardest part, the part that more than once it seemed he could not bear, was the thought that he should never more see Venice again. Since now for the second time the place had made him ill, since for the second time he had had to flee for his life, he must henceforth regard it as a forbidden spot, to be forever shunned; senseless to try it again, after he had proved himself unfit. Yes, if he fled it now, he felt that wounded pride must prevent his return to this spot where twice he had made actual bodily surrender. And this conflict between inclination and capacity all at once assumed, in this middle-aged man's mind, immense weight and importance; the physical defeat seemed a shameful thing, to be avoided at whatever cost; and he stood amazed at the ease with which on the day before he had yielded to it.

Meanwhile the steamer neared the station landing; his anguish of irresolution amounted almost to panic. To leave seemed to the sufferer impossible, to remain not less so. Torn thus between two alternatives, he entered the station. It was very late, he had not a moment to lose. Time pressed, it scourged him onward. He hastened to buy his ticket and looked round in the crowd to find the hotel porter. The man appeared and said that the trunk had already gone off. "Gone already?" "Yes, it has gone to Como." "To Como?" A hasty exchange of words—angry questions from Aschenbach, and puzzled replies from the porter—at length made it clear that the trunk had been put with the wrong luggage even before leaving the hotel, and in company with other trunks was now well on its way in precisely the wrong direction.

Aschenbach found it hard to wear the right expression as he heard this news. A reckless joy, a deep incredible mirthfulness shook him almost as with a spasm. The porter dashed off after the lost trunk, returning very soon, of course, to announce that his efforts were unavailing. Aschenbach said he would not travel without his luggage; that he would go back and wait at the Hôtel des Bains until it turned up. Was the company's motorboat still outside? The man said yes, it was at the door. With his native eloquence he prevailed upon the ticket-agent to take back the ticket already purchased; he swore that he would wire, that no pains should be spared, that the trunk would be restored in the twinkling of an eye. And the unbelievable thing came to pass: the traveler, twenty minutes after he had reached the station, found himself once more on the Grand Canal on his way back to the Lido.

What a strange adventure indeed, this rightabout-face of destiny—incredible, humiliating, whimsical as any dream! To be passing again, within the hour, these scenes from which in profoundest grief he had but now taken leave forever! The little swift-moving vessel, a furrow of foam at its prow, tacking with droll agility between steamboats and gondolas, went like a shot to its goal; and he, its sole passenger, sat hiding the panic and thrills of a truant schoolboy beneath a mask of forced resignation. His breast still heaved from time to time with a burst of laughter over the contretemps. Things could not, he told himself, have fallen out more luckily. There would be the necessary explanations, a few astonished faces—then all would be well once more, a mischance prevented, a grievous error set right; and all he had thought to have left forever was his own once more, his for as long as he liked. . . . And did the boat's swift motion deceive him, or was the wind now coming from the sea?

The waves struck against the tiled sides of the narrow canal. At Hôtel Excelsior the automobile omnibus awaited the returned traveler and bore him along by the crisping waves back to the Hôtel des Bains. The little mustachioed manager in the frock-coat came down the steps to greet him.

In dulcet tones he deplored the mistake, said how painful it was to the management and himself; applauded Aschenbach's resolve to stop on until the errant trunk came back; his former room, alas, was already taken, but another as good awaited his approval. "*Pas de chance, monsieur,*" said the Swiss lift-porter, with a smile, as he conveyed him upstairs. And the fugitive was soon quartered in another room which in situation and furnishings almost precisely resembled the first.

He laid out the contents of his handbag in their wonted places; then, tired out, dazed by the whirl of the extraordinary forenoon, subsided into the armchair by the open window. The sea wore a pale-green cast, the air felt thinner and purer, the beach with its cabins and boats had more color, notwithstanding the sky was still gray. Aschenbach, his hands folded in his lap, looked out. He felt rejoiced to be back, yet displeased with his vacillating moods, his ignorance of his own real desires. Thus for nearly an hour he sat, dreaming, resting, barely thinking. At midday he saw Tadzio, in his striped sailor suit with red breast-knot, coming up from the sea, across the barrier and along the board walk to the hotel. Aschenbach recognized him, even at this height, knew it was he before he actually saw him, had it in mind to say to himself: "Well, Tadzio, so here you are again too!" But the casual greeting died away before it reached his lips, slain by the truth in his heart. He felt the rapture of his blood, the poignant pleasure, and realized that it was for Tadzio's sake the leavetaking had been so hard.

He sat quite still, unseen at his high post, and looked within himself. His features were lively, he lifted his brows; a smile, alert, inquiring, vivid, widened the mouth. Then he raised his head, and with both hands, hanging limp over the chair-arms, he described a slow motion, palms outward, a lifting and turning movement, as though to indicate a wide embrace. It was a gesture of welcome, a calm and deliberate acceptance of what might come.

Now daily the naked god with cheeks aflame drove his four fire-breathing steeds through heaven's spaces; and with him streamed the strong east wind that fluttered his yellow locks. A sheen, like white satin, lay over all the idly rolling sea's expanse. The sand was burning hot. Awnings of rust-colored canvas were spanned before the bathing-huts, under the ether's quivering silver-blue; one spent the morning hours within the small, sharp square of shadow they purveyed. But evening too was rarely lovely: balsamic with the breath of flowers and shrubs from the near-by park, while overhead the constellations circled in their spheres, and the murmuring of the night-girted sea swelled softly up and whispered to the soul. Such nights as these contained the joyful promise of a sunlit morrow, brim-full of sweetly ordered idleness, studded thick with countless precious possibilities.

The guest detained here by so happy a mischance was far from finding the return of his luggage a ground for setting out anew. For two days he had suffered slight inconvenience and had to dine in the large salon in his traveling-clothes. Then the lost trunk was set down in his room, and he hastened to unpack, filling presses and drawers with his possessions. He meant to stay on—and on; he rejoiced in the prospect of wearing a silk suit for the hot morning hours on the beach and appearing in acceptable evening dress at dinner.

He was quick to fall in with the pleasing monotony of this manner of life, readily enchanted by its mild soft brilliance and ease. And what a spot it is, indeed!—uniting the charms of a luxurious bathing-resort by a southern sea with the immediate nearness of a unique and marvelous city. Aschenbach was not pleasure-loving. Always, wherever and whenever it was the order of the day to be merry, to refrain from labor and make glad the heart, he would soon be conscious of the imperative summons—and especially was this so in his youth—back to the high fatigues, the sacred and fasting service that consumed his days. This spot and this alone had power to beguile him, to relax his resolution, to make him glad. At times—of a forenoon perhaps, as he lay in the shadow of his awning, gazing out dreamily over the blue of the southern sea, or in the mildness of the night, beneath the wide starry sky, ensconced among the cushions of the gondola that bore him Lido-wards after an evening on the Piazza, while the gay lights faded and the melting music of the serenades died away on his ear—he would think of his mountain home, the theater of his summer labors. There clouds hung low and trailed through the garden, violent storms extinguished the lights of the house at night, and the ravens he fed swung in the tops of the fir trees. And he would feel transported to Elysium, to the ends of the earth, to a spot most carefree for the sons of men, where no snow is, and no winter, no storms or downpours of rain; where Oceanus sends a mild and cooling breath, and days flow on in blissful idleness, without effort or struggle, entirely dedicate to the sun and the feasts of the sun.

Aschenbach saw the boy Tadzio almost constantly. The narrow confines of their world of hotel and beach, the daily round followed by all alike, brought him in close, almost uninterrupted touch with the beautiful lad. He encountered him everywhere—in the salons of the hotel, on the cooling rides to the city and back, among the splendors of the Piazza, and besides all this in many another going and coming as chance vouchsafed. But it was the regular morning hours on the beach that gave him his happiest opportunity to study and admire the lovely apparition. Yes, this immediate happiness, this daily recurring boon at the hand of circumstance, this it was that filled him with content, with joy in life, enriched his stay, and lingered out the row of sunny days that fell into place so pleasantly one behind the other.

He rose early—as early as though he had a panting press of work—and was among the first on the beach, when the sun was still benign and the sea lay dazzling white in its morning slumber. He gave the watchman a friendly good-morning and chatted with the barefoot, white-haired old man who prepared his place, spread the awning, trundled out the chair and table onto the little platform. Then he settled down; he had three or four hours before the sun reached its height and the fearful climax of its power; three or four hours while the sea went deeper and deeper blue; three or four hours in which to watch Tadzio.

He would see him come up, on the left, along the margin of the sea; or from behind, between the cabins; or, with a start of joyful surprise, would discover that he himself was late, and Tadzio already down, in the blue and white bathing-suit that was now his only wear on the beach; there and engrossed in his usual activities in the sand, beneath the sun. It was a sweetly idle, trifling, fitful life, of play and rest, of strolling, wading, digging, fishing, swimming, lying on the sand. Often the women sitting on the platform would call out to him in their high voices: "Tadziu! Tadziu!" and he would come running and waving his arms, eager to tell them what he had done, show them what he had found, what caught—shells, seahorses, jelly-fish, and sidewards-running crabs. Aschenbach understood not a word he said; it might be the sheerest commonplace, in his ear it became mingled harmonies. Thus the lad's foreign birth raised his speech to music; a wanton sun showered splendor on him, and the noble distances of the sea formed the background that set off his figure.

Soon the observer knew every line and pose of this form that limned itself so freely against sea and sky; its every loveliness, though conned by heart, yet thrilled him each day afresh; his admiration knew no bounds, the delight of his eye was unending. Once the lad was summoned to speak to a guest who was waiting for his mother at their cabin. He ran up, ran dripping wet out of the sea, tossing his curls, and put out his hand, standing with his weight on one leg, resting the other foot on the toes; as he stood there in a posture of suspense the turn of his body was enchanting, while his features wore a look half shame-faced, half conscious of the duty breeding laid upon him to please. Or he would lie at full length, with his bathrobe around him, one slender young arm resting on the sand, his chin in the hollow of his hand; the lad they called Jaschiu squatting beside him, paying him court. There could be nothing lovelier on earth than the smile and look with which the playmate thus singled out rewarded his humble friend and vassal. Again, he might be at the water's edge, alone, removed from his family, quite close to Aschenbach, standing erect, his hands clasped at the back of his neck, rocking slowly on the balls of his feet, day-dreaming away into blue space, while little waves ran up and bathed his toes. The ringlets of honey-colored hair clung to his temples and neck, the fine down along the upper vertebræ was yellow in the sunlight; the thin envelope of flesh covering the torso betrayed the delicate outlines of the ribs and the symmetry of the breast-structure. His armpits were still as smooth as a statue's, smooth the glistening hollows behind the knees, where the blue network of veins suggested that the body was formed of some stuff more transparent than mere flesh. What discipline, what precision of thought were expressed by the tense youthful perfection of this form! And yet the pure, strong will that had labored in darkness and succeeded in bringing this godlike work of art to the light of day—was it not known and familiar to him, the artist? Was not the same force at work in himself when he strove in cold fury to liberate from the marble mass of language the slender forms of his art which he saw with the eye of his mind and would body forth to men as the mirror and image of spiritual beauty?

Mirror and image! His eyes took in the proud bearing of that figure there at the blue water's edge; with an outburst of rapture he told himself that what he saw was beauty's very essence; form as divine thought, the single and pure perfection which resides in the mind, of which an image and likeness, rare and holy, was here raised up for adoration. This was very frenzy—and without a scruple, nay, eagerly, the aging artist bade it come. His mind was in travail, his whole mental background in a state of flux. Memory flung up in him the primitive thoughts which are youth's inheritance, but which with him had remained latent, never leaping up into a blaze. Has it not been written that the sun beguiles our attention from things of the intellect to fix it on things of the sense? The sun, they say, dazzles; so bewitching reason and memory that the soul for very pleasure forgets its actual state, to cling with doting on the loveliest of all the objects she shines on. Yes, and then it is only through the medium of some corporeal being that it can raise itself again to contemplation of higher things. Amor, in sooth, is like the mathematician who in order to give children a knowledge of pure form must do so in the language of pictures; so, too, the god, in order to make visible the spirit, avails himself of the forms and colors of human youth, gilding it with all imaginable beauty that it may serve memory as a tool, the very sight of which then sets us afire with pain and longing.

Such were the devotee's thoughts, such the power of his emotions. And the sea, so bright with glancing sunbeams, wove in his mind a spell and summoned up a lovely picture: there was the ancient plane tree outside the walls of Athens, a hallowed, shady spot, fragrant with willow blossom and adorned with images and votive offerings in honor of the nymphs and Achelous. Clear ran the smooth-pebbled stream at the foot of the spreading tree. Crickets were fiddling. But on the gentle grassy slope, where one could lie, yet hold the head erect, and shelter from the scorching heat, two men reclined, an elder with a younger, ugliness paired with beauty, and wisdom with grace. Here Socrates held forth to youthful Phædrus upon the nature of virtue and desire, wooing him with insinuating wit and charming turns of phrase. He told him of the shuddering and unwonted heat that come upon him whose heart is open, when his eye beholds an image of eternal beauty; spoke of the impious and corrupt, who cannot conceive beauty though they see its image, and are incapable of awe; and of the fear and reverence felt by the noble soul when he beholds a godlike face or a form that is a good image of beauty: how as he gazes he worships the beautiful one and scarcely dares to look upon him, but would offer sacrifice as to an idol or a god, did he not fear to be thought stark mad. "For beauty, my Phædrus, beauty alone, is lovely and visible at once. For, mark you, it is the sole aspect of the spiritual which we can perceive through our senses, or bear so to perceive. Else what should become of us, if the divine, if reason and virtue and truth, were to speak to us through the senses? Should we not perish and be consumed by love, as Semele aforetime was by Zeus? So beauty, then, is the beauty-lover's way to the spirit—but only the way, only the means, my little Phædrus.". . . And then, sly arch-lover that he was, he said the subtlest thing of all: that the lover was nearer the divine than the beloved; for the god was in the one but not in the other —perhaps the tenderest, most mocking thought that ever was thought, and source of all the guile and secret bliss the lover knows.

Thought that can merge wholly into feeling, feeling that can merge wholly into thought—these are the artist's highest joy. And our solitary felt in himself at this moment power to command and wield a thought that thrilled with emotion, an emotion as precise and concentrated as thought: namely, that nature herself shivers with ecstasy when the mind bows down in homage before beauty. He felt a sudden desire to write. Eros, indeed, we are told, loves idleness, and for idle hours alone was he created. But in this crisis the violence of our sufferer's seizure was directed almost wholly toward production, its occasion almost a matter of indifference. News had reached him on his travels that a certain problem had been raised, the intellectual world challenged for its opinion on a great and burning question of art and taste. By nature and experience the theme was his own; and he could not resist the temptation to set it off in the glistering foil of his words. He would write, and moreover he would write in Tadzio's presence. This lad should be in a sense his model, his style should follow the lines of this figure which seemed to him divine; he would snatch up his beauty into the realms of the mind, as once the eagle bore the Trojan shepherd aloft. Never had the pride of the word been so sweet to him, never had he known so well that Eros is in the word, as in those perilous and precious hours when he sat at his rude table, within the shade of his awning, his idol full in his view and the music of his voice in his ears, and fashioned his little essay after the model Tadzio's beauty set: that page and a half of choicest prose, so chaste, so lofty, so poignant with feeling, which would shortly be the wonder and admiration of the multitude. Verily it is well for the world that it sees only the beauty of the completed work and not its origins nor the conditions whence it sprang; since knowledge of the artist's inspiration might often but confuse and alarm and so prevent the full effect of its excellence. Strange hours, indeed, these were, and strangely unnerving the labor that filled them! Strangely fruitful intercourse this, between one body and another mind! When Aschenbach put aside his work and left the beach, he felt exhausted, he felt broken—conscience reproached him, as it were after a debauch.

Next morning on leaving the hotel he stood at the top of the stairs leading down from the terrace and saw Tadzio in front of him on his way to the beach. The lad had just reached the gate in the railings, and he was alone. Aschenbach felt, quite simply, a wish to overtake him, to address him and have the pleasure of his reply and answering look; to put upon a blithe and friendly footing his relation with this being who all unconsciously had so greatly heightened and quickened his emotions. The lovely youth moved at a loitering pace—he might easily be overtaken; and Aschenbach hastened his own step. He reached him on the board walk that ran behind the bathing-cabins, and all but put out his hand to lay it on shoulder or head, while his lips parted to utter a friendly salutation in French. But—perhaps from the swift pace of his last few steps—he found his heart throbbing unpleasantly fast, while his breath came in such quick pants that he could only have gasped had he tried to speak. He hesitated, sought after self-control, was suddenly panic-stricken lest the boy notice him hanging there behind him and look round. Then he gave up, abandoned his plan, and passed him with bent head and hurried step.

"Too late! Too late!" he thought as he went by. But was it too late? This step he had delayed to take might so easily have put everything in a lighter key, have led to a sane recovery from his folly. But the truth may have been that the aging man did not want to be cured, that his illusion was far too dear to him. Who shall unriddle the puzzle of the artist nature? Who understands that mingling of discipline and license in which it stands so deeply rooted? For not to be able to want sobriety is licentious folly. Aschenbach was no longer disposed to self-analysis. He had no taste for it; his self-esteem, the attitude of mind proper to his years, his maturity and single-mindedness, disinclined him to look within himself and decide whether it was constraint or puerile sensuality that had prevented him from carrying out his project. He felt confused, he was afraid someone, if only the watchman, might have been observing his behavior and final surrender—very much he feared being ridiculous. And all the time he was laughing at himself for his serio-comic seizure. "Quite crestfallen," he thought. "I was like the gamecock that lets his wings droop in the battle. That must be the Love-God himself, who makes us hang our heads at sight of beauty and weighs our proud spirits low as the ground." Thus he played with the idea—he embroidered upon it, and was too arrogant to admit fear of an emotion.

The term he had set for his holiday passed by unheeded; he had no thought of going home. Ample funds had been sent him. His sole concern was that the Polish family might leave, and a chance question put to the hotel barber elicited the information that they had come only very shortly before himself. The sun browned his face and hands, the invigorating salty air heightened his emotional energies. Heretofore he had been wont to give out at once, in some new effort, the powers accumulated by sleep or food or outdoor air; but now the strength that flowed in upon him with each day of sun and sea and idleness he let go up in one extravagant gush of emotional intoxication.

His sleep was fitful; the priceless, equable days were divided one from the next by brief nights filled with happy unrest. He went, indeed, early to bed, for at nine o'clock, with the departure of Tadzio from the scene, the day was over for him. But in the faint grayness of the morning a tender pang would go through him as his heart was minded of its adventure; he could no longer bear his pillow and, rising, would wrap himself against the early chill and sit down by the window to await the sunrise. Awe of the miracle filled his soul new-risen from its sleep. Heaven, earth, and its waters yet lay enfolded in the ghostly, glassy pallor of dawn; one paling star still swam in the shadowy vast. But there came a breath, a winged word from far and inaccessible abodes, that Eros was rising from the side of her spouse; and there was that first sweet reddening of the farthest strip of sea and sky that manifests creation to man's sense. She neared, the goddess, ravisher of youth, who stole away Cleitos and Cephalus and, defying all the envious Olympians, tasted beautiful Orion's love. At the world's edge began a strewing of roses, a shining and a blooming ineffably pure; baby cloudlets hung illumined, like attendant amoretti, in the blue and blushful haze; purple effulgence fell upon the sea, which seemed to heave it forward on its welling waves; from the horizon to zenith went great quivering thrusts like golden lances, the gleam became a glare; without a sound, with godlike violence, glow and glare and rolling flames streamed upwards, and with flying hoofbeats the steeds of the sun-god mounted the sky. The lonely watcher sat, the splendor of the god shone on him, he closed his eyes and let the glory kiss his lids. Forgotten feelings, precious pangs of his youth, quenched long since by the stern service that had been his life and now returned so strangely metamorphosed—he recognized them with a puzzled, wondering smile. He mused, he dreamed, his lips slowly shaped a name; still smiling, his face turned seawards and his hands lying folded in his lap, he fell asleep once more as he sat.

But that day, which began so fierily and festally, was not like other days; it was transmuted and gilded with mythical significance. For whence could come the breath, so mild and meaningful, like a whisper from higher spheres, that played about temple and ear? Troops of small feathery white clouds ranged over the sky, like grazing herds of the gods. A stronger wind arose, and Poseidon's horses ran up, arching their manes, among them too the steers of him with the purpled locks, who lowered their horns and bellowed as they came on; while like prancing goats the waves on the farther strand leaped among the craggy rocks. It was a world possessed, peopled by Pan, that closed round the spellbound man, and his doting heart conceived the most delicate fancies. When the sun was going down behind Venice, he would sometimes sit on a bench in the park and watch Tadzio, white-clad, with gay-colored sash, at play there on the rolled gravel with his ball; and at such times it was not Tadzio whom he saw, but Hyacinthus, doomed to die because two gods were rivals for his love. Ah, yes, he tasted the envious pangs that Zephyr knew when his rival, bow and cithara, oracle and all forgot, played with the beauteous youth; he watched the discus, guided by torturing jealousy, strike the beloved head; paled as he received the broken body in his arms, and saw the flower spring up, watered by that sweet blood and signed forevermore with his lament.

There can be no relation more strange, more critical, than that between two beings who know each other only with their eyes, who meet daily, yes, even hourly, eye each other with a fixed regard, and yet by some whim or freak of convention feel constrained to act like strangers. Uneasiness rules between them, unslaked curiosity, a hysterical desire to give rein to their suppressed impulse to recognize and address each other; even, actually, a sort of strained but mutual regard. For one human being instinctively feels respect and love for another human being so long as he does not know him well enough to judge him; and that he does not, the craving he feels is evidence.

Some sort of relation and acquaintanceship was perforce set up between Aschenbach and the youthful Tadzio; it was with a thrill of joy the older man perceived that the lad was not entirely unresponsive to all the tender notice lavished on him. For instance, what should move the lovely youth, nowadays when he descended to the beach, always to avoid the board walk behind the bathing-huts and saunter along the sand, passing Aschenbach's tent in front, sometimes so unnecessarily close as almost to graze his table or chair? Could the power of an emotion so beyond his own so draw, so fascinate its innocent object? Daily Aschenbach would wait for Tadzio. Then sometimes, on his approach, he would pretend to be preoccupied and let the charmer pass unregarded by. But sometimes he looked up, and their glances met; when that happened both were profoundly serious. The elder's dignified and cultured mien let nothing appear of his inward state; but in Tadzio's eyes a question lay—he faltered in his step, gazed on the ground, then up again with that ineffably sweet look he had; and when he was past, something in his bearing seemed to say that only good breeding hindered him from turning round.

But once, one evening, it fell out differently. The Polish brother and sisters, with their governess, had missed the evening meal, and Aschenbach had noted the fact with concern. He was restive over their absence, and after dinner walked up and down in front of the hotel, in evening dress and a straw hat; when suddenly he saw the nunlike sisters with their companion appear in the light of the arc-lamps, and four paces behind them Tadzio. Evidently they came from the steamer-landing, having dined for some reason in Venice. It had been chilly on the lagoon, for Tadzio wore a dark-blue reefer jacket with gilt buttons, and a cap to match. Sun and sea air could not burn his skin, it was the same creamy marble hue as at first—though he did look a little pale, either from the cold or in the bluish moonlight of the arc-lamps. The shapely brows were so delicately drawn, the eyes so deeply dark—lovelier he was than words could say, and as often the thought visited Aschenbach, and brought its own pang, that language could but extol, not reproduce, the beauties of the sense.

The sight of that dear form was unexpected, it had appeared unhoped-for, without giving him time to compose his features. Joy, surprise, and admiration might have painted themselves quite openly upon his face—and just at this second it happened that Tadzio smiled. Smiled at Aschenbach, unabashed and friendly, a speaking, winning, captivating smile, with slowly parting lips. With such a smile it might be that Narcissus bent over the mirroring pool, a smile profound, infatuated, lingering, as he put out his arms to the reflection of his own beauty; the lips just slightly pursed, perhaps half-realizing his own folly in trying to kiss the cold lips of his shadow—with a mingling of coquetry and curiosity and a faint unease, enthralling and enthralled.

Aschenbach received that smile and turned away with it as though entrusted with a fatal gift. So shaken was he that he had to flee from the lighted terrace and front gardens and seek out with hurried steps the darkness of the park at the rear. Reproaches strangely mixed of tenderness and remonstrance burst from him: "How dare you smile like that! No one is allowed to smile like that!" He flung himself on a bench, his composure gone to the winds, and breathed in the nocturnal fragrance of the garden. He leaned back, with hanging arms, quivering from head to foot, and quite unmanned he whispered the hackneyed phrase of love and longing—impossible in these circumstances, absurd, abject, ridiculous enough, yet sacred too, and not unworthy of honor even here: "I love you!"

In the fourth week of his stay on the Lido, Gustave von Aschenbach made certain singular observations touching the world about him. He noticed, in the first place, that though the season was approaching its height, yet the number of guests declined and, in particular, that the German tongue had suffered a rout, being scarcely or never heard in the land. At table and on the beach he caught nothing but foreign words. One day at the barber's—where he was now a frequent visitor—he heard something rather startling. The barber mentioned a German family who had just left the Lido after a brief stay, and rattled on in his obsequious way: "The signore is not leaving—he has no fear of the sickness, has he?" Aschenbach looked at him. "The sickness?" he repeated. Whereat the prattler fell silent, became very busy all at once, affected not to hear. When Aschenbach persisted, he said he really knew nothing at all about it, and tried in a fresh burst of eloquence to drown the embarrassing subject.

That was one forenoon. After luncheon Aschenbach had himself ferried across to Venice, in a dead calm, under a burning sun; driven by his mania, he was following the Polish young folk, whom he had seen with their companion, taking the way to the landing-stage. He did not find his idol on the Piazza. But as he sat there at tea, at a little round table on the shady side, suddenly he noticed a peculiar odor, which, it seemed to him now, had been in the air for days without his being aware: a sweetish, medicinal smell, associated with wounds and disease and suspect cleanliness. He sniffed and pondered and at length recognized it; finished his tea and left the square at the end facing the cathedral. In the narrow space the stench grew stronger. At the street corners placards were stuck up, in which the city authorities warned the population against the danger of certain infections of the gastric system, prevalent during the heated season; advising them not to eat oysters or other shellfish and not to use the canal waters. The ordinance showed every sign of minimizing an existing situation. Little groups of people stood about silently in the squares and on the bridges; the traveler moved among them, watched and listened and thought.

He spoke to a shopkeeper lounging at his door among dangling coral necklaces and trinkets of artificial amethyst, and asked him about the disagreeable odor. The man looked at him, heavy-eyed, and hastily pulled himself together. "Just a formal precaution, signore," he said, with a gesture. "A police regulation we have to put up with. The air is sultry—the sirocco is not wholesome, as the signore knows. Just a precautionary measure, you understand—probably unnecessary. . . ." Aschenbach thanked him and passed on. And on the boat that bore him back to the Lido he smelled the germicide again.

On reaching his hotel he sought the table in the lobby and buried himself in the newspapers. The foreign-language sheets had nothing. But in the German papers certain rumors were mentioned, statistics given, then officially denied, then the good faith of the denials called in question. The departure of the German and Austrian contingent was thus made plain. As for other nationals, they knew or suspected nothing—they were still undisturbed. Aschenbach tossed the newspapers back on the table. "It ought to be kept quiet," he thought, aroused. "It should not be talked about." And he felt in his heart a curious elation at these events impending in the world about him. Passion is like crime: it does not thrive on the established order and the common round; it welcomes every blow dealt the bourgeois structure, every weakening of the social fabric, because therein it feels a sure hope of its own advantage. These things that were going on in the unclean alleys of Venice, under cover of an official hushing-up policy—they gave Aschenbach a dark satisfaction. The city's evil secret mingled with the one in the depths of his heart—and he would have staked all he possessed to keep it, since in his infatuation he cared for nothing but to keep Tadzio here, and owned to himself, not without horror, that he could not exist were the lad to pass from his sight.

He was no longer satisfied to owe his communion with his charmer to chance and the routine of hotel life; he had begun to follow and waylay him. On Sundays, for example, the Polish family never appeared on the beach. Aschenbach guessed they went to Mass at San Marco and pursued them thither. He passed from the glare of the Piazza into the golden twilight of the holy place and found him he sought bowed in worship over a prie-dieu. He kept in the background, standing on the fissured mosaic pavement among the devout populace, which knelt and muttered and made the sign of the cross; and the crowded splendor of the Oriental temple weighed voluptuously on his sense. A heavily ornate priest intoned and gesticulated before the altar, where little candle-flames flickered helplessly in the reek of incense-breathing smoke; and with that cloying sacrificial smell another seemed to mingle—the odor of the sickened city. But through all the glamour and glitter Aschenbach saw the exquisite creature there in front turn his head, seek out and meet his lover's eye.

The crowd streamed out through the portals into the brilliant square thick with fluttering doves, and the fond fool stood aside in the vestibule on the watch. He saw the Polish family leave the church. The children took ceremonial leave of their mother, and she turned toward the Piazzetta on her way home, while his charmer and the cloistered sisters, with their governess, passed beneath the clock tower into the Merceria. When they were a few paces on, he followed—he stole behind them on their walk through the city. When they paused, he did so too;

when they turned round, he fled into inns and courtyards to let them pass. Once he lost them from view, hunted feverishly over bridges and in filthy culs-de-sac, only to confront them suddenly in a narrow passage whence there was no escape, and experience a moment of panic fear. Yet it would be untrue to say he suffered. Mind and heart were drunk with passion, his footsteps guided by the dæmonic power whose pastime it is to trample on human reason and dignity.

Tadzio and his sisters at length took a gondola. Aschenbach hid behind a portico or fountain while they embarked, and directly they pushed off did the same. In a furtive whisper he told the boatman he would tip him well to follow at a little distance the other gondola, just rounding a corner, and fairly sickened at the man's quick, sly grasp and ready acceptance of the go-between's role.

Leaning back among soft, black cushions he swayed gently in the wake of the other black-snouted bark, to which the strength of his passion chained him. Sometimes it passed from his view, and then he was assailed by an anguish of unrest. But his guide appeared to have long practice in affairs like these; always, by dint of short cuts or deft maneuvers, he contrived to overtake the coveted sight. The air was heavy and foul, the sun burned down through a slate-colored haze. Water slapped gurgling against wood and stone. The gondolier's cry, half warning, half salute, was answered with singular accord from far within the silence of the labyrinth. They passed little gardens, high up the crumbling wall, hung with clustering white and purple flowers that sent down an odor of almonds. Moorish lattices showed shadowy in the gloom. The marble steps of a church descended into the canal, and on them a beggar squatted, displaying his misery to view, showing the whites of his eyes, holding out his hat for alms. Farther on, a dealer in antiquities cringed before his lair, inviting the passer-by to enter and be duped. Yes, this was Venice, this the fair frailty that fawned and that betrayed, half fairy-tale, half snare; the city in whose stagnating air the art of painting once put forth so lusty a growth, and where musicians were moved to accords so weirdly lulling and lascivious. Our adventurer felt his senses wooed by this voluptuousness of sight and sound, tasted his secret knowledge that the city sickened and hid its sickness for love of gain, and bent an ever more unbridled leer on the gondola that glided on before him.

It came at last to this—that his frenzy left him capacity for nothing else but to pursue his flame; to dream of him absent, to lavish, loverlike, endearing terms on his mere shadow. He was alone, he was a foreigner, he was sunk deep in this belated bliss of his—all which enabled him to pass unblushing through experiences well-nigh unbelievable. One night, returning late from Venice, he paused by his beloved's chamber door in the second story, leaned his head against the panel, and remained there long, in utter drunkenness, powerless to tear himself away, blind to the danger of being caught in so mad an attitude.

And yet there were not wholly lacking moments when he paused and reflected, when in consternation he asked himself what path was this on which he had set his foot. Like most other men of parts and attainments, he had an aristocratic interest in his forebears, and when he achieved a success he liked to think he had gratified them, compelled their admiration and regard. He thought of them now, involved as he was in this illicit adventure, seized of these exotic excesses of feeling; thought of their stern self-command and decent manliness, and gave a melancholy smile. What would they have said? What, indeed, would they have said to his entire life, which varied to the point of degeneracy from theirs? This life in the bonds of art, had not he himself, in the days of his youth and in the very spirit of those bourgeois forefathers, pronounced mocking judgment upon it? And yet, at bottom, it had been so like their own! It had been a service, and he a soldier, like some of them; and art was war—a grilling, exhausting struggle that nowadays wore one out before one could grow old. It had been a life of self-conquest, a life against odds, dour, steadfast, abstinent; he had made it symbolical of the kind of overstrained heroism the time admired, and he was entitled to call it manly, even courageous. He wondered if such a life might not be somehow especially pleasing in the eyes of the god who had him in his power. For Eros had received most countenance among the most valiant nations—yes, were we not told that in their cities prowess made him flourish exceedingly? And many heroes of olden time had willingly borne his yoke, not counting any humiliation such if it happened by the god's decree; vows, prostrations, self-abasements, these were no source of shame to the lover; rather they reaped him praise and honor.

Thus did the fond man's folly condition his thoughts; thus did he seek to hold his dignity upright in his own eyes. And all the while he kept doggedly on the traces of the disreputable secret the city kept hidden at its heart, just as he kept his own—and all that he learned fed his passion with vague, lawless hopes. He turned over newspapers at cafés, bent on finding a report on the progress of the disease; and in the German sheets, which had ceased to appear on the hotel table, he found a series of contradictory statements. The deaths, it was variously asserted, ran to twenty, to forty, to a hundred or more; yet in the next day's issue the existence of the pestilence was, if not roundly denied, reported as a matter of a few sporadic cases such as might be brought into a seaport town. After that the warnings would break out again, and the protests against the unscrupulous game the authorities were playing. No definite information was to be had.

And yet our solitary felt he had a sort of first claim on a share in the unwholesome secret; he took a fantastic satisfaction in putting leading questions to such persons as were interested to conceal it, and forcing them to explicit untruths by way of denial. One day he attacked the manager, that small, soft-stepping man in the French frock-coat, who was moving about among the guests at luncheon, supervising the service and making himself socially agreeable. He paused at Aschenbach's table to exchange a greeting, and the guest put a question, with a negligent, casual air: "Why in the world are they forever disinfecting the city of Venice?" "A police regulation," the adroit one replied; "a precautionary measure, intended to protect the health of the public during this unseasonably warm and sultry weather." "Very praiseworthy of the police," Aschenbach gravely responded. After a further exchange of meteorological commonplaces the manager passed on.

It happened that a band of street musicians came to perform in the hotel gardens that evening after dinner. They grouped themselves beneath an iron stanchion supporting an arc-light, two women and two men, and turned their faces, which shone white in the glare, up toward the guests who sat on the hotel terrace enjoying this popular entertainment along with their coffee and iced drinks. The hotel lift-boys, waiters, and office staff stood in the doorway and listened; the Russian family displayed the usual Russian absorption in their enjoyment—they had their chairs put down in the garden to be nearer the singers and sat there in a half-circle with gratitude painted on their features, the old serf in her turban erect behind their chairs.

These strolling players were adepts at mandolin, guitar, harmonica, even compassing a reedy violin. Vocal numbers alternated with instrumental, the younger woman, who had a high shrill voice, joining in a love-duet with the sweetly falsettoing tenor. The actual head of the company, however, and incontestably its most gifted member, was the other man, who played the guitar. He was a sort of baritone buffo; with no voice to speak of, but possessed of a pantomimic gift and remarkable burlesque *élan*. Often he stepped out of the group and advanced toward the terrace, guitar in hand, and his audience rewarded his sallies with bursts of laughter. The Russians in their parterre seats were beside themselves with delight over this display of southern vivacity; their shouts and screams of applause encouraged him to bolder and bolder flights.

Aschenbach sat near the balustrade, a glass of pomegranate-juice and soda-water sparkling ruby-red before him, with which he now and then moistened his lips. His nerves drank in thirstily the unlovely sounds, the vulgar and sentimental tunes, for passion paralyzes good taste and makes its victim accept with rapture what a man in his senses would either laugh at or turn from with disgust. Idly he sat and watched the antics of the buffoon, with his face set in a fixed and painful smile, while inwardly his whole being was rigid with the intensity of the regard he bent on Tadzio, leaning over the railing six paces off.

He lounged there, in the white belted suit he sometimes wore at dinner, in all his innate, inevitable grace, with his left arm on the balustrade, his legs crossed, the right hand on the supporting hip; and looked down on the strolling singers with an expression that was hardly a smile, but rather a distant curiosity and polite toleration. Now and then he straightened himself and with a charming movement of both arms drew down his white blouse through his leather belt, throwing out his chest. And sometimes—Aschenbach saw it with triumph, with horror, and a sense that his reason was tottering—the lad would cast a glance, which might be slow and cautious, or might be sudden and swift, as though to take him by surprise, to the place where his lover sat. Aschenbach did not meet the glance. An ignoble caution made him keep his eyes in leash. For in the rear of the terrace sat Tadzio's mother and governess; and matters had gone so far that he feared to make himself conspicuous. Several times, on the beach, in the hotel lobby, on the Piazza, he had seen, with a stealing numbness, that they called Tadzio away from his neighborhood. And his pride revolted at the affront, even while conscience told him it was deserved.

The performer below presently began a solo, with guitar accompaniment, a street song in several stanzas, just then the rage all over Italy. He delivered it in a striking and dramatic recitative, and his company joined in the refrain. He was a man of slight build, with a thin, undernourished face; his shabby felt hat rested on the back of his neck, a great mop of red hair sticking out in front; and he stood there on the gravel in advance of his troupe, in an impudent, swaggering posture, twanging the strings of his instrument, and flinging a witty and rollicking recitative up to the terrace, while the veins on his forehead swelled with the violence of his effort. He was scarcely a Venetian type, belonging rather to the race of Neapolitan jesters, half bully, half comedian, brutal, blustering, an unpleasant customer, and entertaining to the last degree. The words of his song were trivial and silly, but on his lips, accompanied with gestures of head, hands, arms, and body, with leers and winks and the loose play of the tongue in the corner of his mouth, they took on meaning; an equivocal meaning, yet vaguely offensive. He wore a white sports shirt with a suit of ordinary clothes, and a strikingly large and naked-looking Adam's apple rose out of the open collar. From that pale, snub-nosed face it was hard to judge of his age; vice sat on it, it was furrowed with grimacing, and two deep wrinkles of defiance and self-will, almost of desperation, stood oddly between the red brows, above the grinning, mobile mouth. But what more than all drew upon him the profound scrutiny of our solitary watcher was that this suspicious figure seemed to carry with it its own suspicious odor. For whenever the refrain occurred and the singer, with waving arms and antic gestures, passed in his grotesque march immediately beneath Aschenbach's seat, a strong smell of carbolic was wafted up to the terrace.

After the song he began to take up money, beginning with the Russian family, who gave liberally, and then mounting the steps to the terrace. But here he became as cringing as he had before been forward. He glided between the tables, bowing and scraping, showing his strong white teeth in a servile smile, though the two deep furrows on the brow were still very marked. His audience looked at the strange creature as he went about collecting his livelihood, and their curiosity was not unmixed with disfavor. They tossed coins with their fingertips into his hat and took care not to touch it. Let the enjoyment be never so great, a sort of embarrassment always comes when the comedian oversteps the physical distance between himself and respectable people. This man felt it and sought to make his peace by fawning. He came along the railing to Aschenbach, and with him came that smell no one else seemed to notice.

"Listen!" said the solitary, in a low voice, almost mechanically; "they are disinfecting Venice—why?" The mountebank answered hoarsely: "Because of the police. Orders, signore. On account of the heat and the sirocco. The sirocco is oppressive. Not good for the health." He spoke as though surprised that anyone could ask, and with the flat of his hand he demonstrated how oppressive the sirocco was. "So there is no plague in Venice?" Aschenbach asked the question between his teeth, very low. The man's expressive face fell, he put on a look of comical innocence. "A plague? What sort of plague? Is the sirocco a plague? Or perhaps our police are a plague! You are making fun of us, signore! A plague! Why should there be? The police make regulations on account of the heat and the weather. . . ." He gestured. "Quite," said Aschenbach, once more, soft and low; and dropping an unduly large coin into the man's hat dismissed him with a sign. He bowed very low and left. But he had not reached the steps when two of the hotel servants flung themselves on him and began to whisper, their faces close to his. He shrugged, seemed to be giving assurances, to be swearing he had said nothing. It was not hard to guess the import of his words. They let him go at last and he went back into the garden, where he conferred briefly with his troupe and then stepped forward for a farewell song.

It was one Aschenbach had never to his knowledge heard before, a rowdy air, with words in impossible dialect. It had a laughing-refrain in which the other three artists joined at the top of their lungs. The refrain had neither words nor accompaniment, it was nothing but rhythmical, modulated, natural laughter, which the soloist in particular knew how to render with most deceptive realism. Now that he was farther from his audience, his self-assurance had come back, and this laughter of his rang with a mocking note. He would be overtaken, before he reached the end of the last line of each stanza; he would catch his breath, lay his hand over his mouth, his voice would quaver and his shoulders shake, he would lose power to contain himself longer. Just at the right moment each time, it came whooping, bawling, crashing out of him, with a verisimilitude that never failed to set his audience off in profuse and unpremeditated mirth that seemed to add gusto to his own. He bent his knees, he clapped his thigh, he held his sides, he looked ripe for bursting. He no longer laughed, but yelled, pointing his finger at the company there above as though there could be in all the world nothing so comic as they; until at last they laughed in hotel, terrace, and garden, down to the waiters, lift-boys, and servants—laughed as though possessed.

Aschenbach could no longer rest in his chair, he sat poised for flight. But the combined effect of the laughing, the hospital odor in his nostrils, and the nearness of the beloved was to hold him in a spell; he felt unable to stir. Under cover of the general commotion he looked across at Tadzio and saw that the lovely boy returned his gaze with a seriousness that seemed the copy of his own; the general hilarity, it seemed to say, had no power over him, he kept aloof. The gray-haired man was overpowered, disarmed by this docile, childlike deference; with difficulty he refrained from hiding his face in his hands. Tadzio's habit, too, of drawing himself up and taking a deep sighing breath struck him as being due to an oppression of the chest. "He is sickly, he will never live to grow up," he thought once again, with that dispassionate vision to which his madness of desire sometimes so strangely gave way. And compassion struggled with the reckless exultation of his heart.

The players, meanwhile, had finished and gone; their leader bowing and scraping, kissing his hands and adorning his leave-taking with antics that grew madder with the applause they evoked. After all the others were outside, he pretended to run backwards full tilt against a lamp-post and slunk to the gate apparently doubled over with pain. But there he threw off his buffoon's mask, stood erect, with an elastic straightening of his whole figure, ran out his tongue impudently at the guests on the terrace, and vanished in the night. The company dispersed. Tadzio had long since left the balustrade. But he, the lonely man, sat for long, to the waiter's great annoyance, before the dregs of pomegranate-juice in his glass. Time passed, the night went on. Long ago, in his parental home, he had watched the sand filter through an hourglass—he could still see, as though it stood before him, the fragile, pregnant little toy. Soundless and fine the rust-red streamlet ran through the narrow neck, and made, as it declined in the upper cavity, an exquisite little vortex.

The very next afternoon the solitary took another step in pursuit of his fixed policy of baiting the outer world. This time he had all possible success. He went, that is, into the English travel bureau in the Piazza, changed some money at the desk, and, posing as the suspicious foreigner, put his fateful question. The clerk was a tweed-clad young Britisher, with his eyes set close together, his hair parted in the middle, and radiating that steady reliability which makes his like so strange a phenomenon in the *gamin,* agile-witted south. He began: "No ground for alarm, sir. A mere formality. Quite regular in view of the unhealthy climatic conditions." But then, looking up, he chanced to meet with his own blue eyes the stranger's weary, melancholy gaze fixed on his face. The Englishman colored. He continued in a lower voice, rather confused: "At least, that is the official explanation, which they see fit to stick to. I may tell you there's a bit more to it than that." And then, in his good, straightforward way, he told the truth.

For the past several years Asiatic cholera had shown a strong tendency to spread. Its source was the hot, moist swamps of the delta of the Ganges, where it bred in the mephitic air of that primeval island-jungle, among whose bamboo thickets the tiger crouches, where life of every sort flourishes in rankest abundance, and only man avoids the spot. Thence the pestilence had spread throughout Hindustan, raging with great violence; moved eastward to China, westward to Afghanistan and Persia; following the great caravan routes, it brought terror to Astrakhan, terror to Moscow. Even while Europe trembled lest the specter be seen striding westward across country, it was carried by sea from Syrian ports and appeared simultaneously at several points on the Mediterranean littoral; raised its head in Toulon and Malaga, Palermo and Naples, and soon got a firm hold in Calabria and Apulia. Northern Italy had been spared—so far. But in May the horrible vibrions were found on the same day in two bodies: the emaciated, blackened corpses of a bargee and a woman who kept a greengrocer's shop. Both cases were hushed up. But in a week there were ten more—twenty, thirty in different quarters of the town. An Austrian provincial, having come to Venice on a few days' pleasure trip, went home and died with all the symptoms of the plague. Thus was explained the fact that the German-language papers were the first to print the news of the Venetian outbreak. The Venetian authorities published in reply a statement to the effect that the state of the city's health had never been better; at the same time instituting the most necessary precautions. But by that time the food supplies—milk, meat, or vegetables—had probably been contaminated, for death unseen and unacknowledged was devouring and laying waste in the narrow streets, while a brooding, unseasonable heat warmed the waters of the canals and encouraged the spread of the pestilence. Yes, the disease seemed to flourish and wax strong, to redouble its generative powers. Recoveries were rare. Eighty out of every hundred died, and horribly, for the onslaught was of the extremest violence, and not infrequently of the "dry" type, the most malignant form of the contagion. In this form the victim's body loses power to expel the water secreted by the blood-vessels, it shrivels up, he passes with hoarse cries from convulsion to convulsion, his blood grows thick like pitch, and he suffocates in a few hours. He is fortunate indeed if, as sometimes happens, the disease, after a slight malaise, takes the form of a profound unconsciousness, from which the sufferer seldom or never rouses. By the beginning of June the quarantine buildings of the *ospedale civico* had quietly filled up, the two orphan asylums were entirely occupied, and there was a hideously brisk traffic between the *Nuovo Fundamento* and the island of San Michele, where the cemetery was. But the city was not swayed by high-minded motives or regard for international agreements. The authorities were more actuated by fear of being out of pocket, by regard for the new exhibition of paintings just opened in the Public Gardens, or by apprehension of the large losses the hotels and the shops that catered to foreigners would suffer in case of panic and blockade. And the fears of the people supported the persistent official policy of silence and denial. The city's first medical officer, an honest and competent man, had indignantly resigned his office and been privily replaced by a more compliant person. The fact was known; and this corruption in high places played its part, together with the suspense as to where the walking terror might strike next, to demoralize the baser elements in the city and encourage those antisocial forces which shun the light of day. There was intemperance, indecency, increase of crime. Evenings one saw many drunken people, which was unusual. Gangs of men in surly mood made the streets unsafe, theft and assault were said to be frequent, even murder; for in two cases persons supposedly victims of the plague were proved to have been poisoned by their own families. And professional vice was rampant, displaying excesses heretofore unknown and only at home much farther south and in the east.

Such was the substance of the Englishman's tale. "You would do well," he concluded, "to leave today instead of tomorrow. The blockade cannot be more than a few days off."

"Thank you," said Aschenbach, and left the office.

The Piazza lay in sweltering sunshine. Innocent foreigners sat before the cafés or stood in front of the cathedral, the center of clouds of doves that, with fluttering wings, tried to shoulder each other away and pick the kernels of maize from the extended hand. Aschenbach strode up and down the spacious flags, feverishly excited, triumphant in possession of the truth at last, but with a sickening taste in his mouth and a fantastic horror at his heart. One decent, expiatory course lay open to him; he considered it. Tonight, after dinner, he might approach the lady of the pearls and address her in words that he precisely formulated in his mind: "Madame, will you permit an entire stranger to serve you with a word of advice and warning which self-interest prevents others from uttering? Go away. Leave here at once, without delay, with Tadzio and your daughters. Venice is in the grip of pestilence." Then might he lay his hand in farewell upon the head of that instrument of a mocking deity; and thereafter himself flee the accursed morass. But he knew that he was far indeed from any serious desire to take such a step. It would restore him, would give him back himself once more; but he who is beside himself revolts at the idea of self-possession. There crossed his mind the vision of a white building with inscriptions on it, glittering in the sinking sun—he recalled how his mind had dreamed away into their transparent mysticism; recalled the strange pilgrim apparition that had wakened in the aging man a lust for strange countries and fresh sights. And these memories, again, brought in their train the thought of returning home, returning to reason, self-mastery, an ordered existence, to the old life of effort. Alas, the bare thought made him wince with a revulsion that was like physical nausea. "It must be kept quiet," he whispered fiercely. "I will not speak!" The knowledge that he shared the city's secret, the city's guilt—it put him beside himself, intoxicated him as a small quantity of wine will a man suffering from brain-fag. His thought dwelt upon the image of the desolate and calamitous city, and he was giddy with fugitive, mad, unreasoning hopes and visions of a monstrous sweetness. That tender sentiment he had a moment ago evoked, what was it compared with such images as these? His art, his moral sense, what were they in the balance beside the boons that chaos might confer? He kept silence, he stayed on.

That night he had a fearful dream—if dream be the right word for a mental and physical experience which did indeed befall him in deep sleep, as a thing quite apart and real to his senses, yet without his seeing himself as present in it. Rather its theater seemed to be his own soul, and the events burst in from outside, violently overcoming the profound resistance of his spirit; passed him through and left him, left the whole cultural structure of a lifetime trampled on, ravaged, and destroyed.

The beginning was fear; fear and desire, with a shuddering curiosity. Night reigned, and his senses were on the alert; he heard loud, confused noises from far away, clamor and hubbub. There was a rattling, a crashing, a low dull thunder; shrill halloos and a kind of howl with a long-drawn *u*-sound at the end. And with all these, dominating them all, flute-notes of the cruelest sweetness, deep and cooing, keeping shamelessly on until the listener felt his very entrails bewitched. He heard a voice, naming, though darkly, that which was to come: "The stranger god!" A glow lighted up the surrounding mist and by it he recognized a mountain scene like that about his country home. From the wooded heights, from among the tree-trunks and crumbling moss-covered rocks, a troop came tumbling and raging down, a whirling rout of men and animals, and overflowed the hillside with flames and human forms, with clamor and the reeling dance. The females stumbled over the long, hairy pelts that dangled from their girdles; with heads flung back they uttered loud hoarse cries and shook their tambourines high in air; brandished naked daggers or torches vomiting trails of sparks. They shrieked, holding their breasts in both hands; coiling snakes with quivering tongues they clutched about their waists. Horned and hairy males, girt about the loins with hides, drooped heads and lifted arms and thighs in unison, as they beat on brazen vessels that gave out droning thunder, or thumped madly on drums. There were troops of beardless youths armed with garlanded staves; these ran after goats and thrust their staves against the creatures' flanks, then clung to the plunging horns and let themselves be borne off with triumphant shouts. And one and all the mad rout yelled that cry, composed of soft consonants with a long-drawn *u*-sound at the end, so sweet and wild it was together, and like nothing ever heard before! It would ring through the air like the bellow of a challenging stag, and be given back many-tongued; or they would use it to goad each other on to dance with wild excess of tossing limbs—they never let it die. But the deep, beguiling notes of the flute wove in and out and over all. Beguiling too it was to him who struggled in the grip of these sights and sounds, shamelessly awaiting the coming feast and the uttermost surrender. He trembled, he shrank, his will was steadfast to preserve and uphold his own god against this stranger who was sworn enemy to dignity and self-control. But the mountain wall took up the noise and howling and gave it back manifold; it rose high, swelled to a madness that carried him away. His senses reeled in the steam of panting bodies, the acrid stench from the goats, the odor as of stagnant waters—and another, too familiar smell—of wounds, uncleanness, and disease. His heart throbbed to the drums, his brain reeled, a blind rage seized him, a whirling lust, he craved with all his soul to join the ring that formed about the obscene symbol of the godhead, which they were unveiling and elevating, monstrous and wooden, while from full throats they yelled their rallying-cry. Foam dripped from their lips, they drove each other on with lewd gesturings and beckoning hands. They laughed, they howled, they thrust their pointed staves into each other's flesh and licked the blood as it ran down. But now the dreamer was in them and of them, the stranger god was his own. Yes, it was he who was flinging himself upon the animals, who bit and tore and swallowed smoking gobbets of flesh—while on the trampled moss there now began the rites in honor of the god, an orgy of promiscuous embraces—and in his very soul he tasted the bestial degradation of his fall.

The unhappy man woke from this dream shattered, unhinged, powerless in the demon's grip. He no longer avoided men's eyes nor cared whether he exposed himself to suspicion. And anyhow, people were leaving; many of the bathing-cabins stood empty, there were many vacant places in the dining-room, scarcely any foreigners were seen in the streets. The truth seemed to have leaked out; despite all efforts to the contrary, panic was in the air. But the lady of the pearls stayed on with her family; whether because the rumors had not reached her or because she was too proud and fearless to heed them. Tadzio remained; and it seemed at times to Aschenbach, in his obsessed state, that death and fear together might clear the island of all other souls and leave him there alone with him he coveted. In the long mornings on the beach his heavy gaze would rest, a fixed and reckless stare, upon the lad; toward nightfall, lost to shame, he would follow him through the city's narrow streets, where horrid death stalked too, and at such times it seemed to him as though the moral law were fallen in ruins and only the monstrous and perverse held out a hope.

Like any lover, he desired to please; suffered agonies at the thought of failure, and brightened his dress with smart ties and handkerchiefs and other youthful touches. He added jewelry and perfumes and spent hours each day over his toilette, appearing at dinner elaborately arrayed and tensely excited. The presence of the youthful beauty that had bewitched him filled him with disgust of his own aging body; the sight of his own sharp features and gray hair plunged him in hopeless mortification; he made desperate efforts to recover the appearance and freshness of his youth and began paying frequent visits to the hotel barber. Enveloped in the white sheet, beneath the hands of that garrulous personage, he would lean back in the chair and look at himself in the glass with misgiving.

"Gray," he said, with a grimace.

"Slightly," answered the man. "Entirely due to neglect, to a lack of regard for appearances. Very natural, of course, in men of affairs, but, after all, not very sensible, for it is just such people who ought to be above vulgar prejudice in matters like these. Some folk have very strict ideas about the use of cosmetics; but they never extend them to the teeth, as they logically should. And very disgusted other people would be if they did. No, we are all as old as we feel, but no older, and gray hair can misrepresent a man worse than dyed. You, for instance, signore, have a right to your natural color. Surely you will permit me to restore what belongs to you?"

"How?" asked Aschenbach.

For answer the oily one washed his client's hair in two waters, one clear and one dark, and lo, it was as black as in the days of his youth. He waved it with the tongs in wide, flat undulations, and stepped back to admire the effect.

"Now if we were just to freshen up the skin a little," he said.

And with that he went on from one thing to another, his enthusiasm waxing with each new idea. Aschenbach sat there comfortably; he was incapable of objecting to the process—rather as it went forward it roused his hopes. He watched it in the mirror and saw his eyebrows grow more even and arching, the eyes gain in size and brilliance, by dint of a little application below the lids. A delicate carmine glowed on his cheeks where the skin had been so brown and leathery. The dry, anemic lips grew full, they turned the color of ripe strawberries, the lines round eyes and mouth were treated with a facial cream and gave place to youthful bloom. It was a young man who looked back at him from the glass—Aschenbach's heart leaped at the sight. The artist in cosmetic at last professed himself satisfied; after the manner of such people, he thanked his client profusely for what he had done himself. "The merest trifle, the merest, signore," he said as he added the final touches. "Now the signore can fall in love as soon as he likes." Aschenbach went off as in a dream, dazed between joy and fear, in his red necktie and broad straw hat with its gay striped band.

A lukewarm storm-wind had come up. It rained a little now and then, the air was heavy and turbid and smelled of decay. Aschenbach, with fevered cheeks beneath the rouge, seemed to hear rushing and flapping sounds in his ears, as though storm-spirits were abroad—unhallowed ocean harpies who follow those devoted to destruction, snatch away and defile their viands. For the heat took away his appetite and thus he was haunted with the idea that his food was infected.

One afternoon he pursued his charmer deep into the stricken city's huddled heart. The labyrinthine little streets, squares, canals, and bridges, each one so like the next, at length made him lose his bearings. He did not even know the points of the compass; all his care was not to lose sight of the figure after which his eyes thirsted. He slunk under walls, he lurked behind buildings or people's backs; and the sustained tension of his senses and emotions exhausted him more and more, though for a long time he was unconscious of fatigue. Tadzio walked behind the others, he let them pass ahead in the narrow alleys, and as he sauntered slowly after, he would turn his head and assure himself with a glance of his strange, twilit gray eyes that his lover was still following. He saw him—and he did not betray him. The knowledge enraptured Aschenbach. Lured by those eyes, led on the leading-string of his own passion and folly, utterly lovesick, he stole upon the footsteps of his unseemly hope—and at the end found himself cheated. The Polish family crossed a small vaulted bridge, the height of whose archway hid them from his sight, and when he climbed it himself they were nowhere to be seen. He hunted in three directions—straight ahead and on both sides the narrow, dirty quay—in vain. Worn quite out and unnerved, he had to give over the search.

His head burned, his body was wet with clammy sweat, he was plagued by intolerable thirst. He looked about for refreshment, of whatever sort, and found a little fruit-shop where he bought some strawberries. They were overripe and soft; he ate them as he went. The street he was on opened out into a little square, one of those charmed, forsaken spots he liked; he recognized it as the very one where he had sat weeks ago and conceived his abortive plan of flight. He sank down on the steps of the well and leaned his head against its stone rim. It was quiet here. Grass grew between the stones, and rubbish lay about. Tall, weather-beaten houses bordered the square, one of them rather palatial, with vaulted windows, gaping now, and little lion balconies. In the ground floor of another was an apothecary's shop. A waft of carbolic acid was borne on a warm gust of wind.

There he sat, the master: this was he who had found a way to reconcile art and honors; who had written *The Abject,* and in a style of classic purity renounced bohemianism and all its works, all sympathy with the abyss and the troubled depths of the outcast human soul. This was he who had put knowledge underfoot to climb so high; who had outgrown the ironic pose and adjusted himself to the burdens and obligations of fame; whose renown had been officially recognized and his name ennobled, whose style was set for a model in the schools. There he sat. His eyelids were closed, there was only a swift, sidelong glint of the eyeballs now and again, something between a question and a leer; while the rouged and flabby mouth uttered single words of the sentences shaped in his disordered brain by the fantastic logic that governs our dreams.

"For mark you, Phædrus, beauty alone is both divine and visible; and so it is the sense way, the artist's way, little Phædrus, to the spirit. But now tell me, my dear boy, do you believe that such a man can ever attain wisdom and true manly worth for whom the path to the spirit must lead through the senses? Or do you rather think—for I leave the point to you—that it is a path of perilous sweetness, a way of transgression, and must surely lead him who walks in it astray? For you know that we poets cannot walk the way of beauty without Eros as our companion and guide. We may be heroic after our fashion, disciplined warriors of our craft, yet are we all like women, for we exult in passion, and love is still our desire—our craving and our shame. And from this you will perceive that we poets can be neither wise nor worthy citizens. We must needs be wanton, must needs rove at large in the realm of feeling. Our magisterial style is all folly and pretense, our honorable repute a farce, the crowd's belief in us is merely laughable. And to teach youth, or the populace, by means of art is a dangerous practice and ought to be forbidden. For what good can an artist be as a teacher, when from his birth up he is headed direct for the pit? We may want to shun it and attain to honor in the world; but however we turn, it draws us still. So, then, since knowledge might destroy us, we will have none of it. For knowledge, Phædrus, does not make him who possesses it dignified or austere. Knowledge is all-knowing, understanding, forgiving; it takes up no position, sets no store by form. It has compassion with the abyss—it *is* the abyss. So we reject it, firmly, and henceforward our concern shall be with beauty only. And by beauty we mean simplicity, largeness, and renewed severity of discipline; we mean a return to detachment and to form. But detachment, Phædrus, and preoccupation with form lead to intoxication and desire, they may lead the noblest among us to frightful emotional excesses, which his own stern cult of the beautiful would make him the first to condemn. So they too, they too, lead to the bottomless pit. Yes, they lead us thither, I say, us who are poets—who by our natures are prone not to excellence but to excess. And now, Phædrus, I will go. Remain here; and only when you can no longer see me, then do you depart also."

A few days later Gustave Aschenbach left his hotel rather later than usual in the morning. He was not feeling well and had to struggle against spells of giddiness only half physical in their nature, accompanied by a swiftly mounting dread, a sense of futility and hopelessness—but whether this referred to himself or to the outer world he could not tell. In the lobby he saw a quantity of luggage lying strapped and ready; asked the porter whose it was, and received in answer the name he already knew he should hear—that of the Polish family. The expression of his ravaged features did not change; he only gave that quick lift of the head with which we sometimes receive the uninteresting answer to a casual query. But he put another:

"When?" "After luncheon," the man replied. He nodded, and went down to the beach.

It was an unfriendly scene. Little crisping shivers ran all across the wide stretch of shallow water between the shore and the first sandbank. The whole beach, once so full of color and life, looked now autumnal, out of season; it was nearly deserted and not even very clean. A camera on a tripod stood at the edge of the water, apparently abandoned; its black cloth snapped in the freshening wind.

Tadzio was there, in front of his cabin, with the three or four playfellows still left him. Aschenbach set up his chair some halfway between the cabins and the water, spread a rug over his knees, and sat looking on. The game this time was unsupervised, the elders being probably busy with their packing, and it looked rather lawless and out-of-hand. Jaschiu, the sturdy lad in the belted suit, with the black, brilliantined hair, became angry at a handful of sand thrown in his eyes; he challenged Tadzio to a fight, which quickly ended in the downfall of the weaker. And perhaps the coarser nature saw here a chance to avenge himself at last, by one cruel act, for his long weeks of subserviency: the victor would not let the vanquished get up, but remained kneeling on Tadzio's back, pressing Tadzio's face into the sand—for so long a time that it seemed the exhausted lad might even suffocate. He made spasmodic efforts to shake the other off, lay still, and then began a feeble twitching. Just as Aschenbach was about to spring indignantly to the rescue, Jaschiu let his victim go. Tadzio, very pale, half sat up, and remained so, leaning on one arm, for several minutes, with darkening eyes and rumpled hair. Then he rose and walked slowly away. The others called him, at first gaily, then imploringly; he would not hear. Jaschiu was evidently overtaken by swift remorse; he followed his friend and tried to make his peace, but Tadzio motioned him back with a jerk of one shoulder and went down to the water's edge. He was barefoot and wore his striped linen suit with the red breast-knot.

There he stayed a little, with bent head, tracing figures in the wet sand with one toe; then stepped into the shallow water, which at its deepest did not wet his knees; waded idly through it and reached the sand-bar. Now he paused again, with his face turned seaward; and next began to move slowly leftward along the narrow strip of sand the sea left bare. He paced there, divided by an expanse of water from the shore, from his mates by his moody pride; a remote and isolated figure, with floating locks, out there in sea and wind, against the misty inane. Once more he paused to look: with a sudden recollection, or by an impulse, he turned from the waist up, in an exquisite movement, one hand resting on his hip, and looked over his shoulder at the shore. The watcher sat just as he had sat that time in the lobby of the hotel when first the twilit gray eyes had met his own. He rested his head against the chair-back and followed the movements of the figure out there, then lifted it, as it were in answer to Tadzio's gaze. It sank on his breast, the eyes looked out beneath their lids, while his whole face took on the relaxed and brooding expression of deep slumber. It seemed to him the pale and lovely Summoner out there smiled at him and beckoned; as though, with the hand he lifted from his hip, he pointed outwards as he hovered on before into an immensity of richest expectation.

Some minutes passed before anyone hastened to the aid of the elderly man sitting there collapsed in his chair. They bore him to his room. And before nightfall a shocked and respectful world received the news of his decease.

Translated by H. T. Lowe-Porter

THE HUSSAR

by Johann Peter Hebel

When, at the beginning of the French Revolution, the Prussians made war against the French and rode through the province of Champagne, no one imagined that the wind would change and that before long, in the year of 1806, the French would come to Prussia and return the uninvited visit. For not every Prussian behaved as befits an honorable soldier in an enemy country.

Thus, then, a Prussian hussar, who was an evil person, invaded the house of a peaceable man, took from him all his money and much else of value, and finally even his pretty bed with the brand-new bedspread, and mistreated husband and wife. Their boy, eight years old, begged him on his knees at least to give back the bed to his parents. The hussar pushed him away harshly. Their daughter ran after him, caught hold of his cape, and implored him for mercy. But he seized her and threw her into the well in the courtyard, and got away with his loot.

Years afterward, he retired, settled in the city of Neisse in Silesia, and thought little of the crime he had once committed, believing that the grass had grown over it long ago.

But what happened in the year of 1806? The French marched into Neisse, and one evening a young sergeant was quartered at the home of a good woman who attended him well. The sergeant was honorable, behaved decently, and seemed cheerful.

The next morning the sergeant did not come down to breakfast. The woman thought: "He's still asleep," and put his coffee in the oven to keep warm. After a while, when he still didn't come, she went up to his room to see whether he was all right, and softly pushed open the door.

There was the young man, awake and sitting up in bed, with his hands folded, and sighing as if he'd met with some great

---

See page 38.

misfortune, or as if he had become homesick or some such thing. He did not notice that someone was in the room.

The woman went quietly to him and asked: "What has happened to you, sergeant, and why are you so sad?"

The young man looked at her with a tearful expression and said that the spread of the bed in which he'd spent the night had belonged to his parents in Champagne; they'd lost everything in the pillage fourteen years before and had become paupers, and all that was coming back to him now, and his heart was full of sorrow. For the sergeant was the son of the man who had been robbed in Champagne, and he still recognized the spread and the red initials that his mother had sewed on it.

The good woman was frightened and said she'd bought the bed-cover from a hussar who still lived in Neisse, and that she should not be blamed.

The Frenchman got up and had himself taken to the home of the hussar, and recognized the man.

"Do you recall," he said to the hussar, "how fourteen years ago you took away from an innocent man in Champagne all his possessions, even his bed, and took no pity when an eight-year-old boy begged for mercy? And do you still remember my sister?"

At first the old wretch tried to make excuses, saying that in wartime, as everyone knows, not all things go as they should, and what one fellow leaves, another takes, so one might as well do the taking oneself. But when he saw that the sergeant really was the boy whose parents he had plundered and mistreated, and as he remembered the sister, the hussar's voice failed, in remorse and terror, and he fell on his shaking knees before the Frenchman unable to utter anything but "Forgive me." "But," he thought to himself, "this won't help much."

The gentle reader may think, gleefully: "Now the Frenchman will hack the hussar to pieces." But that would not tally with the truth. For when a man's heart is stirred and almost breaking in pain, he cannot take revenge. For vengeance is too small and contemptible, and he thinks: "We are in the hands of God," and he can't bring himself to repay evil with evil. Thus thought the Frenchman, too, and he said: "That you mistreated me, I forgive you. That you mistreated my parents and made them paupers, my parents will have to forgive you. That you threw my sister into the well, where she perished—may God forgive you that." With these words he went away without doing the hussar the slightest harm, and he became well again in his heart.

But the hussar felt afterward as though he'd stood before the Last Judgment and had been found wanting. He did not have one peaceful hour from that day on, and a quarter of a year later, it is said, he died.

Translated by Paul Pratt

This book was set on the Linotype in *Bodoni Book*, a printing-type so called after Giambattista Bodoni, a celebrated printer and type designer of Rome and Parma (1740–1813). Bodoni Book as produced by the Linotype company is not a copy of any one of Bodoni's fonts, but is a composite, modern version of the Bodoni manner. Bodoni's innovations in printing-type style were a greater degree of contrast in the "thick and thin" elements of the letters, and a sharper and more angular finish of details.

The book was composed, printed, and bound by Kingsport Press, Inc., Kingsport, Tenn.

The typography and binding were designed by Herbert Bayer.